# PRAISE FOR BETHANY TURNER

## *Wes and Addie Had Their Chance*

"*Wes and Addie Had Their Chance* is a delight!"

—Sophie Cousens, *New York Times* bestselling author of *This Time Next Year*

"Consider yourself warned: Once you start a Bethany Turner romance, you better clear your schedule because you're not going to want to do anything but read and swoon! *Wes and Addie Had Their Chance* is the perfect return to Adelaide Springs, and the perfect escape for every sweet romance lover!"

— Courtney Walsh, *New York Times* bestselling author

"Just when you think Bethany Turner can't get any funnier or her characters get any more lovable, in walk Wes and Addie . . ."

—Betsy St. Amant, author of *Tacos for Two* and the Magnolia Bay series

"Bethany Turner is an auto-buy for me. In *Wes and Addie Had Their Chance*, she masterfully couples real-world issues and delightful banter in a moving second-chance romance. It is one of the highlights of my reading year, and I highly recommend it to anyone looking for a great love story with laughter and depth."

—Julia London, *New York Times* bestselling author of *Nice Work, Nora November*

"This delightfully swoony rom com had me rooting for Wes and Addie at every turn! If you're a fan of stories with punchy dialog, charming dry wit, and romance that will sweep you off your feet, be sure not to miss this one."

—Katie Bailey, bestselling author of *The Quit List*

"Real, funny, open, honest, and oh-so-entertaining, this book is just like Bethany herself!"

—Zibby Owens, author of *Blank: A Novel*, host of podcast *Moms Don't Have Time to Read Books*

"Another laugh out loud, pitch perfect romance from Bethany Turner."

—Annabel Monaghan, bestselling author of *Same Time Next Summer*

"Bethany Turner is a master at writing romantic tension with the snappy wit of *Gilmore Girls*—all while being laugh-out-loud funny."

—Melissa Ferguson, bestselling author of *Meet Me in the Margins*

## *Cole and Laila Are Just Friends*

"Deliciously romantic and laugh out loud funny, this one had me in its grip until the very end. Cole and Laila are meant-to-be perfection. I loved it!"

—Annabel Monaghan, bestselling author of *Same Time Next Summer*

"*Cole and Laila Are Just Friends* is a glorious ode to '90s romcoms, lifelong friendships, and all the many twists of life that drop us right where we need to be. Full of warmth and witticisms galore, this will-they-or-won't-they love story will capture readers from the first page and spin them capably through the landmarks of New York alongside the most rootable duo I've ever encountered. Sweet and swoony, yet always rooted in human struggles (and stubbornness!), *Cole and Laila Are Just Friends* is the tight, affirming hug we all need right now."

—Nora Nguyen, author of *Adam & Evie's Matchmaking Tour*

"Hands down THE BEST pairing of first-love flutters and soul-deep friendship a romance reader could ask for—a new fan favorite! Funny, moving, and achingly adorable, Cole + Laila = relationship goals."

—Nicole Deese, Christy Award–winning author

"Small town romance? Check. Friends-to-lovers? Double check. Enough romantic tension to keep you turning pages well into the night? That's a big check! I couldn't put down Cole and Laila's love story."

—Erin La Rosa, author of *Plot Twist*

"Bethany Turner has taken my favorite trope, friends-to-more, and created the most heartwarming, joy-filled, tender story. It's absolutely wonderful! Their love for each other brews from the first page all the way through to the beautiful finale. Why it takes them so long to realize how made for each other they are, well . . . sometimes falling in love with your best friend is complicated. With all sorts of pop culture references and a first 'fake' date to beat all first 'fake' dates, this book is Turner at the very top of her game. Do yourself a favor and pick up this gem of a story."

—Pepper Basham, bestselling author of *Authentically, Izzy* and *The Mistletoe Countess*

"I always thought, Once you're in love, the only place you ever fall in love again is the movies. But you can fall in love again reading this book."

—Delia Ephron, bestselling author, screenwriter, and playwright

## *Brynn and Sebastian Hate Each Other*

"Set in a charming small town and populated by well-developed, believable characters, *Brynn and Sebastian Hate Each Other* is a thoughtful and often tender exploration of two wounded souls seeking redemption and learning to trust again. I couldn't get enough of Bethany Turner's witty banter or the loyal found-family and sweet nostalgia threaded throughout this delightful story. A must-read for lovers of romantic comedy with healthy doses of pop culture, humor, and depth . . ."

—Julie Christianson, author of *The Mostly Real McCoy* and *That Time I Kissed the Groomsman Grump*

"From the moment I heard the title and saw the cover, I knew I *needed* to read this book. And if you are someone who loves quirky small town settings, enemies to lovers, and crisp, delightful prose, you do too! You'll be rooting for Brynn and Sebastian, not just as a couple, but as two people in need of a little redemption and maybe a life reset. This is a rom-com that brings some real depth and development but will also leave you smiling. Longtime fans of Bethany Turner and new readers alike will love this one!"

—Emma St. Clair, *USA TODAY* bestselling author

"Bethany Turner has a magical, effortless way with words, and *Brynn and Sebastian Hate Each Other* showcases this perfectly! You also get an adorable small town, enemies-to-lovers vibe, and all the feels you expect when two protagonists figure out themselves as they figure out each other. Add in a cast of unique and delightful secondary characters, and you get a feel-good story sure to delight and entertain."

—Jenny Proctor, author of *How to Kiss Your Best Friend*

## *The Do-Over*

"Turner's (*The Do-Over*) latest is fun, fast, and heartwarming. This book will appeal to anyone who loves enemies-to-lovers romance and to readers who appreciate when a community plays a central role in the story."

—*Library Journal*

"Turner (*The Do-Over*) charms in a squeaky clean contemporary driven by a battle of wits between journalists . . . In addition to the appealing and endearingly flawed protagonists, Turner delivers a strong supporting cast, especially cameraman Orly Hill and generous town mayor Doc Atwater. Readers will long for a quick return to Adelaide Springs and its salt-of-the-earth citizens."

—*Publishers Weekly*

"Readers who haven't yet discovered the savvy, comedic rom-coms of award-winning author Bethany Turner are in for a treat with her latest second chance romance, *The Do-Over* . . . While romantic comedy may not be the genre for every reader, many will enjoy this light-hearted escape, especially anyone looking to drift away with a well-paced, feel-good story."

—*New York Journal of Books*

"Pitch-perfect comedic timing, a relatable heroine, and a refreshing sweetness elevate this novel above the sea of modern rom-coms. The rare author who can make me laugh out loud, *The Do-Over* is Bethany Turner at her best."

—Lauren Layne, *New York Times* and *USA TODAY* bestselling author

## *Plot Twist*

"Turner crafts an entertaining rom-com that spans ten years and keeps the reader guessing who will claim the heroine's heart . . . As the slow-burn romantic mystery of who Olivia will end up with builds to an amusing and satisfying conclusion, Olivia's witty narration will hold readers' attention. This is a treat."

—*Publishers Weekly*

"Turner's humorous latest has an enjoyable New Adult vibe . . . There is a happily ever after, but not the one most readers will be expecting."

—*Library Journal*

"*Plot Twist* gave my rom-com loving heart everything it could hope for: pop-culture references, frequent laugh-out-loud lines, an enduring friendship, a determined heroine to root for, and (of course) a love story with plenty of twists and turns. Bethany Turner's voice is fresh and fun, and it's a joy to read about Olivia as she grows and changes over the course of ten years. A sweet, funny read about the many kinds of love in our lives, perfect for anyone who loves love or dreams about meeting George Clooney."

—Kerry Winfrey, author of *Waiting for Tom Hanks*

"With a decade-long span of pop-culture fun, playful romantic possibilities, and the soul-deep friendships that push us to be real, *Plot Twist* is everything a reader has come to adore from Bethany Turner . . . plus so much more!"

—Nicole Deese, award-winning author of *Before I Called You Mine*

"Funny, clever, and sweet, *Plot Twist* reminds us that sometimes love doesn't look just like the movies—and that it can be so, so much better than we ever dreamed. Bethany Turner has gifted us all with another winning story with her trademark wit, wisdom, and charm!"

—Melissa Ferguson, bestselling author of *The Cul-de-Sac War*

"Bethany Turner just keeps getting better! *Plot Twist* is like experiencing the best parts of all my favorite rom-coms, tied together with Turner's pitch-perfect comedic timing, an achingly sweet 'will they or won't they?' romance, and the BFF relationship most girls dream of. Add in some Gen-X nostalgia, and you have a book you'll want to wrap yourself up in and never leave."

—Carla Laureano, RITA Award–winning author of *The Saturday Night Supper Club* and *Provenance*

"With a sassy Hallmark-on-speed hook and a winning leading lady, Turner loans her fresh, inimitable voice to her strongest offering yet: a treatise on how love (and the hope for love) paints across a canvas of fate and happenstance, and how life undercuts our expectations only to give us the biggest romantic adventures. Winsome and wise, Turner draws on beloved romantic tropes and zesty pop-culture references to provide a surprising comedy that is the sweet equivalent of Beth O'Leary and Emily Henry."

—Rachel McMillan, author of the Three Quarter Time series and *The London Restoration*

# WES AND ADDIE HAD THEIR CHANCE

## ALSO BY BETHANY TURNER

*Cole and Laila Are Just Friends*

*Brynn and Sebastian Hate Each Other*

*The Do-Over*

*Plot Twist*

*Hadley Beckett's Next Dish*

*Wooing Cadie McCaffrey*

*The Secret Life of Sarah Hollenbeck*

# WES AND ADDIE HAD THEIR CHANCE

*A Love Story*

BETHANY TURNER

THOMAS NELSON
*Since 1798*

*Wes and Addie Had Their Chance*



Published in Nashville, Tennessee, by Thomas Nelson. Thomas Nelson is a registered trademark of HarperCollins Christian Publishing, Inc.

Thomas Nelson titles may be purchased in bulk for educational, business, fundraising, or sales promotional use. For information, please e-mail SpecialMarkets@ThomasNelson.com.

Publisher's Note: This novel is a work of fiction. Names, characters, places, and incidents are either products of the author's imagination or used fictitiously. All characters are fictional, and any similarity to people living or dead is purely coincidental.

**Library of Congress Cataloging-in-Publication Data**

Names: Turner, Bethany, 1979- author.
Title: Wes and Addie had their chance : a love story / Bethany Turner.
Description: Nashville, Tennessee : Thomas Nelson, 2025. | Summary: "When he left her at the altar twenty years ago, the last thing they expected was to seek closure and find something more . . ."—Provided by publisher.
Identifiers: LCCN 2024049920 (print) | LCCN 2024049921 (ebook) | ISBN 9781400345892 (paperback) | ISBN 9781400345908 (epub) | ISBN 9781400345915
Subjects: LCGFT: Christian fiction. | Romance fiction. | Novels.
Classification: LCC PS3620.U76 W47 2025 (print) | LCC PS3620.U76 (ebook) | DDC 813/.6—dc23/eng/20241024
LC record available at https://lccn.loc.gov/2024049920
LC ebook record available at https://lccn.loc.gov/2024049921

*Printed in the United States of America*

25 26 27 28 29 LBC 5 4 3 2 1

*To my mom, who never quit asking me,*
*"What about the one with the politician?"*

I'd already encountered several things I had not seen coming. I never would have believed Doc Atwater and Mrs. Stoddard would seem younger than they had twenty years ago. Never ever in a million years would I have believed that Old Man Kimball would sit in my presence without bringing up the $6.42 I owed him for whiskey glasses I had broken in 2001. But those were just surprises. I never could have been prepared for the shock of Addie Atwater and Wes Hobbes not living happily ever after together.

—Brynn, *Brynn and Sebastian Hate Each Other: A Love Story*

# ADDIE

If a guy breaks your heart, it seems only right that he should go on to be unhappy and unsuccessful. That's fair, right? And you know what? It wouldn't hurt if he were also ugly. Prematurely bald. Maybe required the application of some prescription ointment to keep his skin condition in check.

Now, if the guy breaks your heart by leaving you at the altar—humiliating you in front of everyone you know, scarring you for life, and causing you to question and doubt everything you thought you knew about love—shouldn't he also be unable to leave his house without the assistance of some sort of crane? I don't consider myself a vindictive person, but I really don't think that's unreasonable.

I'm forty years old, and my heart has been broken three times. And I guess that's not so bad if we're grading based on quantity alone.

Of course I'm not talking about the emotional devastations of youth that we think are heartbreak at the time but are, in actuality, disappointments at worst or hormonal fluctuations at best. Getting socks for Christmas. Snagging the hem of your prom dress. Planning for months to go to Denver to see The Verve only to discover at the very end of the concert, when they sing "Bitter Sweet Symphony" (the only song you've recognized all night), that you had them confused with The Verve Pipe.

Or is it the other way around? Honest to goodness, I still don't know the difference.

My first true heartbreak was when my mom died. I was eleven, and I didn't understand why everyone was acting like life was just going to go on. Like the sun was going to come up the next day and the world was going to keep on spinning. But of course it did. Even if my life—and every aspect of the whole wide world—felt like something was missing, from sunrise to sunset of every single day, from that point on.

But you know . . . most of us outlive our parents. We're simply not, however, hardwired to be widowed at thirty-eight. That was the third heartbreak. The clock is not supposed to be ticking down while our toothbrush is hanging out of our mouth. We're not supposed to be running so late for work that when our husband FaceTimes us for what will be the very last time, and we have one more chance to tell him how much we love him, we accidentally spit toothpaste on the camera and end the call in a flurry of foam and minty-fresh aroma and never-to-be-fulfilled promises to call back in a few.

So yeah. It was that third heartbreak—losing my husband, Joel, almost two years ago—that hurt the most. That was the one that almost did me in. But here lately, it's the unavoidable reminders of heartbreak number two that are really starting to stick in my craw.

When I was eighteen, I was left at the altar. Literally left at the altar. I think a lot of people use that expression too liberally when they're talking about a breakup after the invitations have already gone out, or the night before the wedding when you still have time to call everyone and tell them not to show up. I think those of us who were really and truly left at the altar—hair and makeup done, dress zipped up, long train perfectly placed on the grass behind us in preparation for our walk through a meadow to the only boy we thought we'd ever love—should file a class-action suit against the women who carelessly throw around the phrase. Calling off a wedding would always be hard, I'm sure, but those of us who had it called off for us, once it had already begun? We alone have earned that particular badge.

Wes Hobbes didn't just break my heart that day twenty-two years ago. He ripped it out of my chest and ran it through a meat grinder. Then, in case there hadn't been enough damage done, he stomped on it a few times and fed it to the wolves—and left me behind to try to salvage the digested remains as they were pooped out in the forest.

Whatever. I got over it. It took a long time, but I really did get over it. I met Joel, I fell in love again, and I got to spend nearly ten years married to the love of my life. Joel Elwyn. A man who never did anything to hurt me. You know, except die. Meanwhile, Wes Hobbes couldn't even do me the simple courtesy of going on to become severely pockmarked and unemployable.

The man who left me at the altar when we were eighteen years old had become Senator Wesley Hobbes, the beloved front-runner for president of the United States. And he was handsome and had all his hair, and his skin was flawless, and if the nightly news and *People* magazine and all the thirsty fan forums online were to be believed, he was perfectly capable of squeezing through doorways without any sort of lever-and-pulley system whatsoever.

Such a bummer.

# CHAPTER 1

# ADDIE

## 330 Days Since She Returned to Adelaide Springs

"Have you guys looked outside?" I called over the bells that jingled as I opened the door to the Bean Franklin. "Don't hold me to it, but I'm almost certain I saw some sunlight peeking through."

"Just a trick of the mind." Fenton Norris pulled his eyes away from the television on the counter just long enough to survey the gray skies through the glass behind me. "This one's set in good."

He was right. Truth be told, I hadn't even looked up from underneath my coat's hood as I jogged from my parking spot on Main Street, but I knew there had been no sun. I didn't have to look up at the sky to understand that sunlight was going to be a rare treat for the next few days, just like it had been for the past several. In Adelaide Springs you could just feel it. These late-January storms made your bones feel wet and cold. And if you could stand the blowing of thirty-miles-per-hour winds (and the snow those winds blew directly into your eyes and up your nostrils) long enough to look around, you'd notice that every bit of scenery that made Adelaide Springs beautiful was missing. The storm was so set in that the twelve- and fourteen-thousand-foot peaks surrounding the town's elevation—at just over nine thousand—were gone, like they'd been part of a movie set that had been torn down prematurely. The bark of the aspens was nearly indecipherable against the pure-white ground and the slightly darker backdrop of the sky. And the people, whose folksy Main Street presence usually made you feel as if the movie set you were on was constructed by Hallmark, were inside, for the most part. Even the hearty, acclimated citizens of a rugged Colorado mountain town knew when to brew their own coffee and fry their own eggs rather than brave the elements.

Not that mornings at the Bean Franklin were ever really about coffee or eggs.

"Oh, come on, Fenton. Don't be so glass-half-empty." I smiled as he sipped his coffee and rolled his eyes at my ironic positivity. Having only been back in the land of snowblowers, hand warmers, and avalanches for eleven months, my acclimation had been slow, and my complaining had been vocal.

I'd known Fenton Norris—or, more accurately, Fenton Norris had known me—since I was born. Like so many of the citizens of Adelaide Springs, he was a fixture. Almost part of the furniture. And no matter how much had changed about the town—and about me—in my years away, some things would always remain. Fenton Norris would always have his eyes on the television and his mind on the weather. The local diner—the Bean Franklin, it was now called—would always play host to a few stalwart regulars in the morning, even when the rest of the town was taking advantage of a well-deserved snow day. And Adelaide Springs would always operate at its own pace.

Slowly.

It wasn't that there weren't things to do, but in Adelaide Springs, people understood there wasn't any real rush to get them done. Most of the town got up with the sun and began thinking about the day. But the best thinking came a little later, over that second or third leisurely cup of coffee. Most mornings you'd find my childhood friend Laila Kimball expertly managing the relaxed chaos that defined breakfast time at the Bean Franklin on nonblizzard days. Roland and Paula Cross's oldest, Dustin, was turning out to be a natural in the kitchen (having learned under the expert tutelage of Laila's husband, Cole). And Laila may have barely known how to boil water, but she could serve the seven or eight tables of two to four people more efficiently than an entire waitstaff at any given chain restaurant in any given city. Not that most of the patrons would have noticed if she'd ignored them altogether. Like I said, mornings at the Bean Franklin weren't really about breakfast.

On a morning like this one, when a lot more of the population enjoyed their coffee at home, it was quiet. Quiet enough to make those of us who had spent the majority of our lives in much noisier environments uneasy. Uncomfortable. Nervous, even.

How long would I have to be back home before the nervousness went away? How many conversations would I have to sit through with these people who had cared about me my entire life before I finally stopped waiting for the dreaded end of superficiality? Before I finally stopped worrying that the next time they opened their mouths, it would be to ask a question I didn't want to answer?

I reached one of three occupied tables and threw my arms around my dad's shoulders from behind. "Morning."

"Hi, sweets." He patted my hands and leaned into the kiss I was planting on his cheek.

As was my covert habit when I hugged my dad, I held him just tightly enough—just long enough—to check his pulse and perform a general welfare check. No matter how much his energy level and abilities seemed to indicate he was fine—*better* than fine for his age, maybe—he always looked frail to me. I'd stayed away so long that he'd gotten old in my absence, and it wasn't easy to reconcile it all in my mind.

Most difficult of all to reconcile was the fear that frailty hadn't been a companion of age but rather of concern and endless worry about his wayward only child who hadn't managed life so well in the months leading to her return to Colorado.

"What's on the menu today? I'm starving."

Josephine Stoddard spoke up from the seat on the other side of my dad. "There's a new one today." She raised her eyes above my head and called to the kitchen behind me. "What are you calling it again, Laila?"

Laila laughed before answering. "The Battle of Goudas-Burg Quiche." She came around the corner and joined us at our table while my dad was still midchuckle. "I know. It's a bit of a stretch. Not to mention off-brand. But I swear, Andi—and Marietta before her—already mined all viable punny American Revolution food ideas. I want to honor the legacy of this place, but I just *can't* with the John Hancock-a-Doodle-Doo Frittatas or Alexander Ham-and-Cheese Omelets or whatever. There's seriously nothing left."

Andi Franklin, the owner of the Bean Franklin, had still been going by Andrea Franklin when I last lived in town. Well, Andrea Gardner, actually, since I left before she married her first husband. She was several years older than us—my school class of five: Brynn, Cole, Laila, Wes, and me—and had always been Andrea when she babysat us. Somewhere along the line, she had become known as Andi, which I couldn't help but think might not have happened if I hadn't moved away. When you only had a few hundred people in your town, there was no need for confusion over names, and Andi was just a little too similar to Addie. There were plenty of names to go around, so it was usually just a matter of letting the small town do its thing and determine who would be known by what moniker. We couldn't have two Mikes, so one had to go by Michael. One of the Roberts became Bob. There was a Katherine, and there was a Kate.

(And for some inexplicable reason, when Thomas and Tallulah McAfee named their newborn son after his father, we all started calling the baby BooBoo, when really Tom or Tommy probably would have sufficed. That baby was now a minor league baseball pitching coach for the Pensacola Blue Wahoos, because, really, what else was the poor kid going to do with a name like BooBoo McAfee?)

And I had always been Addie. Rarely Adelaide. As a child I had often complained about being named after the place where I was born, and Cole had once said, "Just be glad you're not from Booger Hole, West Virginia." From that point on, as teenagers, he'd occasionally called me "Boog" with mischievous affection. Other than that, I was just Addie.

Ah, well. Names change. For all sorts of reasons, but I'm pretty sure always for a reason that changes you in other ways too.

There'd sure been a lot of life changes for Andrea recently. Over the past few years, she'd lost her younger sister, Wray, to cancer, met some environmental lobbyist guy in DC when she was there sorting out Wray's personal affairs, and moved there full-time when she married the guy, whom no one in town had even met.

(Speaking of names changing, Wray had been Wray Gardner-Hobbes ever since she left town—oh, nearly a couple of decades ago now—and at some point along the line married Wes. As in the guy who left me at the altar.)

In any case, the Bean Franklin—one of three restaurants in town and the only coffeehouse—had been left high and dry with Andrea's abrupt departure, but Laila had refused to let the beloved Adelaide Springs institution die.

"I like it," my dad finally contributed after more concentrated thought than most town mayors likely believed the naming of a daily breakfast special deserved. "We couldn't stay Revolutionary forever. It's good that you've brought our quirky little idiosyncrasies into the nineteenth century. You'll be naming some waffles after Archduke Franz Ferdinand before you know it. You're doing great, kiddo."

Laila laughed and wrapped her arm around my dad's shoulder and briefly rested her head on his. "Thanks, Doc."

Eighteenth-century American history—now nineteenth as well?—and breakfast foods. It was impossible to say which my odd little hometown took more seriously.

"So what will it be, Addie?" Laila stood straight again and adjusted her apron.

"Well . . . why not? Let's go with the Battle of Goudas-Burg." *No matter how morbid it feels to say it.* It still definitely beat the occasional Boston Massa-Curry Chicken lunch special.

Laila smiled at me and nodded. "Coming right up."

Her smile was warm—everything about Laila was always warm—but we hadn't quite settled into any sort of comfortable groove since I'd returned to town. That wasn't Laila's fault, I knew. I'd been back for nearly a year, and in that time my childhood friend had asked me to join her for dinner or coffee or shopping probably a dozen times. All in the first few months. Even the kindest and most loyal of old friends gives up after a while, I guess.

My dad turned his attention back to his crossword puzzle, and Mrs. Stoddard studied her coffee cup. I looked behind me to see Fenton staring at the television and Roland Cross looking up at the ceiling. There were only four or five other people in the entire place, and not a single set of eyes met mine as I surveyed the dining room.

Clearly, my presence had interrupted a conversation I wasn't meant to be a part of.

Since I'd returned to Adelaide Springs, that had become a frequent occurrence. I tried not to take it personally. I'd been gone a long time, after all, and many discussions had been had without me. I couldn't expect to be instantly included in everything all the time. That sounded horrible, truthfully. As the daughter of Doc Atwater—the doctor who had delivered pretty much all of us under the age of fifty and who knew every citizen in our tiny town (literally inside and out)—I had grown up feeling a bit like the unofficial town mascot.

As a child I'd eaten at every dinner table within a five-mile radius. I'd opened the door or answered the phone in the middle of the night and overheard my dad walk people through treating infections and getting bleeding / vomiting / panic attacks under control more times than I could count. As a teenager I'd served as an unofficial nurse and witnessed babies being born and broken arms being set—and no one had ever seemed to mind that I was there. I couldn't remember ever being told I needed to keep things confidential, and I couldn't think of one single time when anyone apart from my dad asked me to leave the room or even hinted that my dad should remove me. The sensitivity . . . the importance . . . the privilege of being welcomed into the most private details of our neighbors' lives . . . it was just understood. Though it wasn't so much that it didn't have to be taught as it was that my dad had been teaching me by his own example since the day I was born.

But since I'd come back to Adelaide Springs, it had become very clear that I was no longer the town mascot. If anything, I was the town project. The town sob story, maybe. It felt, sometimes, like they wanted to make me the town charity case, so I worked very hard at making sure they knew I was fine. Totally fine. *Perfectly* fine. And fine felt nothing short of miraculous to me. Why wasn't it good enough for them?

"What did I miss?" I asked of the room at large, and only my dad's eyes flickered to mine before returning to his paper.

"Think it will snow tonight?" Fenton Norris asked.

The thought of having to plaster on the smile and play the role of the happy and well-adjusted widow to appease them was exhausting, but not as exhausting as this game of avoidance they seemed determined to play.

"It's snowing now, Fenton. It's *been* snowing. You literally told me the storm is 'set in good' five minutes ago." I sighed. "So allow me to ask again: What did I miss?"

"It's nothing, sweets."

"You just missed one of Wes's campaign ads on TV." Laila slid a warmed slice of quiche in front of me and then looked around the room with what appeared to be frustration on her face. Maybe disappointment. And no one seemed too eager to meet her eyes either. "Everyone is afraid to mention his name around you, like he's Voldemort—"

"It's been twenty-two years!" I exclaimed as laughter exploded out of me.

The passing of time. *That* was funny. *That* I could laugh at. So we'd just focus on that rather than the fact that falling in love with Joel Elwyn had long ago ensured the pain I felt at the mention of the name *Wes Hobbes* was no more significant than vapor.

And that the loss of Joel Elwyn had ensured I felt nothing at all.

"And it's an election year. If you guys really intend to clam up every time a campaign ad comes on, I guess let's just plan on reconnecting in December."

Laila shrugged. "That's what I said."

"You guys, I don't care about Wes Hobbes one way or the other. I really don't. The name *Wes Hobbes* has no power over me anymore. Wes Hobbes, Wes Hobbes, Wes Hobbes. Say it with me. It's therapeutic." Everyone was looking at me now, that was for sure, so I raised my arms and dramatically gestured as if I were a conductor leading them all in the world-premiere performance of a new symphony. "Wes. Hobbes."

I didn't expect anyone to say it with me, of course, but Laila actually did, our lifelong (if woefully neglected) friendship and solidarity on brazen display. I smiled up at her, and she winked before heading back to the kitchen.

"You know he's running for president, right?" I asked, quite rhetorically, as I stuffed the first bite of loosely-inspired-by-the-Civil-War creaminess into my mouth. "And as of now, odds are he's going to win. There's a chance—*a chance*—I might see his name here and there between now and November, and then maybe even more over the course of the next four years while he's, you know, leader of the free world. What's the plan? Are you going to hide all the TVs and newspapers? Can I expect a redacted ballot when the time comes?"

I took another bite of quiche and this time chewed and swallowed in silence, savoring the way the crust quite literally melted in my mouth. "This is delicious, Dustin!" I called to the kitchen.

"Thank you!" he yelled back. Laila peeked her head around the wall just long enough to add, "The Civil War has opened up a whole new world of possibilities!"

I chuckled and took another bite before looking up at those around me. Jo Stoddard attempting to bore holes into my soul. Fenton Norris shaking his head sadly and looking at me like I was seven and he'd just learned he'd mistakenly killed my pet hedgehog, thinking it was the rabid raccoon he'd been hunting for years but that no one else in town had ever seen evidence of. (True story.) My dad once again pretending to study his crossword puzzle.

"I'm serious. His name means nothing to me. *He* means nothing to me. I mean it."

"Maybe you do." Dad began folding his newspaper. He got it back into its original form, pulled it tightly through his fingers to reinforce the creases, and removed the napkin from his lap and placed it on the table in front of him.

"Of course I do."

"Then good for you, sweets." His eyes finally met mine—did he always look so tired, or only when he was worried about me?—as he sighed. "Maybe someday you can tell us how you did it."

It was a rare, insensitive misstep from Doc Atwater, and he knew it. His eyes immediately softened, and he cleared his throat as he placed his hand on mine on the table. He knew exactly how I had done it. He'd been there through the months of despair followed by the months of wandering and then by the years of anger and denial. By the time Joel came into my life, I'd fought battle after battle to free myself from the power the name *Wes Hobbes* had once held over me.

"Robert E. Leek Soup!" Laila shouted from the kitchen to the world at large, and only my dad seemed to hear her.

He smiled and patted my hand. "I'd eat that." Then he stood to go and pushed his chair in before leaning over to kiss the top of my head. "Love you."

"Love you, too, Dad."

He grabbed his coat from the back of his chair, slipped it on, and walked out to greet the gray, snowy day, looking older than I'd ever imagined he would.

## CHAPTER 2

# ADDIE

**8,203 Days Since Wes Left**

The rabbit ears on the ancient relic of a television sitting on the counter of the Valet Forge Car Service office only picked up six or seven channels. On a cloudy day like this one, I was lucky to get four. My shift at Valet Forge had been going since noon with nary a customer. Now, as the sun began to set, was it too much to ask that one of those TV channels air a hockey game or an episode of *The Simpsons*, or really anything other than shots of my ex-fiancé shaking hands and kissing babies?

I'd meant what I'd said. Every single word. His name had no power over me, and neither did his face. But my brain hadn't yet gotten the hang of not comparing and contrasting the boy I'd known with the most beloved man of Every. Single. News cycle.

I was an analyst. I *had* been an analyst, anyway. A good one. I might have left the agency a year ago, but that didn't mean my brain just suddenly stopped analyzing. So yeah. Each time I saw Senator Wesley Garrett Hobbes of the great state of Connecticut, my brain automatically tried to make sense of it. My job had been all about getting from point A to point B. I hadn't been a spy or anything exciting like that, though I knew a lot of spies (and truly, being a spy wasn't usually as exciting as movies and TV shows made most people believe it was). But I had no doubt most people would view even the real-world version of being a spy as much more exciting than being a CIA analytic methodologist such as yours truly. Keri Russell and Matthew Rhys were way too sexy to ever be cast as analytic methodologists.

So yeah. I was a highly trained expert at collecting data and figuring out what it all meant. What did it mean, for instance, that the young man who had very nearly talked me into wearing cargo pants and Converse, Avril Lavigne–style, to our wedding (with maybe a Britney newsboy cap up top, to make it dressy) was now a style and fashion icon who seemed to be included on every Best Dressed list in existence? We'd seriously come *this* close to an early aughts grunge wedding (in the end, almost as close as we came to actually getting married) just so he could get away with wearing jeans, a Hollister shirt, and his frayed canvas flip-flops. Therefore, my brain found it odd to see him in tailored suits on TV all the time. He gave speeches in suits. He walked and waved in suits. When a not-at-all-prearranged (um . . . *okay*) opportunity arose to kick a soccer ball around with the UConn collegiate team, he did it without even breaking a sweat. In a suit.

That's like point A to point W for my brain, and it can't help but feel compelled to connect the dots. So forgive me for wishing *anything* else was on TV. These days I found connecting dots to be exhausting.

Wes Hobbes. A lock for the nomination. Well on his way to being elected president of the United States before he turned forty-two years old. The same Wes Hobbes who struggled with reading and spent years trying to claw his way to the back of the pack to prove he was a follower rather than a leader and who had once claimed, "Everything I know about geography I learned from *Carmen Sandiego*." My brain would never be able to make sense of that one.

Of course that was the problem, right? There was no journey that made any sense at all in which *that* Wes Hobbes—*my* Wes Hobbes—should have become *this* Wes Hobbes.

No one ever broached the subject of Wes with me, but at least Laila, Cole, and Brynn didn't awkwardly avoid it like everyone else. The four of us hadn't spent a whole lot of time together since I'd been back, but once in a while, when there was a mention on the news of the long-missing fifth member of our graduating class, or when a campaign ad came on, one of them would say something to the effect of, "It's just so weird to imagine our Wes ever *wanting* to be president." They were right. It was. And I would nod along with everyone else, and then we'd change the subject.

But the truth was, I had long ago figured out something very important that hadn't yet clicked for them. It wasn't that *our* Wes had somehow become *that* Wes. It was that *that* Wes had *always* been *that* Wes. And we hadn't known him at all. There was no other explanation that made sense.

The guy we thought we'd known probably wouldn't have wanted to be president, but at the same time, that was just a job. A path. No one, myself included, would have believed in our childhood that I would go on to become an air force pilot and a CIA analyst. Trauma changes you. And maybe whatever happened in Wes's life after he left Adelaide Springs on August 9, 2003, changed him. Made him shoot higher. Turned him into someone who would excel at leading the entire free world. Maybe he could even be trusted not to accidentally start a ground war in Newfoundland without consulting dispatches from the chief at ACME Detective Agency while chasing down a criminal mastermind while wearing a red hat and trench coat. I couldn't claim to know anything about any of that. But I knew one thing for sure: our Wes—*my* Wes—never would have left us. Never would have left *me*. So he must have actually been *that* Wes all along.

---

The gentle *ding* of the door opening pulled my eyes away from the television for the first time in ten minutes or so, and I reflexively hit the power button, causing the image of Adelaide Springs' lost son to fade from the screen.

"Hey, Boss." I smiled at Neil Pinkton as his cheeks turned pink at the greeting.

He sighed and shook his head. "Addie, I told you, I'm not your boss."

I hopped off the stool and leaned across the counter to good-naturedly goad him further—one of my favorite pastimes in recent days. "Let's see . . . you make the schedule, you sign my checks, you know where we keep the good coffee. If that doesn't make you the boss, I don't know what does." Neil rolled his eyes, and the pink went all the way up to his ears, giving me the opportunity to add, "And you roll your eyes at me. My last boss rolled his eyes at me constantly, so there's proof."

"I'm guessing your last boss wasn't a twenty-two-year-old with no idea what he was doing."

My last boss had been a major general who threatened to court-martial us if we didn't turn off the lights over the sink in the break room, but I didn't figure mentioning that would do any favors for Neil's imposter syndrome.

"No. He wasn't. But neither are you. Twenty-two, yes. But you're doing a great job around here. Andrea knew what she was doing, leaving Valet Forge in your hands."

"Thanks, Addie." He paused for just a second and grinned at me before shutting the door behind him. "I don't know what I'd do if you weren't here, that's for sure."

Adelaide Springs didn't have Ubers or Lyfts or buses or taxis. We just had Valet Forge—another essential small-town business abandoned by Andrea Franklin. Laila had stepped in at the Bean without so much as a note of instruction, but Neil had actually gotten a phone call. From what I understood, he and Brynn's husband, Sebastian Sudworth, had been the only ones who had. Neither one of them had shared many details of what was discussed, but just like that, Neil's desire to finish business school online and then find a good job had been put on the fast track.

Well, no, that wasn't true. School was going to take longer to get through now, since I was his only other driver most of the time. Sebastian, who had returned to his successful journalism career full-time, rarely had time to tinker with vehicles or serve on city council or tend bar and sing karaoke, as town chatter informed me he had in the years before I arrived back home (in what I could only imagine must have been his midlife crisis years). Now he and Brynn were in New York more than they were in Colorado. And Fenton Norris had lost his license months ago after, in his words of defense, mistaking a fallen boulder for a garbage can (and still plowing into it for some inexplicable reason), leaving only young Neil and myself to transport the tourists and elderly can't-drive-after-dark locals.

"Happy to do it, Boss."

I liked working with Neil. He had no memories of me. As far as Neil was concerned, I was just Doc's daughter who had come back to town, and who happened to be a former CIA analyst, which he thought was pretty cool. He was one of the few in whom I didn't discourage the CIA-equals-spy delusions. It made the boring afternoons when he was tired of studying and no one needed a ride much more interesting.

"What's on the docket for tonight?" I asked. "Do you have a lot of homework?"

He shook his head, fulfilling the dual purpose of answering my question and shaking the snow out of his shaggy strawberry-blond hair. "No, I don't have any, if you can believe it. But I do have a hot date with QuickBooks."

I used my hands to push myself back up onto the stool. "Oh. Well, that's boring."

He shrugged. "I like it." He placed his laptop on the counter in front of us and typed in his password.

Neil, by living in Adelaide Springs since birth, had now been a full-time part of the town longer than I had, but I was only a couple of years behind him if we combined my original residency with my current one. I certainly knew what it was like to grow up in a town where the residents' median age seemed to skew a decade older every time you bothered to check. Young couples tended to leave for better opportunities, taking what could have been the town's next generation with them. The kids who made it all the way through school here—like Neil and like me—tended to choose one of two well-worn paths after high school graduation. Either they got out the first chance they had, or they settled in and became members of the ever-dwindling population.

Of course things didn't play out exactly like that for Neil or for me. And truth be told, a weird thing had begun happening in Adelaide Springs over the past few years. New life had been breathed into its rigid, geriatric ways. Having two international celebrities call the tiny mountain town home—even if those two celebrities (*Do we call journalists celebrities?*), Brynn and Sebastian, only lived here part-time now—had brought a lot of new attention. Combine that with the return of Township Days—a quirky little festival with absurd origins that dated back to the seventies—and Adelaide Springs was actually growing for the first time in a century.

"There aren't a lot of people your age around here, are there?" I asked the direct question with the obvious answer, causing Neil's grin to fade quickly.

"No." He sighed and turned back to the counter. "In fact, there are exactly none."

I studied him as he slipped the week's fuel receipts from the spindle on which they were stored and straightened them into a neat pile before locking them together with a staple.

"What's the plan, kiddo?"

The final syllable caught in my throat as I said the word. *Kiddo.* I'd heard my dad call members of my generation *kiddo* my entire life. I'd heard him refer to Laila—forty-year-old Laila—as *kiddo* that very morning. Was this how it happened? One day you were the kiddo, and the next you were the matriarchs and patriarchs of an entire community, trading in your snowmobile weekends and ability to rap all the words of Eminem's "Lose Yourself" for achy knees and crossword puzzles and never-ending debates over the virtues of Barbara Mandrell versus Crystal Gayle?

"What do you mean?" Neil kept his eyes on his receipts, but his fingers seemed to forget they were supposed to be inputting numbers.

I took a deep breath and stepped down from the stool again to stand beside him. "If you hadn't been handed Valet Forge on a silver platter, what would you be doing? What *was* the plan for the next few years?"

He spent the next couple of minutes talking about business plans and getting his MBA and sustainability and initiatives and statistics, and I think there was a mention in there of geospatial data, and all I could think about was how I'd never seen someone's face light up so much when they were talking about such boring stuff.

"But I was always going to come back to Adelaide Springs anyway," he concluded with a shrug.

My eyebrows rose. "You were?"

"Sure." He took in a deep breath and released it in the form of a gentle raspberry at his lips. "I think Adelaide Springs is the most wonderful place in the world, and I want to do what Sebastian and Brynn and Cole and Laila and everybody are doing now. Making sure it survives and thrives and doesn't get turned into something it's not. You know?" He cleared his throat and chuckled. "That sounds so stupid."

"No. It doesn't." I smiled at him and swallowed down all the advice I wanted to give. Advice about seeing what the rest of the world had to offer before locking in those thoughts about Adelaide Springs being the most wonderful place. Advice about how difficult it is to forge your own identity in a community that believes it knows you better than you know yourself. Maybe even a little advice about how, much like Valet Forge's long-overdue conversion to QuickBooks, his life in Adelaide Springs might always feel like it was running several decades behind. "Those are some noble and important dreams you've got. Good for you." I gave his arm a gentle, maternal pat. "Whatever you do, you're going to be a superstar at it. I hope you know that."

Who was I to give advice about dreams anyway? As has oft been said, kill my dreams once, shame on you. Kill my dreams twice, move back in with my dad, work a minimum-wage job, and don't waste any more time on dreams.

"Thanks, Addie." He smiled at me as the phone rang. He grabbed the receiver. "Valet Forge Car Service. Where can we take you?"

I kept trying to convince Neil we needed to answer the phones with something snappier. Something more befitting our Revolutionary War namesake. Thus far, however, neither of us had been able to come up with anything that didn't use the words *hypothermia* or *dysentery*.

"Got it. Thanks," Neil was saying on the phone. "I'll head out now." He grabbed the keys to the classic 1974 orange-and-white Ford Bronco from the hook behind him.

"What's up?"

"Roland, calling from the airport. Steve radioed ahead for a passenger arriving at about five forty-five."

I glanced at my watch. Twenty minutes. I stepped down from the stool before placing my open palm in front of Neil so he could hand me the keys. "Let me get it. QuickBooks is waiting for you to show her a good time."

## CHAPTER 3

# WES

### 6 Weeks Until the California Primary

"Yes, Phil, I remember."

Wes was pretty sure that someday, when the time came to write his memoir, it would be published under the title *Yes, Phil, I Remember: One Politician's Futile Quest Not to Be Treated Like a Four-Year-Old.*

"And don't forget you need to get scheduled for a sit-down with Ambassador Harlington the second you're back in DC. In fact, let's go ahead and set that up. You're in Sacramento how long? You'll be back in time to commemorate the anniversary, won't you?" Phil took a deep breath, muttered something, and then exhaled loudly into the receiver, necessitating Wes's removal of the phone from his ear. Sadly, he was back before he could miss a word. "What am I saying? Of course you will. That's Tuesday. You won't be in Sacramento longer than a day or two."

*Right?*

That was the point in the conversation where, if it were like normal conversations and Philip Brewster and Wesley Hobbes were like normal men, Phil would have asked for confirmation of that assertion. If Wesley Hobbes were a normal man, his life would be his own.

Right?

"What if I stayed a little longer?"

Silence emanated. For a long time after leaving Adelaide Springs, the silence had bothered him. Actually, on some level silence had *always* bothered him. He'd never really had those natural instincts that seemed for so many to accompany a quiet life and a slower pace. He'd always felt the need to try to fill the gaps. Depending upon which of his former therapists you asked, he'd been either afraid he was in trouble or afraid of no longer being someone's focus. Either way, the silence triggered fear, and fear triggered his need to hop up on an apple cart, grab a megaphone, and sing "Yankee Doodle Dandy" to try to please someone or other.

"Why would you stay longer? The anniversary is—"

"Tuesday. Yes, Phil, I know."

"Well, then, surely you know that it's not an option for a United States senator from Connecticut, two months out from the Connecticut primary, to commemorate the one-year anniversary of the death of the most beloved governor in Connecticut history with a visit to Harry Potter Land when he should be in Connecticut."

"Could you please remind me which state I represent? It's so hard to keep track. Connecticut, is it?" Wes sighed in response to the tense silence on Phil's end of the line. Except he didn't. He'd gotten pretty good at only sighing internally. It was a useful trick that he figured was going to either save his sanity or result in an ulcer. Only time would tell. "And it's Harry Potter *World*." *Nope, that isn't right either.* "Which is in Hollywood. Allow me to remind you one more time that I'm in—"

"You used to be able to take a joke, Senator. I know. You're in Sacramento."

Except he wasn't.

Wes looked out the window and, though it was getting dark, knew that the geography within view confirmed just how far he'd taken his own joke. Not that it was a joke at all, of course. Nor a prank. A midlife crisis? Maybe. The only thing he knew for sure was that he and Phil were never going to share a laugh over it. There was never going to come a day when Phil would good-naturedly tell the story of that time his presidential front-runner ditched his aides and ignored the schedule and claimed he was valiantly fighting for California's fifty-four electoral votes when, in reality, he had donned a baseball cap, flown coach completely incognito, and smuggled himself back to his Colorado hometown.

"Yeah. Sacramento. And the only magic that's going to be happening here over the course of the next few days will involve sealing up undecideds and bringing in massive campaign contributions."

"Well, I do like the sound of that." Phil laughed. "Okay, so tell me: Why the need for extra days? If I know you, you'll have this all sewn up by noon tomorrow."

"Noon?" Wes chuckled. "There's going to be a ticker-tape parade in my honor before the lieutenant governor has gotten the parsley from breakfast out of his teeth." (The average taxpayer would be shocked to learn the number of people kept on government payrolls for the sole purpose of notifying elected officials when they have something green and stringy hanging from their gums.) "Nevertheless, I want to really stick it to them while I'm here. I don't just want them to vote for me. I want them eating out of the palm of my hand. I want to remind them—"

"Who's 'them,' specifically? The lobbyists or the congressional delega—"

"Yes. All of them. I want to remind every single one of them that I don't like them any more than they like me, but that doesn't change the fact that I'm going to be their president soon. It would serve them well not only to remember that but to start thanking me for even gracing them with my presence. Even if we only have a couple days together, it's on them. It's time to let bygones be bygones, and if they behave, we'll all get to be part of a little feel-good piece on the nightly news."

Wes's campaign manager cackled on the other end of the call like the heartless, maniacal supervillain he was, and Wes thought he might be sick. Not that Phil was the cause of the nausea. Not this time.

"Well, if that's the case, go get 'em. I have to say, it's nice to hear you focused again. Ever since Wray passed, I've been wondering if you even had it in you—"

"You don't need to worry about that." *There we go.* Nausea. Phil's fault. Order was restored.

Being revolted by much of what came out of Phil's mouth was nothing new, of course. But something about hearing him say the name of his late wife caused Wes to feel so much more than just queasiness. The nausea was easy. The sadness and regret were something else entirely.

"Well, I'm going to go ahead and reach out to Harlington's office, and then when you—"

Wes was startled out of listening to the rest of Phil's patronizing instructions about how he should hold his scissors and always remember to put the lid back on the glue stick by a sound akin to that of a 747 idling nearby. He turned to face the bellow and discovered the revving engine seemingly belonged to a normal—if not somewhat massive and ancient—vehicle parked just outside the glass doors of the airport lobby. The headlights were shining directly into his eyes, so he was rendered blind as he raised his hand and waved. The sharp honk of the horn that followed didn't exactly bode well for the service he expected he was about to receive, but there was no one else waiting around. The ride had to be his.

"I'm gonna cut you off there, Phil. My car's here." He'd really hoped to have a few moments of solitude to think about all that was to come without Phil blabbering into his ear, but some dreams were not meant to be. "I'll talk to you later."

"Call me when you—"

Wes ended the call and stuffed his phone into the inside pocket of his suit jacket, then reached down and hoisted up his suitcase and his trusty Tumi leather backpack that rarely left his side. He would never stop being grateful that at least he was the young and "hip" politician who could get away with carrying a backpack rather than a briefcase. It was a small consolation that, on certain days, provided the only fuel in his tank.

"Thank you!" He was pretty sure someone was in that back room behind the counter. He could hear sports announcers effusing from a television, and every so often he heard a desk chair creaking loudly, but he'd witnessed no other signs of life. "Have a nice evening!" Wes's voice cracked, and he took a deep breath and smiled at the sound.

"Signs of life," he whispered to himself encouragingly.

He was actually grateful for the squeaky voice and the moisture on his palms and the way his heart seemed to be attempting to keep pace with a group of sprinting track-and-field athletes only it could see. He wasn't sure whether to attribute the rush of adrenaline to all the lies he had told in order to break free—to *be* free, even if just for a little while—or to finally being back home, but the signs of life were a welcome reminder that he was doing the right thing.

*Home?*

Yes. Home.

"Good evening," he said, waving again and greeting the driver through the old orange-and-white Ford Bronco's slightly cracked-open window. The brunette in the driver's seat stared at him with wide eyes as he passed. "I hope I didn't keep you waiting," he prepared to say as he began to climb in, reacting to the death glare she was giving him—which he initially processed as clear communication that he had, in fact, kept her waiting. But then, quickly, but still just a little too slowly, his brain remembered he wasn't in Sacramento or Hollywood or Hartford or even one of his off-the-beaten-path campaign stops in a far-flung corner of the rural heartland. No, he was in Adelaide Springs, and it was possible he would encounter many, *many* sets of glaring eyes during his visit. Some of them would probably even be familiar to him.

But no set of eyes across the entire nation would ever be as familiar to him as the ones glaring at him now.

Wes lowered his foot from the running board and took a step back to stand beside the driver's door again. "Addie?" he attempted to say into the cold, dark air, but the two syllables seemed hesitant to move past his lips.

The wide-eyed glare fell for just a moment at the sound of her name and morphed into something softer. But in an instant any hint of softness was gone, replaced by what he interpreted as narrow-eyed skepticism and mistrust. Maybe he was attempting to read too much into a nearly imperceptible gamut of expressions that danced across her face for a second, maybe two, but skepticism and mistrust had been what he expected from every set of eyes from his past. He hadn't been expecting Addie's eyes at all, but how much truer must the feelings be for her?

She cleared her throat and turned away to face front, adjusting the rearview mirror before gripping the steering wheel with both hands. "Better climb in, Senator. The meter's running."

# CHAPTER 4

# ADDIE

### 5,561 Days Since the End of Before

I'd never forgotten the day I first saw him on television. It was November 2, 2010, and I was just a couple of weeks away from finishing up grad school.

There are times, when I think back on that part of my life, that I still marvel at where I ended up. And I don't mean the hot-mess omnishambles of my current life. I mean where I ended up when I was still heading somewhere. A degree in operations research from the Air Force Academy led to recruitment to AFIT—the Air Force Institute of Technology—where, in addition to serving my stint as an active officer in the air force, I obtained my MS in operational analysis. I learned to fly and spent time as a pilot, but thankfully, I had commanding officers who saw that I was more of an asset in a cubicle than in a cockpit.

Now, so many years later, I felt like my life could be divided into two different eras: Before 11/2/10 and After 11/2/10. The truth is, I rarely spent time thinking about the Before. It felt so distant. That version of *me* felt so distant. In the Before, I hadn't known for sure what I was going to do with my life, even as I chased those elite degrees, but I had known I was going to do it with Wes. Never mind that by the time we got to the Before-After time split, I hadn't seen him in seven years. I still believed he and I were endgame.

I'd been accepted into the academy before high school graduation, but I never told anyone. At that time, in those moments, in that era, I couldn't even have said for sure why I'd applied. Maybe just out of curiosity. Mrs. Stoddard had certainly encouraged me to go that direction. Actually, she'd first encouraged me to try for MIT, but there was no way I was going to entertain that idea. Wes didn't have the grades or the money to go anywhere out of state, so a college in Colorado was the only option. The Air Force Academy was in Colorado Springs, only four hours away, and tuition was free if you were accepted and committed to serve after graduation, but with Wes's lackluster GPA and SAT scores, he'd had a better chance of getting accepted to Hogwarts. That was the joke he always made, anyway. Still, maybe I should have given the academy more serious consideration when I received my acceptance letter, but Wes was going to Colorado State in Fort Collins.

Therefore, I was going to Colorado State in Fort Collins.

And then, suddenly, I was going nowhere.

It took more than a year for me to come out of the hole. Not that I fully came out of it after a year, mind you, but I thought I had. In reality, I was more like Punxsutawney Phil, peeking my head out and marveling at my own shadow. But it sure felt like progress at the time, even just to rise aboveground and breathe some fresh air and declare that winter was, in fact, going to end eventually. I had no idea what had become of Wes. No idea where he had landed. But I hadn't stopped believing he was coming back. That was the worst part of those first few years, I think. As the saying goes, it's the hope that kills you, and my belief that he would come back never wavered—but the emotions circling that belief oscillated wildly, depending on the day.

I was so mad at him. So hurt. No, actually . . . words like *mad* and *hurt* don't even begin to lend enough weight to how I felt. I had been destroyed. I remember reading *New Moon*, the second Twilight book, when it came out in 2006 or so, and just laughing through the whole thing. Cackling, really. I wasn't laughing for any of the obvious reasons—just the idea that Bella Swan could be sent spiraling into this bottomless pit of despair and depression over some guy she'd known for, what? A year? Wes may not have been a sparkly vampire—although I couldn't help but draw some cold, heartless bloodsucker comparisons—but I knew Bella's pain was nothing compared to mine.

The Wes I had known since I was born and been in love with since well before I knew how to classify the emotion never would have left me like that unless there'd been a very good reason for it. But what reason could there possibly be? He'd done something stupid and careless and unforgivable—but I anxiously awaited the day he would come home so I could forgive him. I anxiously awaited the day we'd begin putting it all behind us.

And then other days I swore I would never speak to him again. I told myself that when he came back—yes, *when*, because even on the worst days I couldn't help but look up expectantly every time a car approached—he could beg and plead and implore all he wanted, but I would never again acknowledge him. It was my turn to disappear from *his* life. It was my turn to leave him to wonder what he could have done differently to make sure things turned out the way they were supposed to. He wouldn't have to wonder about that for as long as I had, of course. He could have bothered to look me in the eyes on our wedding day, regardless of what needed to be said or done after that. That's all it would have taken. We would have figured it out from there.

It was on one of the angriest days that I reapplied to the Air Force Academy. I reveled in the knowledge that he wasn't smart enough to ever join me there. I rested—for the first time, I rested—in the solace that four hours away may as well have been four lifetimes away. He would never find me there, and I could finally move on.

Except I didn't. Not until November 2, 2010, when his face popped up on my television screen for the first time. The first of so many times. *Countless* times. It was Election Day, and all the buzz was about this new guy on the scene. Wesley Hobbes—the handsome, charismatic son of the beloved governor of Connecticut, and at only twenty-five years old and newly elected, the youngest member of the House of Representatives.

Alongside his beautiful wife of seven months, Wray Gardner-Hobbes.

That was it. That was the moment when time split but my heart began healing. All of a sudden, I understood that he was never coming back, and I wasn't crushed. I wasn't crushed at all. I was relieved. I could finally breathe again.

I finished my master's and completed my active service, and then I entertained offers from all three branches of government, several prestigious universities, and at least one European monarchy. Instead, I fought my way into the CIA. Not that I had to *fight*, really. I was right for the agency. They knew it, and I knew it. But no one slid into the CIA. My education and references opened the door, and then I had to prove myself. I'd never wanted anything as much as I wanted that job. It was where I belonged.

So there I was, settling down in Langley, fully aware that Wes was just twelve miles down the George Washington Parkway in the Rayburn Building. It didn't keep me up at night. It didn't keep me from going out with friends to trendy Dupont Circle bars where young politicos were known to hang out. It meant nothing.

And then one day, after I'd been at the agency a year, I delivered a clandestine target analysis report to a collection management officer whose tie was on inside out. Everyone at times worked crazy hours under unfathomably stressful conditions, so I'd seen women wearing one brown shoe and one black shoe. Men who forgot their socks. Missed buttons and rumpled, slept-in slacks. But I'd never seen the small part of the tie in front of the big part, and I couldn't stop staring at it. I don't know why it bothered me so much—had he tied it that way or just slipped it over his head with the wrong side facing out?—but I couldn't let it go. So much so that once I'd clocked out for the day, I hurried back to Officer Elwyn's office to tell him. He was heading out for the day as well, and when we met up in the hallway, he was quick to tell me how much he would have appreciated me telling him about his tie *before* his meeting with the deputy administrator of the US Agency for International Development. I promised to be more forthcoming next time, and he promised to look in a mirror before leaving the house . . . hopefully to pick me up for dinner.

It had meant nothing that my ex-fiancé was twelve miles down the road, but from that point on, it somehow meant even less than nothing. But that was a long time ago. Things change.

Now my ex-fiancé was in the back of my car.

---

I glanced at him in the rearview mirror as soon as the interior light faded and we had only moonlight to reflect any potential connection between our eyes. Moonlight was all I needed to see his gaze locked in place, ready to pull mine in like a tractor beam once I carelessly looked up. I looked down at the gear stick and shifted into Reverse so I could back out of the parking space.

"Where to?" I asked as if he were any other tourist from any other flight.

"Addie, I don't even know what to—"

"Where to?" I repeated as I pulled onto the county road and began heading toward town.

I glanced back at the mirror just as he finally pulled his eyes away. He chewed on his bottom lip before answering. "It's called the Inn Between. Do you know it?"

I'd have known *him* anywhere, that was for sure. Anytime, in any context, in any brightness of light or lack thereof—without question. Even if I hadn't seen him on *Meet the Press* as recently as last Sunday. Not that I saw even an echo of the boy I had loved in the perfectly-orchestrated-for-ultimate-voter-appeal package that was currently staring out the window. But eyes and lips don't change too much, even when gentle creases begin to surround them. And when you'd spent as many hours staring into someone's eyes and kissing someone's lips as I had those of Wes Hobbes, their imprint on your brain couldn't ever really be expected to leave you.

And maybe it made sense that all of that was as true for him as it was for me, but that hadn't made it any less shocking to hear him say my name. Eyes and lips may not change too much, but voices do. Or at least our memories of them do. It was jarring, really. Not because I didn't know his voice. I did. But I'd gotten used to hearing it say, "I'm Wesley Hobbes and I approve this message." Hearing him say my name after twenty-two years felt like a little too much reality a little too quickly.

I'd walked into the airport, overheard him on the phone, and turned around as quickly as I could to scurry back to the vehicle. *Lay low.* That had been the plan. Joel had always told me that "Lay Low" should have been the motto of the CIA rather than "The Work of a Nation. The Center of Intelligence." I was very good at laying low. Usually. But you don't lay low by making eye contact. Still, it was surprising that he recognized me so immediately. In his two decades away, he hadn't once had to watch national coverage of *me* delivering a stump speech.

"Yeah, I know it." I shifted my eyes away from the mirror as his rose in my direction.

"Great. Thanks. Um . . . so how have you been?"

I chuckled humorlessly and signaled to pass the little front-wheel drive Mazda going a snail's pace in front of me as snow began to fall. "We're not doing that."

"We're not doing what?"

"Talking."

"But—"

"Nope."

"Come on, Addie, don't—"

"Wes." I met his eyes in the mirror, and he leaned forward for just a moment, until I added, "Stop talking."

His mouth opened, but thankfully he thought better of saying anything else and instead scoffed, crossed his arms, and turned toward his window.

I had always excelled at patting my head and rubbing my stomach at the same time. Well, not literally. For whatever reason, that particular skill had always been out of reach for me, and any attempts resulted in either a whole lot of patting or a whole lot of rubbing. Never both. But I could pilot an F-15 Eagle through maneuvers while concurrently annihilating whoever was on the headset in a round of Six Degrees of Kevin Bacon. I could comb through hours of poorly translated transcripts of a recording from a cave somewhere in Yemen while simultaneously quoting to myself the entire episode of *Friends* in which Chandler pretends he's moving to Yemen just to get away from Janice.

I *could* do those things. Once upon a time. Now, apparently, I was going to require complete silence in order to drive a familiar road and, you know, *think* at the same time.

I was an analyst. No, I didn't get paid any longer to be an analyst, but that changed nothing. I was an analyst. So it was time to do what I had done countless times before and separate the data from the emotions. It was as simple as dividing the yolk from the rest of the egg. Sometimes messy, sure. Sticky. A delicate process—one that could go wrong so easily and so quickly, and once it did, there was often no turning back. But that didn't make it any less simple. So, setting the emotions aside, what data did I have to work with?

Senator Wes Hobbes was in the back of the vehicle I was driving.

He was alone. In other words, he was sans entourage and security and advisers and press. He was wearing a ball cap with sunglasses resting on the bill.

Steve, the pilot, had radioed ahead to Roland at the airport that someone was arriving. In turn, Roland had called Valet Forge and passed the info along to Neil. But Neil had said nothing to me about it being a VIP, which meant Roland had said nothing about it being a VIP, which meant Steve had said nothing about it being a VIP. That meant that neither Steve, who was not from Adelaide Springs, nor Roland, who was, had recognized the passenger. And they both most certainly would have recognized Senator Hobbes unless Senator Hobbes didn't want to be recognized.

He'd been surprised to see me. That much was certain. Anyone who wasn't a proficient reader of lips (and perhaps also a retired expert in the field of Wes Hobbes) would have missed the barely there whisper of my name, but no one could have missed the startle in his eyes, most commonly found in deer pausing in the middle of the road and children caught with their hands in cookie jars. It remained to be seen if he had been surprised to see me at all, or just surprised to see me then.

My eyes flitted back to the mirror, and I took the opportunity to study him while his focus was on the passing scenery out the window.

*Fascinating.* I think in the past, since the split in time and certainly since I met Joel, I wouldn't have had any difficulty being cordial with Wes if I had bumped into him in a cocktail bar at the Hay-Adams, for instance.

*"My goodness, how long has it been? It's lovely to see you. Joel, you know Wes Hobbes—oh, sorry,* Representative *Hobbes. Or wait—it's Senator Hobbes now, right? Congratulations on that, by the way. This is my husband, Joel. Tell me, how's Wray doing? Please give her my best."*

No, it probably wouldn't have gone exactly like that, but we no doubt would have achieved some equally schmoozy level of DC small talk, and then we would have gone back to our respective tables and each spent a couple of minutes wondering what we'd ever seen in the other. Then we would have stuffed our faces with oysters Rockefeller without another thought or a single flash of nostalgia.

But that would have been DC, and this was Adelaide Springs. Joel was dead. Wray was dead. Wes was about to become president. And I was his chauffeur.

Didn't see that one coming.

And still, I felt nothing. I didn't hate him. I certainly didn't love him. I didn't think, *He looks good*, or *Do* I *look that old?* I didn't even wonder what I had seen in him. No, all I could think about was what a tactical error he was making by coming back here. *Ever*, but especially now, so close to the election.

*"Even if we only have a couple days together, it's on them. It's time to let bygones be bygones, and if they behave, we'll all get to be part of a little feel-good piece on the nightly news."*

The comments hadn't been about us. It wasn't about Adelaide Springs. Whoever he'd been strategizing against during that little snippet of phone call I'd overheard at the airport, he couldn't possibly be so stupid as to talk about his hometown that way.

No, actually, let me restate that. I had no idea what he said about Adelaide Springs. I had no idea what he thought or felt about the little town where he grew up. More than twenty years gone without so much as a mention in a feel-good interview on the *The Drew Barrymore Show*, from what I knew, of where or how he grew up certainly didn't make me think he had been missing me. *Us*, I mean. Adelaide Springs. He wasn't missing Adelaide Springs. But whether or not he was stupid enough to talk about his hometown that way, he *definitely* wasn't stupid enough to believe he could get the people he deserted to "behave" so he could fly away in a couple of days with a few more votes that weren't going to make any difference at all in the election. No. He most definitely hadn't been strategizing against Adelaide Springs.

But it was still a tactical error for him to come back here. Wherever he went, the press was sure to follow eventually. Wes wouldn't lead—no politician in the world would intentionally lead—the press to the closet where all the skeletons were hidden. And maybe it was possible that he didn't realize just how unforgiving his former friends and neighbors were still feeling after all this time.

But he'd realize it soon. Probably as soon as he got to the inn and encountered Jo Stoddard.

Mrs. Stoddard had, at some point or other in our lives, been the closest thing any of the five of us had to a mother. For Wes, it was junior year, when his mom was in and out of the hospital fighting cancer, and senior year, when she lost the battle. It was Mrs. Stoddard who gave him a place to stay and Mrs. Stoddard who helped him with college applications, and it was Mrs. Stoddard who was preparing to share a dance with him at our wedding reception while I danced with my dad.

And then he deserted her just like he deserted me.

He was going to walk into the Inn Between, wanting a room at the only option that came up when he googled "where to stay in Adelaide Springs, Colorado," and he was going to come face-to-face with his past. At least in the Bronco he had the benefit of only coming face-to-back-of-head with his past.

"Hey, Addie," he began softly behind me, shuffling in his seat to lean forward just a bit as I turned off the road and onto the inn's gravel driveway. "I can't just sit here and not say anything."

"You can."

"Okay, but I don't want to. You weren't expecting to see me tonight any more than I was expecting to see you, but we're here now, and I think we should talk."

I came to a stop and shifted into Park before cutting the engine and opening my door. It was such a practiced move. This old vehicle didn't have a trunk I could pop open from the inside, so I was used to getting out, unlocking the trunk, helping with bags, visiting with the tourists for a moment—being sure to recommend the Bean Franklin for breakfast, Cassidy's for lunch, and Milo's for dinner—and then making sure they had Valet Forge's number for all their transportation needs. But this tourist didn't have a lot of bags, I wasn't voluntarily going to sic him on my friends and their various dining establishments, and I sure didn't want to stand around and chat for a moment. And as for his transportation needs, he had long ago proven he could wrangle a ride out of town when he needed one.

I pulled my foot back in and shut the door again. "Have a good night, Senator."

He sighed and unbuckled his seat belt. Then I felt his presence over my shoulder. Too close. Too intimate. And so familiar, even after having been without him longer than I had been with him, that my pulse began racing.

"I get it—"

I laughed. "You *don't*."

"No, Addie, I really think I do. I know I don't have any right to ask you to listen to anything I have to say, but—"

"You need to back away."

I met his eyes in the mirror again, and there was a flash of confusion. But then awareness dawned, and his eyes softened into sadness as he cleared his throat. And then his eyes were gone and he was pressed against the back seat as he whispered, "Sorry."

I didn't know what to do with this data. I didn't know what to do with the fact that I saw pain in his eyes and that I didn't really enjoy hurting him. I certainly didn't know what to do with the fact that it hurt me, too, to treat him like someone I didn't trust. Of course I didn't trust him. I *couldn't* trust him. He had taken my trust and made a mockery of it. But until now I hadn't had to act on that lack of trust.

Every muscle in my body was as taut as a tightrope, and suddenly my emotions felt every bit as precarious as one.

"Get out of the car, Wes."

He sighed. "Okay."

He opened the door and gathered his belongings, which had been on the seat beside him, as he stepped outside. All that was left was for him to shut the door.

*Shut the door, Wes. Just shut the door.*

"Um, do I pay you, or—"

"No charge."

He set his bags on the ground and leaned back inside. "Come on, Addie."

"I insist."

"But—"

I turned in my seat to face him, suddenly feeling like the greatest disservice he had ever done me was not allowing me to end this encounter on my terms.

"Tell me," I seethed. "What sort of federal penalty will I face for the hit-and-run squishing-in-a-car-door of a United States senator?"

I faced forward again before I could see what his initial surprise morphed into, and the instant the car door shut behind me, I was gunning the old Bronco into action and barreling down the driveway and back onto the highway.

And I'd be lying if I said it didn't feel pretty good to be deserting *him* for a change.

## CHAPTER 5

# WES

### A Year and a Half Since He'd Said Her Name

"Addie."

*Addie.*

"Addie."

Her name was the only sound he could make, but he wasn't entirely sure he was making any sound at all. His brain was a symphonic dissonance of those two syllables, over and over, as he watched the taillights reach the end of the driveway. And then his brain finally kicked into gear enough to activate his feet into movement and his voice above a hoarse whisper.

"Addie!"

"Wesley Hobbes, what in tarnation do you think you're doing?"

Any other time, the sternness of Jo Stoddard's voice behind him would have caused him to snap to attention like a little boy playing soldier. But first things first.

"Jo, what is Addie doing here?"

He hadn't said her name aloud since Wray died, and he hadn't said it to anyone outside of Wray in more than a decade before that. Now his brain and his tongue and his vocal cords all seemed fixated on it. Once upon a time, Addie Atwater had been his first language. He'd been fluent in every dialect of her. And yet tonight he'd made contact with her eyes in a mirror and seemingly lost the ability to communicate. At least he couldn't communicate well. He certainly couldn't communicate with her.

He watched her turn onto the county road and fade off into the darkness, and then he asked the question again. "What is Addie doing here, Jo?"

"She lives here. I think the better question at this moment is what are *you* doing here?"

Wes turned to face her and was surprised to realize how far down the driveway he had wandered—watching Addie go, wanting to chase after her, unable to process that desire. He glanced over his shoulder one time to make sure she wasn't coming back and then sighed and began walking toward Jo. "A little warning wouldn't have hurt."

"About Addie?"

"*Of course* about Addie."

"Yeah, well." She shrugged and wrapped her bulky knee-length sweater tightly around her. "You could stand to listen to yourself. A little warning about *you* might not have been a bad idea either."

"What do you mean? You told me I should come home."

Jo laughed. "No. I most certainly did not."

"Yes, you did. Last week. You said I should try talking to Sebastian and—"

"No, no, no. No, sir. You're not putting this on me. First of all, I'm not even sure that half of what I say on the Face-to-Face Time gets transmitted—"

"But you *did*, Jo. You said that if anyone would give me a fair shake, it would be Sebastian Sudworth."

"And you took that to mean you should show up here unannounced like the Ghost of Christmas Past?" She planted her fists on her hips as her lips tightened into a wrinkly cluster that resembled a peach pit.

He arrived back at his abandoned bags and stood in front of her. She was shorter than she'd been. Of course he was probably a little bit taller than he had been, but she was definitely smaller. Whereas they'd once stood eye to eye, and then eye to mouth after his last big growth spurt junior year, they were now a little more eye to chin. That didn't change the fact that she was still the most imposing figure he'd ever known.

Not that her being the most imposing figure he'd ever known made him any less likely to tease her.

"Actually . . ." He cleared his throat and took one more step toward her. "I'm pretty sure the Ghost of Christmas Past was announced. That was sort of the point of Jacob Marley, right?" One corner of his mouth rose, and the other joined in when he spotted her peach-pit lips twitching. He opened his arms and leaned down and pulled her into his embrace. "I've missed you."

"Fine, fine." She wouldn't go so far as to return his hug, but she patted her hands on his back twice before pulling away. "Let's continue this argument someplace warmer."

He picked up his backpack and hoisted one strap over his shoulder before extending the handle from his suitcase and proceeding to roll it over the bumpy gravel. Jo didn't wait for him, so after she'd hurried inside, he found himself standing alone on the porch, looking up at the redbrick walls of the house he had once known so well. There was no way to track all the hours he had spent there with his group of friends when it had belonged to Laila's grandparents. The attic had been their clubhouse where they hung out, watched movies, played games, studied, you name it, from the time they were in elementary school.

Over the course of the past year, he'd made amends with Jo. And making amends with Jo had led to his teaching her to use FaceTime (which he could never, for whatever reason, quite convince her wasn't called Face-to-Face Time) so they could talk. Face-to-face. (Okay, so she wasn't quite as out in left field as, say, his stepmother when she referred to Lady Gaga as Zsa Zsa Gabor.) Maybe that had filled him with a false sense of security about coming back. That was one of the risks of modern technology, he supposed. It was the same phenomenon that made him feel like he and Jennifer Garner really were friends just because he spent so much time watching her pretend cooking show on Instagram. He knew where she kept her measuring cups, so why couldn't he expect her to recognize him if they bumped into each other on the street?

But now he was dealing with the reality of being back. Jo Stoddard in her seventies. The Olivets' house having been converted to an inn.

*Addie.*

"I know for a fact you weren't raised in a barn."

He shook himself out of his stupor and smiled as he walked in through the open door—making sure to be a good boy and shut it behind him.

---

"Who's going first?" Jo asked him as they settled in front of the fire in the front room of the Inn Between.

Wes took the cup of coffee she offered and nodded his thanks before taking a sip. "First? For what?"

"Well, I figure you need to tell me why you're here, and I need to tell you why you should leave."

He chuckled and took another scorching sip before setting the cup on the coffee table in front of him. "Good to see you too."

"Come on, now. You know that has nothing to do with it. I'm not the problem here."

He may not have understood the full scope of the problem as Jo saw it, but he still had no doubt she was correct in that assertion.

"The truth is, I didn't put a lot of thought into it."

Jo blew gently on her steaming mug of herbal tea and cocked a brow over raised eyes. "It's good to see some things never change."

That was fair. In Jo's eyes he probably did appear to be the same flighty, somewhat wild, somewhat dim-witted boy who seemed incapable of treating anything with the seriousness it deserved, be it his homework or his SATs, a mountain bike wreck while he stupidly wasn't wearing a helmet, or his mother's death. What no one had ever understood, though—not even Addie, he was pretty sure—was that he carried it all with him. All the time. What they saw him dismissing on the outside was usually gnawing and churning and slowly destroying him on the inside.

"Why do I continually feel the need to remind you that the good people of Connecticut have elected me to office five times now? I think it's safe to say I've come pretty far."

"Well, that may be, but 'the good people of Connecticut' never had to train a schnauzer to lick your face in the mornings when your alarm clock went off so you wouldn't be late."

Wes leaned forward and grabbed his coffee again. "What? You think I show up on the floor for legislative sessions of my own volition?" A gulp of the hot, rich liquid burned on the way down, and he savored it. "You don't give 'the good people of Connecticut' enough credit."

No one could have been more surprised by his evolution into a three-term representative, two-term senator, and popular presidential candidate than Wes himself. It was just that for ten or fifteen years, he'd forgotten to feel surprised. Or, perhaps more accurately, for ten or fifteen years, he'd realized it was easier not to feel anything.

"Why is Addie here, Jo?"

She took a sip of tea and then rested the cup on her knee. She traced the rim with her finger—round and round and round—before finally saying, "Tell me why you're here, and then I'll tell you why she's here."

"You *know* why I'm here."

"No, I don't. Not really. I know why you want to talk to Sebastian, but I've told you he's only here part-time. And for the record, part-time is not right now." She looked up from her cup with compassion in her eyes. "You had to have known it was a crapshoot, but you came anyway. Rather than have 'your people' reach out to him and try to set something up—which I can't imagine would have been too difficult, given that he covers the news and you currently are the news—you decided to show up here for the first time since you—"

"Thanks, Jo, but I know what I did. You can spare me the recap."

"See, I don't think you do know. Not really."

Until his first tentative phone call to Jo, nearly a year ago, he'd been completely cut off from news of Adelaide Springs. Well, that wasn't entirely true. He'd always received tidbits here and there, but they were filtered at best, run through the meat grinder of personal pain at worst.

Way back in 2005, when Wray Gardner knocked on his dorm room door at Yale, he'd almost wrung himself dry of homesickness. Her arrival marked a transition in his history: from trying not to miss Adelaide Springs to convincing himself that leaving was the best thing he ever could have done. Wray stayed loosely in touch with her sister, Andrea, through the years, but if she ever gleaned news from the home front, she sure didn't share it with him. Of course he never asked. Oh, occasionally over dinner she would let him know that so-and-so had died or this business or other had closed down, but they never dwelled on the topic. And she knew never to utter the names of any of the people who truly mattered. Or who had once mattered, rather. It was just part of the unspoken solidarity between them.

Then Brynn Cornell took the world by storm. Brynn certainly never talked about Adelaide Springs in her early days on *Sunup*, but it was still disconcerting to be assaulted by the appearance of a woman who had once been among his closest friends nearly every time he turned on the television or walked past a newsstand. The extent of his discussions with his wife about the development never went beyond "Was she always a brunette?" or "Do you think she's had any work done?" until one day he walked into the living room and found Wray weeping on the sofa while watching his former friend apologize in front of a mountain.

A week earlier Brynn had bad-mouthed their hometown on a hot mic, and the world had talked about little else ever since. Wray and Wes, meanwhile, hadn't said one word about it to each other—no matter how obsessively they were each following along with Brynn's career-threatening developments. But suddenly, there she was, back on *Sunup*, live from Adelaide Gulch. The same Adelaide Gulch where they'd all sledded on inner tubes as kids. The same Adelaide Gulch where Wes had gotten at least half of the cuts and scratches that he still carried with him as scars.

The same Adelaide Gulch that, as Wes and Wray and maybe even Brynn all seemed to realize in near unison, wasn't the cause of any of their multitudes of emotional scars.

From that point on Wes and Wray seemed to talk about Adelaide Springs all the time. Memories that had for so long been treated as a toxin they couldn't allow into their bloodstreams suddenly took on new life as the antidote to their self-inflicted misery.

Of course by then Wray was already sick, and some antidotes would prove to be more successful than others.

Wes set his coffee on the table once again and stayed leaned over his knees as he asked, "How is she? Is she okay? Did she and her husband move here or—"

"She left the CIA—"

"Hang on. Addie? Addie was in the CIA?"

"I've already said too much." Jo shook her head slowly. "But no. Her husband died. And I don't think she's okay at all."

In his year of FaceTime with Jo, he'd never once asked how anyone was doing. Especially not Addie. It wasn't that he hadn't wondered, but Jo had made it clear from their very first phone call that he was and probably forevermore would be a persona non grata in Adelaide Springs, and that she would most likely be viewed as a traitor for even talking to him. Once, about seven months ago, she had flippantly made mention of Jake and Lucinda Morissey, members of a younger generation he barely remembered, having another child, then immediately hung up in a panic as if she had accidentally muttered every digit of the nuclear codes over the PA system at a mall. She didn't answer his calls for six weeks after that.

So they talked about him. *He* talked about himself, to be more precise. And Wray. It was nice to talk with someone who had memories of her from before. She was three years younger than he was, but of course they'd still grown up together. And yet they'd lived completely different lives—until they intersected at Yale.

He'd asked Wray about Addie once. Right in the beginning. That was the only time. *"Just tell me if she's okay."* Wray told him she had moved away for college and that she assumed she was fine, and that was that. He didn't want to know anything else. There was nothing he could do about any of it, but from that point on he could rest in the knowledge that Addie's life had gone on.

After that he didn't hear her name again for nine years, until Wray asked him, "If Addie got married, would you want to know?" He'd been running for House reelection, and they'd been on a campaign bus heading back to Hartford. He hadn't even looked up from his phone. "You can never have too much knowledge, I guess," he'd said with a shrug. And then Wray had spread out on the couch on the bus, laid her head down on a pillow, and said, "Last weekend, apparently." Then she called out for her personal assistant to wake her when they were ten minutes away from home.

"What do you mean she's not okay?" Wes asked Jo, not at all sure of what to do with this new knowledge. "How long ago did he die?"

Jo sighed and stood, sticking out her hand for his empty coffee cup, which he obligingly gave her. "Ask *her* if you really want to know."

*Huh.* Yeah. That was a nice idea—a nice but terrifying idea—but talking to her hadn't gone very well so far.

Wes stood and followed Jo into the kitchen. "She didn't seem too keen on having a heartfelt conversation with me," he stated mildly, choosing not to share the part where he barely got his toes out of the way before her massive snow tires ran over them. "Any advice on how I should navigate—"

"I don't know. Good grief. You're a grown man. I am no longer responsible for being your emotional compass."

"I know, Jo, but—"

"No *buts*." She set the cups in the sink and turned to face him.

"It was your choice to come back, and you're the one who has to deal with the consequences. And let's face it. There's a backlog of consequences you haven't faced yet, for a backlog of choices."

"I know."

"It's time to either confront all of that or—"

"I said I know, Jo. That's why I'm here." Wes's eyes began to sting, and everything in him wanted to pull his gaze away from her. *Retreat. Retreat!* But he couldn't. "At least I think so. I don't know anything, Jo. I really . . . I just don't know anything anymore."

"Oh, you poor kid," she muttered under her breath before opening her arms to him and finally giving him the hug she'd denied him earlier—and that life had been denying him for the last twenty-two years.

## CHAPTER 6

# ADDIE

### 4,165 Days Since She Reclaimed the Meadow

I brushed the snow off the log before sitting down, but the freezing temps still created a sensation of dampness under my legs. The knobs on the fallen section of tree made for an uncomfortable seat, even if it hadn't been freezing and the wind hadn't been blowing. The breeze passing through the branches above me caused snow to filter down onto my nose and cheeks, which were completely exposed since I'd accidentally left the house without my hat and scarf. And gloves. Yeah, the exposed fingers were already tingling, but at least I could stuff my hands into my coat pockets. It was entirely possible my nose would just turn into a nosecicle and break right off, but none of the current threats of hypothermia and frostbite had felt nearly as urgent as the need to rush out of the house before my dad woke up.

Truth be told, the cold wasn't even bothering me. Not really. All I could focus on was the rising sun glistening off the white peaks of the fourteen-thousand-foot mountain in front of me. Warmth fought for dominance and won as I soaked in the subtle contrast of the white aspens against their matching backdrop and the crystal-clear blue sky above the valley, blissfully unaware of the storm heading its way. Within an hour or two, there would be nothing but gray again as far as the eye could see. But if there was anything I had gotten pretty good at over the course of the past couple of years, it was not looking ahead.

All told, I'd been away for twenty years, and in the slowly progressing months I'd been back, I'd had to put in some effort to reclaim my Colorado. Or, more accurately, I'd had to accept that it would require effort to do so—if I ever decided the effort might be worthwhile. I mean, in so many ways, Adelaide Springs was home and always would be. But it wasn't home to my memories with Joel. Our little house in Bethesda, surrounded by lush greenery that could never survive in Colorado and that had made us feel blissfully alone in the world—that was our home.

Work schedules had kept us from visiting Adelaide Springs very often—one or two Christmases, a week in the summer every few years—and when we did, our time was rarely if ever our own. Dad would take Joel fly-fishing on the Rio Grande while I hung out with Laila and Cole, all of us pretending that our shared youth had knitted us together tightly enough that our lifetime apart was inconsequential. And then, before we knew it, we'd had a good time, fulfilled our relational obligations, and had enough time away from work that our nerve endings were twitching to get back at it.

But this meadow was ours. This meadow. This log where I sat, losing feeling in my thighs. This view. It was all ours. Never mind that it had also been the site of the most painful moment of the first thirty-eight years of my life. The most painful moment of my life until I received word, 717 days ago, that a relatively routine operation in Venezuela had gone horribly wrong.

This meadow had once been my most special spot. So special that I'd chosen it as the location of what was supposed to be my wedding to Wes. But then I'd been left alone there—confused and in shock—and the spot lost all its value. Rather than being the place I went to feel happy and content, it became the memory I fled from. Just like I fled from feeling happy and content, I suppose.

But eleven years later, my new husband had wanted to know

everything about me. He wanted to know everything that had turned me into the woman he had chosen to spend his life with. I couldn't deny that Wes Hobbes and the heartache I'd experienced in the meadow had shaped me, for better or for worse, so I took him there. And I told the whole unfiltered story of August 9, 2003, for the very first time. It wasn't just the first time I shared all the gory details with Joel. It was the first time I shared all the gory details with *anyone*. I'd never had to tell it before. Before Joel, there hadn't been a person of significance in my life who hadn't been there that day to witness it themselves.

We spent hours on that log, on a much warmer day than today, and lying in the grass and walking through the wildflowers. When I started crying, I was surprised to realize I wasn't crying for Wes or because I could still feel the pain and humiliation, or even because the young version of myself had lost so much time and innocence. No, I cried because I hated that Wes Hobbes had ruined my favorite spot for me. He stole so much from me, but eleven years later, my meadow was all I wanted back.

And Joel reclaimed it for me. He recited what he could remember of poems by Lord Byron and Langston Hughes and Emily Dickinson, filling in the gaps with Dr. Seuss and Leonard Cohen and a little bit of Tupac. We daydreamed together about a day when we would bring our future children back to Adelaide Springs and introduce them to the beauty of the place, and maybe we'd even build a little cabin in the mountains. We climbed trees and made birdcalls and very nearly had his-and-hers heart attacks when a massive hawk momentarily seemed to fall for our feeble bird-calling deception. And then, of course, we laughed until we fell over, recounting the disgraceful way two respected, highly trained members of the United States intelligence community would have willingly traded state secrets to get away from that giant swooping bird.

In the length of one afternoon, Joel Elwyn had managed to make my meadow magical again.

So much so that even now, sitting on that log, attempting to ignore the icy wind whipping into my eyes from the east just long enough to witness the conclusion of the sunrise over the mountains, the countless memories I'd made there with Wes in the ancient past didn't spring to mind. For years my ex had been twelve miles down the road and we'd never bumped into each other once, but Adelaide Springs wasn't even twelve miles from city limits to city limits and back again. The population of the entire town would be dwarfed by an hour's worth of visitors to the Smithsonian's Air and Space Museum, and I'd been unable to avoid him beyond his first five minutes back. Chances were I'd see him again, and when I did, I'd grin and bear it much better than I had the night before—maybe while reciting some Tupac in my head.

My phone rang just as the final rays of sunrise ended their game of peekaboo with the mountain and began a new game with the clouds, preparing to fight for dominance of the day. I sighed and said goodbye to solitude as I glanced down at the screen and stood from the log.

"Good morning, Neil."

"Hey, Addie. I'm sorry to bother you so early. I know you're not on call until eight, but—"

"It's fine." I stepped gingerly over tree roots so covered in snow that anyone who was less familiar with this meadow than I was would probably trip and go flying. "What do you need?" I froze as my hand reached out for the door handle of the vehicle. There was a decent chance, I realized, that I knew exactly what was on Valet Forge's early-morning docket. "Do you need me to run a pickup to the inn?"

"Yeah. If you can."

I shivered—the shiver having nothing to do with Wes, just the screechy grinding metal sound of the ancient vehicle door opening—then chuckled to myself. "Yeah . . . I had a hunch."

The chuckle, of course, had everything to do with him.

I didn't love the way I'd lost my cool with him. I didn't love that I'd been the one unable to remain civil. Sure, there was no way around the discomfort—it *would* be uncomfortable. But in that moment, as I climbed up into the truck, I chose to be grateful for an opportunity to redeem myself. It was also another opportunity to gather data, and data was my friend. There was nothing to fear. Nothing to dread. Nothing to avoid.

"I was heading out to get it, but then we got another call. If you can get the one at the inn, I'll take the other one. It's somebody stuck in a snowdrift, needing a tow—"

"I'll take that one."

*Coward.*

"Aren't you in your little hybrid thing? You won't be able to tow in that—" He was interrupted by the unmistakable sound of my dad's 1976 Chevy roaring to life with all the subtlety of a hungry lion. "Ah. You're in Beulah. Still, I don't mind."

"No, really, it's no big deal. I've got everything I need with me." I glanced through the window behind me as I backed up, trying to see into the truck bed and hoping I hadn't just lied to Neil in my cowardice. "Besides, it's a nice morning. It'll be good to get some fresh air."

*Pathetic. Absolutely pathetic. You're better than this, Adelaide.*

"Well, it's eighteen degrees and dropping, but to each his or her own. You're sure?"

I stopped at the end of the gravel. "I am. Where am I heading?"

"Off of Banyon."

Beulah's tires spun, and then I turned right onto Elm Street with a jolt—not even completely sure where I was heading yet but thoroughly disappointed in myself for how relieved I was to be heading there.

## CHAPTER 7

# WES

### Nearly 3 Years Since He First Asked the Question

Wes had long ago stopped trying to feel things, instead spending his energy on *doing* things. *Doing* didn't always turn out the way he hoped, but it usually didn't destroy him as much as *feeling* did. But as he watched the last of that morning's sunrise—overturned in a snowy ditch on the side of a mountain and undeniably stuck in a position where there was very little he could do—he allowed himself to grab onto the feeling of peace that was overtaking him.

He saw the sunrise all the time, of course. Nearly every day, he supposed. He walked past or jogged past or drove past or flew past it, but anymore it seemed like wherever he was, he was always on his way to somewhere else.

There were all sorts of things he hadn't ever felt as strongly outside of his hometown. Why shouldn't the peace and comfort that accompanied taking the time to watch the sun do its thing be among them? Of course, now that the moment had passed, he was filled with that same stupid gnawing in his gut. Even when there was literally nowhere he could go and nothing he could do. Would he ever remember how to watch a sunrise or a sunset, or even the second-by-second ticking of the clock, without an overwhelming sensation of guilt?

Probably not. That was what his father had instilled in him, right?

*"Rest is a weak man's most reliable friend."*

*"Celebrations are reserved for those who are happy staying right where they are."*

*"The only thing standing between where you are now and where you want to be is a preference for contentment."*

Governor McNeese had a million such nuggets, and he had never been shy about sharing them—with his son, with his constituents, with unhoused citizens standing in line outside a soup kitchen. And they loved him for it.

Why had they loved him for it?

*Why did* I *love him for it?*

He had asked himself that question so many times in the year his father had been gone, and even more in the eighteen months or so prior to his passing as Alzheimer's yanked away the suave, charismatic cushion that had always softened the blow of the governor's painful words.

"He can't help it." His stepmother and Phil and his father's doctors had all said those words to him more times than he could keep track of. And Wes knew they were right. Alzheimer's was a cruel, unfair, devastating disease that took no prisoners and yet, simultaneously, created prisoners of them all. He could never—he *would* never—blame his father for the pain inflicted as the disease waged war with the once-brilliant man's brain. But "*He can't help it*" hadn't been the oft-repeated cliché that caused him, for the first time, to start taking a long, hard look at who he had become under his father's tutelage. It was that other one.

*"You know that's not who he really is."*

Alzheimer's may have removed the cushion of well-crafted words and yanked away the veil of emotional intelligence and social decorum, but it hadn't made his father mean and spiteful and narcissistic. That was, in fact, who he really was. That was who he had always been. And once Wes began acknowledging that to himself and, over time, talking through it with Wray and his therapist to the point of fully accepting its truth, that had been the question he'd been left with.

*Why did I love him for it?*

Not that he'd questioned why he'd loved him. No, he was his father. He'd spent eighteen years of his life not knowing the man, and even then, he'd loved him. When his mother tried to discourage him from learning about him, and when she warned him no good would come from whatever he discovered . . . When she cautioned him that he would only get hurt . . . When she'd point-blank told Wes that his father was a man incapable of actual human emotions . . . Still, he'd loved him. Maybe this man—whoever he was—had not done right by his mom, but it would be different for him. Somewhere out there, a father was desperate to know his son. Somewhere out there was a man who had changed and grown and who wanted nothing more than to make up for lost time. Wes couldn't accept any other reality. So he loved him. And then he found him, and he loved him even more.

And the more the governor fed him fatherly wisdom like "*Love is defeatist*" and "*I'll be proud of you when I can't differentiate between you and my own reflection*," the more Wes loved him (but not really, of course, because love was defeatist). He emulated him. Practically worshipped him. And it wasn't very long until those things became interchangeable with love. Maybe even preferable to love. And then it wasn't very long until he realized how much of his life he'd wasted on love. *No wonder* he'd always been such a loser.

An icy gust from the east stung his eyes, and he pulled his Persol sunglasses down from his head. That was probably past due anyway, considering the sun was fully over the mountaintop now and illuminating the last sliver of blue in a sky quickly being overrun by gray.

His pondering and reflection got pushed away as quickly as the storm blowing in when he heard a Boeing 757 landing directly behind him. Oh, wait. It was only an old beat-up farm truck—

*Hang on.* He *knew* that old beat-up farm truck. He turned fully away from the sun as the blue Chevy rambled across the speed bumps created by the melted snow and slush that had frozen again overnight, and headed straight toward him.

"Crap!" he exclaimed to the vast isolation surrounding him before recovering as quickly as he could and attempting to plant a smile on his face. A funny thing had happened over the course of the past months, though. He had become acutely aware of the fact that he didn't know how to smile. He'd forgotten how to do it naturally, in any sort of way that wasn't accompanied by "I hope I can count on your vote this November" subtext. And the more aware of it he'd become, the more awkward he felt each time he tried to smile for real.

As the truck executed a perfect three-point turn and backed up in front of him, he looked around one more time and took in his surroundings. Nothing about this morning was going the way he had intended, obviously, but Addie coming to his rescue just took it all to new levels of failure and humiliation.

"Good morning!" Wes called to her as she hopped down from the cab of the truck. He waved and then crossed his arms and rested them on the metal roll cage of the UTV's open cab.

He'd recognized her instantly last night, but as he watched her grabbing equipment from the back of the truck, he was taken aback by how little she resembled the girl he had almost married. Her face was turned away from him, but the line of her body was on display—even beneath layers and a winter coat—as she stretched into the truck bed. Maybe he couldn't really see the shape of her figure, but the physical strength and assuredness with which she carried herself was foreign to him. The Addie he'd known hadn't been weak, physically or otherwise, but he remembered her being so delicate. There was nothing delicate or fragile about the woman currently hoisting chains over her shoulder and striding confidently toward him through a couple of feet of snow.

"Tell me right now," she said to him in greeting, "was this a ploy to get me out here?"

Wes guffawed at the thought. "No."

"What? Why's that funny?" She clipped the chain to the front of the side-by-side.

He raised the sunglasses back to his head. "It's not." He glanced at the hot chocolate stains all down the front of him and at his feet. Sopping wet, he precariously balanced on the highest metal pieces he could stand on without slipping. "It's just that if I were going to orchestrate something, it wouldn't be this. I'm not exactly positioned to make a good impression here. In fact, nothing personal, but when I called Valet Forge, I think I sought about five different levels of confirmation that the guy on the phone would be the one coming."

The corners of Addie's lips twitched as she made eye contact with him for the first time. "Fair enough." She pulled her hand up to create a sun visor and squinted as she faced him. "This may be on me, now that you mention it."

"How so?"

"Well, right back at you with the 'nothing personal,' but there were two calls for rides this morning, and I insisted I should take this one because the other was a pickup at the inn—"

"Which you assumed was me?"

"Which I assumed was you."

She looked tired. She looked tired in the ways you could never tell a woman she looked tired. Wray had taught him that lesson very early in their marriage. Even when you had the best of intentions and just wanted to show concern and facilitate rest, you always had to consider what it was that had made you realize she was tired. If she yawned, fine. You could talk about her being tired if she yawned. But if your context clues involved puffiness or wrinkles or heavy lids, all of which Addie currently sported, it was important that you kept your mouth shut. He might mean, *Are you doing okay?* but she would hear, *You look so old! When did you get so old?*

Addie didn't look old. It wasn't that. But there was no doubt she carried a weariness he'd never seen on her when they were kids.

*Obviously.* Weariness and exhaustion were distinct pleasures of adulthood, weren't they?

Wes wanted to roll his eyes at his internal Captain Obvious monologue, but Addie was still looking at him, and it was taking all his mental fortitude to try to remember how to smile like a normal human being.

"Who are we kidding, Addie?" He drew his eyes away from hers and chuckled. "I think, for both of us, it was pretty personal." He looked back up as her arm dropped to her side, a passing cloud taking over her hand's sun protection responsibility. "But I wasn't wanting to avoid you, for the record. Not altogether, anyway. But in this particularly humiliating situation? Well, I suppose it's fair to say I very much wanted to avoid you."

They stared at each other in silence, a smile planted firmly on his lips. (And Wes could only hope against hope that the smile didn't resemble that of a B-movie monster learning to feel.)

"So what happened here?" she finally asked, stepping forward to survey the side-by-side for damage. "You're not hurt, are you?"

He shook his head. "No. I mean, my pride's bruised . . ."

"And that's as it should be." She stepped back toward the truck to secure the chains and called over her shoulder, "You do know that these things are specifically designed to handle these exact conditions, right? It's kind of like sinking a raft when all it's doing is floating across a swimming pool."

Growing up, Wes had always been the most athletic of them. Adelaide Springs didn't have enough students for school teams, so you had to travel an hour or two or join church leagues if you wanted to compete in team sports. As fun as it was to lob softballs at senior citizens with all the high-speed velocity of that feather that floats around Forrest Gump, he'd realized at a pretty young age that team sports weren't where he was going to burn off all his excess energy. Instead, he'd turned to tennis and skiing and snowboarding and whatever else made his pulse race.

Of course it helped that all of those solo things could be done in tandem with his friends. With Addie. She certainly hadn't been as daring as he had, so she'd passed on accompanying him down the scarier ski courses. Brynn had been his fellow adrenaline junkie, and it wasn't at all unusual for them to fearlessly race each other down a black-diamond slope only to find Addie, Laila, and Cole at the bottom enjoying hot chocolate, having already had enough excitement on the bunny slopes for the day. It had been a long time since he'd been allowed to ski down any real slopes, but he really believed that if he was given the opportunity, it would come right back to him.

Considering he'd felt exactly the same way about driving a UTV on Banyon in the thick of winter, he might hold off on booking his ticket for Aspen.

"I just overcorrected. It was stupid. Something ran out in front of me, and I was coming up on the curve . . ." Wes looked ahead to the thousand-foot drop-off he had been approaching when he panicked. "I didn't realize how sensitive the steering is on this thing, I guess."

She shrugged and made her way back to him. "Don't beat yourself up too much. It happens. That's why no one really travels on Banyon this time of year. You can't see much, and the road never sees sunlight. I think the elk have begun taking it for granted that they have the road to themselves."

He circled his arms around himself as a whip of wind attacked them off the mountainside. "I wish it had been an elk. At least an elk is a respectable adversary."

"Deer?"

Wes shook his head. "Rabbit."

"Well, then, that *is* embarrassing." Addie knelt down and made one last adjustment to the chain. "So are you going to get out of there, or do you want me to flip it with you still in it?"

Oh. Yeah. How idiotic he must have looked, still standing there in the capsized side-by-side, his body peeking out from the chest up, just watching her work. "I'm so sorry." He pushed up and climbed out on top of it, then jumped into the snow. "How can I help?"

"You can help me flip it over. And while we're doing that, you can tell me what in the world you're doing out here. Where did you even get this thing?"

Wes followed her lead and crouched on the side popping out of the ditch, and they got it mostly upright pretty easily. A little too easily, truth be told. So easily he was afraid she was thinking what he was thinking: he could have done it himself.

"I borrowed it from—"

"This is Jo's," Addie said at the same time.

"Yeah."

She looked the UTV up and down and then looked Wes up and down. "Did you steal it?"

"What? No! Of course not. I borrowed it." Addie crossed her arms and raised an eyebrow, so he clarified, "With her permission. I didn't steal it. Good grief, Addie."

Her second brow joined the first in what he interpreted as a transition from mistrust to surprise, and Wes realized in the second before Addie spoke that he had accidentally thrown Jo under the bus. Or at least he'd begun to. Maybe he could still save her.

"You've seen Jo?"

He nodded. "I have. I mean, at the inn, of course. And she—"

"Did she tear you to shreds? I bet she tore you to shreds."

He didn't expect sympathy, of course, and he definitely wanted to avoid putting Jo in the hot seat for being in contact with him and inviting him to town—even if the last time he'd seen her before going to bed she was still insisting she had done no such thing—but he could have done without the smile that was overtaking Addie's face at the thought of him being torn to shreds.

"No, she didn't 'tear me to shreds.' Why would she?" Well, if *that* wasn't just the stupidest thing he possibly could have said. "I mean, not that she doesn't have any reason to. Not that *you* don't have any reason to, for that matter. Because you do. Have reason to. To, um . . . tear me to shreds or whatever. To be mad at me, I mean."

"You're saying this to me as if I'm not aware that any anger I might feel toward you is justified? Thanks for that." She rolled her eyes. "Give me your gloves."

Wes looked behind him—why, he wasn't quite sure—and then back at her. "What?"

"Come on." She put her right hand in front of her, palm up. "Give me your gloves. I forgot mine."

Okay, that moment wasn't *quite* as embarrassing as pretty much every other moment he'd experienced with her in the last twelve hours or so, but he didn't exactly feel good about himself as he surveyed his own situation (Saint Laurent wool coat buttoned up to his chin, cashmere Burberry scarf circled around his neck, hands covered in wool-lined leather gloves, still basically just standing there watching her work) and compared it to hers (no scarf, no hat, no sunglasses, no gloves, her hands flexing continually to keep blood circulating).

"Of course." He snapped out of his less than chivalrous inactivity and pulled off his gloves. "Here." He took a step toward her and held them open, one after the other, for her to slip her hands into. "Sorry."

"Thank you."

She pumped her hands into balls a few more times inside the gloves before leaning over to verify the connection of the chain to the now-upright side-by-side. It was then, when she pulled the palm of the right glove away from the metal chain and it created that lovely sound that usually accompanied shoes being lifted from a poorly mopped bathroom floor, that she looked up at him again.

"Why are your gloves sticky?"

Wes stuffed his bare hands into the pockets of his coat and bobbed up and down. "Hot chocolate. It spilled when—"

"When the bunny rabbit jumped out and scared you?"

It was funny: as he looked at her, the years simultaneously piled up on top of one another and disintegrated before his very eyes. He'd never seen this woman, as she currently existed, in his life, but he absolutely would have known her anywhere. Her body had changed, her face had changed, her voice had changed, but that look? The one she was giving him right now—one of impatience and frustration and lack of amusement (which had always brought him great amusement)? That was his Addie.

"It really is good to see you, Addie Atwater."

"It's Elwyn now, actually. And if you don't mind, I would really appreciate help understanding why Jo not only didn't rip you to shreds for showing back up here but was also happy to let you take her side-by-side out for a joyride."

Her pupils dilated, and her arms crossed, and her brow furrowed, and he could hear her insisting he shouldn't settle for staying in Adelaide Springs and taking a job in maintenance with the city. He could see her insisting they didn't need money to be happy. He could almost smell the pumpkin pie she'd been baking for Thanksgiving when he told her she shouldn't throw away scholarship offers just to be with him.

Regardless of her last name, an annoyed Addie was apparently the same yesterday, today, and tomorrow.

Wes shrugged. "We talked last night when I got checked into the inn—"

"Had a good little chat, did ya?"

"Yes, actually. And this morning I asked her if I could borrow the UTV in exchange for shoveling the sidewalks and plowing the driveway."

Addie's shoulders dropped down from her ears. "Oh."

He didn't have to ask her to translate the "Oh." They were no longer dealing with Jo just being kind to Wes—Wes, whom, he was pretty sure, no one else in Adelaide Springs would see as deserving of kindness. He'd leave Jo to sort that out with her neighbors in her own time. Right now, it seemed that Addie was satisfied there had at least been a very Jo-like requirement of manual labor behind her offering of kindness to the pariah.

"And as for *why* I borrowed it—"

"That's enough talking. It isn't worth the frostbite."

Another gust of wind assaulted them, and she pulled her hands up in front of her face and huffed on them, attempting to warm them up through the gloves. Disgust registered in her expression as her hands stuck together (again, just enough to evoke that unpleasant bathroom floor imagery), and Wes laughed at her as a little stickiness (which was, admittedly, building upon itself as wind and dirt and moisture compounded into hot chocolate–based goo) completely undid the competent woman who had just been maneuvering chains and hitches and truck beds like a boss.

"Get these things off me!" she shrieked as a small twig got stuck on the fingers of one glove and then the other.

"Hold up." He leapt over a mound of snow and reached her just as she growled at the gloves, now in one chaotic clump on her hands, causing her fingers to splay like the talons of an old, disfigured witch in a Disney cartoon.

"Hot chocolate," she muttered under her breath.

He pulled her clustered fingers closer to his chest, and her grumbling stopped. Everything stopped. Her grumbling, her twitching, maybe her breathing . . .

*His* breathing, come to that.

Wes freed one gloved finger at a time and transitioned his involuntary holding of breath into a conscious decision so as not to accidentally startle her into refusing his assistance. She kept staring down at her hands between them, her brow furrowed, even as he hovered over the knuckles of her left hand and thought about when he'd slipped a white-gold band (with the tiniest diamond that he'd known wasn't good enough for her) onto her finger and promised her he was hers for life. His need for oxygen began warring with his desire to dwell in the memory as long she would let him, but he steeled himself and pulled her hands apart.

Neither of them could help but react to the hideous *glurp* that resulted. Wes exhaled his held breath as laughter while Addie closed her eyes and shook her head.

"Why couldn't you drink coffee like an adult?"

He shrugged.

"Get them off of me," she instructed, spreading out her hands toward him, and he obliged, pulling on the gloves from the tips of her fingers. He stuffed the gloves in his pockets and stood there, unable to pull his eyes away from her, especially as the corner of her mouth twitched again and her lips curled up. Just slightly.

"Stop smiling," she told him, "or I'll unhitch this thing and leave you to dig yourself out with your bare hands."

She began walking back to the cab of the truck without unhitching a thing—though he most certainly had not fulfilled his half of the bargain.

## CHAPTER 8

# ADDIE

**7,148 Days Since They Tore Down the Diner on Kearney**

I sniffed (*ouch—snotcicles*) and wiped my eyes before opening the truck door. "Get in before we freeze to death."

"Don't I need to push or something?"

"No, the truck will handle it."

"Well, I'll just stay out here and be ready to climb back into the—"

"Are you *wanting* to drive the rest of the way up Banyon, considering you literally went off the road at the very first curve?" I dangled a leg from my seat as I looked back over my shoulder at him. "Because if that's what you want, I am more than happy to leave you to your sticky mess and—"

"No, no. Sorry. Yes, thank you. I'll take the ride."

He began walking around the back of the side-by-side to get to the passenger side of the truck—like an idiot—rather than just stepping over the chain connecting the two vehicles. I considered throwing out a word of caution and advice but ultimately thought better of it. Instead, I climbed in the rest of the way and watched him in the rearview mirror as he struggled to lift his feet through the snowdrift. The snowdrift that got deeper and deeper as he got closer to the mountainside. I had to hand it to him, he wasn't a quitter. Not when it came to this, anyway. It would have been so much easier, at any point, just to accept defeat, turn around, and go the other way. But no. I don't know—maybe he thought that would be too humiliating. If he'd been able to see what I saw, I think he might have eaten that particular slice of humble pie rather than descend deeper and deeper into a work of art that was part La Brea Tar Pits and part Luke Skywalker on the ice planet of Hoth.

I cranked at my window, but it was frozen shut, so I leaned across the bench seat and opened the passenger door. "Go around, dummy!"

"What?" he yelled into the wind as he attempted to lift his foot in snow that had now buried him clear up to his hips.

I shouted louder. "Go around!"

There was no point in it now, of course. He'd passed the point of no return. He knew it. I knew it. And doggone it if I didn't start laughing when he called out, "Would Edmund Hillary give up? Would Jacques Cousteau? Where would we be right now, Addie, if Lewis and Clark had decided to 'go around'?"

He finally reached the door of the truck and stepped up before brushing off thick powder from the waist down. He joined in the laughter at his own expense as he held on to the grab bar and collapsed into the seat beside me. "That went well, don't you think?"

---

By the time the side-by-side was pulled out of the ditch and we were plodding along at a safe pace back toward the inn, the laughter had faded, taking all the comfort with it. Gone was the brief moment in time in which we were too focused on the present to think about the past. Not that I was thinking about the past per se. There was no particular memory in my mind—good or bad. It was more that, for me, Wes only existed in the past. For a few brief moments, dopamine and endorphins and adrenaline had worked their magic and *now* had been all that mattered. But once the spell was broken, I was sitting beside a guy who, at worst, represented a truly miserable time in my life and couldn't be trusted or who, at best, was a politician with as-yet unclear motives and most definitely could not be trusted.

Or maybe I had that the wrong way around. In my mind, the best and worst of Wes Hobbes were interchangeable . . . and all pretty bad.

"What are you doing here, Wes?"

"Do you mean *here*? As in sticky and cold from head to toe?"

"No, I mean *here*. Adelaide Springs. Surely you didn't come all this way after all this time to fight a losing battle for another vote or two."

He chuckled softly. "Are you saying I'm not going to find any 'Vote Hobbes' yard signs around town?"

"I'm saying the people of this town wouldn't vote for you on *Dancing with the Stars*, much less for president."

"Um, *ouch*. I'm actually a very good dancer, if you must know."

"You are not."

"I am."

"*You* are a very good dancer?"

"Well, I'm better than competent."

"Since when?"

"Since spending three years as one of two men tasked with partnering with approximately ninety-four women in the young adult class of Madam Kiki's Art of Dance Studio of Greater Hartford, thank you very much."

I took my eyes off the road just for a moment, just long enough to try to interpret what he was playing at, and I'd never seen a more earnest expression on anyone's face in my entire life. A chortle built up in my chest for just a second before bursting out of me.

"You're serious!"

"Yes, I'm serious! I would never joke about Madam Kiki." He adjusted and rested his left knee on the seat as he twisted to face me. "I mean, I exaggerated about the ninety-four women, but there were fifteen, easily, and Beauregard and I—"

I gasped. "No."

"Yes. His name was actually Beauregard. Beauregard Linklater, I kid you not."

"What were Mr. and Mrs. Linklater thinking?"

"Well, they obviously hated little Beauregard from birth. There's no other explanation. Anyway, Beauregard and I were supposed to divvy up all the ladies, but Beau had asthma and tended to max out at three or four a night."

I smiled as I leaned forward over the steering wheel and strained to see the entrance to the Inn Between. Once I spotted it, I flicked on my turn signal—not that anyone else was on the roads, and not that they would have been able to see my taillights until it was too late if they were—and settled back into my seat. After removing all traces of the smile, of course.

"Okay, so maybe we'd be forced to support you in your pursuit of the Mirrorball Trophy, but the White House, Wes?" The truck came to a stop, and I shifted into Park before turning toward him, matching his knee-propped posture. "Regardless, the votes of a couple hundred voters don't matter when you've already got Colorado sewn up. So why are you here? What's the angle, Senator?"

"There's not an *angle*, Addie. I mean, okay, does it make for a freakishly small world that Adelaide Springs is home base for a journalist I'm hoping to—"

"I knew it!" I exclaimed. Even as disappointment coursed through my body upon realizing that I had not, in fact, known anything.

I *should* have known it. I felt really off my game for not having figured it out. I'd focused on the wrong part of that "we'll all get to be part of a little feel-good piece on the nightly news" comment I'd overheard at the airport. I'd wasted time thinking about the chumps he was trying to get to "behave" when I should have been focusing on the "little feel-good piece." There was no one in the world more beloved for *exactly* that type of journalism than our old friend Brynn Cornell—the sunny host of *Sunup*, the number one morning news/entertainment program in the country.

But as I looked at him, and he didn't shy away from looking at me, I felt like something still didn't add up.

My role as an analytic methodologist very rarely required me to come face-to-face with a target, but I had spent countless hours—days, *weeks* of cumulative hours—watching video feeds of people who couldn't be trusted (unless they could, because desperation sometimes caused even the vilest to grasp at redemption). I stared into their eyes when they didn't know they were being watched and, more often than not, in those moments they told me most of what I needed to know without ever saying a word. I had always figured my job was easy in that way. Certainly easier than what agents in the field were called to do—look into the eyes of some of the most brilliant people in the world (because dummies rarely survived long enough to merit CIA involvement) when everyone's life is on the line and determine, in real time, whether they could be trusted. Not in the future. Not under different circumstances. Right then. Right there. And certainly easier than what Joel had done as the management officer for a great number of those agents. How many times had he sent someone into the field hoping his contact could be trusted? How many times had he sent someone into the field—a real, live, breathing person, often with a family at home—knowing full well his contact *couldn't* be trusted?

As I studied Wes's unflinching eyes, seeking answers, I couldn't imagine what desperation could have led him back to his hometown of a few hundred people who had refused to speak his name for more than twenty years. The last polls I'd seen had 57 percent of Americans voting for him if the general election were held today, and he hadn't even won the nomination yet. (Though most of his respectable opponents had dropped out of the race before Christmas, so winning the nomination was not going to be a challenge.) In an America as divided as we had ever seen in our lifetime, electing Senator Wesley Hobbes as president seemed to be the one thing the majority of people could agree on. He didn't need our votes. That much was obvious. And he didn't even need a feel-good news story.

Brynn wasn't the journalist he wanted to talk to, I finally realized.

And Adelaide Springs was, after all, home base for more than one in-demand reporter.

"You snuck out here, incognito, not knowing who you would run into or what their reaction would be—"

"Oh, I think I know what their reactions will be."

"And still you came." My voice was soft and no longer in attack mode. I genuinely wanted to figure out what I was missing. "Just to try to talk with Sebastian?"

Whereas Brynn was known as America's Ray of Sunshine and did ads for orange juice and approached her weekly recaps of *The Bachelor* with the same level of seriousness that other journalists applied to their election-night coverage, her husband was arguably the most trusted and revered newsman of his generation. Sebastian Sudworth had been a Pulitzer Prize–winning international reporter and had now found a larger audience as the hard-hitting, take-no-prisoners host of the world's top-rated current affairs podcast, *Conscience: Fair Reporting in an Unfair World*.

Wes sighed, pinching the bridge of his nose as he closed his eyes and breathed in through his nostrils and out through his barely separated lips. Then he tilted his head and looked at me through one squinted eye. "I'm dropping out of the race, Addie."

I felt my eyes grow wide in surprise and forced them back into an unaffected and mistrusting squint. Both of his eyes were wide open and studying me now, waiting for a reaction, but apparently I had recovered quickly enough that he didn't observe one. I finally swallowed down the breath that had caught in my throat as the hand that had been squeezing the bridge of his nose dropped to his thigh and he pulled his eyes away.

"No one knows. Well, almost no one. My campaign manager certainly doesn't know. He thinks I'm in California right now, as a matter of fact. And it's . . . it's, um . . . delicate. So yes, I'm hoping to find a sympathetic journalist in Sebastian Sudworth—"

I cut him off with my scoff. I still wasn't sure what all could be trusted and what couldn't, and there were at least a hundred missing details, but it was easy enough to point out the ridiculousness of his statement while I kept trying to sort it out. "You think Sebastian is going to be sympathetic? I think you're barking up the wrong tree there. Fair, unbiased reporting is sort of his brand, you know. Besides, I realize you may not know this, but he's practically the patron saint of this town now. They love him *much* more than they love any of us who grew up here, and I think that's because he loves Adelaide Springs with a passion that every last one of us would have made fun of when we were younger. He's not going to be sympathetic to anyone who hurt his friends the way—"

"The way Brynn did?"

Wes knew as well as I did that I wasn't about to say Brynn's name, but our eye contact remained intact as he allowed what he had just said to sink into my brain.

*Touché.*

Brynn and Sebastian had met when she came back to Adelaide Springs in an attempt to salvage her career, after a hot mic on *Sunup* revealed her true thoughts about her hometown—and revealed her to be a bit of a mean girl in the process. I hadn't been here then, when all of that was happening, but you couldn't escape the coverage. It was the most exciting love story anyone around here had witnessed since Martina Layton moved to Montrose to marry that volunteer firefighter who rescued her when she tried flambéing bananas Foster with half a bottle of Everclear, so it got told quite a lot. When you threw in the fact that Brynn's memoir, which recounted the story in detail, spent a few months on all the bestseller lists, it was safe to assume that *everyone* knew their story. Including Wes.

"Okay, yes, Sebastian came around on Brynn, but that's not because he was *sympathetic*. Brynn changed."

"*I've* changed, Addie! But that's not even what I mean." He rubbed his face feverishly and then faced forward. "I'm not looking for sympathy for myself. I'm really not."

It was possible I was asking the wrong questions, I realized. Focusing on the wrong things. I'd just been handed information that, if true, was going to send the entire world reeling. Was he really dropping out of the race? If so, there was only one logical reason why. He knew something that, as of right now, voters did not. He knew he didn't stand a chance, even while Washington power players gathered their sacrificial offerings to lay at his feet. What was the going rate for a cabinet position these days, anyway? Ten virgins and a couple oxen? The entire political landscape of our nation would change with the announcement, and shock waves would follow throughout the entire world. And he was seeking a sympathetic journalist to help him break the story.

"Who?"

He kept staring at the layers of snow and slush being cleaned away with each cycle of the windshield wipers. "Hmm?"

"For whom are you seeking sympathy?"

His eyes glanced to the right, and then his head followed. I waited while he took in deep breaths and let them out slowly, fogging up the window each time. This was it. Whatever he was hiding, whoever he was trying to protect, as part of whatever scandalous misdeed was about to pop out of his closet and consume news cycles and possibly earn entry in future history books—alongside a democracy's worth of bribes and mistresses and treason and addictions—was being considered alongside meticulously deep breaths right now.

And for reasons I didn't understand, my heart hurt for him as he suffered whatever pain he was trying to breathe his way through.

"First things first: Why are you 'sticky and cold from head to toe'?"

The fog he'd been creating on the window with the in-and-out consistency of a beating heart dissipated, and he turned back to face me. "I'm sorry, what?"

"You heard me."

He chuckled softly. "I told you. Hot chocolate."

I crossed my arms. "Yes, but why were you drinking hot chocolate in an all-terrain vehicle you're not remotely qualified to handle?"

The smile was evident on his face as he looked down at his hands resting on his leg, but it was subdued nearly to the point of vanishing by the time he looked back up at me. "I wasn't drinking it. It was for you."

My eyes narrowed into slits. "What do you mean it was for me?"

"I remembered how much you used to like the hot chocolate from that diner on Kearney—"

"That diner isn't even there anymore."

He nodded. "Yep. I know that now. But there's that little gas station at County Road 22."

"That isn't exactly on the way back into town."

"It is if you take Banyon." Wes shrugged, and a sheepish smile slanted at his lips. "And it was well worth it—for the variety they offer, if nothing else. Today's specials were powdered cappuccino, coffee with the grounds dumped right into the pot as an extra treat, and, of course . . ." He reached into the pocket of his coat and pulled out a messy, sticky, crumpled cup. "Hot chocolate."

He handed the cup to me, and I took it, pinching the rim with my thumb and forefinger at the one clean spot I could see. "And why were you trying to get me hot chocolate?"

"Well, like I said, I remembered how much you—"

"Stop." I held up the hand not holding the pathetic shell of a former cup, and he heeded the warning in my voice. "We're not walking down memory lane here, Senator. That's not an option on the table. So if you were hoping to capture me in a net of nostalgia or something—"

"No, Addie. No. That's not what I meant at all. That's not what I'm trying to do." He rolled his eyes upward and seemed focused on the light blue cloth interior of the old truck. His teeth grabbed at his bottom lip as he closed his eyes, and his eyes remained closed as he finally spoke. "I just wanted to say I'm sorry. And obviously, I'm sorry for a lot of things—"

"And hot chocolate's going to make all of that okay?"

"No." His eyes opened slowly. "Of course not. I just hated that you had to drive me around—"

"It's my job."

"What I mean is, I'm sorry to have just shown up out of the blue. I didn't even know you were back in town, and I certainly didn't know you would be my driver."

My chest constricted as the implication of what he said—of one tiny part of what he said—washed over me. *"I didn't even know you were back in town."* Which meant he knew I had left town. Which meant that at some point or other, he'd heard—asked?—something about me. Funny. For all the thought I had put into avoiding news of him and being unable to avoid news of him, for all the time I had wasted imagining scenarios in which he came back to me and all the time I spent trying to convince myself I never wanted to see him again . . . I had never once considered that maybe he'd checked up on me. I had never once wondered if he'd ever so much as googled me.

"It's not a big deal. We've now *not* known each other longer than we ever knew each other, so let's not be weird about this, alright?" I faced forward and turned up the defrost to begin clearing the fogged windows. "You could have just as easily been picked up by any other random person from your past—"

"Don't do that, Addie." He cleared his throat and blinked rapidly. "Regardless of anything that happened between us, can we please not act like you're in the same category with anyone else in this town?"

"No, of course not." I leaned down and stuffed the crumpled cup into the trash bag on the carpeted floor between us. "I'm fully aware I'm the only one in the 'Get out of here as quick as you can before you get stuck marrying her' category."

*Shoot.*

I pulled the handle on the door and then threw my shoulder into it when it wanted to stick closed. The snow and ice were coming down so quickly that I stepped into a foot or more of white on the driveway path Wes had plowed earlier that morning, but I was pretty sure the heat coursing through me was going to create puddles of water in my wake.

If only he'd had the decency to stick around long enough to break my heart to my face. If only he'd treated me with even a modicum of the respect I deserved. Then he could have said, "It's not you, it's me," or "I hope we can still be friends," or "You know I'll always care about you," or any of the clichéd, meaningless, insulting things that people say, and I wouldn't have to put up with sticky gloves and crumpled cups and him acting like I'd been as special to him as I'd always believed I was.

Still, I wasn't mad because he'd said what he'd just said. Not entirely, anyway. I was mad because I'd been the first to bring up the "wedding that wasn't"–sized elephant in the room.

"Here, let me get that," he said as he appeared beside me at the back of the truck. I had pulled my hand away from the metal in the instant I touched it, recognizing the contradictory burn of my fingers as a warning that my skin was going to freeze to the chain if I lingered. By the time Wes got out of the truck, I was straddling the hitch and had stretched the hem of my sweatshirt down below my coat to use the soft cotton as a very ineffective layer of protection.

"I've got it," I insisted.

I must admit I didn't hate that he ignored my insistence. He slipped his sticky gloves back on and disconnected the chains and hooks and piled them into the back of the truck.

"Thank you," I muttered with a tone usually reserved for words like, "I know you are, but what am I?" and "Take a picture. It will last longer." Then I was climbing back into the truck, and he was standing at my door.

"Don't go. Not like this."

"I have to get to work." That wasn't strictly true, since Neil was working today and all the calls were being forwarded to his cell. I'd stopped him before he could give me answers to questions—big, potentially democracy-altering questions—I was, in fact, curious about. But it was the fear that I might finally get some answers I wasn't sure I was ready for—so many years after I'd finally stopped asking the questions—that made me want to run away.

No . . . that wasn't it exactly. I think I was in such a hurry to get away because I knew that if I slowed down, I might have to admit that my curiosity had been awakened—*reawakened*—about more than just the political scoop of the decade.

"Okay." He stuffed his hands into his pockets, but his reflexes were sharp as he reached back out and grabbed the door before I could slam it shut. "Then have dinner with me. Tonight. Just so we can talk. And we don't have to talk about anything you don't want to talk about."

I laughed and momentarily forgot about attempting to pull the door shut. "There's nowhere in this town we could go without being seen, and the moment you're seen—"

"I'm not hiding from anything, Addie."

It took me a moment, as the wind rushed between us, to realize that was all he'd said. The *Are you?* hadn't come from him. It was apparently a question I was asking of myself. And if there was one thing I knew, it was that there were already too many unanswered questions. I wasn't in the mood to add another to the list.

"I'll pick you up at seven, presuming you have something nonsticky to wear."

Then I motioned for him to step away from the door, which he did, and slammed the door shut and looked over my shoulder as I shifted into Reverse. But not before I caught the subdued smile spreading across his face.

*Dang it.*

# CHAPTER 9

# ADDIE

**524 Days Since Senator Hobbes Became Untouchable**

I'd lost my mind. It was an indisputable fact that if I really, truly had just agreed to have dinner with Wes—as it seemed I had—then I had completely lost my mind.

The bell over the door jingled as I entered Elevate, the cute little boutique Laila had opened a year or so ago. I'd only been in there once or twice and I wasn't quite sure what I was doing there now. All I knew for sure was that I needed to talk to someone, and grown-up Addie didn't have a person she went to when she needed to talk. Not about stuff like this. Whatever "stuff like this" was. But for the first eighteen years of my life, *someone* had always been Laila and Brynn. Back in those days I used to lose my mind over him in very different ways, but still . . . there was no one in town with more experience than Laila at helping me sort through a little Wes Hobbes freak-out.

"Hey, you," she greeted me, stepping behind the counter from the back room. "This is a nice surprise."

Brynn and Sebastian may have been the power couple who put Adelaide Springs on the map, but Cole and Laila were the ones keeping it alive and thriving from day to day. In addition to stepping in at the Bean Franklin on the other end of Main Street, Laila had Elevate, which was right next door to Milo's Steakhouse, owned and operated by Cole. Between Laila's boho-chic designs and Cole's talent in the kitchen, they had already begun drawing in tourists from miles around. I had no idea what else they had in store for the few remaining vacant storefronts they had taken ownership of following the death of Cole's grandfather a year or two prior, but it was easy to tell they were just getting started.

"I need to talk to you. Do you have a few minutes?"

"Of course. What's up?"

I stood along the wall and combed my fingers through a display of silky scarves. "Wes is here."

The only sound in the store was Taylor Swift playing on the little Bluetooth speaker in the corner. And I didn't rush things. I knew she would have her own thoughts and emotions to process. It hadn't been just me he had walked out on that day, after all.

I pulled a pair of khakis with extra pockets off the shelf and held them at my waist in front of me. I hadn't gone in there to shop, certainly, but those pants were supercute.

*When was the last time I bought clothes because they were cute?*

Actually, I realized, I hadn't bought any new clothes for any reason since Joel died. I guess I hadn't seen the point.

"What do you mean Wes is here? Where?"

"Here. Adelaide Springs. I just left him about ten minutes ago."

"*Left him?* What do you mean you just left him? Left him where? Why were you with him? What is he . . . *What?*"

I finally looked at her and realized I may have been a bit too nonchalant in my delivery. This was not nonchalant news to Laila. The color had drained from her cheeks, which were shiny due to the tears suddenly running down them.

"Oh, Lai, I'm sorry." I set the khakis down on the counter and crossed behind to grab her hands in mine. "I didn't deliver this news very well, did I?" I spotted a stool in the corner by the closed-circuit security feed and pulled it over for her.

As she sat, she asked, "How are you so calm about this? Are you okay?"

I shrugged. "Yeah, I am. I'm fine."

"This is the first time you've seen him, right?"

"Well, no, actually. I picked him up at the airport last night."

"Last night?!"

I chuckled. "Yeah. But I meant for Valet Forge. Not because I'm his person who picks him up at the airport or anything."

She brushed the tears from her cheeks and took a deep breath. "Okay, Addie, I actually was asking if this is the first time you've seen him since 2003."

"Oh yeah, for sure."

"And you picked him up at the airport last night?"

I nodded. "Yes. And then this morning he got stuck in a ditch on Banyon—"

"I heard about that!" Her eyes were so wide they practically swallowed her other facial features. "That was *Wes*?"

I didn't have to ask what she'd heard or how she'd heard it. I could imagine the churning sound as the Adelaide Springs gossip mill sprang to life with the simple news bulletin that some idiot had flipped a previously-thought-nearly-unflippable UTV. It was shocking to me, actually, that the mill hadn't already been hard at work distributing the news that Wes was in town. Despite being someone we all trusted with our lives, Josephine Stoddard was also a bit of a harmless busybody who rarely missed an opportunity to make sure everyone knew what she knew. Was Jo Stoddard actually keeping juicy gossip to herself? That was new.

"That was Wes," I answered Laila, but apart from that, my old friend had lost my focus for the time being.

Wes was staying at the inn, of course, and there was no reason to suspect there was more to that story. There was nowhere else in town to stay. But letting him borrow her UTV? Okay, sure, he'd plowed the driveway for her. Great. But this was the woman who used to write "Property of J. Stoddard" on the sides of all the No. 2 pencils in her classroom and make us sign a "contract of mutual respect" when we borrowed one.

"Why is he here, Addie?"

I blinked back into focus and turned to her. "I'm not sure, exactly." I wouldn't reveal anything he had told me in confidence, of course, but I didn't see any harm in sharing theories I had basically (eventually) constructed on my own. "I'm pretty sure he's hoping to talk to Sebastian—"

"That makes sense, I guess."

"—but I know there's got to be more to it than that."

There had to be a scandal lurking in the shadows, right?

Of course it remained to be seen if the rules were different for our first widowed presidential front-runner in a couple of centuries. Wray had been gone for, what, a year and a half already? Wes was a single man. Presumably it would take a different sort of scandal from the type my mind went to first to bring his candidacy to a halt.

There was no way to say it without sounding cold and heartless, but the fact was Wray's death had been the development to launch Senator Hobbes into the untouchable political stratosphere. I'd done a little bit of research into his polling trajectory last night after getting home, trying to make sense of how he thought a trip to Adelaide Springs could possibly benefit his race, and his campaign really was a fascinating study. His approval ratings in Connecticut had been hovering around 70 percent for a long time, but Wray's numbers, as the senator's stylish and charming wife who championed literacy and child hunger causes, had been closer to 90. When news of her breast cancer diagnosis broke a few months after he was elected to his second Senate term, and just weeks after the two of them stood on the steps of their white colonial in New Canaan and declared his candidacy for president, they both checked their "mere mortal" status at the door—as far as the citizens of Connecticut seemed to be concerned, anyway.

No, he wouldn't pause his campaign. The future of our nation was at stake.

No, he wasn't stepping down from the Senate. Their love for the people of Connecticut was what kept them going in the darkest moments.

No, the death of his beloved wife didn't change everything. She'd never forgive him if he quit now.

Each sound bite was more heartrending than the last, but the young, handsome political superstar—the only son of the most popular governor in Connecticut history, whose own devastating battle with Alzheimer's had taken a severe turn for the worse in roughly the same time frame as Wray lost her health battle—refused to turn his back on his family, his state, or his country. And the entire world seemed to love him for it.

Or, as was actually the case—since politics is just an art form centered around knowing when and how to appropriately express your displeasure—his detractors and opponents had been put in the impossible position of not being able to speak out against him without appearing cold, callous, and petty. By the time an acceptable period of mourning passed, it was too late. The damage had been done to every other campaign. Would-be candidates dropped out before they began, and Wes had only to avoid shooting himself in the foot before Election Day.

So I guess it did make sense, actually. If a super PAC for the other side discovered, for instance, that he'd once stepped out on Wray—a woman who had seemingly been elevated to sainthood upon her death—or maybe if he'd moved on too soon with a pretty young girlfriend, they'd finally have some ammunition. If he got out ahead of it now, he could run again in four years. Eight, maybe. Maybe that was his plan. He'd still be in his forties, still be that picture of robust health and energy that stood in such stark contrast to so many others vying for the top office, and he could reinvent himself as the man who carried on and thrived after tragedy.

"Do you think someone found out about you?" Laila asked after we were each lost in our thoughts for I'm not quite sure how long.

My brain reflexively ran an inventory of the not insubstantial list of hidden things that might be worth finding out about me—and then I remembered Laila wasn't aware of any of those things.

"What do you mean? Found out *what* about me?"

"You know . . ." She stood from her stool and folded the khakis I had carelessly set on the counter. "Do you think they found out about how he skipped town? I know it was a long time ago, but it still doesn't look good, I wouldn't think. If somebody wanted to use it—make him look like a jerk who doesn't treat women well, or show that he's not so loyal and committed after all . . ."

*Well, huh.* That little secret about me—which was actually about Wes—had been left off my hastily compiled list a moment ago.

"I don't know." Laila brushed her hand across the air in front of her face. "That's probably stupid. I don't know anything about political stuff."

*No.* It couldn't be. *Could it?* It wasn't possible. I mean, it wasn't even a story. Yes, for me it had been a seismic incident of epic proportions that had split me right down the middle, but we were kids. It was an awful thing he did. Truly horrible. But if we were all judged for the rest of our lives for the mistakes we made when we were eighteen years old, no one would ever even consider running for office. Heck, no one would ever get out of bed in the mornings. No . . . it couldn't be that.

*"I'm not looking for sympathy for myself. I'm really not."*

Was he hoping Sebastian would be sympathetic toward *me*? That didn't make any sense. There wasn't a potential telling of the story, as far as I could come up with, that *wouldn't* be sympathetic toward me. I had been the one sitting under that tree in my wedding dress as the evening rain began to fall and the dirt under me turned to mud. I was the one who refused to leave that spot because I still believed he would show up. No matter who told the story, I was pretty sure there would not be a lack of sympathy for *me*.

Unless, of course, Wes was hoping the husband of our childhood friend would be sympathetic enough to give him a platform to drop out of the race without ever bringing me into the story at all.

"What's wrong?"

I startled at her voice, and the slight shake of my head caused a salty tear to break free and land on my lip. I rubbed my palm across my cheek and sniffed. "I have to go. Sorry. Can we talk more later?"

She was staring at me like I was Daryl Hannah in *Splash* and she was Eugene Levy regretting the role she had played in getting me put into a tank. "Addie, are you okay? What is it? Did I say something wrong?"

"No. Of course not. Really, I'm fine. I'm just . . . thinking. Really, let's talk more later, okay?"

She nodded. "Sure. Whatever you need."

I hurried to the door, turning back to wave as I reached it. "Thanks, Lai. I'll, um . . . I want to buy those pants later, okay?"

She grabbed them off the counter and walked toward me. "Here. Take them."

"No, I couldn't."

"Really, it's fine. Pay me later. Whatever. Just take them."

Warmth for her eased its way up through my chest, and another tear fell. I really did not understand what was happening. "Thanks." I reached out and placed my hand on the pants but hesitated when my eyes caught a display on the wall. "Actually, if it's not too much trouble, could I grab a couple pairs of gloves too?"

## CHAPTER 10

# WES

**18 Months Since the Voice Mail**

~~There has been no greater privilege in my life than representing the great state of Connecticut. Therefore, it is with a heavy heart that I~~

~~As much as I genuinely intended to carry on and fight the good fight, I've realized that without Wray by my side~~

In the iconic words of New Haven's favorite son, Michael Bolton . . .

Wes didn't immediately dismiss that one. As a Connecticut transport in the early aughts, it hadn't taken him long to figure out that the pride the state had in Michael Bolton ran true and perplexingly deep. But he couldn't help but laugh as he ran through the Bolton discography in his mind. Which song should he quote?

"When I'm Back on My Feet Again"?

"How Am I Supposed to Live Without You?"

His constituents would love it, even if "Said I Loved You . . . but

I Lied" seemed like a better song with which to conclude his once-promising and illustrious career in politics. If he was going to burn the whole thing to the ground, why not hide the water and extinguishers?

Still, no matter how much the thought made him laugh as he sat there brainstorming what would be his final speech, he knew he wanted to go out on a high note. Or at least by taking the high road. Not to salvage any future political aspirations but to show the proper level of respect for all parties. He owed it to Wray. He owed it to the people who were still out there campaigning and working hard for him, having no idea they were all about to be unemployed, just because *he* was about to be unemployed. He owed it to the people of Connecticut.

Mostly, he owed it to Wray. That was the debt he needed to focus on. Otherwise, he was afraid it would be far too easy to crumple up his in-progress Michael Bolton speech and start jotting down thoughts for a "Time, Love and Tenderness"–centric Inauguration Day instead.

He sighed and pushed aside the Inn Between notepad before standing from the desk chair in his room and walking toward the nightstand where his phone sat charging. Charging and buzzing. Always buzzing. He liked to think he wouldn't miss that—when his phone stopped ringing. When the only calls he received were requests to serve on second-tier philanthropy boards or maybe, once the dust had settled, deliver a TED Talk. His phone had been an extension of his hand for so long he really was a bit worried he wouldn't know how to function without that urgent buzzing against his skin and in his ear—at this point he really *felt* it more than heard it—at all hours of the day. From the time he landed in Adelaide Springs, he'd certainly made himself less available than he'd been in years, and even having it charging across the room while he scrawled notes at the desk had been a sort of test for himself. He'd mostly passed, he felt, despite the compulsive need to check his messages being his current motivation for crossing to the nightstand.

*Phil.*
*Phil.*

*Senate whip.*
*Phil.*
*Hartford office manager.*
*Daughters of the American Revolution.*
*Phil.*
*Phil.*
*GQ. (How'd they get his number?)*
*Phil.*
*Phil.*
*Phil.*

Wes groaned and threw the phone across the room. Or he tried to, anyway. It might have gotten past the floor at his feet if he'd unplugged it first.

He knew he couldn't keep Phil in the dark much longer. The truth was, he was going to need his help to pull things off as elegantly as he hoped to. But there was no aspect of it all that he was dreading more than telling his campaign manager he'd just been wasting his time. That he'd been wasting *so many people's* time. In some ways, Wes suspected Phil had a hunch. Maybe not that he was preparing to drop out of the race, but certainly that something was amiss. No, he couldn't have known he was preparing to step away with a forty-two-point lead for the nomination heading into the primaries. Only a crazy person would do that, and of all the things Phil probably thought Wes was, he doubted crazy was among them.

A natural. Born for this. Even *ordained*, whatever that meant. These were the ways Phil Brewster described Wes—at fundraisers, on *Meet the Press,* to Wes himself when he needed a pick-me-up. And all of those terms were on Phil's vocabulary list because Governor McNeese had spoken them into being, chanting them over his son and to anyone who would listen from the day they'd met in 2003.

*Well, that's not entirely true.* He'd come at it from the opposite perspective, just long enough to gluttonously feed all of his son's fears about himself that he would never amount to anything. And then, when Wes had imploded under the weight of his inferiority and worthlessness and guilt and regret, the governor set about convincing him he was destined for greatness. Among the most painful experiences of his life had been finally seeing his father's "love" for what it was, but he tried to comfort himself with the rationalization that there wasn't an eighteen-year-old in the world who wouldn't have fallen for it. At least not if they'd been as desperate for a dad as young Wes Hobbes had been.

Wes picked his phone off the floor and disconnected it from the charger before flopping onto the bed, his head on the pillow, and pulling up his voice mails. He skimmed through, intending to start at the beginning of all he'd missed in the last few hours, but instead he did what he did so often lately and scrolled back in time to just weeks before Wray died. Just days before he checked her into the hospital and never brought her home again.

*"Hey, Hobbes. I've got some things to say, and I can never quite get you to listen. I know you think I need you to be strong, and in your mind, I think that means tricking me into believing none of this is as bad as it seems. So we never get to have the real conversation. That's fine. But I just need to say—I need you to hear me say—that you're enough. If anyone tells you different, don't walk . . . run. But guess what? You are not God's gift to mankind. You're not dipped in gold. If anyone tells you different, don't walk . . . run. You're as imperfect as the rest of us, but you do try harder than most. I'll give you that. So figure out what matters to you, Wes, and give it your all, and I promise you, you'll be okay. Just stop letting everyone else tell you who you are. Just . . . stop. Be Wes Hobbes. Wes Hobbes is good and fun and smart and cares about things. Wes Hobbes is my favorite person in the world, and it's time for him to figure out what sort of legacy he wants to leave. And yeah, I'm really sorry I won't be here for you. But you don't need me. You don't need your dad. You don't need focus groups or polling numbers. Just . . . Babe, listen to me. Trust yourself. And if you can't trust yourself, trust me, just this one more time. It's going to be fine. You're going to be fine. Alright? And no matter what, I love you. For better or worse."*

He set the phone aside—so careful, as he always was, to make sure he closed out of the voice mail properly so he didn't accidentally delete it—and then pulled one of the pillows out from under his head and covered his face with it before giving in to the sobs that always hovered just under the surface as he listened to Wray's ragged breaths and fading energy.

He'd never imagined he would miss her as much as he did. He'd always cared about her, of course. He'd even grown to love her, though theirs was never going to be a great love story for the ages. They were partners for years. Allies. Their mutually beneficial, symbiotic relationship was the stuff DC fairy tales were made of, and they both would have sworn during the course of those early years that they didn't need or want anything else. They both had other desires, of course, but those were secondary. What they had was what mattered, and while other young married couples daydreamed about future children and grandchildren and all the adventures they'd have together, Wes and Wray dreamed of making real strides toward equal pay for equal work and ending childhood hunger and easing racial tensions. They registered for wedding china while pointing out various characteristics of pieces that they would want to integrate into their White House set. And they were there for each other in every circumstance, just like other couples, even if in their case that meant making sure their assistants and social secretaries knew that being each other's plus-one received highest priority on the calendar.

And then cancer reared its ugly head, and where others may have gotten lost in self-pity or thrown themselves into accomplishing as much as they could in whatever time they had left—at least Wes was pretty sure that's how *he* would have responded—Wray scaled back. Reevaluated. Focused. Savored. She sent handwritten notes—hundreds of them in those last months—to charities she believed in and role models who had inspired her. She cleared her schedule and covertly cleared his so they could spend an entire afternoon each week playing board games in his office in the Rayburn Building while Senate aides scrambled to explain his absence.

And she started talking about *home*.

Wes pulled the pillow away from his face at the sound of an urgent knock on the solid oak door to his room. He remained immobilized, listening, until she spoke.

"Wes, are you in there?" Her voice was a stage whisper. "It's me. It's Addie."

"Coming," he called out and then set the pillow, wet tears–side down, back on the bed and hurried to the door. Well, he *began* by hurrying, then caught his reflection in the mirror. *Oh yeah, totally looking sane there, Hobbes.* "Be right there!"

He stepped into the bathroom and splashed cold water onto his face and rubbed at his eyes. In the process of rubbing, he inadvertently got a whiff of his coffee breath bouncing off his hand, so he quickly squeezed some toothpaste onto his finger and slid it onto his teeth before swishing it around and spitting it into the sink.

Well, it was *supposed* to go into the sink, and chances were good he would have accomplished that simplest of tasks if he hadn't grown overly ambitious and attempted to run a comb through his hair at the same time. It all proved too much for him, and white toothpaste slobber spilled all down the front of his blue dress shirt.

*Trust me, America. I'm doing you a favor here. Your commander in chief should be able to spit into a sink.*

He unbuttoned the top two buttons of his shirt and pulled it over his head just as Addie stage-whispered, "Everything okay in there?"

He sighed at his reflection and chuckled before turning the crumpled shirt right-side-out again and slipping it back over his head. "She's seen you look worse," he said to himself.

# CHAPTER 11

# ADDIE

**8,206 Days Since Their Last Fight**

"Hey," he greeted me as he opened the door. "I didn't expect to see you for another . . ." He raised his wrist as I pushed past him into his room.

"Yeah, yeah, I'm early." I wasn't there for obvious observations. "Are you dropping out of the race to protect me?"

His eyes flew open, and he leaned out the door to look down the hallway before reentering and shutting the door behind him. "I wasn't kidding when I said no one knows yet, Addie, so if you don't mind—"

"I just need a yes or no."

He compulsively brushed at a spot on his shirt. "I'm sorry, what was the question again?"

I crossed my arms and rolled my eyes. "Are you dropping out of the race to protect me?"

"Okay . . ." He eyed me warily and walked past me to the desk. "That's what I thought you said. Um, no."

"Because if you are, I don't need you to protect me, Wes. I'm a big girl, and I can handle whatever they throw at me."

"I'm sure you can."

"And I'm not saying you should stay in the race. I don't care if you stay in the race or not. I really don't. But—"

"But I shouldn't drop out to protect you?"

"Right."

He gave me a thumbs-up. "Got it."

"So?"

His eyes flitted from side to side. "So . . . *what*?"

"Are you going to?"

"Am I going to drop out?"

"Yes."

He nodded. "Yes."

"To protect me?"

"No."

"You're sure?"

"Quite."

I released the entire contents of my lungs and nodded once, sharply. "Okay. Good. Thanks." Then I turned back to the door and reached for the knob.

"Wait a minute." His soft laugh got a step closer. "Are you at least going to tell me where that came from?"

That was fair, I supposed. I faced him again. "It was just a theory Laila had."

His Adam's apple bobbed up and down as he swallowed, and the smile faded. "About what? You mean . . . you and Laila were talking about why I'm dropping out? You told her?"

My eyes flew open, and I took a step toward him, horrified, as I realized what he was thinking. He was thinking exactly what he *should* have been thinking, based on the incomplete pieces of the puzzle I'd given him. "No! No, I definitely didn't. Sorry." I covered my eyes with my hands, still hearing it the way he must have heard it. "I wouldn't, Wes. Really. All I said was that I thought you were hoping to talk with Sebastian and that I felt there had to be more to it. That was it."

Calm returned to his eyes, and he leaned his shoulder against the wall. "And Laila jumped to me dropping out all on her own?"

I felt my hackles rise for a moment, thinking that he was doubting my story, but it didn't take long at all to realize there was no hint of cynicism in his voice. "Nothing ever came up about you dropping out. Not from me or her. She just thought maybe one of your opponents or somebody found out about our past . . . the way we ended . . . and they were going to use it against you."

Wes nodded and tilted his head from side to side while his eyes rose and seemed to do computations in the air. "Huh. Yeah. If that came to light, it might not look great."

"I mean, not that it *should* be a big deal after all this time, but for the purposes of a cutthroat political campaign—"

"Of course it should still be a big deal, Addie." His voice was quiet and gravelly. "It *is* a big deal."

I pulled my eyes away from his and turned back to the door and opened it. "Don't do that. I don't want to have this conversation."

"Hey." He rushed over and put his hand on the door, causing it to close again. "You brought it up. And now that it's been brought up, don't you think—"

"What? I'm not allowed to leave now?"

*Don't be a jerk, Addie. You know very well he didn't mean anything by it.*

His gaze darted from my eyes to his hand, a foot above my height, pressing the door closed. He sighed, and his shoulders fell. "Of course you can leave. Sorry."

"Thank you."

For a long time, when we were kids, it had looked like I was going to be tall and Wes wasn't. In fifth grade, Cole shot up like a weed, but I was the next tallest for a couple of years after that. Then Brynn got tall. Cole got even taller. Laila and I had several more moderate growth spurts. And we were all taller than Wes. And then in eighth grade, a magical thing happened. At least I thought it was magical. Cole had been less than impressed as Wes seemed to grow about a foot and a half overnight and Cole became forevermore the second tallest of our group.

Now, as he lowered his arm and stepped away, I had to swallow down an unwelcome appearance by fifteen-year-old Addie's hormones—or at least the bred-in-the-bone memory of those hormones. There wasn't much in the world those hormones—*that* Addie—would have liked more than having Wes's all-grown-up stature towering over her, blissfully keeping her from leaving.

"Oh. Here." I reached into the pocket of my coat, briefly squeezed my fingernails into my palm to make sure I was steady on the outside, even if I felt slightly less steady on the inside, and pulled out a pair of men's gloves and handed them to him. "Not quite as fancy as your leather ones, of course."

"These are great!" He slipped them on and wiggled his fingers around as the type of smile usually reserved for a gift of concert tickets or a puppy spread across his face. "How much do I owe you?"

"Don't worry about it."

"Are you sure? These really are great."

"Well, they aren't sticky. That's something."

He laughed. "That's definitely something."

"And bonus, they're designed and made by our own Mrs. Kimball, so—"

"Mrs. Kimball?" The smile stayed in place, and new curiosity began dancing in his eyes. "Cole's wife?"

I stared at him, waiting for him to catch up and put two and two together, but then realized there was zero reason whatsoever he would be able to do the math. He didn't have all the figures.

"Um, yeah. Laila."

He literally stumbled back a step as curiosity was replaced by wonder and astonishment. "*No.*"

"Yep. *Finally.* A little over a year ago."

"Wow." He sat on the edge of his bed, still studying his gloves. "Took 'em long enough. I mean, we used to talk about them getting together—"

"Who did? You and Cole?"

"Oh no. Cole was clueless. You know that. But you and I used to talk about it. And Brynn. But I don't think I ever thought it would actually happen."

"No, neither did I. If anything, I just assumed neither of them would ever end up with anyone, and they'd move to Miami and eat cheesecake together until they died, like some romantic tension–oblivious Golden Girls."

Wes laughed as he took off his gloves. "Do you remember when Lai talked us all into performing that horrible lip-sync routine to that Spice Girls song in eighth grade?"

"Oh, good grief!" I chuckled as the memories of Cole and Wes dressed as Baby and Scary, respectively, flooded my mind. "'Say You'll Be There,' right? She really could get us to do anything."

"She could get *Cole* to do anything, and then they'd gang up on us and we were all done for." He smiled wide and shook his head as he set the gloves on the bed beside him. "Thank you for these. Really."

"You're welcome."

We were having dinner in a few hours. Whether or not that was a mistake remained to be seen, but still . . . so it was. Dinner was the time set aside for me to ask questions and for him to provide answers. But we were here now. Alone. Dinner would be very different. I still hadn't even figured out where we could go. He'd said he wasn't hiding, and I didn't think I was either. But that didn't mean I was ready to deal with the reaction this town would have to seeing Addie Atwater and Wes Hobbes together again.

I crossed over to the desk and grabbed the chair, taking quick note of the pads of paper that had been scrawled on and crossed through, and turned it around to face him. "So why are you dropping out?" I asked as I sat.

"Thank you for not telling Laila."

"Of course."

"I'm just saying, I know how close the two of you are—"

"You don't know anything."

He chewed on his bottom lip and nodded. "You're right. Sorry. I just mean I know how close you *were*, and I don't think there was ever much you didn't tell her and Brynn back in the day, so I appreciate the discretion."

"Quit trying to change the subject, Wes."

He took a deep breath as his head fell back. "I'm not." He faced me again. "I'm actually trying to politely ask if I can trust you with what I'm about to say now."

I scoffed. "If you can trust *me*?"

"Yes," he replied, completely unfazed by my short-fused umbrage. "Like you just said, I don't know anything. I don't know *you*, quite frankly."

It felt like the air had been knocked out of me, and my head began spinning, and suddenly I was in the kitchen at my house. My dad's house, rather. I mean, I wasn't literally there. His words hadn't opened a portal to a different multiverse or anything. (Jeez, Joel had turned me into such a nerd.) But it felt almost as real.

It was August 8, 2003. The night before our wedding. Wes was on one side of the marble island, and I was on the other, but we might as well have had an actual island between us.

*"You're not listening to me."*

*"What? Of course I am. I'm nervous, too, Wes."*

*"I'm not nervous, Add. This has nothing to do with being nervous. I just want to make sure you're sure."*

*"Sure that I want to marry you? How could you even ask me that?"*

*"No, not that you want to marry me. That you want to marry me tomorrow."*

*"Why? Don't you want to marry me?"*

*"I love you, Addie. I love you so much. I love you forever. You know that."*

*"Then we're fine."*

"Addie? You okay?" Back in his room at the inn, Wes was leaning in, concern in his eyes. "You look like . . . Are you going to be sick? Can I get you anything?"

*What was that?* "Um, yeah . . . I'm fine." I swallowed hard. And then again. The third time, the nausea dissipated. "Maybe some water?"

"Of course." He jumped up and grabbed a little clear plastic cup and removed it from its wrapper, then filled it with water from the bathroom sink and brought it to me. "Here." He placed his hand gently on the back of my head for less than a second before realizing what he was doing and pulling it back as if he'd been bitten. "How about a wet washcloth? Would that help?"

I gulped the water down and shook my head. "I'm okay now. Thanks." He still stood over me, concerned, so I put a little more effort into selling it. "I'm fine. Really. It was just . . ."

The truth would be so easy in some ways and so impossible in others. I hadn't thought about that day for years. The way we'd fought. The way I'd cried. The way we'd both been so exhausted by the time we got to that point in the conversation. The way the fight had left us—and the way I stormed off to my bedroom a few minutes later without telling him I loved him. The way my last words to him that night had been a dismissive, "I'm not sure I even know who you are."

They were my last words to him for twenty-two years.

Still, even then, as far apart as we'd been and as angry as I'd felt, the thought of him not showing up in the morning never entered my mind. It was beyond unfathomable. It was an impossible truth.

"I just don't think I've had enough water today."

Wes took the cup from my hand and had it refilled and back to me within seconds. He watched me as I drank, ready to fill the small cup again, but when I shook my head, he sat back down across from me.

"There's a story that's going to break," he began, and I set the cup down on the desk behind me. "I'm not sure when, exactly. I've been going crazy, actually, just waiting. It's hard to imagine we'll make it past Super Tuesday, so . . . soon. It's, um . . ." He began fiddling with that weird extra collar button sewn into the bottom of men's dress shirts. "It's not going to be good for me. I've been feeling for a while like this isn't what I want anyway. I mean, running for president. So

I was already weighing my options. This just . . . Yeah, it takes the choice out of my hands. And that's fine. Really. But, um . . ." He lowered his eyes to watch his fiddling fingers. "I'd just rather try to control the narrative as much as I can. And I'm thinking Sebastian Sudworth may be my best hope of doing that."

"Did you have an affair?"

His head snapped up, and his red-rimmed eyes met mine. "What?"

I shrugged. "I'm sorry. I'm not trying to be insensitive." Although, let's face it, I wasn't trying superhard to be sensitive either.

He blinked repeatedly. "No. I, um . . . No."

"Sorry. That was . . . Sorry. You don't have to tell me, obviously."

His phone buzzed, and he groaned and walked over to it and held it long enough to turn it off, then threw it back onto the bed. He walked over to the window and pulled back the curtain—the snow was still coming down in the type of storm that I was certain had brought the town to a standstill—and stared out at the blanket of white. And I just watched him.

It wasn't my first time looking at him since he got into town, of course, though I suppose it was the first opportunity I'd had without him being aware. It wasn't so much about seeing him in person for the first time in more than two decades, though. That wasn't what made my jaw and my nerve endings and my heart all tighten. It was seeing him in contrast to the clear image of the eighteen-year-old young man I'd seen so vividly in my mind just a couple of minutes ago.

That young man, standing across the island from me, had been dressed in a shirt and tie and actual dress shoes, though until then his version of dress shoes had been his black-and-white-checkered skate shoes. His blond hair—that blond hair I had spent countless hours running my fingers through while we watched movies and his head rested on my lap—had been trimmed and combed and slicked back. At our rehearsal dinner, Cole—his best man, of course—had asked him if he'd left any hair gel for the rest of the wedding party, and we'd all laughed. All except for Wes, who was uncharacteristically offendable that night.

Now, with his wrinkled shirt and his sock-clad feet and his disheveled hair, he reminded me of my Wes more than the person I'd fought with that night, and certainly more than any image I'd ever seen of the senator on television or on the cover of *Time* or *Newsweek*.

I couldn't explain it, but I knew this guy. The one staring out the window. The one who had seemed so genuinely touched by a gift of—at this point—unpaid-for gloves. The one who, I was willing to bet, was used to not having anyone to share his secrets with.

If nothing else, after a lifetime together followed by a lifetime apart, we had that in common.

"I was in the CIA."

I felt his eyes focus back on me as I took my cup to the sink and refilled it. "To be honest, I wouldn't have predicted—"

"What? That I'd actually make something of myself after you left?" I groaned softly and my chin fell sharply to my chest.

"No! Addie, I didn't mean anything remotely like—"

"I know." I turned off the faucet and faced him again. "I seem to be incapable of keeping snarky thoughts to myself around you. Sorry. All I meant—and the only reason I brought up the CIA at all—is that I'm pretty good at keeping secrets."

"I bet you are." He watched me with a sad expression on his face as I came back around the corner from the bathroom, and then he sat on the edge of the bed just as I sat back down in my chair.

I chose not to add on, "Of course I also got kicked out of the CIA," and instead kept my mouth shut and waited for him to carry on when he was ready.

"So look, here's the thing," he finally said. "Wray and I didn't have what you would call a traditional marriage."

"How so? Were you into kinky stuff or something?"

It was a good thing I was the one drinking water. He spewed, nonetheless, and I laughed as he recovered by coughing into the corner of his elbow. "Um, no. But thanks for helping to prepare me for some of the hard-hitting questions I may get asked by the media."

"My pleasure."

"What I mean is, we got married because . . . well, because we both thought we needed to get married. She was my best friend from the time she showed up at Yale to the day she died. Maybe my only friend. We were partners. There was trust and respect, and . . . I needed a perfect DC wife, and Wray was . . . yeah, she was made for that life. The public service life, I mean. So much more than I was, truthfully. She *cared*, Addie. She had her own ambitions, but it wasn't ever about power or control for her. If she'd been a little more power hungry, she would have made a much better candidate than I ever did, trust me. But it just wasn't about that for her. She needed to be in the conversation, because everything she had to say made the conversation better."

My thoughts and memories of Wray Gardner were, like so many aspects of my life, divided into two eras. When we were kids, she'd been two or three years younger than us. Not so young that we had to babysit her but young enough that we sort of just viewed her as a nuisance. An annoying brat who wanted to hang out with us and whom we allowed to do so from time to time if she stayed out of our way until we needed her to get us more soda from the fridge.

And then I just didn't ever think about her at all until I saw her on TV with Wes.

"Did you cheat on me with her? Is that why you left?"

"Oh goodness, Addie, no. She was a kid, and I'd never looked at her. I'd never looked at *anyone*." He pulled his eyes away and sighed. "No, I promise you nothing ever happened. There wasn't even the idea of anything ever happening. I don't think I even had a full conversation with her until Yale. That's the truth."

I took a swig of water and then stood for another refill. God bless the tiny little cup and its gift of frequent opportunities to walk away from discomfort. "Anyway, you were saying your marriage was not a traditional one."

"Right." I walked back in as he was running his hands through his hair, disheveling it further. "So yeah, I needed a political-asset wife, and Wray needed a cover-up-story husband. It was perfect."

"A cover-up story? Why? What was she covering up?"

He released another heavy sigh. "This is her story, Addie. I need you to know that."

"I said you don't have to tell me anything you don't want—"

"No, it's not that. I'll tell you." His eyes locked with mine as he restated the sentence with a new emphasis. "I'll tell *you.* But I don't tell people this because *she* didn't tell people this. And that's why I'm in a tight spot now—"

"Wray was a lesbian?"

He bit his bottom lip and nodded.

I scooted back in my chair and crossed my ankle up onto my knee. "Huh."

"Yeah."

"Okay . . . Okay . . ." I tried once again to think of it all from the perspective of a political strategist. "That's awkward to manage, I'm sure. I mean, yeah . . . there's lots to consider there. But I don't see any reason why this has to end with you dropping out of the race."

"Well, like I said, I was probably going to do that anyway. But it needs to be now. I need to get ahead of it."

I nodded, finally understanding. I thought. "That's the story that's about to break?"

Wes's lips formed a tight line, and his nose scrunched up. "No, actually. I'm pretty sure no one knows. I mean, Andrea didn't even know."

"How did her own sister not—"

"Because Wray didn't want her to. She didn't want *anyone* in this town to know. She didn't want to deal with being judged and ostracized—"

"Oh, come on, Wes. No one would have—"

"Are you serious, Addie?" He pushed off the bed and returned to the window. "Look, this town was always made up of kind people who meant well. I'm not denying that. And I don't know what it's like now. But back then?" He shook his head and leaned against the wall, facing me. "Maybe they would have accepted her, maybe they wouldn't have, but she felt like she had to get out. And let's not revise history here and forget that at various times for various reasons we all felt that way. I was the only person she knew outside of Adelaide Springs, so I was the person she tracked down. And then from that point on, we were both so focused on what we could accomplish together that we never turned back."

He was right, of course. We'd been blessed to grow up in a community in which you didn't lock your door at night and everyone knew everyone. Everyone looked out for everyone. But there weren't ever any big surprises. If you were one of them, they would fight to the death for you. And if you weren't? Well, I wasn't aware of anyone ever being run out of town or anything like that, but new people didn't usually stick around. And as painful as it was to admit, it probably wasn't just because you had to drive nearly an hour to pick up a decent pizza.

"Okay, but then she left. She was at Yale. She was in Washington. DC is not Adelaide Springs, Wes. She could have—"

"Well, *now*, sure. Maybe," he added a little less confidently. "But this was twenty years ago."

I sighed. "Of course. You're right." I'd been a woman in the military and then in the intelligence community long enough to understand that even those who advocated for change and had the power to do something about it sometimes—all too often—still fell back on asking the only person in the room wearing a skirt—who outranked at least a few of the men with empty cups—to pour the coffee. And it hadn't been anywhere near twenty years ago that my compliant pouring had last been followed up with, "Thanks, hon." My circumstances and Wray's may have differed, but I could understand her desire to keep those circumstances from interfering with the things she wanted to accomplish.

"By the time the world—or at least DC—might not have cared quite as much, we were pretty settled in." He stuffed his hands into the pockets of his slacks. "Neither of us forced the other into anything we didn't want. It was not traditional, and maybe it isn't what other people in our situation would have done, but we got to focus on the work, and that was what mattered to us. It worked for us. Really. For a long time. Until . . . well, until it didn't."

"What changed?"

He sat back on the bed, this time against the headboard with his knees propped up against his chest. "Would you believe it was a potent combination of cancer and Brynn Cornell?" He laughed gently.

"What? What does Brynn have to do with any of this?"

"Cancer makes you reevaluate everything. At least it made Wray reevaluate everything. Not the choices she'd made—the choices *we* had made—just why we had made them. She began seeing my father a little more for what he was, and she saw how long we'd both been ignoring our scars rather than trying to get any healing from them. And then everything that happened with Brynn on *Sunup*, putting down Adelaide Springs and everything, happened, and she—Wray, I mean—forced us to have a conversation we'd managed to avoid for fifteen, sixteen years or so."

"About what?"

He wrapped his arms around his knees, and one corner of his mouth rose in a half smile. "You, mostly."

"Me?"

"Yeah. You. And Andrea. Cole. Laila. Jo. Everybody, I guess. But yeah . . . you."

I didn't have to ask for more details. Not that I would have anyway, of course, but there was no need. I didn't know what pain he had been dealing with. What unresolved emotions he may have needed to tackle. But I understood that he and Wray had finally had a conversation equivalent to the one Joel and I had in the meadow.

*And let the healing begin.*

"So if that's not the story, Wes, what's the story? I don't understand. No one knew she was gay. You said it's not about an affair. No one knew the two of you were anything other than a perfect DC power couple on their way to the White House."

"Exactly. We were a perfect DC power couple, and when she died, I was the perfect grieving widower. The perfect grieving widower who experienced an unprecedented bump in the polls, it's worth mentioning. You could even argue that I'm the front-runner *because* of how perfect Wray and I were together and because of how perfectly destroyed I was when I lost her."

"Okay, yeah, so? It's not like you murdered her to get ahead in the polls. I mean, you didn't, right?"

He chuckled. "No. I didn't. But pretty soon it's going to leak that while my wife was on her deathbed, finally losing her brave battle with breast cancer, hooked up to machines and having only a couple of weeks left to live, I walked myself down to the courthouse and filed for divorce. And that's something everyone on both sides of the aisle can agree is pretty unforgivable."

## CHAPTER 12

# WES

**Nearly 23 Years Since He Lost the First Woman He Loved**

That had been his worst day. A day when every regret for every stupid thing he'd ever done and every weak or impulsive decision he'd ever made came home to roost. He'd had to acknowledge that he really was going to lose her. It became impossible to deny that any longer, watching her frail, disappearing body lift briefly off the sheets with each agonizing, assisted breath. Watching the life disappear from her eyes more and more each time she opened them between restless naps.

That day he'd finally felt the full force of the guilt he'd been burying or swallowing or justifying for most of his life. How could he not think of his mom and *her* ragged breaths, *her* fading eyes, and remember how he'd found excuses to stay out late so he wouldn't have to be inconvenienced by how sad her suffering made him?

And then once that knife of shame and regret was in his gut, how could he resist twisting it until he finally acknowledged that he'd been lying to himself for years? He'd convinced himself he'd left the way he did to make things easier for Addie, but the truth was, he'd been in self-preservation mode then too. He'd run rather than face her suffering too.

And for months he'd walked the same path with Wray. Sure, he was there physically. He sat with her through treatments and held her hair back when chemo made her sick. He learned how to tie her head scarf the way she liked it when the hair was gone and she didn't have the strength to lift her arms to tie it herself. But through it all, he'd also talked about the future and refused to acknowledge she might not be there for it. And maybe that would have been what some people needed him to be in that situation, but it wasn't what Wray needed. It wasn't what she wanted.

Wes hated that it had taken the pain of losing yet another woman he loved for him to finally realize he hadn't even tried to be the man any of them needed him to be.

Months prior, Wray had told him it was time. She was going to file for divorce and do an interview—something high profile but kind. Her heart was set on Brynn, but Wes thought that was a mistake. He thought the entire idea was a mistake. It was easy to see now that he was being selfish, but he had to believe—he *did* believe—it wasn't all about him. He didn't want her subjected to the scrutiny. An in-depth interview—even with a friendly face—in which she explained the nature of their marriage and carefully constructed the image of Wes as blameless, as she insisted she wanted to so he could still pursue his political aspirations, would be taxing at best. Disastrous at worst. And she needed to save her strength to fight and recover.

Because she was going to recover, he knew. He just knew it. And then, on that day—his worst day—he finally understood that she wasn't.

"That's what Wray wanted?" Addie asked softly. "The divorce, I mean."

"That's what Wray wanted." He slipped his feet off the far side of the bed and leaned over, staring at them. "That's what she had wanted for a while, but I refused. I think, as much as anything, I didn't want her to do it for me. I think I thought she was freeing me up for whatever came next. Making sure I wasn't portrayed as the bad guy. Making sure I could still get elected. And yeah, that was probably all part of it. But it didn't occur to me that maybe she didn't want her life to end while she was living a lie. Not until the day I took her to the hospital for the last time. And so that was the day I filed for divorce. I wanted her to be free of the lie. Then the rest would be hers to do with as she pleased." He looked over his shoulder to Addie. "It didn't occur to me that I'd be *here* at some point. That she would die before she had a chance to define how she would be remembered. And it certainly never occurred to me that I'd keep pushing or getting pushed—I don't even know the difference anymore—toward the presidency, and that with Wray gone, the compass would just spin and spin."

Addie stood from the chair and joined him on the side of the bed. "Scoot," she instructed him, and he scooted to the top of the bed while she remained nearly at the foot. Wes turned toward her and propped his knee up on the bed between them, duplicating the position he'd adopted as they talked in the truck earlier.

*This is nice.*

The words were jangling around in his chest like an errant pinball, desperate to escape the endless bouncing, bouncing, bouncing against the sides, never scoring a single point. That was all he wanted to say. That it was nice to be spending time with her again. That it was nice to be talking to her again. It was nice to spend time with someone he trusted, despite the fact that he now knew his personal assistant and his barber and the attendant at the Rayburn Building parking garage better than he knew the woman he had just told all the untellable things to.

But everything in him was on high alert, cautioning him not to say the words, no matter how harmless they seemed to him.

"How's your dad?" He hadn't meant to change the subject so abruptly, but he needed to say *something* that wouldn't make her super aware of how much he'd missed her. "I mean . . . he's still around, right?"

"Oh yes. He's the mayor, in fact. He hasn't changed much at all, really. Except he seems older every time I look at him, even if I can't pinpoint any differences."

"Is he still practicing medicine?"

Addie nodded and placed her palms on the bed behind her, leaning back. "I don't think he feels like he has much choice. He's still the only doctor in town."

Once he and Wray had begun talking about home, there was no other name that came up in Wes's memories and regrets as often as Doc Atwater's. Apart from Doc Atwater's daughter's, of course. The thought that he may have the opportunity to speak with him and apologize for breaking his promise to always take care of their girl both terrified him and filled him with gratitude.

"I was sorry to hear about *your* dad, by the way. His death, I mean."

"Were you?" Wes picked up his new gloves from the center of the bed and ran his finger along the stitching. "It would be perfectly understandable if you weren't."

They *had* to talk about it, right? When he'd decided to come to Adelaide Springs, yes, he'd been hoping to talk to Sebastian Sudworth (he *had* to talk to Sebastian Sudworth—there was no plan B), but he knew Jo was right. She'd never encouraged Wes to just show up, and the fact that he had, if that was really the reason why, was absurd. *Of course* Sebastian wasn't in town. It was absurd to think—the odds were astronomical, probably—that he would actually catch him here and be able to walk up to him on Main Street and say, "I'm Senator Wesley Hobbes. You know, the guy who deserted most of the people you know and love. Can I buy you a cup of coffee and fill you in on a really big favor I'm hoping you'll do for me?"

He'd known when he made the decision to come—though, really, could he call it a "decision" since he'd sort of just told a bunch of lies and ended up on a plane?—that it wasn't going to be easy. That it might not work. That Sebastian might not be here. That he probably wouldn't be. Wes had known that he had enough clout to pick up the phone and get Sebastian Sudworth on the line.

So why had he come?

Addie rested her cheek on her shoulder and met his eyes. "To be honest I didn't really care one way or another. But that's not the sentiment Emily Post advises us to pass along in our condolences over the loss of one's father."

"Emily Post would be proud. Thank you."

He'd come to begin making it right. He'd only hoped for an opportunity to *begin*. He would apologize as many times as he needed to, to as many people as he could. Not that an apology would make what he had done okay. They might not even be willing to hear anything he had to say, but he had to start somewhere. He had to try. And then someday . . .

*Addie.*

He never would have imagined that *someday* would be *today*. But here she was. Now. Talking with him. Sitting on a bed with him, however innocently. Smiling at him. *No one* would have imagined that. Sure, she was hating him at the same time, he was fairly confident, but there seemed to be an uneasy and incredibly unexpected truce between them. At least for the moment. If he did nothing else right for the rest of his life, he would not mess this up. He wouldn't rush her or force her to talk about things she wasn't ready to talk about. He wouldn't even tell her how nice it was just to be in the same room with her again. Yep, if he could just prevent himself from saying stupid things, then they'd have a chance to talk about important things eventually. He was sure of it.

*That's all you have to do, Wes. Don't say stupid things.*

"And I was sorry to hear about your husband."

She rose up slowly from her relaxed, comfortable position that had helped lull him into a false belief it was safe for him to open his mouth. "How do you know about Joel?"

Well, okay, then. If he was being honest, he'd made it longer than he thought he would without saying stupid things.

"I don't. I mean, I do. Obviously. But all I know is that he passed away."

She stood from the bed and returned to the chair, but she didn't sit down. She just stood behind it and gripped the chipped wood so hard her knuckles turned white. "And how do you know that?"

He lied for a living. All politicians lied for a living. And that wasn't to say they were all corrupt or evil or self-serving monsters. Some of them—and Wes liked to believe he was among the illustrious number—actually did all they could to make the world a little bit better, one bill or vote or initiative at a time. No matter why he had gotten into politics in the first place, and no matter why he had run for office originally or why he'd been preparing to do it again, he'd always taken his responsibility seriously. But that didn't change the fact that he lied for a living. It was part of the game. Each campaign promise was a lie—not because you didn't truly hope to fulfill it, but because ultimately you had so very little control over anything.

How many times had he and his cohorts told the press they were "optimistic" a deal could be made as they walked onto the Senate floor, when the truth was agreements had already been made or squashed in offices or on golf courses or over drinks in the days leading up to the public actions?

It wasn't exactly a badge of honor, but the fact remained: Wes Hobbes was a very good liar. But he wouldn't lie to Addie. He couldn't be completely sure, but something in his soul confirmed that the math would check out on his hypothesis: Addie Atwater was the only person in his entire life, in the entire world, to whom he'd only ever spoken the truth.

"Jo told me."

"Wow. In her sunset years, Jo has become quite generous with information she has no right sharing *and* her recreational vehicles."

Wes stood and circled the bed to stand before her, the chair between them—its four legs on the floor the only aspect of her stance preventing her from looking like a lion tamer keeping him at a safe distance. "I was just surprised to see you here. In Adelaide Springs, I mean. Last night. And Jo told me you moved here after your husband died. That's it."

"That's it?"

"That's it." *Well, shoot.* "And that you were in the CIA. So I did know that already. Sorry. But *that's* all. Honest."

"What? How did *that* come up in the conversation, pray tell?"

"Same thing. Why you're here. You were in the CIA, and then you left the CIA."

"Well, that sounds like *two* things to me, for a total of three."

"Now that's just absurd, Adelaide. I daresay even I am smart enough to connect the dots and figure out that if you left the CIA, that means you were *in* the CIA. We're still at two things."

"You don't have any right to go around asking questions about me. You understand that, right? You don't get to breeze back into town after twenty-two years—"

"I'm not 'breezing back into town.' Good grief!" he growled at her and grabbed the back of the chair, his hands between her hands. His knee on the seat and her face just inches away. "Yes. I understand. I have no right to details of your life. I get that. I walked out. I gave up whatever right I had to ask why you're here or offer my condolences over the loss of your husband. And I certainly gave up my right to apologize and tell you how much I regret all of it. To tell you how I would give anything—*anything*, Addie—to be able to go back in time and not be such a stupid, idiotic, clueless eighteen-year-old kid. Cool. I get it. Thanks. Thanks for explaining that to me."

Neither of them blinked or cowered or took a step back from the far-too-intimate space they were sharing, though Wes's mind was reeling, and his pulse was racing, and he was trying to remember how to compute geometric equations. She was closer to the door, and there was a chair between them, and she was going to turn and make a run for it any second, he knew. He wouldn't block her way (that hadn't gone so well the last time he'd accidentally done it), but he had to give himself a fighting chance at getting to the door before she did. That was geometry, right?

Being the son of Governor McNeese might have come with an inordinate number of disadvantages, but passing Yale courses that he may have deserved to fail was not one of them.

"Addie, look, I'm sor—"

"I'm just glad we're on the same page."

And then she kissed him on the tip of his nose.

Instantly, Addie's eyes flew wide, as did her mouth, though no words came out. Wes, meanwhile, released the chair and gasped for breath as laughter overtook him. He stumbled backward until his legs hit the bed, and then he collapsed onto it. There was something—some tiny but assertive do-gooder in his brain, like that nerdy little bookworm cartoon on those posters in the school library growing up, telling them to shush—cautioning him to stop laughing. To double down on his geometric equations. But seriously, he was about as likely to stop laughing as he was to suddenly understand how to figure out the surface area of a trapezoid.

"Shut up," she finally said, but laughter was bubbling out from beneath the words, and Wes was able to silence the nagging bookworm once and for all.

"That's what you did when—"

"Oh, I know." She groaned through her laughter and stepped away from the chair. She then walked over to the floor-length mirror, crossed her arms over it, and lowered her forehead onto her arms—still laughing.

They had been nine years old, hanging out in the clubhouse, as they called it, on the top floor of Laila's grandparents' house—

He suddenly breathed in air so quickly it choked him, and he coughed as he jumped up from the bed.

"Are you okay?" Addie asked, turning away from the mirror to check on him.

"Is this the clubhouse?" he hacked out between throat-clearing coughs.

She chuckled. "No. That's the other room, down the hall."

"Oh." He slumped back onto the edge of the bed. "Bummer."

They'd been nine years old, and she was already his favorite person in the world. She told him all the time, even then—even when they were younger than that—that she was going to marry him someday.

The idea of all of that was ridiculous to him, of course—not that he could actually wrap his head around it at all. No, it meant nothing. That was just Addie being Addie. It didn't scare him off. It just didn't register. And she kept on being his best friend—not that he ever called her that. He called Cole his best friend, because at that age it mattered. His best friend couldn't be a girl. That wasn't how it worked. (Never mind that Laila was Cole's best friend and Cole never shied away from admitting it. That wasn't uncool. That was just Cole and Laila being Cole and Laila.)

Then one day, it was just Wes and Addie in the clubhouse, waiting for Brynn to get back from the bathroom and for Cole and Laila to get back from the kitchen with popcorn, and Addie said, "I think we should be boyfriend and girlfriend."

Once again, it didn't scare him off. It just didn't mean anything. He told her he didn't want a girlfriend, and she told him that was okay. "Never mind," she'd whispered, and then she'd gone over to look out the transom window at the moon.

He felt bad for making her sad, so he joined her at the window and said, "But if I ever do have a girlfriend, it will probably be you."

And that was the moment. She turned to face him—she was about six inches taller than he was then—and said, "I'm glad we're finally on the same page." And then she kissed him on the nose.

He had no idea if nine-year-olds could actually fall in love, and certainly none of his feelings for her shifted into a recognizable higher gear until a few years later, but still. If he had to look back and pinpoint a precise moment when Addie Atwater became the great love of his life, that was it.

"A Whole New World" from *Aladdin* had been playing. He wasn't sure why he remembered that all of a sudden, but despite the fact that the *Aladdin* soundtrack had *always* been playing around that time, the irony was no longer lost on him.

"I don't think Jo locks the doors to the rooms when there aren't guests staying in them. I'm sure you could go look in the clubhouse if you wanted."

When they got older—when all those gears had been shifted as high as they could go—he'd rarely, if ever, missed an opportunity to pull her into every empty room of this house or any other as they passed by unlocked doors. Just to steal a kiss without their friends teasing them about their PDA or to tell her he loved her. Sometimes just to spend thirty seconds looking at her without distraction.

Wes swallowed down the lump in his throat and smiled as he looked up at her. "Nah, that's okay. It just would have been sort of cool if both times you kissed my nose, thirtysomething years apart . . ."

"Yeah."

He tilted his head and studied her. "Now that we both fully understand that I am not to pry or show any interest whatsoever in your life, mind if I ask if you and Joel had kids?"

The smile on her face got a little more subdued, but it didn't go away. He took that as an encouraging sign. "Nah. We tried for a while, early on, but didn't have any luck. And then at some point, I think we realized we were okay without them. Like, it would have been nice, but there wasn't anything missing between us. You know what I mean?"

Somehow, though his marriage had to be examined through a very different lens, he felt as if he did. "Yeah, I think so."

She returned his gaze, and he couldn't help but marvel at the easiness between them. "I think it's okay for you not to hate me," he offered. "Now, I mean. I feel like . . ."

*What are you doing here, Wes? What are you hoping to achieve with this one?* If he'd been sitting beside someone who was cracking up watching a movie, would he lean over and tell them it was okay to think the movie was funny? If he did, nothing was going to get the other person to stop laughing faster. "Never mind. I don't know where I was going with that."

"Yeah, you do." She crossed her arms and jutted her chin toward him. "Say it."

"It's just . . ." *Okay, she said to say it. So say it.* "We're obviously two very different people than we were growing up. Whether that's a good thing or a bad thing, I won't pretend to know. And I know there are a million things we aren't saying to each other that we probably should. But as stupid as I'm sure it sounds, separate from—or I guess on top of—all the feelings from the past . . . I like you. Now. I'm enjoying talking with you, despite the fact that I enjoy very little of what we've talked about. It's just . . . it's nice to talk to someone I know I can trust. And yes, I know that's super weird, because in some ways it *is* like we just met, and in other ways—"

"I know."

"I'm not trying to minimize or dismiss anything. I'm not suggesting we just pretend it didn't happen or that we move past it." He had lost the thread of whatever he had wanted to say, not that he had really known what that was. "Just . . . I guess if nothing else, I hope you know that today . . . all the talking . . . it feels like a gift. For me, I mean. That's all I'm trying to say."

Addie pulled her eyes away from his when they had lingered just a little too long. "We're still on for dinner?"

"Absolutely. Yes. I'd love it. Besides, Jo has banned me from the UTV, so I don't have anywhere else to be."

Her eyes met his again as the trace of a smile crossed her lips. "Okay," she whispered and scooted the chair back under the desk. "See you then."

She walked to the door and had her hand on the knob as she turned back to face him and shook her head. "I don't hate you. I could never hate you. Trust me, I spent a long time trying. And I'll admit it: I haven't completely hated spending time with you today. But I also have to admit . . ." Her nose scrunched up. "I hate that I haven't hated it. I don't know how to make sense of that. So sure, let's have dinner. But anything beyond that . . ."

"I'm not asking for anything beyond that."

She nodded and looked down at her feet briefly and then faced the door again. "See you tonight."

"Add?"

She froze in place but didn't face him. "Hmm?"

Wes cleared his throat and bit down on the inside of his cheek in an attempt to distract from the burning in his eyes and the throbbing in his temples. "I just . . . I really just want to know if you're okay. Am I allowed to ask if you're okay?"

He watched her shoulders rise swiftly to her ears and then fall slowly as she released a heavy breath. "Come now. We don't want to use up all our conversation starters before dinner." Then she stepped through the door and closed it behind her.

## CHAPTER 13

# WES

### 269 Months Since He Last Tied a Windsor

"Where in the world have you been?" Phil asked him in greeting as he answered the phone. "Do you have any idea how close I was to notifying the sergeant at arms that you went missing?"

Wes put his phone on speaker, turned up the volume, and set it on the desk beside him. "Oh no. Please don't. I'd hate to involve the lady responsible for protecting the Senate gavel."

"Don't get cheeky, Senator. You know as well as I do that the sergeant at arms oversees Senate protocol—"

"In *addition* to babysitting the gavel? I stand corrected."

"—and as soon as she was made aware, she'd have to notify the vice president. And then the vice president—"

"Would do nothing. You know he hates me."

"That may be, but that doesn't change the fact that this stuff matters. I believe we've all been more than understanding—"

"Who's *we*?"

"*I've* been more than understanding. There. Is that better? First your wife and then the governor . . . I know it has been a difficult time for you. But fair or not, your life is not just your own. You know that.

It belongs to the people of the fourth district of Connecticut, and you don't just get to wander off and not answer your phone—"

"I checked my messages, Phil." Wes stood in front of the mirror and held a silver necktie up to his collar with his left hand, then lowered it and held the black one up with his right hand. "I didn't miss a single call from the people of the fourth district of Connecticut. If *they* had called, I definitely would have called them back."

"Fine. Joke all you want. But we've now gone an entire news cycle without anything new from you, and your opponents are beginning to circle like there's blood in the water. There's no guarantee that your victories in Iowa and New Hampshire will carry you through South Carolina—"

"I know. It's crazy. Almost like South Carolina is an entirely separate state with different voters and everything." He threw the silver tie over the back of the chair and looped the black one around his neck.

Phil sighed on the other end of the line, and Wes pictured his red, exasperated face as if it were right there in front of him. He'd certainly seen it enough—not just over the course of the past couple of years, as he dealt with the declines and deaths of Wray and his father, but really since the day they met.

"Sorry, Phil. You're right. I've been a bad little senator, and I promise to behave much better—" Wes caught the lie as it came out of his mouth and quickly attempted to rephrase it into truth. *Tricky.* "I know I'm not always easy to put up with. I appreciate you, Phil. I really do." He'd almost uttered some true but cryptic statement like, "You won't have to put up with me for much longer," but he knew Phil would have taken that as, *When I'm elected, I'm not bringing you on as White House chief of staff after all,* and he would have considered that a fate worse than death, most likely.

When he first met Philip Brewster, Wes had been eighteen, regretting his decision to go to Connecticut with his newly discovered father and nearly convinced he needed to go to trade school and learn to be a welder or something. He had absolutely no ambitions for his life, and truthfully, he was fairly confident a career as a welder was out of reach for him. Welders had skills and worked hard, while Wes believed the only thing he'd been born knowing how to do was love Addie Atwater, and the only skills he'd picked up in his eighteen years of life since were making out with her and abandoning her.

It may have been his father, already in his second term as governor of Connecticut (one of thirteen states without gubernatorial term limits), who plotted the course for Wes's life and opened the doors, but Phil had been the one to do the heavy lifting. As the governor's deputy chief of staff, he couldn't have been pleased with his new assignment—playing Henry Higgins to a small-town, homesick, and brokenhearted Eliza Doolittle with a C-minus average—but Wes had sensed a shift in his allegiance around the time he was elected to his second House term. That was when Phil asked him, for the first and only time, if he wanted to be president.

Wes had come to understand pretty early on that that was his father's desire for him. When he threw himself into his schoolwork to keep his mind off Addie and began to make decent grades for the first time—and, more important to him, actually began to learn some things—the desire began shifting into cautious optimism. The addition of Wray into the mix helped convert the cautious optimism into a full-fledged plan. From that point on, he wasn't still or quiet long enough to truly think about anything. Until the day Phil cleared Wes's schedule, drove him the hour to Mystic Seaport under the guise of a photo op at a War of 1812 exhibit at the museum, and then asked him if we wanted to be president while they sat on a dock and ate lobster rolls.

Wes had begun to answer without thinking. When was the last time he'd been asked to *think* about any of it, after all? Of course he wanted to be president. He believed he could make a real difference. It would be an honor to serve his nation in that way when the time came. If he was one of Pavlov's dogs, questions about his future in politics were the bell, and his stump speech was the saliva.

But Phil stopped him and stood up, telling him he didn't want an answer until they got back to Hartford. Then he went to the museum, leaving Wes to eat alone by the water and walk through the village and *think*.

On the way back to the city, Phil had talked to him about anything—*everything*—apart from the question he had asked. When they parked at the Capitol building, the only thing Wes knew to say was, "I want to be president. When did that happen?"

Phil nodded and said, "Though I've seen no data to support my hypothesis, I'm convinced that Washington, DC, corners the market on daddy issues per capita. But you're one of the few I believe can work his daddy issues to his own advantage." Then he'd stuck out his hand, and they'd shook on the pursuit of a shared dream.

From that moment on, Phil Brewster was *his* man. Not his father's.

"Water under the bridge," Phil said now on the other end of the call. "How goes it in Sacramento? Maybe we're not quite to the point of filing a sergeant at arms missing-persons report just yet, but there really have been rumblings. I need your face on television."

Yeah, television wasn't going to work. Not when his backdrop would have to be either snowy mountains that clearly couldn't trick anyone into believing they were the 831-foot Carpenter Hill, which had the distinction of being the highest point in Sacramento, or one of any number of stuffed and mounted dead animals, which had the distinction of being Jo Stoddard's design element of choice.

"With those new ads the PAC seems to be running every two minutes, I think my face is on television plenty."

"Then do *Press the Nation*."

Wes groaned. "I hate doing *Press the Nation*. Herbie Eccleston is a ratings-chasing kiss-up who doesn't even understand the electoral college but tries to pass himself off as a pundit."

"Oh, come on. Herbie's not so bad. Besides, most of the electors in the electoral college don't understand the electoral college."

"Still. Herbie Eccleston, Phil? Really?"

"Herbie Eccleston has eight million daily listeners, Wes. He's got the number one current-affairs podcast."

He didn't. He was number two, after Sebastian Sudworth. But Wes couldn't focus on that right then. He had finished tying the tie and slipped the knot up against his neck, and he was currently trying to make sense of what he was looking at in the mirror. "I just tied a Windsor knot."

"I'm sorry?"

He tilted his head and ran his thumb and forefinger along the bulkier triangular shape as he studied it. "My tie. I tied a Windsor."

"Good to know. Is that what you want me to take to Reuters? 'Senator Wesley Hobbes of Connecticut gained another four points in his bid for the presidency this week. Pundits credit his Windsor knot'?"

He had probably tied at least ten ties a week for the last fifteen years, and every last one of them had been tied with a Kelvin knot. (Wasn't sure when he'd decided he wanted to be president. Also wasn't sure when he'd turned into a guy who knew the names of tie knots.) Wray had called it his signature knot. It was just an inside joke between them, because she had said she drew the line at being like those politicians' wives on TV who straightened their husbands' ties in a contrived show of intimacy. *"If your people ever want me to do that, just tell them I've never been able to master your signature knot."* It was a joke. It was funny. It made him miss her deeply when he thought of it. But it didn't change the fact that the Kelvin knot sort of *was* his signature knot.

And he'd just tied a Windsor.

He pulled at the tail, and it released and unfurled in one smooth motion. He'd forgotten how much he enjoyed that sensation.

*Doc.*

Doc Atwater had been the first man to help him tie a tie. That first time, Wes's mom had dropped him off at the Atwaters' house for the middle school dance, which Doc was driving all five of them to. Cole was wearing a bolo tie he'd borrowed from his grandfather, but Wes hadn't thought about the necessity of a tie at all. Addie, Laila, and

Brynn were all in Addie's room finishing getting ready, and Doc had pulled Wes aside and handed him one of his own ties. Wes had stared at him blankly—embarrassed, he supposed, by the expectation that he should know what to do with it.

Doc, of course, had defused the situation before Wes could even figure out why he was ashamed of himself (because he didn't know he should wear a tie? because he didn't have money for one? because he didn't have a dad to teach him these things?) and walked him over to the mirror on the wall between the living room and the kitchen. Cole had watched and learned, too, as Doc did it for him twice and then guided him as he attempted it on his own. That attempt was a mess, but the girls were heading toward them, so Doc tied it quickly and perfectly, and only he and Cole were any the wiser that Wes had committed the faux pas.

By the time he took Addie to senior prom, he had spent hours practicing the reliable Windsor knot, and he felt so cool when, at the end of the night, when things got a little less formal, he was able to release that baby with one simple tug. And he felt even cooler when he was able to hastily tie it again before dropping Addie off, so that Doc didn't suspect his tie was undone for more salacious reasons.

And then, on his last evening in Adelaide Springs, just before their wedding rehearsal, he'd had the closest thing he'd ever had to a panic attack as he tried on his rented suit one more time. He'd been in the back of his mom's restaurant. The Bean Franklin it was called now, Jo had told him. Then it had been Marietta's, but really, it had been nothing. His mom was gone, after all.

His hands had been trembling so much that the tie would slip through his fingers every time he tried to get a hold on it. Exhaustion was piling on top of jitters and missing his mom and fears about the future and the anxiety he was feeling trying to get to know the father he had searched for his entire life and who had finally shown up in a moment when he just couldn't handle one more thing.

"Doing okay, kid?" Doc had asked him, and Wes had jumped at the sound of someone else's presence in his bubble of anxiety.

"Um . . . yeah. Sure. Thanks." But his voice had been trembling even more than his hands, and Doc knew better.

"Big day tomorrow." He'd stepped in front of him and slipped the tie from around Wes's neck. He'd carefully straightened it before reaching over and lifting the collar of Wes's shirt and perfectly aligning the tie beneath it. "Big few days for you, actually. You sure you're alright? No one would blame you if you weren't."

How could he tell Doc the thoughts that were going through his head? He didn't even want to acknowledge them to himself. "I'm a little nervous, I guess."

Doc nodded and brought the wider end of the tie through the loop. "That's to be expected. I remember the night before I married Addie's mom, I threw up in a shrub in front of the church." He chuckled and carried on tying. "I'd been so sure about everything, and then, all of a sudden, I wasn't sure about anything. Are you feeling some of that?" Wes nodded. "Yeah. Well, you can't always have it all figured out. That's just the way it is."

"What if . . . ?" Wes cleared his throat and tried again. "What if you were right? What if everyone was right?"

"About you two being too young?" Doc pulled the end through the loop a final time and kept adjusting until it was perfect. Although Wes had been pretty sure, even then, that it was perfect from the start. "Parents . . . older people . . . we always have to state our thoughts. Especially when our kids are your age. We know that our time to help guide you is almost up, and we want to teach you every single thing we can while we still have the chance. At the end of the day, do I wish you'd decided to wait a little longer? Sure. Part of me wishes she'd never get married and she'd just stay home with me forever. I can't deny that. But you listen to me, kid." He moved his hands to Wes's shoulders and met him eye to eye. "My hesitation . . . my worry . . . it's never once been about you or about the two of you together. Knowing it's going to be the two of you together might actually be the only reason I'll be able to sleep at night when she heads out into the world. I couldn't be more proud to have you as my son."

"I think that's my line now," Governor McNeese had chortled as he came around the corner. And then Doc had stepped away to check on Addie, and the governor had untied Wes's tie with a derisive, "A Windsor knot? Oh no, son. Let me show you the proper way to tie a tie."

In twenty-two years away, he hadn't once tied a Windsor knot. In twenty-four hours back, his fingers had forgotten they'd ever known anything different.

"Hey, Phil, I need to run."

"So can I tell Herbie to expect your call? And it wouldn't completely break my heart if I woke up to a front page featuring a picture of you shaking hands with Richardson, you know."

"Who?" Why had he undone the perfect Windsor he had subconsciously tied? He once again couldn't get his hands to stop shaking long enough to grab the material, much less tie it into an intricate knot.

"I'm sorry, did you just say *who*?"

Wes yanked the tie from around his neck, crumpled it into a ball, and threw it onto the bed. "Um, sorry. Yeah, just distracted. Governor Richardson. Obviously. I'll see what I can do." Governor Richardson. Of California. Who worked in Sacramento. Where Wes was supposed to be. *Right.*

He looked at his watch—six fifty-eight—and hurried over to the window. The sky was perfectly clear after the day's blizzard, which Wes knew meant the temperature would have dropped thirty or forty degrees since the sun went down. Addie sat in the truck waiting for him, motor running.

"I'll call you tonight, Phil."

"I'm holding you to that."

"Absolutely. If I don't call, feel free to sic Senate gavel lady on me."

## CHAPTER 14

# ADDIE

### 334 Days Since She Boxed Up Her Dresses

"Oh, good grief. What are you wearing?" I muttered as I watched him wave to me from the porch of the Inn Between, button up his coat, and begin carefully making his way down the steps, keeping an eye out for icy patches.

"Hey." He smiled and climbed up into the truck beside me.

"You look nice."

"Oh, thanks." He buckled his seat belt, faced me, and did a quick survey from head to toe and back again. There he was looking like he'd just come from *Forbes* magazine's "Most Eligible Senators" photo shoot while I was trying to recall if I had remembered to put on deodorant. Heat rose in my cheeks, and I involuntarily held in my stomach—not that he would be able to detect my actual body hidden beneath my oldest pair of jeans, my favorite baggy sweater of Joel's, and my parka built for function, not form—as he replied, "You too."

I didn't recognize my body in the mirror lately. That'd been something I was coming to terms with even before having to face the perceived image of myself through the eyes of someone who had last seen me when my metabolism burned off food faster than I could eat it and my lungs had only ever known how to function with reduced oxygen at high elevation. Years spent at sea level had combined with grief and depression and poor choices to turn me into a woman who couldn't drop the extra fifteen pounds no matter what she tried, and who honestly hadn't tried very hard at all. Adelaide Springs didn't have a gym, and I just couldn't get myself excited about running down the street, on display for all to see, while I dripped sweat and gasped for air like my tank supply had reached critical levels in a space movie.

"I'm overdressed, aren't I?" Wes asked, chuckling softly.

I laughed and shifted the '76 Chevy into gear after stealing one more glance at his blushing face. "But you really do look nice. You know, if we're heading to dinner at Pineapple and Pearls."

He stopped laughing, and his eyes snapped in my direction. "You know Pineapple and Pearls? I *love* Pineapple and Pearls."

I hadn't really intended to hint at any details about my life, but then again, I also hadn't intended to be hanging out with him like we were just normal, unscarred-by-past-trauma old friends either. What could it hurt to let him in on the secret that I was aware of—and extremely judgmental of—the upscale, pretentious Capitol Hill establishment that he apparently *loved*?

"Of course you do," I muttered and pulled out onto the county road.

"Have you been there?"

I guffawed at the thought. The thought of spending five hundred dollars for dinner, yes, but mostly the thought of the running commentary Joel Elwyn would have provided at a place where the dress code encourages emerald-green tuxedo dinner jackets and gold-sequin dresses.

"Um, no. Joel, my husband, um . . . He was more the twelve-dollar pizza at home, watching television, maybe drinking a beer type." That overly simplified description felt wrong. "He just . . . Well, we both had pretty stressful jobs. Him especially. Schedules were crazy, and if we actually got the chance to both be home in the evening, there was no chance we were going to waste it bottlenecked on the Beltway."

"Hang on. You lived in DC?"

"Bethesda, but yeah. I told you I was CIA."

"Well, yeah, but . . ." He scoffed and lifted his hands in front of him. "I don't know. I guess it just didn't click. I mean, *I* live in DC—part-time, anyway."

"Yes. I'm aware. Last I checked, that was sort of home-base operations for the United States Senate, right? I did sort of assume you spent some time there."

He chuckled and covered his face with a hand. "Sorry. I'm dumb."

"You're not dumb. I'm just giving you a hard time." I turned onto Main and slowed down to better maneuver the icy, narrower street. "My job was a little lower profile by design, so I know this is new information you're processing. I, on the other hand, couldn't have avoided news of you even if I wanted to."

"And?"

"And I really would have liked to, yes." I pulled into a diagonal parking space in front of the Bean Franklin and shifted the truck into Park. "So look, before we head over to the restaurant—"

"Oh, is this not where we're eating . . . ?" His voice trailed off as he pulled his vision away from me and looked out the front window instead. "Wow. Okay. That's . . . Huh. That's weird."

I glanced from him to the storefront to see what he was looking at, and by the time my eyes made it back to him, his eyes were shimmering under the bright moon and the streetlights. In an instant I realized what I had carelessly and flippantly subjected him to.

"Oh, Wes, I'm sorry. I just wanted to park and talk for a second. I didn't even think—"

His hand landed on mine, and our eyes locked as I prepared to shift into Reverse. "No, it's fine. It's good. It's . . ." He released my hand, but my eyes were still held captive. "I miss her."

"Me too."

Once upon a time, I'd thought that taking over Marietta's would maybe be our life. As Wes's mom got sicker and I spent more and more time there helping her out, and as she shared with me the intricacies of running the local dining institution—who was allergic to what and how each person in town liked their eggs and their coffee—I'd thought maybe Wes and I would carry on her legacy.

He wouldn't hear of it, of course.

There were three types of people in Adelaide Springs: those who had never known anything else and had no desire to leave, those who were desperate to get out, and those seeking a fresh start or a second chance. Marietta Hobbes fell firmly into the third category, while her son was the textbook example of the second. I, meanwhile, had my own exclusive fourth category: I would go anywhere or do anything if it meant I got to spend my life with Wes Hobbes.

"I can't believe your dad still has this truck."

I blinked in confusion at the startling non sequitur. "What?"

"What did he used to call it? Bertha? Gertrude?"

"Beulah! And that's not what he 'used' to call 'it.' That is her name!"

"Of course. Forgive me."

"I'm just saying, you need to watch yourself, Hobbes. Beulah is sacred. I learned to drive in Beulah—"

"*I* learned to drive in Beulah," he countered, throwing his head back and laughing.

"Did you?"

"Yes. Your dad would take me out driving while Mom was at chemotherapy."

And just like that, the laughter was gone. He leaned forward and looked up at the awning. "I forced myself not to think too much about her for a long time. It was easy enough, honestly, because I was busy thinking about you, and then I was always focused on . . . well, on *me*. But I've been thinking about her a whole lot more lately. Since Wray got sick, really."

I cleared my throat softly. "I'm sorry you had to go through that again. Losing someone to cancer, I mean."

"I was determined to do it better with her."

"Better? Better how?"

The breath I hadn't realized was being held captive in my chest finally released as he pulled his eyes from mine and looked back toward the Bean Franklin with a sigh.

"I don't know. I just wasn't very *present* with Mom, I don't think."

"You were a kid. How many of us are ever actually present as kids? I think you did the best you could."

He was still staring through the front windows and probably seeing straight into the past. Marietta sending the five of us outside when our laughter got so loud she couldn't hear customers' breakfast orders. Marietta twirling from table to table, kissing the tops of our heads or squeezing our cheeks as she passed. Marietta snapping her fingers at us when we got a little too touchy-feely, practically sitting on top of each other in the corner booth. I'd worked so hard for so long to eliminate my special goggles to the past—the ones that filtered out the present and could see only memories of Wes when they surveyed the corners of this town—but now they were covering my eyes and seemingly taunting me with a refrain of "*As if you could ever really forget.*"

"Mostly I just think of how disappointed she'd be in me."

Marietta Hobbes had been one of the quirkiest people I'd ever met in my life. The quirkiest and the kindest, and certainly the funniest. It was Marietta who had loved puns and gone absolutely berserk with them in her naming of daily specials. It was Marietta who helped me deal with my first period, when it was just a little too much for my normally unflappable but recently widowed doctor dad. And it was Marietta who kept selling Mary Kay long after it had stopped being profitable for her to do so, simply because Laila's mom was distracted by a terrible marriage, Brynn's mom was *awful*, and my mom was dead. Someone needed to teach us how to take care of our skin and apply makeup tastefully, so she gave us lessons and all her product samples.

"'There's great allure in styles demure. But if you're brazen, you'll be a raisin.'"

Wes faced me with narrowed eyes. "I'm sorry?"

I laughed. "Something your mom taught us about applying makeup. She also said, and I quote, 'In eras recent, we keep it decent. In days of yore, they played the whore.'"

Laughter burst from him, and he swiped at his eyes, destroying a tear I'd been keeping my eye on. "Yep. That sounds about right."

"She also taught me this acronym to use as a checklist to help determine if I was ready to have sex—"

"ABSTINENCE VERSUS RESPONSIBILITY?"

I slapped his arm in a fit of hysterics as he said the words.

"Yeah, I got that one too. I always figured she thought by the time I got through all the letters, I'd lose interest."

We sat there laughing together and reminiscing about Marietta until Owen, the owner of Cassidy's Bar & Grill, walked by on the sidewalk in front of us. So much was suddenly happening in my brain. I was waving to Owen, and I was watching Wes to see if he'd meant what he'd said about not hiding. He hadn't so much as flinched at the possibility of being spotted. But mostly, seeing Owen reminded me of why I'd pulled into that parking spot in the first place.

"We're having dinner with Cole and Laila. Are you okay with that?"

He did a double take and shifted in his seat toward me. "Seriously?"

"Yeah. And just to be fair, I don't know exactly why they want to see you. I mean, I think they're hopeful that things with you are, you know . . ."

"On the up-and-up?"

"Yeah. But I don't think they're really convinced. I'm guessing they want to see for themselves."

"I'd love to see them." He swiped at his eyes one more time and smiled.

And I couldn't stop looking at him as he faced forward again, once again staring out the window, looking at the Bean Franklin but no doubt seeing Marietta's.

He was *so* overdressed in his undoubtedly custom-tailored, slim-fitting gray suit and starched white dress shirt. Sans tie and open at the collar, it was actually dressier somehow. Like he was a modern Hollywood icon casually formal on a red carpet. His Italian (just a guess) loafers would have been much more at home on a red carpet than on the poorly shoveled sidewalks of Adelaide Springs, that's for sure.

"You really do look nice," I said softly and then snapped my head back to the front, horrified, and gave the rearview mirror all of my focus.

"Thank you. I don't have real clothes, I'm realizing."

It wasn't surprising that I found him attractive, I assured myself as I backed out onto Main Street. Not surprising or weird or even unexpected.

I mean, it *was* unexpected. There is no adequate way to convey just how unexpected it was. To me. But it really shouldn't have been. For one thing, he was attractive. With certain guys, it just wasn't subjective. He was one of those guys. Trust me. I'd seen him with braces and going through puberty and during the unfortunate mullet stage. I'd also seen him the day his braces came off and he smiled more than he ever had before.

And now he had the same slightly lopsided lips and piercing blue eyes that had made me weak in the knees as a teenager, but he was also stylish and confident and rocked the six-pack abs of which dreams are made. (And no, for the record, I hadn't seen adult Wes without his shirt on, but sometimes you just know these things.) On top of all of that, he smelled like he was sitting in a leather armchair next to a fireplace at a manly Buddhist temple designed by Tom Ford, smack dab in the middle of the redwood forest. (Not that I hadn't been into him during his Drakkar Noir days, mind you. I very much had.)

*What are you doing?*

*Nothing. I'm doing nothing. So quit asking yourself stupid introspective questions, Adelaide.*

I squirmed uncomfortably in my seat and attempted to swallow down the lump that had formed in my throat without also accidentally swallowing my tongue, which, for whatever reason, suddenly felt like it was blocking my airway.

"I could run home and change real quick. A dress or something. So we match, I mean. Well, not *match*. I'm not suggesting your cummerbund should complement my dress or anything."

He laughed. "Seafoam. Those were my marching orders. I had to go all the way to Grand Junction to find a place with a seafoam cummerbund and tie."

"And all for a dress I hated."

I'm pretty sure I heard him gasp. "Why did you hate it?"

"It was way too short—"

"Beg to differ."

"—and way too tight—"

"Beg to differ."

"—and *definitely* far too low-cut."

"Um, do I even have to say it?" Our gaze met for a moment, and I caught his mischievous smirk and rolled my eyes at him, which caused him to laugh softly. "But seriously, all teenage lechery aside, you completely took my breath away. Not just in that dress, to be fair, but the dress . . ." He whistled softly through his teeth.

*Seriously, Addie, what are you doing?*

The introspective question didn't seem quite so stupid the second time around.

"Yeah, I'll just wear this." Heat flooded my cheeks as disappointment in myself washed over me. Had I really been considering rushing home and trying to make myself pretty for Wes Hobbes? And why did the memories of when looking pretty for him mattered to me create a different sensation of warmth?

*Doesn't matter. Moving on.*

Did I even own a dress? Well, yeah. Sure I did. But they were all stashed away in a storage unit in Bethesda, Maryland, where I continued to waste far too much money each month rather than face whatever painful memories of Joel awaited me inside the ten-by-fifteen space. An entire life together reduced to nothing more than hastily packed boxes and inadequately protected furniture.

And that was all that was going on here, of course. I released a deep breath, slowly and quietly so Wes wouldn't take note of it. I willed the conflicting heats of disappointment and desire to dissipate back into the cold that was so much more befitting the company and the clear, icy night.

I hadn't been with a man since Joel. And I don't just mean I hadn't *been* with a man, though *that* probably goes without saying. I hadn't even spent time in the presence of any men. Not men who counted as men, anyway. I'd hung around the extremely happily marrieds (Cole and Sebastian) a little bit. The extremely olds (Fenton) a little bit. And the extremely you're-such-a-little-boy-I-just-want-to-bake-you-cookies-and-ask-you-about-your-day-at-schools (Neil) a little bit. But Wes didn't fit into any of those categories. I certainly hadn't spent time with any others whom I would have to describe as the please-just-let-me-watch-you-do-pushups kind.

And in not *being* around any men, I'd naturally felt as if I'd lost all *interest* in men. So this was good, really. I was still alive. I was still breathing. I could still appreciate a chiseled jawline and broad shoulders. Bully for me. But I couldn't allow myself to forget that this particular chiseled jawline and set of broad shoulders and lean, strong hands and fingers that seemed to be continually itching for action—even when they were mindlessly tapping away on his knee, as they were now—belonged to the man who didn't so much as leave me a note or a message on my answering machine. So . . . fine. I could begrudgingly admit to myself that I'd felt more alive in the past twenty-four hours than I had in all the twenty-four hours of the last two years combined. And yes, like Wes had said, it was maybe even okay not to hate him. We were no longer two small-town Colorado kids brought together by having an entire life in common, but it did feel good, after nearly a year back with old friends I no longer knew, to be able to make a Pineapple and Pearls joke. But that was as far as it could go.

Which was probably why it was a really good thing that we were having dinner at one of the very few locations in town where Wes Hobbes and I had never made out.

## CHAPTER 15

# WES

### A Really Long Time Since He'd Felt Warm

"Have you brought me here to kill me and dispose of the body?" Wes asked Addie as they pulled up to an old stone building that looked like something out of *Butch Cassidy and the Sundance Kid*. The metal bars across the windows and the one small bulb lighting the door added to the movie-set feel—which, of course, in this area of Colorado, worked. It was also entirely possible that rather than just being designed to replicate a movie set, it was an actual historical location where Butch and Sundance had hidden.

"I wouldn't go so far as to say I have completely ruled it out, but no," Addie replied, "that's not the primary item on the agenda for the evening. As of now."

He used his arm to wipe away the fog on his window and studied the building in front of him for context clues. *Milo's* was written in a modern cursive font on a small shingle to the side of the door, but apart from that, there was nothing. Though the longer he stared at the building, and then as he finally began looking up and down the sidewalk and spotted the other storefronts, awareness took hold.

"Did this used to be the day care?"

"Good memory."

"So what is Milo's?" he asked.

"It's the best food within a hundred miles is what it is. Cole's restaurant."

"As in he owns it?"

Addie nodded. "Owns it, chefs it—is *chef* a verb?—remodeled it, turned it into a destination location . . . you name it. It's the first place in Adelaide Springs that's a little less 'the greatest generation' and a little more 'the greatest generation's deadbeat grandkids make good.' He's going to have a Michelin star or two before long. I just know it."

Funny. He'd never made any guesses in his mind about what Cole Kimball might have gone on to do with his life, but if he'd been forced to predict something back when they were still kids, he probably would have landed on police officer or park ranger, maybe. He had always been a protector. The de facto leader of them all who seemed to carry with him all the responsibility that the other four were more than happy to shirk.

The sound of Addie's door creaking open caused him to follow suit. As soon as he met her on the sidewalk, he threw his hand up and then quickly unbuttoned his coat, pulled it off, and reached it out to her. "Can you hold this a second?"

She chuckled as she took it and laid it over her arm. "What are you doing?"

Wes buttoned one more button toward his collar, so he was exposed only to his collarbone rather than the top of his chest, and freed the tail of the shirt from his slacks. He pulled the rest of the shirt from its neatly tucked-in confinement as he headed back to the truck, then slipped out of his suit jacket and opened the passenger-side door. As he carefully folded the jacket over the seat back—he may have been trying to be more casual, but the suit was Tom Ford, and he was no monster—he spotted Addie's scarf and gloves on the bench seat and grabbed them. And as the wind whipped up his shirttail and attacked his exposed skin, serving as a painful reminder of just how cold it was and that sometimes tucked-in shirts served a dual purpose, he slipped the gloves and scarf under his chin long enough to roll his shirtsleeves midway up his forearms and then shut the door and hurried back over to her.

"A little more 'man of the people'?" he asked, holding his arms out to fully reveal his new look. He smiled at her, but she just stared at him, and he tried to interpret her silence. The way her bottom lip was being bitten to within an inch of its life made him fairly certain she was holding back some snarky comment or other. Ah well. If that was it, he appreciated the effort she was putting into not making *too* much fun of him.

"Not very convincing, huh? I know." He found the two ends of her scarf and held one end in each hand, then took a couple of steps toward her and curved it gently around her neck, circling his hand around her head once to loop it. And then, in a move even more familiar than tying a Windsor knot and just as ancient, he brushed his fingers around the back of her neck and tenderly freed her chin-length strands from the confines of the scarf.

*Oh. Sorry. Old habits die hard, I guess.*

Those were the words in his brain, but he couldn't get his mouth to say them. Not when he still had a lock of her hair dancing in the wind between his fingers and he couldn't quite figure out how to pull away at an appropriate pace. And definitely not when he could feel the heat radiating from her cheeks without even touching her skin. Not when he was beginning to wonder if he'd grievously misinterpreted what it was that her teeth were attempting to hold her lips back from.

"Ahem."

Well, *that* sure helped him figure out some quicker pacing. He stepped away from her and turned to the door, where the sound had come from, and in an instant was assaulted by the comfort that accompanied the best, happiest, most worry-free moments of his life. Cole and Laila. Even as kids, they'd all so rarely said one of their names without the other, and there they were, standing together, looking so different than he remembered them in the ways that didn't matter, but exactly the same in all the ways that did.

Laila was staring straight at Wes, tears in her eyes, while Cole's gaze darted from Wes to Addie and back again. He was still the protector, Wes understood immediately. *They're* her *friends now. Not yours.* It was important that he remember that, he knew, rather than slipping into a false sense of comfort and nostalgia within himself. They were kind enough to want to have dinner with him . . . to see for themselves and make their own determinations as to who he had become. He was grateful for that. But he couldn't lose sight of the fact that he'd abandoned them too. And not only were they left with their own pain and anger and resentment and who knew what else, they'd also been the ones left behind to try to help Addie pick up the pieces of the world Wes had shattered.

"I, um . . ." Wes cleared his throat. How could he begin this conversation?

*Great place you've got here.*

*'Bout time you two got together.*

*Thanks for the gloves, Laila. They're really great.*

He might have gone with that one if not for the fact that he wasn't wearing the gloves. They were in the pocket of his coat, which Addie was still holding.

*Yep. That's right.* That's *why I've lost feeling in at least the top two layers of skin.*

And the gloves in his hands were Addie's lavender ones. He should really get those to her. She was probably freezing. Although her hands were tucked under his coat, so maybe she was okay.

*He* was freezing. Maybe that was why he couldn't think. Maybe that was why all he wanted to do was run away and find warmth and curl up in a ball and . . .

*Warmth.*

Nothing was more prevalent in Laila's eyes than warmth. Concern, yes, but coated in warmth. Uneasiness, sure, but bolstered by warmth. Pain and sadness and skepticism and nervousness, all engaged in battle with warmth. Warmth and, if he wasn't mistaken, *hope*. And whereas Addie's eyes (and words) had cautioned him, from his very first moments back in town, that she would not entertain his despair over what he had done to her, Laila's eyes seemed to be inviting him to join her at the corner of regret and reconciliation.

"I'm so sorry, you guys." Wes choked down a sob fighting its way out of his chest, or from so much deeper. "I'm so sorry for what I did. For how I did it. I'm so sorry for everything."

Laila was there before he could even register what was happening, and he had to pull his arms out from between them in order to return her embrace. Wes rested his head on the top of hers and held her and even found himself comforting her as she gave in to the emotion—rubbing her back, smoothing down her hair, being sure not to dribble snot onto her. And then, best of all, laughing with her when he voiced his concerns about dribbling snot on her.

He was pretty sure the smile plastered on his face would never leave, and by the time they pulled apart from each other and he looked up, he had actually been lulled into the comfort he'd warned himself against. He'd been so sure he was about to share the perfection of the moment with Addie and Cole, but they were gone.

"Where'd they go?" he asked.

"Hmm?" Laila looked behind her. "Oh. Well, you know." She began bouncing on the balls of her feet now that the two of them were no longer sharing body warmth. "It might take Cole a little longer."

"Oh." This was not a surprise, Wes reminded himself. There was nothing at all unexpected in what Laila said. "Of course. Sure."

More than anything right then, he wished he knew if Addie had gone in after Cole, to comfort him, or if it had been the other way around.

"Come on." Laila tucked herself under his shoulder and wrapped her arms around his waist. "Let's go inside where it's warm."

He really hoped that would be the case.

## CHAPTER 16

# ADDIE

**718 Days Since She Realized There's Never Enough to Do**

"You okay there, Kimball?" I asked Cole as I entered the kitchen. I'd been so caught up in watching—*processing*—Wes and Laila's reunion that I hadn't realized Cole had left until I heard the door shut behind him. By the time I got into the kitchen, after hanging up Wes's coat, he was beginning to plate our dinner.

"Sure," he replied without looking up. "Why wouldn't I be?"

I shook my head gently. "No reason." I joined him at the prep counter and picked up the tongs to begin mixing the salad he had prepared. "You're not buying it?"

"Buying what?"

"I don't know." I picked up a slice of cucumber and slipped it into my mouth. "The latest redemption and reunion tour from the Adelaide Springs class of 2003, I guess. Not buying it?"

He looked up at me for just a moment and then returned his eyes to the plates and grumbled under his breath. "I don't know."

I shrugged and started tossing again. "Laila seems happy to see him."

"Of course she is. Laila is good and trusting and loving and chooses to believe the best about everyone."

"And you not so much?"

He pulled the serving towel from his shoulder and wiped his hands with it. "Well, no offense, but up until a few minutes ago I would have thought *me and you* not so much."

"A few minutes ago?" I set the tongs down and crossed my arms as I faced him. "What changed a few minutes ago?"

We both tilted our heads toward the front as we heard the door open. "You two looked pretty cozy," he whispered. "What's that about?"

"Oh, that?" I waved my hand in front of me. "No. Don't read anything into that. He was helping me with my scarf." *Not that I needed a scarf, mind you, considering I was about to melt into a puddle of attraction, confusion, and questionable life choices.*

"Oh. Okay. Sure."

I lowered my voice an octave and impersonated him. "'Oh. Okay. Sure.' What's that supposed to mean?"

Cole's eyebrow rose as he considered my question. Or, I was guessing, considered *me*.

I was in a unique position among our class of five, I knew. Brynn and Wes had both left without saying goodbye. Cole and Laila stayed. But I left and still occasionally came home for Christmas. I had moved away and moved on and had a life they knew very little about, but we still had the bond of the first half of our lives. Having said all that, we certainly hadn't figured out what the new version of our friendship looked like.

And I knew that wasn't for lack of trying on Cole and Laila's part.

For the first couple of months, they had given me space. Hugs whenever they bumped into me on the street. Invitations to dinner. Kind, optimistic understanding when I turned down almost all said invitations to dinner. And then they'd begun doubling down on their efforts a bit more. Laila sent notes home to me via my dad, and Cole dropped off samples from new recipes he was trying on the porch.

Ultimately, my avoidance of the Kimballs (I hated calling it *avoidance*, though of course it totally was) had absolutely nothing to do with them. The Sudworths had made attempts to connect when they were in town, too, and I was equally good at avoiding them.

*Newlyweds.* They weren't all supposed to be newlyweds at our age any more than I was supposed to be a widow. Friendships outgrow their normal life cycles under the best of circumstances, even when everyone follows the same pattern. But when one friend's love story—one friend's life as she knew it—is ending while all the others' are beginning, what do you have to grab onto?

Cole sighed and shook his head. "Forget it."

"Forget what?"

"It's just . . . I don't know, Addie. I guess it's just that I had a lot of years of experience walking in on you and Wes in the middle of being you and Wes, so don't feed me this 'helping you with your scarf' nonsense. I really just don't understand how he can show up here out of the blue and just like that . . ." He snapped his fingers. "I mean, aren't you mad?"

"At Wes?"

"*Of course* at Wes!" He looked over my head toward the dining room door and then gently grabbed my elbow and pulled me farther back into the kitchen. "Maybe it's none of my business." He ran his hand through his dark waves and then crossed his arms. "No, you know what? I'm sorry, but I do think it's my business. Just a little bit. Because I was the one standing beside you, holding out hope that he'd come back when everyone else—even hopeful, bighearted, loving Laila—began trying to recover by acting like he'd never existed. And—"

"I don't need you to protect me, Cole. I'm a big girl."

"I know that."

"And the fact is, no, it isn't any of your business. And as for whether I'm mad at Wes?" I laughed bitterly. "There are so many other things to be mad about. Wes isn't even a blip on my anger radar anymore. Truly."

Cole took a deep breath. "Hmm. Okay."

"What? Go ahead. Say it."

His lips scrunched over to one side of his face as he once again gave thoughtful consideration to all I had said. "I missed Brynn when she left, and I missed you when you went off to the Air Force Academy and beyond. And yeah, if I'm being honest, I was mad at both of you. Brynn for just taking off and you for cutting us off. Not staying in touch."

"Cole—"

"But it was okay, you know? It was awful, and it was especially awful because I had to watch Laila suffer through losing you both, but it was okay. I understood. Or I thought I did, at least. Brynn's life—her mom—was horrible. We all knew that. So no matter how upset I was that she left the way she did, there was always a part of me that was glad she got away. And I told myself there were too many memories for you here. I told myself that no matter how much we loved you and wanted to be there for you, you just couldn't separate us from him." He shrugged. "I really don't know if that was it or if it was just a line I fed myself in order to feel better, but it was how I coped."

"I think you were probably onto something," I whispered.

"But *him*?" He motioned toward the dining room with his chin. "I had nothin'. I still have nothin'. And look, Addie, I want him to be back. I really do. I mean, I saw it with Brynn, so yeah, I believe it can happen. But I'm sorry; it's going to take a little more than an apology from a man I barely even recognize—a polished, practiced politician, mind you—for me to trust him again. And maybe you know something I don't. I know Laila said you've spent some time with him. Obviously, I haven't. All I know for sure right now is that whatever Laila and I walked in on a few minutes ago looked a whole lot more like the past than what I had imagined in the present. So . . . okay. It's none of my business. Fine. You can obviously handle this however you like. I, for one, don't know how I would handle losing him again. For right now, I think I'm better off letting him still be gone."

I nodded. "I get that."

"Everything okay back here?" Laila asked as she poked her head around the corner.

Cole looked up at her and his face lit up, as it still always managed to in her presence, even after all these years. "Yeah. We'll be right out."

She bounced away, back to the dining room, and Cole and I sighed in weighty unison, then chuckled about it. We might not have spent nearly as much time together in the second half of our lives as we had the first, but we still understood each other enough to accurately interpret the moment. We worried about Laila's tender heart getting trampled on, but we would never want her to be anything other than who she was—open, vulnerable, genuine. And I knew Cole considered himself charged with guarding the perimeter of her heart. It was his job to fight off threats so that Laila could keep being Laila.

"Thank you for caring so much, Cole. Really. And for the record, I'm not putting any of my eggs in the basket of 'our Wes' being back, or anything like that. I just think I sort of like spending time with this new guy who came to town. If I'm being honest, it's been a while since I've enjoyed"—*if I'm being honest*—"anything."

There it was. That look of pity that usually filled everyone's eyes when they talked to me. The one that said, *Bless her heart. Her husband died, you know.* To Cole's credit, he made it go away quickly. For most people it seemed like a prerequisite and a kindness they thought they were bestowing on me when, really, being caught in the sympathy tractor beam was agony for me and only made them feel better about their own lives. I knew that wasn't the case with Cole, but I was still relieved when he wiped away the sadness and sympathy and replaced it with the focused eyes and furrowed brow that I knew represented his concern. Concern that came from love.

"Just be careful." He reached out and squeezed my hand and then began issuing orders. "Grab that salad, and let's get out there. We have VIPs dining at table seven. And a United States senator, too, if the rumors are to be believed."

---

"Well, *some* things never change," I said to Wes once we had climbed back into Beulah.

"What do you mean?"

"You and Laila. Half the time Cole and I just sat there looking at each other, having no idea what the two of you were laughing about."

He chuckled and latched his seat belt. "I'd forgotten how much I love her. The big memories are you or Cole, or sometimes all five of us, of course. Daredevil stuff with Brynn. But I'd forgotten just how many of the best moments were spent laughing with Laila, the two of us in our own little world—usually making fun of how serious you and Cole were about everything."

I threw my arm over the back of the seat and looked behind me to begin backing out. "Yeah, that was always what we figured."

"Isn't it weird," he began, "seeing them together like that? Is it weird for you? I mean, on one hand, it's about time."

"Amen to that."

"But it's still weird, right?"

"Not as weird as you and me *not* being together."

I said it so casually, without even thinking. I said it with a continuation of the humor and camaraderie that had mostly ruled the evening. I said it. *I* said it.

I couldn't believe I had said it.

"I didn't mean that like it's weird that we're not together."

"No. Totally."

"I just meant—"

"I know what you meant, Addie. Really." I glanced at him, and his eyes were wide and vulnerable and, I'm pretty sure, imploring me not to retreat, because *of course* I wanted to retreat. "Just . . . with it being the four of us again, it was easy for it to almost feel like the old days. Right?"

"Right." I nodded. "That's all I meant."

"I know. I totally get it." He faced forward again and nodded slowly. "I was thinking that too. And I think that's a natural thing for us to have been feeling."

We sat in silence until I turned off Main Street onto the county road back to the inn. It was right about then that I started laughing, seemingly from nowhere.

"What?" he asked.

"That was a very nice politician's way of handling that situation. Are you sure you don't want to be president?"

Truth be told, his skills had been on display all evening long. It hadn't been difficult to decipher Cole's skepticism, but rather than pushing him toward reconciliation or trying to make things less awkward—which in nearly all circumstances made things more awkward regardless of who was making the attempts—Wes had been respectful of the skeptic. Not once had he attempted to pull Cole into a moment of nostalgia, but by the end of the evening, Cole was the one starting sentences with words like, "Do you guys remember when . . ."

"Honestly?" Wes asked after several seconds had passed. Several seconds in which I had been thinking about how, long before we'd gotten to dessert, the ticking time bomb threatening the evening had been defused by a combination of Wes's refined diplomacy, Laila's effusive joy, and Cole's ability to prepare a steak that would send even Eeyore to his happy place. (Although I don't think donkeys in the Hundred Acre Wood eat beef, now that I think of it. Or any donkeys, really. Please forgive the poorly executed idiom, PETA—and the estate of A. A. Milne.)

"Honestly what?"

"You asked if I was sure I don't want to be president."

"Oh." *Oh.* "Um, yeah, sure. Honestly."

"I mostly don't. I know I can't be. I won't be. And I'm fine with it. Mostly."

"But?"

"But I'm going to miss it. Politics, I mean." He sighed. "No. Not politics. Not the glad-handing. Not campaigning. *Definitely* not campaigning. But I like negotiating. I like sponsoring a bill I believe in and following it all the way until it becomes a law. An actual *law*, you know?"

"Like on *Schoolhouse Rock*."

He laughed. "Yes. Exactly. My life is very much like *Schoolhouse Rock*."

I pulled up in front of the inn and shifted into Park just as he asked, "Do you miss the CIA?"

I released air through my lips, creating a raspberry sound, and turned to face him. "My, my. What a complicated, existential question that is, wrapped up in a deceptively simple, ho-hum topic of conversation."

His eyes took on that *Please don't retreat!* quality again. "Sorry. I'm not trying to pry."

"No, I know. It's just . . . Well, it really is complicated. I loved my job. And then . . ."

The agency had offered to find me someone to talk to immediately after Joel died. I don't know. Maybe I should have taken them up on the offer. The problem, though, was that when the CIA offers to provide someone for you to talk to, it's not going to just be some in-network mental health professional they found in the Yellow Pages under "Therapists" or "Trauma Specialists" or even "Last-Ditch Efforts to Prevent the Complete Loss of Sanity." You couldn't talk to any of those sorts of people, or even the people who love you, because you'd only be able to pour out a heavily redacted version of your heart.

So they encourage you to talk to the one or two highly trained mental health professionals in the entire world who have high enough security clearance to hear the entire story, which is all fine and dandy and maybe would help. Except somewhere in the back of your mind you know that these people you're supposed to trust and be your truest self with so you can heal and move forward are on the payroll of the organization that (accidentally, indirectly, and so regrettably) got your husband killed.

But then again, so are you.

So you convince yourself you don't need to talk to anyone. You convince yourself all you need is a little time. A little time and to stay busy. That's the key, you know. And then all you have to do is find a way to dull the pain during the moments when there isn't enough to do. Easy. Until you realize there's never enough to do. There will *never* be enough to do. And pretty soon you have to acknowledge that whatever it is you're using to dull the pain . . . there's never enough of that either.

"Um . . . my husband was CIA too. A collection management officer."

"Were you at the DO too? Is that where you met?" My eyes popped open, and the words began flowing out of him more quickly. "Sorry. Not prying. If you don't want to tell me how you met—"

"No, it's not that." I shook my head. "I just . . . Sorry. It was just weird hearing someone mention the DO, I guess. It's been a while since I've talked with anyone who even knows what a collection management officer is, much less which department they work for."

The Directorate of Operations, sometimes referred to as the Clandestine Service, was, in fact, the arm of the CIA with all the spies. And while I had always been able to easily dismiss the idea that *I* was a spy (because no, I wasn't—I just computed and analyzed the information the spies gathered and figured out why it mattered and how we could use it), Joel had started out at the agency as a case officer. And when you used the official term of *case officer*, most people retired the John le Carré or Tom Clancy levels of excitement that had been building in their brains. They assumed a case officer was more like a social worker. A social worker for terrorists, maybe, but still, not all that exciting.

But make no mistake. Up until the year I met him, fumbling around in his new office at Langley, struggling to get the hang of his promoted position as a collection management officer and so distracted he'd put his tie on inside out, my husband had been a spy.

"Yeah. That's where I met him. He was the new CMO and I was a methodologist." I lifted my eyes to Wes's, prepared to explain the role of a methodologist, but he was nodding in understanding, so I continued. "It was just one target analysis report out of thousands of target analysis reports. I don't even remember which continent the target was on or if it involved national security or foreign policy, but I remember the look on his face as I handed him that manila folder.

I remember how he took the time to smile at me, and I remember thinking no CMO had ever even made eye contact with me before."

Wes smiled at me. "It was pretty instant, huh?"

I smiled back. "Yeah. It was pretty instant. So . . ." I cleared my throat and tried to refocus on what Wes had asked. He'd probably thought it was such a simple question. "Sometimes I miss the work. I miss taking all the available facts and figuring out what they mean as my *job* rather than just a hobby that makes me analyze and mistrust everyone and everything around me."

He sighed. "Some things just became very clear to me."

"What do you mean?"

"Well, I understand why you were always so good at board games, for one thing."

He wasn't wrong. "You were also just really bad at them."

"That may be, but seriously, I get it now. Years of Balderdash and Stratego and Battleship—"

"Guess Who?"

"Yes! Guess Who?" He started laughing, and I couldn't help but join in. "I don't think any of us ever even beat you at stupid freakin' Guess Who?"

As the laughter subsided, I shrugged and looked down at my hands in my lap. "I don't know. Maybe the CIA was what I was always supposed to do, but maybe I was just supposed to meet Joel Elwyn. And that's the real answer to the question, I guess. Whether or not I miss it, I mostly just miss who I was when I was there . . . with him."

I was suddenly afraid to look at him. I couldn't remember the last time I had talked that much about Joel. There was so much I wasn't allowed to say, so it was usually easier to say nothing at all. People had asked me questions, but after enough one-word answers and subject changes, I guess they got the hint.

But Wes hadn't asked me about him. I had been the one to bring up Joel's name, and I didn't understand why, but for the first time in a really long time, I wondered what it would be like to answer even more questions that no one was asking.

And that, I knew, was my cue to put an end to the conversation.

"Well, I should probably—"

Wes's hand grabbed mine just as I began moving it back to the steering wheel. I couldn't help but look at him then, though I immediately wished I hadn't.

There was no pity in his eyes. Only concern. Understanding, maybe? Not that he and Wray had had a normal sort of marriage, to put it mildly, but he'd loved her. Surely he came closer to understanding than any of the newlyweds, caring and compassionate though they tried to be.

"Addie . . ."

"I can't talk about it, Wes." I pulled my hand away from his. "I appreciate the . . ." What? What did I appreciate? "The, um . . ." The "My Spouse Died and All I Got Was This Lousy Secret That's Going to Tear My Heart Apart" T-shirt? *Well, huh. He did know something about* that, *didn't he?* "Just . . . I appreciate it. But I can't talk about it. I just can't."

"Addie . . ." He lowered his head slightly and forced my eyes to meet his. "I know."

I threw my arms around him, surprising myself even more than I surprised him, I'm pretty sure, and then pulled away before he could hug me back. "Go away now," I muttered with a self-conscious chuckle as I faced forward again.

The fact that he grabbed his blazer from the back of the seat, quietly told me good night, and got out of the truck without another word was almost enough to make me want to ask him to stay.

CHAPTER 17

# WES

**17 Years Since His Date with Mrs. Stanley Livengood**

Wes had his phone pulled out of his pocket before he'd shut the truck door behind him, and it took everything in him not to dial as he jumped over icy patches on the sidewalk. By the time he reached the porch, he was calling Phil's number, even as he turned back and waved goodbye to Addie with a smile on his face as if he had all the time in the world and nothing was more important in that moment than her.

Well, that much was true, at least.

He crossed the threshold into the inn and lifted his phone to his ear as the ringing began.

"How was homecoming?" It was Jo's voice that he heard first, causing him to end the call on his phone just as Phil said, "Hello." "Were you crowned king?"

Of course she knew the four of them had had dinner together. *He* hadn't known it was going to happen, but of course Jo knew.

"Nah. Cole got it again." He clicked the side of his phone to silence the buzz of Phil calling back. "Well, good night, Jo." He took three large, quick steps toward the staircase and couldn't help but roll his eyes when she stopped him.

"Hang on, now. Just a minute. What's your hurry? Aren't you going to tell me how it went?"

"It was good, I think. It was good to see them. Good night."

"Wesley Hobbes, you stop right there." It would have been funny if it hadn't been, at that particular moment, so frustrating that he wanted to scream.

"I'm sorry, Jo. I'm not trying to be rude, and I'm happy to tell you all about it, but I have a really important phone call to make. Can we talk in the morning?"

"Of course." She stood from the couch and looked up at him from the base of the stairs. "I just thought you might like to know that Fenton Norris spotted you and Addie outside of Cole's restaurant and mentioned it to Doc when he saw him at Cassidy's." She yawned then—the most forced yawn he'd ever seen in his life, and he'd sat through more than his fair share of State of the Union addresses. "Well, sleep tight." Then she headed toward the kitchen, no doubt expecting him to follow her.

That was definitely a situation that was going to need to be dealt with, but at the moment it was far from the most pressing.

"You, too, Jo. Good night!"

Then he took the steps two at a time, dialed Phil back, and hoped he could at least get through the call before Doc Atwater showed up at his door to finally chew him out for breaking his little girl's heart.

---

"Whose voice was that a minute ago? Was that Secretary Hubbard? You're not still at the State House, are you?"

"Phil, listen. I need you to do something for me." Wes stepped inside his room and shut the door behind him. "I need you to call Heather—"

"Heather?"

"Yeah. Heather McCord. Deputy staff director for Intelligence."

"As in the agency or—"

Wes groaned and kicked off his shoes. "No. Senate Intelligence Committee. I need her to send me the archives on Operation VE Ladder so I can check on something involving an old friend."

Phil was calm. Too calm for Wes's liking, considering he wanted results in his inbox immediately. "And what exactly is Operation VE Ladder?"

"It's classified is what it is. Just call Heather."

Wes knew how much Phil hated being kept out of the loop on anything. And since the general belief was that they were only one more election away from both having top-secret clearance, Phil's desire for insider knowledge continued to grow. As the chief of staff, Phil would never be told that anything was off-limits ever again. But they weren't there yet. They were *never* going to be there. And even if he could have talked with Phil about this one, he wouldn't have.

But he was hoping against hope that he was allowed to talk about Operation VE Ladder with Addie. She almost certainly hadn't had the security clearance necessary for him to unpack the operation dossier with her like they were both members of the Intelligence Community Book Club, but she'd been briefed. To some extent, as Joel Elwyn's widow, she must have been briefed. He needed to find out what she knew so that he knew what he could say.

*"Addie . . . I know."*

He'd been trying to figure out how he knew the name since she'd first corrected him that morning—"*It's Elwyn now, actually*"—when she rescued him from the ditch on Banyon.

*Was that only this morning?* Was it possible that the reintroduction of Addie Atwater into his life had actually slowed down the speed of Earth's daily rotation? He'd certainly always assumed that if he ever showed his face in Adelaide Springs again, it would result in a cataclysmic, apocalyptic event. So, maybe. Then again, no matter how long the day had seemed, the moments he'd spent in her presence had passed far too quickly, so he wasn't going to alert the authorities that the end of the world was in sight just yet.

By the time she'd revealed Joel's first name that afternoon, there in his room at the inn, it had been driving him nuts. The low-key sort of nuts where it doesn't completely consume you. There's just a slow and steady mental audit of every person you've ever met happening way off in the background of your mind. When she'd said they had lived in Bethesda, the mental Rolodex was put back in storage for the time being. For one thing, that satisfied his general knowledge, if not his specific knowledge. They were in DC. He could have stood behind him at the dry cleaner, or "Elwyn, party of two," might have been said just before "Hobbes" at a restaurant.

And that, of course, was where he got distracted and stopped caring so much about where he'd heard the name. She'd been right there, in the same metro area, and he'd never known it. Had he ever stood behind *her* at the dry cleaner?

Although, come to think of it, when was the last time he took his own clothes to the dry cleaner?

But it had all clicked into place so quickly right there at the end. Not when she told him Joel was CIA too—though he really should have known then—but in that last moment of beautiful vulnerability, when she'd said his entire name. A name he had heard countless times and seen in print even more throughout weeks of closed hearings of the Senate Intelligence Committee.

He took his responsibility seriously, and he'd mourned the loss of American life, of course. But the disaster that was Operation VE Ladder had added countless nonnegotiable appointments to his calendar at a time when he wanted to be devoting his time and attention to Wray's recovery. He'd resented the hearings at the time. There was no doubt about it.

But in the amount of time it took Addie to utter the three syllables of Joel Elwyn's name, he understood. Wes understood that while he was no doubt responsible for far too many of Addie's scars, he might actually be able to bring just a little bit of healing to the gaping wound he hadn't caused but that was on display right in front of him.

"It's twelve thirty in the morning on a Sunday. Obviously no one will be in the office until—"

"Call her at home, Phil."

"I don't have this woman's home number—"

"So find it." Wes was Phil's boss, of course, but their dynamic wasn't as simple as that either. How could it be, considering Phil had been a high-ranking member of the power-playing DC politico network while Wes's acne was still clearing up? He squeezed the bridge of his nose and sat on the edge of the bed with a soft sigh. "Find it, and I'll call in to *Press the Nation* in the morning."

"See? That's how this works. Something for you, something for me, everyone's happy. I'll make sure she has it to you within the hour."

Wes sighed and lay back on the bed. "I have to talk to Herbie Eccleston at 6:00 a.m., Phil. Not everyone is happy. But thanks."

"Five."

"Sorry?"

"*Press the Nation* is on at eight, so that will be five for you in California."

*You're getting sloppy, Wes. You have to do better than that.*

Wes felt as if he could audibly hear the angel on his shoulder whispering, "*Or you could stop lying about being in Pacific time instead of mountain time, confess what you're doing and why you're doing it, and let Phil and everyone else on your staff—not to mention 98 percent of the voters, or whatever ridiculous number the polls currently have you at—find another candidate to back before you wind up starting your inauguration speech with the words, 'My fellow Americans, I've been meaning to tell you . . .'*"

"Right. Five."

"You'll make old Herbie's week, that's for sure." Phil was quiet for a moment before asking, "An actual old friend or a political asset?"

"I wouldn't consider Herbie much of either."

"No, I mean whoever's mixed up in the operation."

"Oh. An actual old friend. An ex." He punched the mattress as soon as the words were out of his mouth. He'd given just a little too much there, and he knew it. "So anyway, have her send it as encrypted as it needs to be, of course. The sooner the better. Thanks, Phil. And send me the details for *Press the Nation*—"

"An ex? Since when do you have exes?"

*"You're such an idiot,"* the devil and angel on his shoulders seethed in unison.

"I have exes."

"You have an *ex*, I'm pretty sure. Singular."

"That's not true." It sort of was. "I mean, serious exes, sure, but I dated other women." Two first dates at Yale before Wray showed up, thank you very much. "Plenty of women." He was almost positive he'd gone to dinner with some third woman in grad school, though he couldn't remember her name. And there may have been a group of them at dinner, actually. "Anyway, enough. I'm done talking about this."

Oh yeah. It was a study group. And the third woman was a sixty-year-old doctoral candidate named Mrs. Stanley Livengood.

The truth was, he had "dated" more women during the early years of his marriage than he had in all the years prior. Wray always told him he had a free pass for life, as long as he never got caught, and he took advantage of that pass for the first few years, when he was still young and stupid enough to enjoy the danger that accompanied his end of that bargain. He never did get caught, but he tired of the risk.

He also, somewhere along the way, realized it just wasn't how he was wired. He knew there were probably a lot of people out there who enjoyed dating (or whatever the kids were calling it these days) for the sake of dating (or whatever the kids were calling it). But that wasn't him. What was the point if it could never lead anywhere? Worse, what if he did accidentally fall in love with some woman along the way? Someone who was never meant to do anything more than fill the void that existed between the love of his life and his wife. And then, at some point, he just completely lost interest. In all of it. He cared about Wray. He cared about the White House. He cared about making the governor proud of him.

Good enough.

"Let me ask you something." Phil adopted what Wes had long ago come to understand was his "fatherly" tone of voice. "You'd tell me if there was anything I needed to worry about, right?"

*Clearly not.*

"Of course. Thanks, Phil. We'll talk in the morning."

## CHAPTER 18

# ADDIE

**10,689 Days Since It Became Just the Two of Them**

I opened the door to the ornate log house I'd grown up in and silently peeked my nose in to make sure I was alone. My Prius was parked out front, so I knew Dad was home. He'd been insisting on driving my car and sending me with Beulah all winter long because he "valued the better gas mileage." (Yes, of course. That made total sense, considering the two miles he drove every day, and had nothing whatsoever to do with Beulah being a more reliable vehicle in winter driving conditions and his desire to keep me encased in Bubble Wrap straight on through my AARP years.) But if he was asleep, I was as good as alone.

I was greeted by the creaks and pops that accompanied the ticking of the clock in the kitchen and a fire burning in the woodstove, but otherwise . . . silence. I shut and locked the door behind me (Dad insisted the locking was unnecessary, and I knew he was probably right, but I'd seen too much of the world to ever return to those Adelaide Springs sensibilities) and hung my coat on the hook by the door. Then I tiptoed in, silently begging the old hickory beneath my feet to vocalize its age just a little bit less.

"I don't think I've caught you sneaking in after curfew since you were a teenager."

I gasped in response to my dad's greeting from the upstairs banister.

Well, so much for that.

"Could that be because I haven't *had* a curfew since I was a teenager?"

"Maybe that has something to do with it." He smiled at me. "How are the roads?"

"Awful, and it's not looking like we'll get above freezing tomorrow. And then did I hear another storm is blowing in?"

"That's what Fenton says, so I doubt it."

I laughed and blew a kiss up to him. "See you in the morning." I began walking down the hallway to my room, but I didn't get very far.

"Adelaide Pearl Atwater, you stop right there."

I stopped dead in my tracks, a shiver of ridiculous, unfounded good-girl angst running down my spine. My dad had always been soft-spoken. Gentle. But there was an unmistakable authority that shot through the center of his words like a steel rod whenever he meant business. Not to mention when he used my middle name, of course. I took a step backward, then another, and looked up at him again. "Yes, sir?"

"Sorry. Elwyn," he backpedaled with a smile, dissipating all the seriousness like a gust of wind across a field of dandelion puffs.

"That's more like it. Atwater-Elwyn is also acceptable."

He shook his head. "No, that won't work. That's your professional name, and on a professional level, you outrank me." He made his way down the stairs, the audible creaks of the wood coming across like a dubbed soundtrack of his joints until they warmed up and loosened about the time he got to the downstairs landing. "I can't lecture you if you outrank me."

"Oh, I'm about to get a lecture, am I?"

"I suppose that's up to you." He kissed the top of my head as I leaned on the railing and looked up at him. "Could just be a conversation if you weren't doing all you could to avoid me—"

"I'm not avoiding you!"

That might not have been entirely true. I thought back to this morning and how I'd been in such a hurry to get out of the house before my dad woke up that I'd forgotten my gloves. Then there were the new gloves I had purchased rather than swing back by the house in the light of day and risk seeing him. And even, I supposed, the fact that I had used a little bit of secret-agent voodoo to convince my friends to host Wes and me at their restaurant on what had been planned as a rare night off for them. (Secret-agent voodoo, if you're wondering, looked a lot like me saying, "I'm not sure where to take Wes for dinner tonight," and Laila saying, "You guys should come to Milo's! Cole will cook. It's settled.") However it ended up happening, let's just say I didn't *not* know that my dad would be eating at Cassidy's, the only other dinnertime restaurant in town.

Dad cocked one eyebrow as he passed by me and then spent a few seconds stoking the fire. When he was satisfied with his work, he sat down on the couch.

"Do you miss flying?" he asked, surprising me with the abrupt subject change. What was with people this evening asking me if I missed my past?

At least this answer was a lot simpler.

I sat on the other end of the couch, slipped my shoes off, and pulled my legs up under me, facing him. "I really don't." *Flying.* I hadn't spent time consciously dwelling on memories of flying in years. "I dream about it sometimes. The good and the bad. Sometimes I'm trying to survive maneuvers or my throttle freezes up or I'm surrounded by lightning. But usually I'm just soaring out over a peaceful body of water, like I'm Meryl Streep in *Out of Africa*."

"Gazelles and elephants and all?"

I shook my head. "No, sadly. Robert Redford isn't even there. Just . . . flying. Pretty boring, really."

"I think that sounds pretty great."

I wrapped my arms around my knees and tried to guess what was behind this topic of conversation. So far I had no insight, but I knew my dad was a man of few words, and the ones he spoke were almost always intentional and meaningful.

"Do *you* miss it?"

He nodded slowly and stared at the fire. "I do. I don't know why, but I've been thinking about it a lot lately."

The air force was, I guess, one of the things we most had in common, and it was also one of the many things we never talked about. I wasn't sure why we never talked about it, but I couldn't even remember the last time it had come up between us. It had been years, probably.

"I don't know," he continued with a sigh. "Maybe it's just because I'm getting old and the clock seems to be speeding up. Makes you nostalgic for the periods of life when you thought you might live forever."

I scooted over to the middle cushion and snuggled under his arm as he lifted it to welcome me. "Flying was just a means to an end for me, I think. I got my hours, did what I needed to do, and then got a desk job the very first chance I got. To tell you the truth, I don't think I ever stopped being scared half to death every time I went up."

He pulled away slightly and looked down at me. "You never told me that."

"Of course I didn't, Sergeant Atwater." I lifted my left hand and saluted him very half-heartedly, causing him to chuckle. "I remember when I was little, Mom was always telling me these stories about how heroic you were in Vietnam. She showed me letters you wrote to her and to Grandma, and everything was epic. How could I possibly tell you that before my first solo flight I threw up for six hours straight, and then by the time I got back on land, I had to be hooked up to an IV and a medic had to babysit me because I kept passing out?" I covered my face in still-fresh humiliation. "I'm not sure who it was, but while I was recovering, I heard someone say the words, 'This one may not be cut out for the air.' In the United States Air Force. Seriously, how could I have told you that?"

"Well, Lieutenant Atwater-Elwyn." He copied my half-hearted salute. "You could have realized that I'm your father first. Besides, I wasn't actually all that accomplished or heroic. Your mother lied a lot." I laughed as he looked down at me again and winked. "No . . . ," he tagged on softly, settling farther into the couch. "I suppose I did okay."

"Yeah. Pretty okay. I'm fully aware I only outrank you because of the nonflying stuff. If I hadn't walked through a few well-timed open doors and been freakishly good at the boring paperwork everyone else hated, I probably would have retired airman first class—if first class isn't pushing it a bit."

"At any rate, I'm sorry we didn't talk about it more." He took a deep breath and paused in that way he always did that I had come to understand meant he was taking the time to carefully choose the next words out of his mouth. "Are there other things we should have talked about more?"

Doc Atwater was more sensitive than many men of his generation, but I knew certain things weren't easy. Certain things had never been easy. He'd raised me alone from the time I was eleven, and for a bristly retired air force medic, he'd handled the "girl stuff" pretty well. Of course, if we're being honest, I'd made it pretty easy, all things considered. I'd never rebelled, really, because I didn't want to disappoint him. I'd been a good student, had helped him in the clinic, had handled most of the cooking and household chores, and even managed to have a group of friends who did all they could to help too. Not that I could take any credit for that. We'd been a good group of kids who loved one another pretty much from the time we were born, and they'd also all happened to love my parents.

Basically, the theme of my childhood after Mom died was that my dad and I were a team, in it together. From day one. And no matter the pain we were each dealing with, we looked out for each other.

"Like what?"

I rolled my eyes at myself as soon as I asked the question. *"Like what?"* Yeah, great question. Whatever could he be referring to? The fact that in the last twenty-two years, I was pretty sure Wes's name had been said between just the two of us approximately . . . let's see here . . . oh yeah, *never*? Or maybe he thought that after avoiding his calls for eight months (when Joel was dead and I wasn't allowed to tell anyone), then suddenly calling to tell him my husband had died (once I got the all-clear and the fully vetted cover story from the agency), then avoiding his calls for *another* three months (when I was spiraling out of control), then showing up on his doorstep with assurances I was fine and healthy and just looking for a change of scenery, I had left some things unsaid. Hard to tell, really. *"Like what?" Yeah, I wonder.*

"I'm not sure I did what I should have done to support you when you got back," he said. "I should have done more."

I sat up straight and looked at him. "I don't think that's true at all, Dad. You've been great."

"I mean . . . with the drinking. Or your sobriety, rather. Your journey through that. I'm not sure I've known quite how to support you through it all." He cleared his throat and lowered the arm that had been around my shoulders. "Clearly I don't even know how to broach the subject now."

Oh yes, I supposed there was at least one more entry on the list of things my dad and I never talked about. There were those last thirty days before I came back to Adelaide Springs (when I was getting clean and sober and digging myself out of the spiral at a DC rehab).

Oh. *That.*

For the record, it wasn't that I never talked about it. I talked about it every Sunday evening during Celebrate Recovery meetings at a little church in South Fork. It also wasn't that I intentionally avoided talking about it with my dad. It just never came up. (And if I'm honest, I didn't absolutely hate that it never came up.)

The CIA cover story as to the nature of Joel's death was that he'd been killed by a drunk driver, and that fake story about Joel's death informed part of the fake story about my sobriety. How could I not stop drinking after that? How could I risk being the one to lose control and take a life? The agency didn't mandate that part of the story, but I must admit it was convenient. Such a large part of the true story was classified, and there was just no possible way for me to be fully honest with anyone. Admittedly, that made getting sober tricky. But isn't it always?

Still, every Sunday night I was completely open and honest about my alcoholism and my sobriety and even my grief. I just left out the details that required an SF-86, an NAC investigation, and a polygraph.

"You're coming up on a year, aren't you?"

"Three hundred and sixty-one days."

"I'm proud of you." He grabbed my hand and squeezed. "You know that, right?"

"Yeah, of course. Thanks, Dad. But . . . what's got you thinking about all of this?"

He released my hand and leaned forward, resting his arms on his knees. "What's the plan, Addie?"

"The plan for what?"

"For you. Look, sweets, I love having you home." He tilted his head to look at me. "I do. But I know you're not happy here."

"What are you talking about? Sure I am."

"Okay, if that's true, explain it to me."

"Explain what to you?"

"How you're happy."

I chuckled lightly and jumped up from the couch. "*How* I'm happy? What is there to explain?" I walked over to the fireplace and stoked the logs that were burning just fine without any help from me. "How are *you* doing? That's what I want to—"

"Adelaide!" My dad raised his voice to me. *My dad raised his voice.* I couldn't remember the last time. I couldn't remember many times at all, actually. Ever.

I turned around slowly as jolts of heat rushed up my neck to the top of my head, causing it to throb. "*What?*"

There was a little too much sass in my voice. I knew it in real time, but I couldn't shut it down. Also in real time, I reminded myself I was a grown woman, and I didn't have to watch my tone. (Yeah, that was stupid and a little too *The Outsiders* for me. The thought of disrespecting my dad would never not horrify me. Real time.)

"Why can't we just *talk* anymore?"

*What is happening?* "Of course we can talk, Dad. I don't know what you—"

"Fenton said he saw you outside Cole's restaurant with someone he swore he thought was Wes Hobbes. And I told him he must be mistaken."

The throbbing in my head intensified. "Dad—"

"But Jo confirmed he's staying at the inn and that you've been spending a fair amount of time together."

"*Excuse me?* That's none of Jo's business." I turned back to the fire, fairly certain that if it did need a boost, I was going to have some flames shooting from my eyes pretty soon. "And frankly it's none of yours either," I muttered under my breath.

My dad was moving slower these days. I'd noticed he got up to go to the bathroom more during the night. Certain foods didn't agree with him anymore. But by golly, he had the ears of a bat in its prime.

"How can you say that to me?" he asked, standing and walking toward me. "How can you possibly say that to me?"

I dug my fists into my hips as I turned around. "It's my life, Dad."

"But I was there, Adelaide. I saw what he did to you, and I saw you struggle to pick up the pieces. For years. Yes, you're a grown woman, but you're also still my little girl, sitting under that tree in her wedding dress in the rain."

"I know, but—"

"I'm so proud of you and your 361 days. I may not be the best about talking it out, but I know how hard you worked to get healthy. And I know you think it's not my place, but I just have to question the wisdom of spending time with someone who caused you so much pain. Everything else I think and feel about him aside, if he's a threat to your sobriety—"

"A threat to my sobriety? Is that what you think?" My hands left my hips, and I folded my arms across my chest. "You think I'm going to drink because of *Wes*?"

"Well . . ." His eyes glistened orange with the reflection of the fire, and his Adam's apple bobbed as he swallowed hard. "Isn't that how it started?"

That was such an oversimplification, and he had to have known it. He *had* to have. Even taking into account all the things I'd never talked about with him, he was a doctor. And he'd known my mom's mom, and her mother before her. He'd lived with my mother who, in so many ways, adopted the life of a Prohibition-era teetotaling nun in order to avoid the heirloom passed down through the generations the way other families might pass down a pocket watch.

I'd known it. They'd made sure I knew it.

But by the time I was out in the world on my own for the first time, I was willing to do anything to stop feeling sad all the time, and also somehow desperate to feel *something*. I was tough and cocky and naive and convinced I had survived the worst thing anyone had ever had happen to them. I understood now, as I never could have then, of course, how blissfully unaware my misery made me. So did I drink for the first time in college, while still throwing myself into anything and everything that took my mind off Wes? Yes. But don't a lot of people try things in college? Not that I recommend the getting-drunk-at-an-off-base-party-the-weekend-before-midterms method of exploration and self-realization. And did I realize the next morning, when I was puking my guts out and worried I was going to get caught and thrown out of the Air Force Academy, that the pain and sadness had gotten turned off for just a little while? Absolutely.

And that was how I knew. I didn't fully understand it then, of course. Yes, the warning signs had been there. Yes, there were lessons from previous generations that I could have heeded. But again, I was young and damaged and stupid enough to truly believe I was tougher than any genetic predisposition toward addiction. There was no harm in it, I told myself. I was doing myself a favor, really, by giving my brain a chance to stop working so hard for a change. So yeah, I didn't know it then, obviously, but I knew now, with absolute certainty, that Wes didn't turn me into an alcoholic by leaving me. Addiction had been lying in wait, knowing that if it was patient, it would get its opportunity to pounce. And the fact was that while I didn't feel I owed him a thank-you card or anything, I had eventually come to realize, after attempting to pin it all on Wes for a very long time, that if I'd lived in a different environment as a teenager—maybe in a different town or with a different dad or different friends or a different boyfriend who, unlike Wes, may have pressured me or been a negative influence—it was entirely possible the beast would have awakened sooner. Regardless, it would have come alive at some point, and that could have just as easily been when I wasn't heartbroken and empty.

"It's not fair to blame Wes for my alcoholism, Dad, any more than it's fair to simply blame genetics or the guy who gave me my first drink in college or the cashier at the liquor store where I bought my last bottle of vodka 363 days ago. It's really not." I took a deep breath and attempted to rein in the frustration I was feeling. "And I'm pretty sure you know that."

He'd lost a little of his height, but he still had a good six inches on me, allowing him to hold the upper hand in our stare down. But I knew I wasn't going to budge. I loved my dad as much as any daughter possibly could, and I had never lost sight of what an incredible person he was. I could remember so many times as a kid when people would show up at our door or the phone would ring in the middle of the night. I never once saw him respond to any interruption of dinner or sleep or family time with anything other than compassion. *"I'm going to let you in on a little secret, Addie,"* he'd said when I was seven or eight. *"People would be a whole lot happier if they'd just remember that the world is an awfully big place, and not a single one of us is at the center of it."*

I respected my dad more than anyone else I'd ever known, but I wasn't backing down. Not on this. I'd fought too hard for the understanding I had of myself. It was far too valuable for compromise.

"Did your mom ever tell you about the time my plane went down near Kham Duc?"

He asked it so randomly, so calmly, as if he were inviting me to play a hand of gin rummy. As if we hadn't been engaged in an epic showdown for the ages—at least by Atwater household standards—and I was so confused that I blinked repeatedly.

"What? No. What are you talking about?" I shook my head as the reality of what he said registered. "Your plane actually went down? Are you kidding?"

"You know me. I joke about the Vietnam War all the time."

He walked into the kitchen, and after a brief moment of focused breathing without him watching me, I followed. "How have I never heard this story?"

"It's not my favorite thing to talk about, as you can probably imagine." He stood at the sink and filled a glass with water. "And your mother . . . well, let's just say she probably preferred to pretend this one never happened."

Bemused, I pulled out a stool and sat at the island. "Tell me."

"There's not much to tell, actually." I scoffed, and he chuckled. "No, really. I'm not being evasive. I only know so much about what happened. It was about the time of the evacuation, and my job was just flying patterns back and forth, mostly for intimidation purposes. Just relatively routine flyovers. And then I lost my engine."

"Were you shot at?"

He shrugged. "Might have been, but I sure didn't hear anything. Could have been a bird or an air pocket or faulty mechanics. I really don't know. All I knew was I had no choice but to land in the swamp before I crashed in the swamp and then just hope and pray I hadn't been spotted."

"Were you? Spotted, I mean?"

"Nope." He took a sip of his water and smiled. "Told you there wasn't much to tell. I got picked up about thirty minutes later, got treated for a broken collarbone and a few cuts and bruises, and that was it."

I released the breath I had been holding as if I hadn't known that, one way or another, he'd made it out okay. "Well, allow me to thank you for not telling me that story before I enlisted. I'd *still* be on an IV from all the vomiting."

Even just hearing him tell the story more than fifty years later and picturing the plane losing control . . . feeling the helplessness he must have felt . . . caused my stomach to churn and my throat to go dry. I reached across the island and grabbed his glass, helping myself to a sip of his water.

Dad waited until I had finished drinking before he continued. "The nightmares and the images that I'll never get out of my head, the sound of enemy fire and the silence where there should have been the roar of an engine . . ." His eyes closed tightly. "The silence. I don't know how to explain it, Addie, but the silence is so much worse than even the most dreaded of sounds." He shook his head as his eyes fluttered back open. "I've been trying to figure it out, but I just can't make sense of it. Maybe you can help me."

"Make sense of what?"

"How can I possibly miss it? How can I look back on the horror of that experience, the pain it caused, the trauma—for me and your mother and really just anyone who cared about me—how can I look back on that and wish, even with some small part of me, that I could do it all again? It just doesn't make any sense."

*Dang it, Dad.*

"Well, *that* was manipulative," I whispered, counting on his bat-like hearing this time.

"I'm not trying to manipulate you. I'm just trying to help you see what I see."

"That is not what's happening here." I spun on the stool and stepped off to the side, then scooted the stool back under the island as calmly as I could.

"I don't understand why you'd agree to be in the same room with him, Addie, much less have dinner. Spend time. I'm just asking you to help me understand—"

"You don't have to understand!" I shouted. "It doesn't have anything to do with you!" He opened his mouth, and I knew he was preparing to issue the same protest from earlier. No way. "*Yes*, you were hurt too. I get that. I do. And I'm sorry that you were hurt. I'm sorry that my pain caused you so much pain. I really am. But, Dad, I'm pretty sure Wes isn't the same person he was then, and I know for a fact that I'm not. But even if we were, even if nothing had changed at all . . . it's *really* not any of your business. I love you, but you have to stop treating me like a child."

The conversation had begun with a joke about breaking curfew (a joke that I now understood hadn't been much of a joke at all, from his perspective), and I had a sinking feeling in my stomach that it was about to wrap up with a good old-fashioned "as long as you live under my roof."

*And maybe that's the problem.*

"I'm going to start looking for my own place. Tomorrow."

"Now, Addie—"

"No." I shook my head. "Don't. It's fine. It's for the best." I hurried out of the kitchen and slipped my shoes back on, grabbed my coat off the hook, and had it zipped up about the time he appeared back in the living room.

He sighed. "Where are you going?"

Every day he looked older to me, and tonight I knew I'd caused the clock to spin forward far too quickly.

I choked down the "none of your business" that I knew I'd regret and instead said, "I just need a little space. I'll see you tomorrow."

And I have to admit that as I pulled out of the driveway not even a minute later, I was suddenly very concerned that my dad might have been onto something. I mean, I didn't want a drink. I honestly wasn't too worried about that. Not right then. No more than I always forced myself to be, just because the worst thing I could do was think I had nothing to worry about.

But I very much found myself wanting to run to Wes.

I'd meant what I said. I really didn't believe it was my responsibility to help my dad understand. But it was probably advisable that *I* at least began trying to figure out what the heck was happening.

CHAPTER 19

# WES

**Nearly 30 Years Since Conditions Were Right**

"What would you say, then, Senator, to those who insist your push for campaign law reform is simply the beating of a hollow drum?"

*I think I would say, "Aren't all drums hollow?" What is that even supposed to mean, Herbie? Is it, perhaps, your hollow brain we should be concerned about?*

He wished he could say that, but of course he never would. Even speaking as a dead man walking in politics, he would never.

Wes was reclined on his bed at the Inn Between, ankles crossed, one hand under his head on the pillows and one holding his phone to his ear. His dress shirt was splayed open, his socks sat on top of his shoes on the other side of the room, and his hair was still wet and disheveled from his shower. And while some might say that not even bothering to get fully dressed to speak live to the eight million Americans listening to *Press the Nation* might be a good indication he had completely checked out, Wes didn't feel that way at all.

Yes, he'd been avoiding media at all costs for a few days, but not because he no longer had things to say. He had lots to say. There was a lot he had hoped to accomplish. There was so much he cared about. So many ways he had planned to make a difference. But just like he didn't believe a lame-duck Congress should attempt to alter the fabric of their democracy after the people had voted them out, he didn't feel right about influencing a national narrative when he knew—and they did not—that he was going to refuse to step up to the plate for them.

But when Herbie Eccleston lobbed the ball at him low and slow, what choice did he have?

"I think you're referencing the argument of some of my opponents who say I only care about campaign law reform because it sounds good to the American people."

"Yes."

"The argument of my detractors, as I understand it, being that I scoured the polls for the issues that most people agree on and then wholeheartedly threw my support behind the beliefs of the people."

"Yes, Senator. To shore up votes. How would you respond—"

"How would I respond to the criticism that during the campaign I have spent time focused on issues that the majority of Americans have said matter to them, that they actually agree on—and that I agree with them on, too, by the way—and that I believe are actually within our power to do something about?"

Wes rested comfortably in the discomfort of a couple of extra seconds of dead air and then smiled when Herbie cleared his throat and said, "Yes."

"Well, I think I would answer that question with a question: If my opponents don't care about the things the American people care about, why do they even want to be president? Or the better question, perhaps: Why in the world would we want them to be?" Wes rolled over to lie on his side and propped his head up on his hand, supporting his weight on his bent elbow. "Look, Herbie, for years we've been arguing about how much money can be spent on campaign ads, how much money someone can donate to a candidate without disclosing the amount, PACs and super PACs, how taxes work on all those donations . . . and I'm not going to pretend to understand all the ins and outs of all those rules. That's what the lawyers and the accountants are for—and let's face it, half the time they're making it up as they go. But what I do know, and what I understand—thanks, primarily, to listening to the American people—is that while we're passing campaign reform laws that affect a small percentage of citizens, a whole lot of time is being wasted. The campaign cycle gets longer and longer, and my critics know as well as you and I do, Herbie—and the American people certainly know it—that we've created a system in which we start running our reelection campaigns before the Bible's put back in the glass case on Inauguration Day. It's a monster of our own creation, and it's time we listen to the people who gave us our so-called power. And by the way, we're not actually the ones with the power. They are. The people who choose us to represent them. So I just don't think it's a bad idea to give the voters what they want from time to time—especially if what they want is for their government to put aside politics as usual and actually *govern* for a change."

Wes pulled his phone away from his ear and glanced at his watch in the moment of silence before Herbie said, "That's all the time we have today on *Press the Nation*. Many thanks to our guest, Senator Wesley Hobbes."

"Always good to chat with you, Herbie." Wes heard shuffling in the hallway and sat up and threw his legs over the side of the bed, adding, "Thanks for having me," in the second before he ended the call. He threw his phone on the bed and hurried toward the door.

Every morning Jo freshened up the bouquets she kept in vases on tables around the inn, gathered from flowers she grew in her greenhouse out back, keeping the entire space bursting with colors and scents that would have otherwise seemed unattainable in the dead of Colorado winter. Last night he couldn't get away from her quickly enough. While he didn't regret the urgency with which he had handled things, a sleepless night had allowed him plenty of opportunity to reflect on some of the other choices he'd made. And as Jo Stoddard herself had reminded him countless times throughout his adolescence, if you're right but you're rude, then you're wrong.

"Hey," he said, opening the door. "I'm sorry about the way I ran off last night."

Jo wasn't beside the door arranging the flowers as he had expected, so he took a step out into the hallway and turned the other direction.

Oh, *hello.* There was Addie, wrapped in a towel knotted at her chest and another towel around her head, forming a makeshift turban.

"Sorry. You're not Jo."

"And you're not dressed," she replied, pink crawling across the top of her chest and up her neck like rapidly growing ivy.

Wes looked down at himself. He was *mostly* dressed. He hadn't gotten around to buttoning up his crisp white dress shirt just yet, and the button of his slacks was still undone, but he was fully zipped. Really, by comparison, he was positively Elizabethan. All he was missing was a jerkin and some wrist ruffs.

"I hate to break it to you, but neither are you."

Addie's eyes flew wide, and she pinched the folded spot of the towel with one hand and with the other reached behind her for the doorknob of the room that had once been their clubhouse. As soon as the door creaked open, she scurried inside. The next image he saw of her was her tilted head peeking around the opening of the door and the towel falling off her head when she tilted it just a little too far.

"Sorry. There's no shower in this room. I thought if I got up early enough . . . But apparently . . . Anyway . . . why are you up so early?"

"East Coast phone call." He laughed softly at how flustered she was, then looked down at his shirt and buttoned it up halfway. Then, after making a show of closing his eyes and covering them with one hand, he took a few steps and knelt to pick up the hair towel for her. He'd had to peek through his fingers to make sure he was reaching out to the right spot, of course, but he was pretty sure she would accept the brief glimpse he'd received of her bare legs over the possibility of incidental contact as the result of a well-meaning but misguided hand.

He placed the towel over her outstretched arm between the narrow opening and stepped back toward his room. "Mind if I ask what you're doing here?"

"It's stupid. My dad and I got into a fight." She directed a puff of air from her mouth to a wet strand of hair dangling in front of her eyes, but it didn't budge.

This time Wes didn't bother covering his eyes, but he didn't have any trouble at all keeping his focus on those sad brown eyes of hers as he rushed back over and gingerly tucked the heavy wet lock behind her ear.

"Want to talk about it?"

"Oh, I don't know . . ."

"I was hoping to talk to you about some things anyway. What do you say we both finish getting ready, and then I'll treat you to breakfast and we can talk about *all* the things?" *All the things.* Okay, that couldn't happen at the Bean Franklin or anywhere that other people might be. "I'll make you breakfast, I mean. Downstairs. Sound good?"

He watched her as her eyes danced to and fro in micromovements. Her brain had always moved so quickly. When they were young, he'd been intimidated by that. It wasn't easy for him to keep up. He didn't understand then that when he said something—anything, really—she moved beyond the words to begin interpreting meanings that maybe he'd intended but maybe he hadn't. She would think ahead to future consequences based on scenarios she'd created, inspired by words he'd never realized carried so much weight.

He'd wondered, more than once in the years since, if things might have turned out differently for them if he'd realized, just a little bit sooner, that even the couples who really loved each other had to put in the work to understand each other. Just because they knew each other better than anyone didn't mean they always spoke the same language.

He recognized the shift in her eyes. Back then, that moment when her eyes began avoiding his and she began withdrawing into herself represented her self-doubt. At least he was pretty sure that was what he had figured out. He didn't know that then, of course, but he'd realized it later. Maybe he'd said he wasn't in the mood to watch a movie, for instance, and in her mind she'd translated that as, "Why would I want to watch a movie with you? The fact that you want to watch a movie at all demonstrates to me how different we are. In fact, I'm pretty sure I don't love you anymore. Maybe I never did. Also, have you put on weight? Peace out, yo." And sure, maybe that was all a bit extreme, but he'd had a lot of time to replay and analyze segments of every conversation they'd ever had. He would swear that a time or two she'd interpreted whatever harmless (to him) thing he was trying to say as pretty much *exactly* that.

That was the one thing he would do differently if he had it all to do again. He would be patient and take the time to understand how his words made her feel. And then, once he did that, of course he would learn how to communicate better. He would be patient with *himself* and take the time to say the right words. He'd put in the effort. He would also make sure she knew that there was nothing she could ever say or do that would cause him to stop loving her. And of course it would have been much easier to convince her of that if he hadn't, in fact, walked out on her with what must have felt very much like a "Peace out, yo."

Okay, so there was actually a lot he would do differently. And if he could pick only one thing, he would have stayed. It seemed so simple now, though it certainly hadn't then.

"Hey." Wes smiled as Addie maintained her sliver of presence in the doorway and wet hair fell in front of her eyes once more. He was so tempted to brush it away again, but he was legitimately worried any sudden moves might startle her at this point. She appeared to be so lost in thought. Maybe so lost in guessing at and analyzing his motives. And he wished he could ease her mind and clarify that it was no big deal and that she was overthinking it. But this conversation over breakfast had the potential to be a very big deal. "I really do need to talk to you. It's important. But also, for the sake of full disclosure, you should know I can't really cook. I will gladly pour cereal or, if the conditions are right, toast you some Pop-Tarts."

"And what exactly *are* the proper Pop-Tart conditions?"

"I mean, I'm *tempted* to say 1996, maybe? A little Matchbox Twenty on the radio? Last night's *X-Files* cued up on the VCR?"

She chuckled and stood straight. "Cereal will be fine. Be there in a minute."

---

He rolled up his sleeves as he ran down the stairs and then hopped to the bottom landing from the third step. Jo was standing over an end table in the living room, carefully arranging a stack of magazines, and looked up at him in disapproval when he landed with a gentle thud.

"I'll thank you not to scuff up my hardwood floors."

Wes hurried over and stood behind her, resting his chin on her shoulder. "And I'll thank you not to be mad at me for how rude I was last night."

She raised her hand and slapped him gently on the cheek three times. "I'm more worried about my floors." He backed up, and Jo turned and faced him. "Everything okay?"

"Addie is going to be down in a minute." He leaned in and spoke quietly. "Is anyone else around? Would it be okay if we had the dining room to ourselves for a little while?"

"Now those are two very different questions, and I'm not sure the answer of one has much to do with the other." She began walking to the kitchen, and Wes followed her. "The Wainscots just checked out—"

"Already? It's 6:30 a.m."

"We're called the Inn Between for a reason, you know. We were their stopover on the way to Denver. They were the only other guests, and I'm just about to go have breakfast at the Bean. So yes, you'll have the place to yourself." She picked up two oven mitts and slipped them on before lowering the oven door and pulling out a casserole dish. "But as to whether or not that will be okay . . . I guess that depends on whether you want to be in the middle of what's going on with Addie and Doc."

He tilted his head and leaned back against the counter. "What do you mean? Why would that—" *Oh.* Of course. "They're fighting because he found out I'm in town?"

Jo closed the oven and tsked as she removed the oven mitts from her hands. "It's really not for me to say. You know I don't like to put my nose where it doesn't belong."

"Yes." He nodded and smiled as he picked a crispy piece of burnt cheese off the side of the dish. "Your discretion is legendary."

---

"I mean, I kind of had my taste buds all set for Raisin Bran or something, but I suppose this will do." Addie took another bite of the sausage and green chile frittata and moaned in satisfaction. "You're not only a better chef than I expected, you're very speedy."

They sat across the large oak dining table from each other—Addie dressed again in her jeans and sweater from the night before, hair still damp, and Wes properly buttoned.

"Well, it was the least I could do. Especially considering I might be at least somewhat responsible for the fact that you're staying at the inn and wearing yesterday's clothes?" He grimaced.

Addie rolled her eyes. "Jo and her big mouth."

Wes chuckled. "Yes. So I suppose the truth is more accurate. It was the least *Jo* could do."

She raised her cup of coffee. "I'll drink to that."

They ate in silence, and he watched her focus on her plate. Occasionally her vision and attention would wander off to a far corner of the room. They were alone, just like he'd wanted, and the only thing keeping him from diving straight in was how much he was enjoying staring at her without her knowledge.

He'd never known anyone as beautiful as her. And the thing was, she probably never would have been hired as a runway model or even been "discovered" by some guy pulling together a local ad for Woolworth's, back when there used to be local ads for Woolworth's. *Back when there used to be Woolworth's.* Brynn had always been the local beauty of that nature within their group. And then Laila was the one who made every guy she encountered fall just a little bit in love with her by simply smiling and lighting up the air all around her.

Addie was different. There was so much depth behind every smile and so much substance wrapped up in every glance. She had big brown eyes that, frankly, had seemed a little too big for her head when she was young—though she'd grown into them nicely. And maybe her mouth was just a little too wide, if you were searching for flaws. Of course, when she laughed and that mouth was on full display, you understood how perfectly those full, slightly asymmetrical lips suited her. She'd hated her nose and the way it turned up a little at the end, and the tiny little gap between her front teeth, but Wes had always thought those two "flaws," as she had viewed them, were among her sexiest features. And now he marveled at how youthful they made her appear, even while she carried the burdens of adulthood.

"Um, Addie?"

The tines of her fork were resting on her bottom lip when he got her attention. She pulled her eyes away from the far window of the dining room and looked at him, but the fork stayed in place. "Hmm?"

"I need to tell you something." He set his fork down beside his plate and switched over to the chair at the head of the table so he could sit beside her instead of across from her. "And I need you to know that I didn't know this until last night. Well, this morning, actually." He sighed and ran his hand through his hair. "No, last night. When we were talking about whether or not you missed the CIA and you mentioned that Joel was CIA too."

"What are you talking about?" She set her fork down with a shaky clank on her plate, and Wes instantly understood that he was already on the verge of messing this up. Not that there was any sort of rule book for this sort of thing, as far as he knew. "What didn't you know?"

He turned in his chair to face her at the corner of the table. "I'm on the Senate Intelligence Committee." He desperately hoped his eyes conveyed compassion and care. That's what he was feeling. That was definitely the reason he had been scouring through thousands of pages of encrypted files from a locked-down server on his phone all night.

His forty-one-year-old eyes would have thrown a parade in his honor if he'd switched over to his laptop, but something about opening classified government files on a computer using guest Wi-Fi at an inn in Adelaide Springs, Colorado, just felt like a no-no, whether it actually would have been a problem or not. Not that using the data plan on his phone was necessarily any more secure. "And last night, when we were talking, I finally remembered where I'd heard the name *Elwyn*."

Her fingers continued to tremble, and the tips turned white as she squeezed the edge of the table in a failed attempt to still them. "You're on Senate Intelligence? Is that true?"

His heart fell inside his chest at her question. *"Is that true?"* He didn't blame her for asking. No matter who he was to her, in the past or the present, this was a tricky situation. Even if she had only been the wife of a CIA officer who lost his life in the line of duty, she would understand the importance of discretion. She wouldn't be keeping the secrets surrounding her husband's death just because she was told to. Just because she had agreed to. Not even because actual, legitimate penalties and jail time were on the line. No, secrets were kept because Joel Elwyn may have no longer been in the field, but hundreds of other spokes of the same wheel—not to mention the hundreds of other wheels all around the world—were still out there spinning. Gathering. Protecting. Reporting. Trying to survive. Saving countless other lives in the process.

Wes couldn't imagine that anyone could marry into the upper echelons of the agency without an inherent understanding of that, and an inherent understanding of what their loved one put their life on the line for every single day.

Of course Addie hadn't been only a CIA *spouse*.

She'd kept the secrets, and she'd kept them well. Secrets that seemed inhumane to ask anyone to keep but that the select few would lay down their lives for. She'd known the risks involved in marrying Senior CMO Joel Elwyn—she'd had to have known them—but how could anyone ever really understand them until all of the worst possible logistical scenarios and a blown clandestine identity and a scared punk who found himself in the wrong place at the wrong time—with a newly acquired FN Five-seveN semiautomatic pistol in his pocket—all came together on a cloudless February night on the streets of Caracas?

Joel had spent his years in the field, valiantly serving his time as a case officer. By the time he was promoted to CMO and given an office at Langley, he had completed hundreds of missions in dozens of countries. Operation VE Ladder got handed off to him as an ever-growing disaster taking its final, hopeless breaths. Failure seemed eminent. But Joel Elwyn refused to accept that.

As CMO, Joel was responsible for making sure the mission succeeded. He knew the risks, but he still chose to send in the best person for the job.

And now Wes's childhood sweetheart—the only woman he had ever been in love with, the one person he'd wanted to protect but whom he'd betrayed with the most cowardly decision he ever made—was having to ask him if what he was saying was true. Because of course she didn't trust him. She'd acclimated to a life in which she didn't trust anyone, he was guessing. But he was the one in whom her distrust was most deserved.

"Yes, Addie, it's true."

The trembling went far beyond her hands now, and she was biting down on her bottom lip, trying to still it. Tears had pooled in her eyes and were making a valiant effort to hold tight, but they'd defied gravity long enough. She sniffed, and the vibration caused the moisture to fall from her eyes in solid streaks down her cheeks.

"I'm so sorry, Add. For *all* of it." Wes slipped off his seat and kneeled in front of her, grabbing his unused napkin from the table as he did. "I can't even wrap my head around how strong you've had to be. How strong you are. To have lost him, but then not to be able to tell anyone?" He dabbed the green cloth napkin against her cheekbones, and new tears spilled onto it before the existing had been absorbed.

And still, he saw her clamping down harder on her lip. Squeezing the table so aggressively that he was beginning to worry she would injure herself. (Or at least worried that Jo would injure her if she damaged her table.) Breathing as shallowly as a highly trained diver, maintaining all her oxygen for the possibility of a terrifying, life-threatening eventuality.

"You really know?" Her voice was resolute but so quiet through her barely separated lips.

He scooted closer to her on his knees, having no idea if he had any right to do so, but quickly discovering his intuitive need to help her know he was there for her was leaving him no choice.

"I do. I sat through the hearings. I saw the photographs. I read the testimonies."

"If that's true, why are you just now—"

"Like I said, *Elwyn* sounded familiar, but . . ." He shrugged. "For whatever reason, it didn't click until you said his full name. And then I had to find out what *you* knew so I knew what I could say."

"How did you—"

"I read through all the files again last night."

*Stop talking over her*, he lectured himself. He wasn't meaning to. Adrenaline was one rude party guest sometimes. "I never knew it was you. And if I'm being honest, I don't know if I'm sorry I didn't know or grateful. I don't know how I . . ." He closed his eyes briefly and tried to block out that pointless attack on his conscience, courtesy of a hypothetical. How would he have managed things if he had known that Addie Atwater was "the Elwyn widow," as she was referred to in the briefings?

*It doesn't matter now. It's not about you.*

He looked at her again. "I know that Joel wasn't even supposed to be there, and he only stepped in to keep the mission from failing when the other agent missed his mark. And Joel *did* keep it from failing, Addie. I know that for a fact. There are fourteen other operatives who still haven't been exposed and who are still alive because he saw

Ladder through to the end. And I know that as cruel as it was to make you wait eight months before acknowledging his death—"

"Two hundred and fifty-eight days."

He nodded and brushed his thumb against her chin, catching a teardrop before it fell from her face. "That gave operatives enough time to maintain contacts and gather enough intel to stop the transport into the US of about twenty tons of cocaine and close to as many weapons." Wes took a deep breath and gently absorbed her tears with the napkin again while her eyes scrunched closed and the trembling overtook her entire body. "But I'm so sorry, Add. I'm so sorry about Joel, and I'm so sorry you haven't had anyone to—"

He was so unprepared for the way she lowered herself out of her chair onto her knees and threw herself into him that he not only let out a very onomatopoeic *harrumph* as the air was knocked out of him, but also had to splay his hand behind him on the floor to maintain his balance and prevent them both from toppling over. But her arms around his neck and her sobs against his shoulder demanded better of him. Wes pushed off from the floor with his palm and wrapped her against his chest.

"It's okay," he whispered against her hair as she clenched the front of his starched and pressed dress shirt in both of her fists and wept with all the freedom she'd been so long denied. He sighed and wiped away a tear of his own and pulled her in even closer before kissing the top of her head, stroking her hair, and finally accepting that there would never be anyone in the entire world he cared about as much as he cared about her.

# CHAPTER 20

# ADDIE

### 8,972 Days Since Their First Kiss

"Gimme." I reached my hand out toward Wes and wiggled my fingers, and he placed a chocolate-chip cookie in my palm. That didn't stop my finger-wiggling, so he gave me another, and I pulled my hand back, satisfied. For the moment anyway.

"Jo's going to kill us," Wes said, his mouth full of cookie. His fifth, at least.

I sat across from him on the dining room floor, my legs crossed under me. (Quick sidebar: How are we, as mature, well-meaning, socially responsible adults, supposed to refer to that style of sitting nowadays? Obviously, we should never use the culturally insensitive colloquialism of our ignorant youth. And not to sound uppity, but as a retired US Air Force first lieutenant with a master's from AFIT, I feel that "crisscross applesauce," frankly, is somewhat beneath me. If anyone has the answer, please let me know.) He set down the increasingly sparse platter of cookies, which Jo had probably intended to (a) share with more than two people and (b) last more than one sitting, and reclined back onto his elbows. His white shirt, originally so "ready for a day on the campaign trail," now screamed "my drunk wife and I just got into an altercation in a Tennessee Williams play," with its partially untucked front and plethora of creases and mascara stains and one broken button in the middle.

"Kill *me*, maybe. You, on the other hand, can do no wrong in Jo's eyes."

Wes had always been her favorite. Oh, sure, like all great educators—a category in which I unequivocally included Mrs. Stoddard—I knew she would deny having a favorite student. At least she would deny it to me and her other nonfavorite former students. But I knew it. We all knew it, back in the day. And while each of my friends handled that a little differently (Cole teased Wes relentlessly, Brynn continually attempted to dethrone him and attain the crown for herself, and Laila was just wholly unaffected by it all), I was always glad that was the case. It was always worth celebrating, I thought, when someone else acknowledged the remarkable person he was and recognized all he had to offer.

He'd certainly had a difficult time recognizing any of that within himself.

"I feel like I should tell you something." He scooted back a touch to rest his head up against the wall, but he stayed in his reclined position. "I've been in touch with Jo for a while. I mean, not a superlong while. Just since a little after my father died."

"I figured," I told him with a shrug. And maybe I hadn't actually gotten quite to the point of *figuring* yet, but I certainly wasn't surprised to hear it. "It makes sense that you'd want some Adelaide Springs intel before coming back here."

"No." He shook his head and sat up fully. "No, it wasn't about that at all. Honestly . . . honestly it was just about me, Addie." He looked down at his shirt, spotted a chocolate-chip smudge, and began to raise his hand to try to wipe it off. But before his hand even reached his shirt, he seemed to decide it was pointless. That shirt was probably a lost cause. He lowered his hand back to the dining room hardwood floor and scooted back against the wall instead. He sighed and looked up from his hopeless shirt to meet my eyes. "After Wray died, and then even more after my father died, I just really started wanting to come home."

*Home.*

"How can you still view this place as home?"

His pupils dilated in response to my question, and I couldn't help but wonder which emotion was causing the physiological response. It had always been fascinating to me, watching surveillance footage and zeroing in on a target's eyes. No matter how skilled and practiced the target, very rarely did I come across one whose pupils didn't react in some sort of indicative way. Oh, sure, that could mean so many different things—fear, anxiety, lies, arousal. You might be surprised to learn how often all of those inciters were simultaneously present at the height of danger for some people, and how in the particularly savvy (and, usually, evil), it was often impossible to sort them all out.

But I didn't get the impression Wes was making any strong attempts to be savvy at that moment. And by that point I was pretty convinced he wasn't truly evil. I was also fairly easily able to eliminate arousal from the mix at that particular moment. If he was the husband in the Tennessee Williams play, I was the drunk wife who had once been the cutest little lady in the whole county but who now resembled Glenn Close in *Fatal Attraction*, somewhere between boiling the rabbit and being drowned by Michael Douglas.

"Don't you?" he asked.

I tried to think about that for a minute—to give it the consideration it deserved—but the answer was so obvious that I couldn't even pretend to be unsure. "No. I don't." Adelaide Springs had stopped being home a long time ago.

Wes's dilated eyes—*sadness*—stayed locked with mine as he reached out to the plate and grabbed another cookie. But he didn't eat this one right away. Instead, he just spun it mindlessly through his fingers. "Is that because of me?"

My initial urge was to shut it down. Again. I didn't want to talk about our past—although it wasn't *our* past that was the issue, I was pretty sure, so much as the part of *my* past that was caused by him. But then, really, wasn't it *all* caused by him? Or at least influenced by him? The lost years, yes, and the pain that I had been so certain was never going to relent, but also the years that came after the pain. *Joel.* And if there was only one thing I knew with complete certainty, it was that I wouldn't have traded my years with Joel. I would have given just about anything to avoid the pain of losing my husband. Anything other than never having found him in the first place.

"Partially, I guess," I answered him, feeling a little bit like a new fawn, testing out my legs, not quite certain they'd hold me. But Wes had given me the gift of the past hour or so. He'd given me the gift of understanding and empathy and a non-government-redacted moment of grief. If he needed to confront this—if he needed to confront *us*—it suddenly seemed like the least I could do. "If I'm being honest, I was pretty sure, for a long time, that I never wanted to show my face here ever again. I couldn't imagine facing the memories. And honestly, it was just weird being here without you."

He nodded and looked down at the cookie in his hands. "I get that. It was weird being, well, *anywhere* without you too."

*Give him this.* It wasn't really my brain telling me to give him the shot at catharsis or closure or reconciliation or whatever it was he was chasing. My brain—logic, analysis, data—was my guiding force and had been for so long. But this was more like a voice from deep inside. Or rather, it *was* my brain, but my brain was telling me it was okay to allow my heart a seat at the table this time.

I didn't owe him anything. I mean, I owed him gratitude for the events of the dining room, there at the Inn Between, and I felt no qualms about giving him that. Beyond that? I owed him nothing. But even if my brain was still struggling to draw a line to connect all the dots of Wes Hobbes—my first love, the guy who'd disappeared, a polished politician so unlike the person I had known, and possibly a middle-aged man in the throes of a midlife crisis—my heart was beginning to see him for what he was. Somewhere under all the other stuff—because of it . . . despite it—he was still Wes.

I cleared my throat as I pushed myself up and grabbed onto the dining table for support when I realized my feet had begun falling asleep. I wiggled my toes in my sneakers and then slid them off and gently kicked them against the wall when they suddenly felt too constricting. I stretched my arms over my head and then brushed cookie crumbs off my sweater. *(Note to self: sweep before Jo gets back.)* Then I walked over to his side of the wall. I didn't have to say "Scoot" this time. He looked up at me and set the cookie in his hands down on a napkin beside him, then pushed the plate of cookies in front of the china hutch and scooted over in the same direction, making room for me along the wall.

I slid down next to him and, as we both stared straight ahead, asked, "Do you want to talk about it?"

He nodded slowly. "I do. And I also very much don't."

"Well, then, we're halfway in agreement. But let's do it anyway."

He propped up his knees and wrapped his arms around them. "Can I just . . . I mean, first of all, before I say anything, can I just issue one disclaimer?"

"Sure."

"I just . . . I need you to know that there is nothing left in me—*nothing*—that believes I did the right thing by leaving. I wasn't even sure then, really, and then I guess I sort of convinced myself somewhere along the line. But now?" He shook his head. "*Nothing.* So any sort of *anything* that sounds like I'm trying to justify . . . I'm not. I'm just explaining where I was at the time. I need you to know that."

"Got it." I found myself counting slowly down from ten, trying to prepare myself for whatever he was about to say. Reminding myself it didn't matter now. Repeating the thoughts from a few minutes prior, though with a slightly different spin. *If Wes hadn't left, I never would have met Joel. If the pain of losing Wes was necessary in order to find Joel, I wouldn't give it up for anything.* "So tell me. What happened?"

He leaned forward and rested his chin on his knees. "The governor. He, um—"

"I'm sorry. Who?"

"My father. Governor McNeese."

"You call him 'the governor'?"

Wes sighed and tilted his head to look at me. "He wasn't exactly the warm and fuzzy papa-bear type of dad, I guess you could say. In private, I could call him 'Dad,' but yeah, publicly . . . 'the governor.' It's been a hard habit to break, I guess. But also, after a while, it just felt right. So anyway, he showed up for the wedding."

"Yep. I was there for that part."

"Right. Sorry."

He had searched for his father for so long. When he was young, he used to bombard Marietta with questions all the time. And every time it would upset her. Wes would talk to me or to all of us about it, and he always felt guilty for making his mom sad. And yeah, pretty much without exception, when he talked it out with us, he would realize (or we would help him realize) that his timing had been awful. He would bring it up when Marietta was worried about money or exhausted from all she was doing on her own. It was so easy to see from the outside, especially now, but the fact was, he'd just been a kid who couldn't be expected to know how to read a room and choose his moment.

And regardless of her son's less than ideal approaches to the conversation, I was convinced then and still now that Marietta never intended to tell her precious little boy about the other half of his DNA. She did the very best she could on her own, and after moving west right after she found out she was pregnant, she'd managed to build a home and a family and a life for the two of them in this little Colorado mountain town in the middle of nowhere. But Wes never gave up the search. He just gave up on the idea of his mom providing any clues.

It was just days after she died, while we were sorting through her things, that Wes found the picture of college-aged Marietta Hobbes, giddy and starstruck, looking up at a handsome congressman in his thirties. The "McNeese for Congress" button on her dress and the wedding band on his finger painted a rather salacious picture that Wes wasn't too eager to buy into, but it didn't take me any longer than a second of staring at that photo to recognize Wes's eyes and nose and chin. I knew every single feature of Wes's face, and even if then Congressman McNeese had been in a lineup with a thousand other potential DNA matches, I wouldn't have hesitated. I knew.

By the time Wes learned of him, of course, he was the governor of Connecticut and very easy to track down. Getting him to acknowledge Wes was a bit trickier, but he eventually agreed to a DNA test that, of course, was conclusive. Three days after they both received the results, Governor McNeese arrived in Adelaide Springs—two days before our wedding.

"And the thing is, Addie, from the time he got here, all he talked about was my potential, my potential, my potential." He rubbed his face and twisted to look at me. "This guy who didn't even know me was telling me I was smart and 'a good-looking kid' and that, hey, I was his son, after all, so of course I was going to go far."

"He was right, obviously," I said softly, tilting my head over slightly to tap him on the shoulder. And then, for whatever reason, I left it there. A tapping head became a resting head, just for a few seconds.

I say "for whatever reason," but really, it's no mystery. I had always believed in his potential. Maybe I wouldn't have guessed he would be the front-runner for president someday, but really, who guesses that about anyone? No matter what he believed about himself, I had always seen how incredible Wes was. And the fact that he thought so little of himself had always been the thing that caused me the most sadness and frustration.

I also couldn't deny that it hurt, just a little bit, to know he had finally believed it when it came from someone else. Someone who had been in his life for two days as opposed to our eighteen years together.

"Was that it?" I asked, lifting my head from his shoulder once I realized he'd gone very still. I hadn't meant to compound new discomfort upon this already most uncomfortable of conversations. "You decided to go 'chase your potential'?" I detected the snark in my tone and shook my head. "Sorry. I swear I didn't mean for it to come out that way. Though, I guess if I'm being honest, I'd have to say that ticks me off somewhat." *Oh, good job, Addie.* That's *better than a little snark in your tone.* "Sorry. Don't mind me. Go on."

"No." He spun around ninety degrees and faced me full on, his legs crossed under him. "Say it."

"It's really not worth it—"

"Please, Addie. Say it. Whatever you need to say. *Please* say it."

I also turned ninety degrees and looked straight at him, our knees touching. "I guess I'm just disappointed. That's all. I guess after all this time, I maybe just wanted to believe that you didn't actually run away from the person who believed in you more than anyone else in the world just because someone else's validation was finally worth listening to."

He pulled his bottom lip between his teeth and nodded. "I get that."

"So was that it? Was that really it, Wes? Did I not . . ." *Dang it.* How could I possibly have any tears left? "Did you not know how much I loved you, or—"

"I knew."

"Or did you just realize . . ."

"What?"

"Nothing."

"*What,* Addie?"

"Did you realize you wanted something different? Was that it? Because how could you not have known that I would have—"

"You would have gone with me? Is that what you're asking? Are you asking if I knew you would go with me if I left? If I asked you to?"

"Yes. Because of course I would have—"

"Of course you would have. I knew that."

"Then why—"

"Because it was never about that!" He pushed away from the wall and stood, walking over to the chair he had been sitting in less than two hours ago—and yet somehow a lifetime ago—when we were eating breakfast and I seriously thought the most emotionally taxing thing of the day was going to be a tiff with my dad. "It was the opposite of that. It was . . ." He stood behind the chair and squeezed the back. "I'd been telling you for weeks I thought we were rushing into getting married."

I shook my head. "No. You never said anything like that."

"Yes, Addie, I did. Maybe not in those exact words, but I talked about waiting. I talked about waiting until after college—"

"Okay, yeah, I do remember that." I jumped up and walked over to him. "But we decided there wasn't any point in waiting—"

"*You* decided there wasn't any point in waiting."

"No, Wes, *we* decided. We'd be able to get married housing at CSU, and that would be cheaper. And we knew—or at least *thought*—we were getting married eventually anyway, so it made sense to go ahead and do it. Remember? I can't believe you're trying to rewrite the history here."

He squeezed the bridge of his nose. "I'm not. Just . . . listen. What I'm trying to say—"

I crossed my arms and planted my sock-clad feet. "Don't try to say it. Just say it."

"Okay, but remember my disclaimer."

"Wes!" I groaned his name and threw my hands up. "Come on. Enough already. Just say it."

"You were throwing your life away!" He raised his clenched fists into the air. "You'd been accepted to the Air Force Academy—"

I gasped. "You knew?"

"Of course I knew. *Of course* I knew. You could have gone anywhere. Done anything. We all knew it. This entire town knew it. And I was the schlub holding you back."

"No one thought that, Wes."

"*I* thought that, Addie! *I* did." He ran the back of his hand angrily across his eyes and began pacing the room, from Jo's prized imperial elk head (affectionately named Elkrique Iglesias by the Adelaide Springs class of 2003, thank you very much) to her framed Thomas Kinkade knockoff in which the leg of a kid in the background was twisted the wrong way and a cross-eyed golden retriever was wearing a bonnet (less affectionately referred to as "Creepy" by Wes and Cole). "And I couldn't get you to listen to me—"

"Oh, so it's my fault?"

"Disclaimer!" he shouted in a long-drawn-out singsong tone that, I must admit, almost made me laugh. But he was so caught up in his yelling and his high-level angst it would have just been rude. "No. It's not your fault. It's mine. I should have stayed. I should have somehow figured out a way to make you hear me. But we were kids. *I* was just a stupid kid, Addie. Which, let's face it, is further evidence that we weren't ready to get married. And suddenly the governor was here, and—"

"I'm sorry, I just have to say it's really disturbing to me that you call him 'the governor.' Didn't you ever watch *The Walking Dead*? The governor was the guy with random body parts in fish tanks—"

"I'm so glad my dysfunctional relationship with my father is amusing to you."

"Sorry." I smiled at him, but then I saw the pain in his eyes and reined it back in. "No, really. I'm sorry. So suddenly your father was here and, what? You had a way out?"

He winced. "Ouch."

*Man, way to flip the emotional temperature on a dime.* "I didn't mean it that way. I just . . ." *Well, hang on a sec.* "Yeah, okay. Yeah . . . maybe I did. You didn't want to get married—"

"It wasn't that I didn't want to get married."

"—and you thought I wasn't capable of making any of those big, life-defining decisions for myself—"

"You know that's not what I meant, Addie."

"—or at least you thought we weren't strong enough to make them together—"

"I wasn't thinking like that then! Again, we were kids. It's easy to look back now and see how wrong I was. I know that. But then, all I knew was that my mom was gone, and suddenly I had a father. And he wanted me to go live with him. And at the exact same time, I couldn't make you see how you deserved so much better than me."

I scoffed and took a step toward him. "That's the stupidest thing you've ever said to me, Wes Hobbes. And you once told me *Death to Smoochy* was Robin Williams's tour de force, so clearly we have an impressive backlist of stupid things to choose from."

"*Death to Smoochy* is an underrated cinematic masterpiece about cynicism and greed, but agree to disagree, I guess," he mumbled softly. "And you know what? That's so easy for you to say now."

"No, I thought *Death to Smoochy* was awful then too."

"Not the movie, Addie. Me. Us. Admittedly, I've done a little better for myself than anyone could have guessed. It's amazing what money and connections and a father you always know will care about you just a little bit less if you don't continually achieve can do for a guy. But then? Are you kidding me? I never would have become anything. And don't get me wrong—I don't think I'd have minded that so much, in hindsight. But you?" He chuckled, but the sound was laced with exasperation. "You have always been remarkable. And I'm sorry I left, Addie. I'm so sorry I left. But if you think for even one moment that it was because I didn't want to spend my life with you or because I didn't love you enough—"

For the second time in a matter of hours, I threw myself into his arms, knocking the wind out of him, and he exhaled against me just as my lips met his. And it was, quite frankly, the worst, most awkward kiss of my life. It was like I'd forgotten *how* to kiss, really. No. You know what? I'm being far too kind to myself calling it a kiss. I'm being far too cruel to the act of kissing to lump this atrocity into its storied and glorious legacy. It was like in the old-time classic movies when two sets of tightly closed mouths and freakishly open eyes just stayed in place, and you never noticed how weird actually kissing like that would be because you were too caught up in the crescendoing orchestrations and the way the shadows of the black-and-white film made everything seem sultry, even when it was really, really not.

Wes was clearly in shock. Of course he was. And I was sort of . . . well, not in shock really. I was more sort of paralyzed. Like, I wanted to pull away, but my brain couldn't get my body to kick into gear and do anything. In fact, all my brain could focus on was how I was going to get out of the situation. And I don't mean the kiss itself. Oh no. That would have been a *good* thing to be focused on. That was exactly what my brain *should* have been devoting all its energy to. (Although, really, how difficult should it have been to instruct myself to stop impersonating one of those suckerfish that clean the algae off the tank and just pull away and run?) But no. My brain—my usually-not-too-shabby brain that had once been trusted with State secrets, if you can believe that—thought it was a good time to plan ahead. My brain seemed to believe the end of the kiss-of-prepubescent-nightmares was inevitable. A sure thing. And apparently, I was confident enough about that to start trying to figure out how to get out of the awkwardness that was oh so guaranteed to follow.

I was trying to come up with a witty exit line and yet . . . *I was still attacking his face*!

Finally he pulled away, which I was grateful for. I mean, my teeth were starting to hurt. Never a good sign. But it was also horrifying, of course. And even more horrifying (although "more horrifying" was sort of like "more dead"—not really possible) was that my brain was already moving the film forward here, too, in light of the new development.

He was a good guy now. I was convinced. I even found myself sort of having to admit to myself that I liked him. Whatever. And worst of all, when he'd opened his bedroom door that morning with his shirt unbuttoned, I'd received the six-pack-abs confirmation I had neither sought nor desired. Again . . . whatever. So *of course* he was going to be charming and swoony and a gentleman and let me off the hook easily in a way that was going to simultaneously endear him to me further and make me hate him just a little bit.

If nothing else, I had to beat him to the punch on that one.

"Well, that sucked. I mean, it was no *Death to Smoochy*, but it was pretty bad."

Yep. That's what I said.

"Addie—"

"Look, Wes, I'm sorry, okay? It's been an emotional day already. That's all. I didn't sleep much, I'm still wearing yesterday's clothes, and I swear even Elkrique Iglesias is judging me right now." I lowered my voice an octave. "'I've been dead and mounted on a wall for thirty years, and I'm a better kisser than you.'"

*Regrettable.*

I put my hand over my eyes, as if blocking out the sight of him would hopefully make me invisible, and said, "Okey dokey. Well, I'll just be going." Turning away from him, I began walking out of the dining room. I wasn't willing to completely uncover my eyes, but I needed to see where I was going, so I looked down at the ground and cupped my hand like a visor. That's when I remembered I'd left my shoes behind. Ah well. When one is climbing into a departing lifeboat on the *Titanic*, one simply does not go back for one's opera glasses. "Forget this happened. Forget you ever met me. In fact, I think it's probably best—"

"Nope." He grabbed my loose hand and spun me around—which occurred in very fast and dramatic fashion, owing to socks on the hardwood floor and all—and I gasped as he used the momentum of the spin to draw me in against him. He lowered himself to my eye level and wrapped both his arms around my waist, then pulled my body flush with his and rose slightly, taking me with him so I was on my toes. "Don't you dare go and start thinking on me, Adelaide. Not just yet."

His lips parted slightly, and I instinctively took in a breath, and my eyes fluttered shut in the instant before his mouth captured mine. The fingers that had been covering my eyes combed their way into his hair while the other arm, which had been dangling since he released my hand, looped around his shoulders.

Suddenly not even my toes were touching the floor, and before I realized what I was doing, I had looped my legs around his waist. Well, I think that's what my legs were going for, anyway. But I was shorter than him, of course, and they'd more sort of latched on around his thighs, like I was attempting to climb up a fireman's pole. And because I was holding on for dear life and clamping his legs together a little bit, Wes began having a difficult time walking us toward the couch, as he had begun to. Not only that, but he was having to lower his head farther and farther in his attempts to keep our lips engaged as I slid down his body.

He chuckled against me, and I was sure I had ruined the entire thing. And unlike the horrific suckerfish experience, I hadn't wanted this to end. Lucky for me, Wes had no intention of giving up so easily. I simultaneously gulped in an inordinate amount of air and felt all the oxygen leave my body in surrender to him as he lowered into a squat and looped one arm under my hips and hoisted me up until my legs were (finally, mercifully) wrapped around his waist. His eyes remained locked with mine as he carried me over to the leather couch by the fire, lowered me down, and then sat beside me.

"That was all I was going for. Was that so difficult?" I asked.

Then his twinkling eyes disappeared so that his lips and mine could carry on in their attempts to get reacquainted.

## CHAPTER 21

# WES

### Make That 9,306

"No . . . no, no, no." He muttered the word against her lips as his phone continued to buzz in the other room, and Addie laughed harder each time at his bullheaded determination to keep kissing her.

"Just answer it. Whoever it is, they've called ninety times now."

Wes traced a trail from the corner of her lips and across her jawline to her ear. "Just ignore it."

"I can't. Why don't you turn it off if you're not going to answer it?"

"Well, the full answer to that would probably require some deep psychoanalysis, which I'm sure would trace back to the governor"—he cleared his throat—"sorry, *my dad* telling me that the measure of a man is the commitments he honors, and if you allow an opportunity to pass by, you have no one to blame but yourself if another one never comes along. But the honest-to-goodness answer right now is that my phone is in the dining room and your lips are in here, and I've made my choice." He looped his arm around her neck and pulled her back to him again to place the punctuation mark on his declaration.

"I feel like we're pushing our luck, anyway," she murmured as Wes traced the line of her neck with his finger, and then his lips followed the trail his finger had laid out. "I half expect Jo to come back and catch us making out."

"Wouldn't be the first time." The phone buzzed again, and he lowered his forehead to her shoulder and groaned. "I'm sure it's just my campaign manager."

She placed her hands on his shoulders and pushed him away, leaving him to stretch his lips out in a comical attempt to return to her. "Yeah, so where are you on that whole thing?"

"What whole thing?"

"That whole running-for-president thing."

He shrugged. "I'm not." He leaned against her, causing her to erupt into a fit of giggles as her strength gave way to his and he was once again kissing her.

"But no one else knows that still, right?" she asked softly. "As in ballots are being printed with your name on them, and campaign staffers are neglecting their families in order to devote every hour to pounding the pavement and knocking on doors in support of Hobbes for President, and meanwhile you're in hiding, holding on to information that's going to impact lots of people."

Wes sighed and furrowed his brow at her before sitting up and leaning back against the couch. "Way to ruin a mood, Adelaide."

"Yep." She sat up and joined him in a normal upright position, like the responsible adults they were. "Nothing like a little the-future-of-our-country-is-at-stake reality check to ruin a perfectly good make-out session."

"First of all, that was a perfectly *fantastic* make-out session, thank you very much."

He really just wanted to stop there. Well, to stop there with his words, anyway. He would have been very content to never stop kissing her. It was mind-boggling to him how, after all this time—after their bodies had changed, their personalities had changed, and they'd each had other experiences with other people—they still fit together like they had the very first time he ever kissed her, in their meadow on the outskirts of town.

"Do you remember our first kiss?" he asked, turning to face her. Reality could wait just a little longer.

"*Do I remember?* Of course I remember. It was summer in the meadow. I was fifteen. The Fourth of July."

Except at the exact same time she said, "The Fourth of July," Wes said, "Your birthday," causing them both to scrunch up their faces and stare at each other in confusion.

"It was the Fourth of July, Wes," Addie insisted. "July 4, 2001. There were fireworks, remember? And as big of a deal as you and my dad usually made of my birthdays, I don't remember anyone ever actually putting on a fireworks display."

"No way." He shook his head fiercely. "I mean, I remember kissing you in the meadow on the Fourth of July during fireworks, for sure. More than once. But our first kiss was on your fifteenth birthday. August 4, 2000. It was raining for the first time in forever, and it was so hot and humid, and you were sad because you were missing your mom, and your dad had given you that necklace—"

"I'm pretty sure you're just stealing a plotline from an episode of *Dr. Quinn, Medicine Woman*."

He laughed and shook his head. "No. Are you serious? You don't remember this? It was your mom's necklace, remember? And it had lost some of the jewels, and Doc had replaced them with sapphires because that was your mom's birthstone."

"Well, yeah, I remember the necklace, but—"

"Okay." He propped his knee up on the couch and leaned toward her. "And remember you walked out of your party, and no one knew where you had gone, but I found you in the meadow, and we rode our bikes farther out—"

"To the waterfall." She nodded. "But you didn't kiss me."

Wes had been practically bouncing in enthusiasm as recognition began flaring in her eyes, but just like that, the excitement was gone. His bouncing stopped, and he sat back on the couch, facing forward again. "Wow, Addie. Just . . . *wow*. Glad it was such a big moment for you."

She laughed and lifted his arm and curled under it so she could look straight up at him. "I have *vivid* memories of our nonimaginary first kiss."

"It wasn't imaginary!" He sat up again, taking her with him. "Okay, picture it with me here. We were at the waterfall—"

"Hot, raining, birthday, necklace, dead mom, sad . . . With you so far."

"And then I said we should probably get back before Doc started worrying, and your bike got stuck in the mud."

She began tracing the outline of his hand with her fingertip and nodded. "Right. I remember that."

"So I picked it up and carried it, and we had to walk all the way back, and by the time we got back to the meadow, it had stopped raining, and it was dark, and I held your hand—"

"To guide me through the puddles."

"What? *No!* It wasn't to help you through the puddles. I mean, maybe it was, but I was very intentionally holding your hand, and then I kissed you. Then I walked you to your house, we never spoke of it again, and I officially asked you out, like, eight months later. And then our *next* kiss was on the Fourth of July."

Addie's finger stilled on his hand. "Oh. You're talking about *that*? That wasn't a real kiss."

"Excuse me?"

"You hugged me, and it was dark, and we kind of bumped into each other—"

"'Bumped into each other'?!" Wes jumped up from the couch, causing Addie to erupt in a fit of giggles. "We did not 'bump into each other.' I kissed you! I meant to do it. I mean, I'm not saying it was one for the ages or anything. I didn't know what I was doing. But we most certainly did not 'kind of bump into each other.'"

His profuse use of air quotes made her laugh even harder, and she leaned forward to grab a tissue from the coffee table to begin wiping away the moisture in the corners of her eyes. "I'm sorry," she choked out, quite unconvincing in her declaration of regret. "I honestly thought it was an accident, and I never mentioned it because I didn't want you to be embarrassed." She stood up and walked over to where he was standing with his elbow resting on the mantel. "Forgive me?"

She traced her finger along a winding vein from his elbow to his wrist and looked up at him with those big eyes that, for the first time in the couple of days he had spent with her, didn't look sad, and it became increasingly difficult to even carry on pretending to be upset. He tucked a strand of her hair behind her ear, and she leaned into the palm of his hand. But just as he was preparing to demonstrate that all was forgiven—not to mention demonstrate that, hopefully, he knew how to kiss her in a way that was much more memorable now—her phone rang in her pocket. Without a word, but with an undoubtedly mischievous grin on her lips, she pulled it out and answered the call.

"Hello?"

"One time," Wes whispered, shaking his finger at her and backing away. "You're weak, Atwater. It rang one time."

"Oh . . . um, yeah . . ." She was still watching him, but their teasing came to an end as her expression morphed into something neutral in response to whatever was being said on the other end of the line. "Yeah, I think I can track him down." She raised her eyebrows and shrugged in his direction. "Okay, sure. If I see him, I'll let him know. Okay . . . sounds good. Yeah, I'll talk to you later." Addie ended the call and stuffed her phone back into her pocket.

"Everything okay?"

"Laila said she needs to see you."

"Hmm. Okay. Did she say what about?"

She shook her head. "Nope. Just that she needs you to head over to Milo's as soon as you can."

Wes nodded and half smiled at her. "Okay. I guess I should go. Just . . ."

"What?"

"If I leave now . . ."

"Are you wondering if the bubble will pop?"

He nodded. "I am." And he was pretty sure he was willing to

neglect the rest of the world and stay by the fire at the Inn Between forever if that was the only way to stay in the bubble with her.

She scrunched up her nose and her lips and wiggled them back and forth. "I don't know. Can't say for sure, obviously, but this hasn't really felt very bubble-ish to me. I mean, it *has*, but in a good way. Like a Glinda the Good Witch sort of bubble that can float from place to place and be controlled. Not a John Travolta *Boy in the Plastic Bubble* sort of bubble, where the bubble is the only thing keeping us alive. You know what I mean?"

He smiled and couldn't help but wonder if it ever would have even been possible for him to fall out of love with her. "As ashamed as I am to admit it, yes. I know exactly what you mean."

---

Wes observed the minimalistic facade of Milo's Steakhouse in the light of day and was even more impressed than he had been the night before. In fact, now that he was able to take in the entire row of buildings—where he knew there had been countless businesses housed through the years, though he could remember the specifics of very few—he felt pride swell up inside him. He was proud of his friends, sure, even if they (or at least one half of "they") weren't quite ready to acknowledge him as a friend again. But he was also proud of Adelaide Springs.

All of them, he was pretty certain, had had a love-hate relationship with their hometown when they were younger. He certainly had. No matter how much they'd been happy there, no matter how much they loved the people, a person couldn't help but sometimes feel a restlessness growing up in a town with just a few hundred people and very limited entertainment options. Well, limited unless you enjoyed the mountains and the river and the endless miles of hiking possibilities and a sky that seemed to show off just out of habit.

Thus the love-hate. He did enjoy those things. He always had. He had loved getting dirty and wet and exploring every nook and cranny of canyons and riverbeds. But yes, once in a while it would have been really nice to be able to take his girlfriend to a fine dinner and a movie without having to spend a small fortune on gasoline. It wouldn't have broken his heart if he and his mother could have done all their shopping right there in town rather than having to make a full-day event out of it, stocking up for weeks at a time.

But to look at Adelaide Springs now—still tiny, still intimate, still bursting with natural beauty and grandeur, but also expanding and attempting to remain relevant—made him feel proud, even if he knew he had no right to claim for himself any of the pride the citizens of the town should feel.

"There you are!" Laila rushed out the door and wrapped her arms around his waist. "I'm glad Addie was able to track you down."

What were they going to think? Well, he didn't have to think too hard to figure out what Laila would probably think. Wes was quite certain Laila would view him and Addie getting back together as a triumph of first love and a celebration of the bond they all shared, or something equally "glass half full" and optimistic. Something equally Laila-ish. Cole, on the other hand . . . That one might be a little trickier. It wasn't that Cole had been unfriendly to him at dinner the night before. Far from it. He was actually pretty sure Cole wasn't wired for unfriendliness any more than his wife was. And there had been a few moments when one of them—let's face it, usually Laila—would mention a funny memory from their past, and even Cole would laugh. A couple of times Wes and Cole had even turned to each other and referenced some guys-only inside joke aspect of the anecdote. It was good. It had felt *really* good to Wes. But Cole had been his best friend for a lot of years, and then Wes had abandoned him, just as surely as he'd abandoned Addie. And now, when he found out he and Addie were back together . . .

*Hang on.* Were he and Addie back together?

As much as he understood and appreciated her bubble theory, all of a sudden all he could hear was *pop*, *pop*, *pop* as all that was to come scrolled in front of his eyes. Not so much like his life flashing before him. More like a list . . . an endless list . . . of all he had to sort out and deal with, scrolling and scrolling in smaller and smaller font size like the *Star Wars* credits.

"Where's Addie?" Laila asked, pulling away from the hug.

"Huh?" Wes looked down at her and saw her eyes directed behind him at the old Chevy pickup truck. "Oh, yeah, she didn't come. She just let me borrow Beulah."

Laila sighed and nodded. "Don't feel bad. You can't expect her to be okay spending *too* much time with you yet. But hey, she let you drive Beulah! That's no small thing."

"That's no small thing," he agreed, grinning at her and squeezing her hand before she pulled away completely. "So what's up?"

"Well . . ." She motioned for him to follow her inside. "I have a surprise for you."

Wes spotted the instantly recognizable face of someone he'd never met before at a table in the center of the room. The man stood as they entered and took a step toward them as they approached, his arm outstretched.

He introduced himself as they shook hands. "Sebastian Sudworth. Nice to finally meet you, Senator."

## CHAPTER 22

# ADDIE

### 2 Days Since She Wanted to Run Over Him with Her Car

There was this one time when we were in high school when a bear got into our tent and completely ravaged everything while we were down at the river fishing. Let me just say that walking back into Jo's dining room to clean up didn't *not* make me think of that memory. It was a mess. But I found myself smiling as I swept and whistling while I wiped down the table.

Wes Hobbes and I had just spent perhaps the most emotionally raw and real few hours together of our entire shared history, and my head felt cluttered by the presence of the various life stages of me all reacting to that development in their own way. Little Addie with her crush basically since birth was giddy. Teenaged and in love Addie felt hopeful and optimistic and so at home. Brokenhearted young-adult Addie was fussing at herself for being so weak and letting him in again. And of course modern-era Addie was just super confused. But even in the midst of all the clutter, peace and clarity were most prominent, rising to the top like the smoke in a burning building. Except the smoke was a good thing. And the peace and clarity and happiness and endorphins were all working together to make me not dwell on the fact that in this analogy, whatever was happening between Wes and me was represented by a house burning down.

I took one last look around the dining room and spotted my shoes against the wall. I slipped them back on and turned my attention to the kitchen—just a few dirty dishes, *much* less bear ravaged—and then indulged in another moment by the fire. It felt weird just to sit. It wasn't like there was a whole lot to do most days, but usually I still found ways to busy myself. But I'd checked in with Neil that morning, and no flights were scheduled today so it was unlikely he would need me at Valet Forge. And I wasn't exactly in a rush to hurry home and have another confrontation with my dad. And of course I couldn't have gone anywhere even if I wanted to, I reminded myself, since Wes had Beulah. There was absolutely nothing better to do than sit here and enjoy the fire and think.

*"Don't you dare go and start thinking on me, Adelaide."*

I sighed indulgently, in the privacy of the empty inn, and stretched out to a fully reclining position on the leather couch. If I closed my eyes, I could still see his lips curling up as he made a valiant attempt not to laugh at me—not that I would have cared if he had. It felt safe and comfortable, and from the moment I was in his arms and he was kissing me, I was as certain about him as I had ever been. I knew him, and he knew me. Not as well as Joel had known me, of course . . .

*Joel.*

My eyes opened again, and the light peeking through the window cleared away the silky, gauzy, hazy warmth that accompanied thoughts of being in Wes's arms and replaced it with the cold and isolated feeling of not being in Joel's. Of never being in Joel's arms again. I had just barely begun the process of truly accepting the isolation. Of adapting to it. Of coming to terms with never feeling warm or silky again, and certainly having no desire to, since I'd yet to master the spell or discover the magic words or build the time machine that would bring Joel back to me.

I felt the silent question well up in my chest—*Should I feel guilty?*—

and then chuckled as the answer reverberated through my heart, undoubtedly in Joel's voice:

*For this? No way. We'll talk later about you forgetting to water my lady's slipper orchid after I died.*

I allowed my eyes to float closed and thought of Wes again. This was good. This was safe. There were things each of us was hiding from every other person in the world, but not from each other.

*He doesn't know you're an alcoholic, but other than that . . .*

I squeezed my eyes tighter and told the nagging voice to shut up. That voice didn't belong to Joel; it belonged to party-pooper Addie, and she wasn't welcome. Not yet. Besides, it wasn't like I was hiding my alcoholism from him. It just hadn't come up. And yes, I knew it would need to. Soon. Probably *really* soon. I had no idea what he and I were flirting with here, but I'd meant what I said: whatever it was didn't feel like something that could only survive inside the bubble. And if we were going to even consider making a go of it, he would need to know what he was signing on for right off the bat.

Nine days out of ten—no, more than that . . . ninety-nine days out of a hundred—I didn't even think about alcohol. I understood what my addiction had cost me: my career, my reputation, quite a few friends, and certainly any hope of finding a way to carry on in DC after Joel died. The thought of going through any version of any of that ever again was reprehensible to me, and I genuinely felt no desire to drink. Not on the bad days and not on the good days. I figured that probably made me one of the lucky ones, and I'd committed to never taking that for granted. On ninety-nine of the days, I didn't think about alcohol, but I thought about addiction on all one hundred of them.

Just because I felt no desire to drink, I knew I wasn't out of the woods. I would never be out of the woods. If I was going to fall off the wagon, it wasn't going to be because I wanted a drink. It would be because I thought I'd be able to handle having a drink. After all, I'd been a high-functioning alcoholic who genuinely believed I didn't have a problem for nearly twenty years before I truly lost control the first time. Maybe I'd be able to control it again for a while, but maybe not. Regardless, even one sip would mean I'd have to start counting days all over again, and I'd worked too hard for that cumulative number. So I never stopped thinking about numbers of days. I never downplayed my dependency in my own mind. And if Wes was going to be in my life . . .

My eyes flew open, and I found myself staring at the ceiling. Was I seriously contemplating a relationship with him? What could that even look like? Okay, so maybe he wasn't running for president. Great. What was he going to do? Would he want to finish out his Senate term? We hadn't even talked about that, had we? Or maybe he'd said something. I couldn't even remember. I was so tired from the past couple of days. Oh, who was I kidding? I was so tired from the past couple of years. And I'd been listening to the words coming out of Wes's mouth with very different ears on Friday, when he was in the back of the Bronco, than I had on Saturday. One day in which I had gone from strategically trying to avoid him to being mildly moved by (if also very leery of) his idiotic hot chocolate gesture to talking with him in his room like old friends to hugging him at the end of an evening during which I couldn't help but remember how good it had felt to be loved by him.

And now, Sunday. Fueled by revertive rebellion at being told what to do and the sight of a truly exquisite bare torso, what had I become?

I mean . . . a *woman*, I guess. Hadn't really felt like one of those—in certain ways, anyway—for a while. In fact, I hadn't expected to ever again.

*Give yourself a little more credit than that, Addie.*

It wasn't really about the torso at all. Although, *seriously*! What had it been? Sixty seconds? How were all those muscles burned into my brain like I'd been staring at the sun too long?

But no. More than abs, it was about Joel.

Wes had been so gentle with the information. So compassionate. And yeah, at first I hadn't wanted to trust a word coming out of his mouth. Even after all the events of Saturday. No unbuttoned shirt could ever be enough to make me treat any of that as any less important than it was. In 718 days, no one had mentioned Venezuela or Operation VE Ladder to me outside of a clinical, controlled environment in which they had all the control and I had none. And I really did suspect at first, for just a moment, that Wes had dug up dirt to try to get close to me. That was what I repeated to myself over and over in those first few seconds when he began talking: *What's the angle?*

But then I'd looked into his eyes, and all I could see was the person I had to believe—who I couldn't *help* but believe—had once loved me. And all he wanted was to let me know he was willing to be there since no one else could be.

"Um . . . excuse me. Do you work here?"

I am not a girl who startles easily, but I'm pretty sure I jumped about a foot straight into the air before standing up and walking toward the front door. "I am so sorry. I didn't even hear the door open."

An older man in a nice suit smiled at me. "No apology needed. I apologize if I spooked you. I'm just wanting to see about getting a room for the night."

In the old days, Jo ran her reservations and occupancy details out of a black-and-white composition notebook. I was pretty sure if that were still the case, I would have been able to figure out her system and get the man a key. But I'd heard that Sebastian had convinced her to modernize, and a computer log-in screen requiring a password was staring at me from the check-in desk.

"I wish I could help. The owner is out right now." I glanced at my watch. It was right about lunchtime, and if she'd spent the morning holding court at the Bean Franklin, as she was known to do, I could imagine Jo would be making her way back to the inn soon. "I can tell you with absolute certainty, however, that there are rooms available. If you wanted to head to town to grab some lunch or a cup of coffee, you're more than welcome to leave your bags here." I looked down at the single bulging briefcase on the floor by his feet. "Or your bag, rather. Unless you have more in your vehicle? I'm happy to help you bring things in."

"That's very kind of you, but this is all I've got. And I don't have a vehicle."

I tilted my head. "If you don't mind me asking, how'd you get here?"

"The car service in town. What was it? It had a pun . . ."

I smiled. "Valet Forge. I actually work there. If I had a vehicle with me right now, I'd be more than happy to drive you somewhere."

"Again, you're very kind, but I wouldn't want to trouble you." He pulled his phone out of his inside suit jacket pocket. "I'll just call them back."

"Here, allow me." I pulled out my own phone and dialed Neil, but curiosity stopped me from hitting the green button. "I know I'm probably playing into small-town busybody stereotypes right now, but I have to ask how you got to town. The airline told us there weren't any scheduled flights today."

"Oh. Well. I flew privately." The man began looking around the open space of the inn—up the stairs, back to the kitchen, over to the fireplace—and I got the impression he'd given me all the information he was willing to give.

"I see. Sorry to pry."

He shook his head and smiled again, though it felt a little less genuine than it had before.

I hit the green button, and Neil answered on the first ring. "Hey, Neil. I'm at the inn. Jo's not here. Are you available to come back for the client you just dropped off? Mr., um . . ." I lifted my chin over the phone and said to the tourist, "I'm sorry, I didn't catch your name."

"Brewster. Philip Brewster."

I nodded once. "Mr. Brewster? Great. Thanks, Neil." I hung up and slipped the phone back into my jeans. "He'll be here in just a couple minutes. Feel free to make yourself at home."

"Thanks so much."

Rather than take a seat, he made himself at home by walking closer to the stairway and looking up. And then craning his neck to try to look into the dining room.

Well, as I'd heard Jo say on more than one occasion, the only kinds of tourists we don't want are the ones without money. And this guy's fancy tasseled loafers and Frank Clegg alligator briefcase certainly gave the impression he wasn't one of those kinds of tourists.

I was still covertly watching Mr. Brewster lean over the banister to look up the stairs one more time when Jo came through the door, unwrapping her scarf from around her neck as she entered.

"Hey, darlin'. I didn't expect you to still be here. Thought I saw Beulah down in front of Cole's place."

Okay. I did *not* want to explain that to her right then.

"Jo, this is Mr. Brewster. He's hoping to get a room for the night."

"Oh, pardon me. Didn't see you there, Mr. Brewster. Let's get you checked in." She hung her coat up on the rack and started to shut the door but stopped suddenly, looking toward the driveway. "Neil's here. Is he picking up or dropping off?"

"Mr. Brewster was going to head into town—"

"I appreciate your help," he said, picking up his briefcase and following Jo to the registration desk, setting his ID and credit card on the counter. "But if I can get a room and a cup of coffee, I think I may just settle in and get some work done."

I nodded. "Of course. Well, if you need a ride later, you can always give us a call. He's Neil, and I'm Addie."

Mr. Brewster turned slowly away from the desk and faced me again. "Addie? Did you say your name is Addie?"

Jo could run her business however she liked, but if it were me, I might have had a policy of not accepting tourists without money, and maybe also not looking too kindly on the ones who stare at you like they're wondering if you'd fit into a specially made box they keep in their basement.

"Yes. Addie Elwyn."

"Addie Elwyn," he whispered almost silently.

"Have we met before, Mr. Brewster?" I knew we hadn't, but I was trying to give his unusual behavior the benefit of the doubt.

He smiled again then, and it didn't seem as forced as before, although it didn't exactly put me at ease either. But suddenly he seemed to morph right before my eyes into Mr. Normal and Harmless Guy Passing Through Town. "No. Sorry. It's just a unique name I haven't heard very often before. Add to that the fact that it's been a long day of travel." He yawned as if on cue. "Don't mind me. That cup of coffee will help."

I glanced up at Jo to see if her stranger-danger radar was going off at this guy, but she wasn't even paying attention to anything other than her computer screen. And I knew she'd handled all sorts. If she'd been worried about any red flags, she would have had her eyes glued to him.

"Alright, then. Um, Jo, I think I'm going to ride into town with Neil. Unless you need me to do anything for you?"

"You go right ahead." She looked up at me over the monitor. "You staying here again tonight?"

I sighed and shrugged. "I'm not sure yet. I'll let you know as soon as I know."

"No rush. The room's yours as long as you need it." She turned her attention back to the computer, then grabbed a key for her guest and handed it to him. "Now, Mr. Brewster, do you want to head straight to your room, or would you like a snack first? I have a plateful of freshly baked chocolate-chip cookies just waiting to be devoured."

*Welp, that's my cue.*

I was out the door and into the car with Neil before she could discover that the bears in this situation might have cleaned up after themselves, but they'd also helped themselves to a whole lot of cookies.

## CHAPTER 23

# WES

**38 Days Until Super Tuesday**

Wes was confused. Instantly, undeniably confused.

"It's nice to meet you too." He finished shaking Sebastian's hand and then looked from Sebastian to Laila and back again. "It really is. I guess . . . I don't know, I guess I'm just wondering why Laila referred to you as a surprise for me."

"You were hoping for a chance to talk with him, right?" Laila stepped forward and stood between them.

"Jo." Sebastian peered over at him with a tilted head and a squinted eye. "Jo told me you wanted to talk."

Wes sighed. *Of course.* "Did she, um . . ." He glanced over at Laila again and then back to Sebastian. "Do you know *why* I was hoping—"

"No, sir. She didn't mention any specifics at all. Just that you were in town and hoping you might run into me while you were here. That was good enough for me, because the truth is . . ." He motioned back toward the table, and Wes followed him over and sat across from him. "I've really been hoping for a chance to chat with you too."

A couple of minutes later, after Laila had offered them both coffee and Wes had taken her up on it, she left them alone in the dining room with an assurance that she and Cole would be in the kitchen preparing for the lunch crowd but not listening to a thing—and a warning that they opened for lunch in fourteen minutes, so if they wanted privacy, they might need to talk quickly.

"Is Brynn with you?" Wes asked after taking his first sip of coffee.

"Not this time. She has to be on air tomorrow morning in New York. I just needed to take care of a few quick things for the *Adelaide Gazette*."

"The *Adelaide Gazette*? That's still a thing?"

"I'm trying to make it a thing. But with flying back and forth, and her job and my job, and both of us writing books and all of that . . . well, I haven't quite given it the attention it deserves." Sebastian shrugged. "What about you, Senator? What brings you back to our beloved Adelaide Springs?"

Wes leaned back in his chair and sighed. "Off the record or on?"

"I won't lie. I think I might be interested in a chance to talk on the record. But as far as I'm concerned right now, I'm visiting with one of my wife's oldest friends, and I'm fairly certain she would stab me in my sleep if I dared screw you over." He leaned in and rested his elbows on the table. "Speak as freely as you like. Off the record. None of it's going anywhere."

Wes chuckled, a sort of sad realization dawning on him, causing a lump to form in his throat. "Brynn's the only one who abandoned *me*, you know? I just realized that. And I don't mean . . . Well, obviously I don't have any hard feelings now. What right would I have to have any hard feelings toward anyone? But yeah. She left before I left. She might be the one person in this whole entire town I don't owe an apology to."

"She would jump at the chance to see you. I promise you that. Once Addie came back, I think Brynn and Laila sort of felt like you were the only thing missing. Not that they could voice those feelings to anyone except each other and me, of course."

"No." Wes laughed. "Obviously not. I imagine saying my name in this town was sort of like saying 'Macbeth' in a theater—"

"Laila likened it to saying 'Voldemort,' but yeah, same idea."

Wes liked Sebastian right way. Just as he had somehow instinctively known he would. He looked forward to getting to know him better and even sharing with him and Brynn how Brynn's well-publicized journey back to Adelaide Springs had begun breaking through the layers he and Wray had built around themselves. But a quick glance at his watch informed him he only had ten minutes of privacy left.

"Off the record, I'm dropping out of the presidential race. And I'm hoping you can be the one to help me announce it on the record."

Sebastian held his position, nodding slowly, and then he stood up and stepped behind the bar and poured himself a cup of coffee. He took a gulp of it while he stood, then walked back over, sat back down, and set the coffee on the table in front of him. "Can I ask why?"

"Why you?"

"Why drop out?"

It was then that Wes realized he was having one of the most important conversations of his career, if not his entire life, with perhaps the most respected journalist of his generation, and he was wearing a shirt that looked like it had been run over by a dirt bike, and then by a dump truck for good measure, just in case it wasn't dead yet.

It said a lot to him about Sebastian's character that he had managed to maintain eye contact with him.

"A divorce filing is going to be made public—pretty soon, I'm guessing. Honestly, I don't know how it's stayed concealed this long."

"Well, for the first few months I imagine it was held up in very confusing probate. After that, from what I understand, Wray's family filed a successful motion to have the case sealed or deferred or something. I'm not sure I have all the facts about that just yet."

Wes's mouth opened, but no words came out. Sebastian sat there slowly drinking his coffee, waiting.

"So . . . you . . . How do you know? It's . . . Are you saying it's already public?"

"Not yet, but it's about to be. I got a lead in my inbox from an untraceable source. Tuesday marks the expiration of the motion the family filed—"

"The family? You mean Andrea?"

"In the name of full disclosure, you should know Andi's my friend, so this part's a little awkward for me. But yeah. She's Wray's next of kin." Sebastian swallowed down another steaming gulp of coffee. "And it's an annulment. Not a divorce. That's an important distinction, since annulments in Connecticut have to go through superior court."

Wes had been a wreck that day. There was no denying that. He hadn't slept, and his wife—his best friend—was dying. But he hadn't been so out of it as to accidentally file for an annulment instead of a divorce.

"No. I definitely filed for divorce."

Sebastian's eyes rose slowly over the cup in front of his face. "I'm sorry. Did you say *you* filed for divorce?"

Was it possible Sebastian Sudworth wasn't quite as sharp as he seemed on TV? "Yes. On August 6, while Wray was literally on her deathbed, I went to the courthouse and filed for divorce. And if you want a more concise answer to your previous question about why I'm dropping out of the race, there it is."

"Huh." Sebastian kept studying Wes while he drank his coffee. And the silence went on a little longer than Wes was comfortable with.

"What? What is it? What does 'huh' mean?"

Sebastian cleared his throat and set his coffee back on the table. Then he leaned forward again into his prior posture, arms on the table. "Are you really unaware that Wray filed for an annulment on July 30?"

Stunned silence permeated the room, and Wes felt all the color drain from his face as his mouth once again fell open and no words came out.

"Okay, I'm going to take that as a yes."

"I don't understand," Wes managed to get out with a croaky voice. "Why would she do that?"

"Why did *you* do that?" Sebastian countered.

"For her. I . . . In retrospect I don't know if it was the right move or not. I really don't know. But at the time, I did it for her."

"Well, I don't know what to tell you, Wes. I never met Wray. I don't know anything about your marriage apart from what I read in an annulment filing. But if that's the case, I'd say it seems at least feasible to think that maybe she had the same idea. Is it possible she was doing it for you?"

Of course it was. *Of course it was.* He reached into the pocket of his slacks and pulled out his phone, and muscle memory scrolled him straight to her final voice mail to him.

July 30.

Of course it was.

*"Just . . . Babe, listen to me. Trust yourself. And if you can't trust yourself, trust me, just this one more time. It's going to be fine. You're going to be fine. Alright? And no matter what, I love you. For better or worse."*

Wes wiped his eyes with his shirtsleeve. This shirt deserved a humanitarian award of some kind or other for the day it had had. "On what grounds?"

"The annulment?" When Wes nodded, Sebastian answered, "Fraud. Based on her sexual orientation."

"It actually said that? I mean, Wray actually said that?"

"Yeah. It was all documented in the filing. And look, like I said, Andi's my friend. Doesn't mean I walk step for step with her on everything. Also doesn't mean I have all that much insight into what she was thinking. I've only talked with her a few times since Wray died. Since she left Adelaide Springs. So honestly, I don't know what she was thinking. I don't know if she was wanting to cover up her sister's sexual orientation or if she just wanted to make sure you didn't get out of footing the bill for the funeral. I really couldn't say, and it's not my place to try. But here's what I do know." Sebastian scooted his chair closer to the table. "I've been following your career a long time, and I've seen you bring together politicians from both sides of the aisle to work on bills that matter. I've seen your polling numbers, and I know that this country somehow agrees on you when they can't agree on whether or not the sky is blue. And yeah, I get it—it would not have been a good look to have filed for divorce from your dying wife, especially if you weren't willing to out her, which I assume . . ."

"I never would have. Absolutely not."

"And for my money, that shows somewhat uncommon integrity among your peers, my friend." Sebastian shrugged and scratched at his beard before stretching his arms and settling folded hands over the back of his head. "Look, I believe in being an unbiased voice, and I'll never publicly support any candidate. Not even my wife's childhood friend. But I'm just saying, this is manageable. If nothing else, Wray gave you a choice. Maybe you drop out of the race, maybe you don't, but you do have a choice now."

"Surely my divorce filing is still going to come out—"

"So what? You were just making an emotional attempt to help fulfill her dying wish."

Wes couldn't believe he was listening. Considering. He couldn't believe that his pulse was picking up speed and his imagination was running away with him. Wray had given him a choice. He knew he should be grateful—he *was* grateful, for what he knew was her heart behind it, if nothing else—but everything had sure seemed a lot simpler when there were no options.

He needed to talk to Addie. And his heart beat even faster at the realization that Addie was in his life. Once again, after so long, Addie could be the person he talked to. He wouldn't make the same mistake he'd made twenty-two years ago. He wouldn't try to figure it out on his own. Never again.

"I really appreciate this, Sebastian." He lifted from his chair and stretched out his arm. "Truly."

"Of course." Sebastian stood and shook his hand. "And whatever you decide, I will happily sit down for an interview. It's an interesting story either way."

Wes punched him on the arm as he passed, headed to the door. Sebastian stopped him before he got there.

"Hey, Senator? Can I ask you one more question? Still off the record?"

Wes turned to face him. "Sure."

"What's the status with you and Addie? I know there's a lot of history there. And based on the buzz at the Bean this morning . . ."

He whistled through his teeth. "That's how you get the Pulitzers, huh? Go straight for the jugular?"

Sebastian laughed and raised his hands in front of him. "If it's too personal . . ."

"It's not that. I'm just honestly not too sure yet." Wes shrugged, then coughed to clear away the lump that formed in his throat at the sudden composure-threatening memory of her legs wrapped around him. "We've definitely made progress."

"Got it." Sebastian downed the last drop of his coffee, then picked up his cup and Wes's and began walking them behind the bar. "You know, the thought does occur . . . Second chance with a childhood sweetheart . . . dedicated public servant . . . air force veteran . . . young widow of another dedicated public servant . . ." He stacked the cups in the bin and shrugged.

"Sounds like the stuff of which First Lady dreams are made," Cole said as he came out of the kitchen, wiping his hands on a towel and then throwing the towel over his shoulder. Wes and Sebastian turned and looked at him in surprise, and Cole raised his hands in front of him. "Sorry, wasn't eavesdropping. I didn't hear anything before ten seconds ago. But it wasn't difficult to get the gist of what was being said."

"Well, don't worry. We're a long way from even thinking about any of that." That was the right thing to say, he was pretty sure. At least to Cole. Even if the reality was that now that the seed of a thought had been planted, he might have difficulty remembering how to think about anything else. "Thanks again, Sebastian. We'll talk soon." He nodded his head toward Cole. "See you, man."

"Hey, before you go . . . I want to apologize. For last night, I mean."

"For what?" Wes shook his head. "No, you don't owe me any apologies. I really appreciate you being willing to—"

"No, listen, Wes." Cole came around from behind the bar and stood between Wes and Sebastian. "This one . . . I mean, *you.* This one's tricky. For me. You know? It, um . . ." He ran his hands through his hair, then leaned up against the bar. "It might take me a little time. Okay? But Seb reminded me of something I said when Brynn came back." Cole stared at the floor for a moment and then looked up at Sebastian. "I forgot what it was." He turned to Wes. "Which is a shame, because I've apparently gotten pretty eloquent in my old age."

"He said that you don't refuse to take a chance on the people you love just because there might be some pain involved."

Cole nodded at Sebastian. "That's right. That was it."

Wes cleared his throat. "Darn near poetic."

"It was, wasn't it?" Cole smiled at Wes as their eyes met. "So yeah, things turned out okay with Brynn. And the fact is, you're my family every bit as much as she is. I'm willing to take a chance." He pushed himself off the bar and stretched his arm toward Wes.

Wes took Cole's offered hand and shook it. "I can't ask for more than that. Thank you."

Sebastian came up between them as they shook hands and placed an arm on each of their shoulders. "You know what? I think I know the perfect way to commemorate this beautiful moment."

Wes looked to him with curiosity, but Cole groaned and pulled away. "Don't fall for it, Wes." He looked at his watch and then walked to the door and unlocked it. "He's going to suggest—"

"Karaoke," Sebastian said, in unison with Cole. "What do you say, Senator? A little 'Delta Dawn,' perhaps?"

Wes turned to Cole with a furrowed brow and chuckled. "I guess I don't get the joke."

"Oh, if only he were joking," Cole said before patting Wes on the shoulder and calling out, "Welcome home, pal," as he headed back to the kitchen.

## CHAPTER 24

# ADDIE

**4,757 Days Since She Met the Love of Her Life**

"Thanks, Neil." I opened the door of the Bronco and stretched out one leg before adding, "Are you sure you don't need me today?" Sunday evenings were my one unreachable time. That had been well established during my months back in Adelaide Springs, even if only my dad knew where I was during those few hours. But I was usually good to be on call during the morning and afternoon.

"Nah, thanks. I'm really half tempted to just run back to the office, grab my laptop, and then park in front of the inn until that guy calls again. Surely it's just a matter of time."

I stepped out fully and then turned back and leaned my arm against the frame. "Yeah, what was your impression of him? Any weird vibes?"

Neil shook his head. "Not weird, no. No weirder than any other big-city business types."

"Did he tell you what he's doing here?"

"No. I barely got two words out of him. He definitely wasn't the 'What do you recommend I do while I'm in town?' type of tourist." Neil leaned across the seat toward me and spoke more quietly. "And did you get a load of that plane as it flew in?"

"No. He mentioned he flew privately—"

"My hoity-toity aunt from Tampa flew privately that one time she visited us a couple years ago, and it was still just a janky charter service that had you feeling under your seat for loose screws that had fallen out. The plane this guy flew in on?" He whistled through his teeth. "This was not that. Roland said it was the same kind of private jet Tony Stark has in *Iron Man*, but he was exaggerating a lot. It was just some little Cessna, I think, but still . . . pretty sweet."

"And it just dropped him here, of all places? Were they grounded for mechanical reasons or something?"

Neil sat back up. "Oh, maybe. Hadn't thought of that, but could be. The plane is still at the airport, so that would make sense, I guess."

I nodded. "Yeah, that's got to be it. And it would certainly help explain why Mr. Brewster wasn't in the best of moods. In fact, all things considered, he was a lovely guy. Probably a lot nicer than I would be if I got stuck here." I bit my tongue to hold in all the jokes I wanted to make about that explaining my occasional bouts of crabbiness over the past year and simply thanked Neil again and shut the door.

A gray cloud passed over the sun just as I stepped onto the sidewalk, and the instant temperature drop reminded me I'd left my coat at the inn. But doggone it if I didn't feel pretty warm again just two seconds later when the door to Milo's opened and Wes stepped out.

"Well, hi there."

My voice took him off guard, and he appeared confused for just the length of a blink as his eyes rose from the sidewalk to my face. As soon as he registered my presence, a smile spread across his face, and I couldn't help but smile right back, like a giddy mirror with a crush.

"Hi there, yourself. I've missed you."

"It's been less than an hour."

"Well . . ." He stuffed his hands into his pockets and took a couple of ambling steps toward me. "In fairness, I've been missing you for over half my life. Might take me a minute to shake the feeling."

I chuckled, wishing I could turn away to hide the heat I felt rising in my cheeks. "That's not true."

"What's not true?"

I shook my head. "Nothing. That was a nice, romantic thing to say, and I don't need to pick it apart and analyze its accuracy. Your Honor, I request that 'That's not true' be stricken from the record and replaced with 'Aww!'" My smile grew wider as I took a step back from his continued approach.

"What? You don't believe I've missed you for over half my life? Do the math, Addie. It is, sadly enough, true."

I took another step back—not that I wanted to get away from him, but I felt like I was hanging on the precipice between needing a little distance and tackling him to the ground and forcing him to make out with me on the sidewalk of Main Street. A choice had to be made.

"It's not the 'twenty-two is greater than eighteen' math I question, Senator. It's more your overly generous rounding up of the numbers."

It was too soon to be joking about all of this, right? Even in a harmless, flirty way, after the events of the morning in which, I was pretty sure, I had forgiven him for the atrocities of twenty-two years ago—or maybe even realized that I'd pretty much granted him forgiveness before he ever asked for it. It still felt wrong to discuss it so freely. So casually.

*No, wait.* It *felt* like it should feel wrong. It felt like almost everyone I knew would think it was wrong. (Of course some of them would also think it was wrong of me to forgive him. Or talk with him at all. Or do anything other than drop him into a shark tank strapped to a freshly slaughtered sea mammal of some kind or other.) But as he took one more slow, deliberate step toward me, and I took one last step back, bumping up against Beulah's hood, I couldn't have forced any of it to feel wrong if I had tried.

"I know it's my own fault, so I'm really not seeking any sympathy here, Addie." He stepped closer, and my breath caught in my throat. There was nowhere else for either of us to go. "But believe me when I say I missed you every single one of those eight thousand days."

I swallowed hard as his eyes fluttered down to study my lips. "You did the math?"

"Okay, I confess. That was just an estimation. Feels about right, though."

His fingertips landed on my hips and inched me toward him. And I swear I tried to turn my head to see if anyone was around, but the only parts of me that could move were my hands, landing on his chest and slipping up around his shoulders, and my feet, gladly helping him pull me as closely as he dared.

"Remember what your mom used to say?"

His lips got closer to mine as he smiled. "Which thing in particular?"

"'Affection in private displays great respect; before it goes public, take time to reflect.'"

He dropped his arms from around me and took a step back as the laughter began, and I smiled as I studied the activated creases at the corners of his scrunched-up eyes. "She was so weird!"

"Yep. The best kind of weird."

*The best kind of weird.*

That was the perfect way to describe Marietta Hobbes, and it was the perfect way to describe how it felt to be standing on Main Street in Adelaide Springs, once again hypnotized by the beauty of her son and all the affection I felt for him. And while it had just been a few seconds ago that I wanted nothing more than to kiss him again and to invite the passion that had overtaken us at the inn to work its magic once more, I was suddenly overcome by desires that somehow felt so much more intimate—even if this PDA would scandalize no one.

"Hey," I whispered, and he raised his head to look at me, the grin still spread out across his entire face. Then I looped my arms around his neck, crushed my body against his, and hugged him. And there was a brief moment (if the way he nuzzled his lips against my ear and the way his fingers danced across my back are to be believed) that he remained caught up in the rekindling fire of the minute before. But then his breathing regulated, and his shoulders relaxed, and his arms enveloped me, and I knew we were on the same emotional page. In embracing each other, we were embracing both the love and heartache of the past and the unexpected comfort and solidarity of the present.

"You know I *didn't* miss you all of those days. Right?" I whispered into his ear. "I mean, it's a romantic sentiment and all, and I'm sorry to not be able to play along, but I cut it off at about the twenty-five-hundred mark."

He sighed against me. "That makes me really sad."

My jaw tightened, and the tops of my ears began burning as I pulled back to look at him, and the words came rushing out of me before I even mapped them out in my head. "You don't seriously think I sat around mourning the loss of you *forever*, do you?"

His eyes flew open. "No. Of course not. I didn't mean—"

"Because, seriously, if so . . . how *dare* you?"

I attempted to pull away, but his arms didn't loosen their grip. And truthfully, I didn't try too hard. The love and heartache of the past. The comfort and solidarity of the present. It was all still there somehow, and as much as I sort of thought I needed to be offended, I suddenly wanted nothing more than for the sadness in his eyes to go away.

I spoke again, just as confident in my words and the emotions behind them as before, but I was okay letting the fight that had been building up in me slip away. "Look, I like the way things are going with us. I do. But I need you to understand that as much as I loved you then—and trust me, I did love you so unbelievably much—I don't love you now."

His eyes were locked with mine, and it should have been so awkward, but I was as comfortable sharing intimate space and air with him as I was sharing the back seat of my vehicle with total strangers. And that was the truth of it, wasn't it? Yes, the developments were new. Forgiveness was new. But Wes and I were not.

"I'm not trying to be cruel here," I continued, much more gently. "The fact is, I thought you were the love of my life. And then I met the love of my life. To me, that doesn't minimize the way I felt about you. It really doesn't. It was every bit as real and true. But I did move on. And Joel—"

"Addie, can I say something? Please?"

I gulped away the throat-closing feeling that welled up at the softness in his eyes and his voice and nodded.

"I understand that Joel is the great love of your life. I'm sorry if I gave the impression a minute ago that I thought you should have stayed hung up on me forever. Nothing could be further from the truth. I *know* that what we had was real and true, and I know now that it was ridiculous to think you would just immediately move on. But at the time, I had myself convinced it wouldn't be all that difficult for you. So I don't know how accurate you were being with that twenty-five-hundred-days comment—"

"Two thousand six hundred and forty-two."

I really needed to be more careful about keeping all these day calculations to myself so I didn't develop a reputation as the Rain Man of the Gregorian calendar.

He nodded slowly and bit the inside of his cheek. "I would give anything to be able to go back and take away those two thousand six hundred and forty-two days of pain. I'm so sorry."

"Hey . . ." I rested my hand on his face and brushed my thumb along his cheekbone. "That's the past."

He tilted his head and fluttered kisses along the inside of my wrist before grabbing my hand in both of his and holding it against his chest. "But I just need you to know—and I promise I'm not trying to prove anything here or say anything other than the words I'm actually saying. I just need you to know that you *are* the love of my life. I never got over you, and then I gave up on trying. And I really am so glad you found Joel. And I'm so sorry you lost him. Nothing I ever say or do will be about trying to replace him or surpass him or anything ridiculous like that. It's just . . . I do want you to understand you're it for me." He raised my hand to his lips again and held my fingers against them. "You're just . . . *it*."

I cleared my throat. "Well, um, I have to say, that does help me understand a bit more why you married a lesbian."

I instantly began wondering if I could forgo my usual Celebrate Recovery addiction small group that evening and launch a new group instead. ("I'm Addie, and I struggle with alcohol addiction and an overwhelming need to avoid moments of vulnerability by making bad and usually inappropriate jokes.") But Wes began laughing right away, thank goodness.

"You're not entirely wrong."

I leaned my forehead onto his chest. "No, I'm sorry. It sounds like you and Wray were a lot more than . . . I don't know." I still didn't understand what exactly they had been, really, but he had clearly cared about her very deeply. "I don't mean to sound disrespectful about any of that."

He wrapped his arms around my shoulders and sighed. "Look, I get it. And the truth is, yeah, Wray was fully aware of how I felt about you. She was the only person I never had to hide that from. I told you it worked for us, and that was a big part of the reason why. She and I were on the same page, working toward the same things." He took a step back and looped his hands around my neck, his wrists resting on my shoulders. "Maybe even more than I knew, as it turns out."

I looked up at him. "What do you mean?"

Wes exhaled and shook his head. "Well, according to what I just found out from—"

"Now hold on. Just settle down."

We both looked down Main Street at the sound of Jo's voice, but it wasn't Jo who kept our attention. She was calling after my dad, who was hurrying toward us faster than I'd seen him move in decades.

"Get your hands off of her!" he shouted, and Wes pulled away and raised his hands into the air.

At any other time, under any other circumstances—with any other looks on Wes's face or my dad's—I would have made some joke about my dad treating us like children and Wes sort of acting like one. But as Wes whispered, "I'm so sorry," out of the corner of his mouth,

I understood he wasn't stuck in the past at all. Not right then. He did, however, fully understand that the present had just been made a bit more difficult.

"Dad, just relax."

"Relax? *Relax*, Adelaide?" He reached us and immediately got in Wes's face. I couldn't remember Wes ever being quite as tall as my dad, though he'd gotten pretty close with his last growth spurt I had been present for, but now he had a good inch or more on him. "How dare you even show your face in this town?"

Jo caught up finally and began pulling on Dad's arm, attempting to get his finger out of Wes's face, but ultimately not getting him to budge. "Doc, you stop this right now."

Wes, meanwhile, put up no resistance, but he certainly didn't cower. "This really isn't how I hoped our reunion would go, Doc—"

"*Reunion?* Is that what this is to you? Do you think you get to come back here and say hello to old friends and get caught up and pick right back up like nothing ever happened?" He shoved Wes toward the wall of the restaurant, causing me to gasp and Jo to run inside—for reinforcements, I discovered a moment later when she came back out with Cole and Sebastian, Laila trailing close behind. It was all happening so quickly, and by this time Wes's back was against the wall, and the front of his shirt—golly, that poor shirt—was clenched in my dad's fists.

"Hey, Doc, why don't you come inside and cool off?" Cole placed a hand on my dad's shoulder, but nothing changed.

"I get it," Wes told him. Then he swallowed hard. "I get it, Doc. You hate me. You *should* hate me. Can we please just go talk—"

"You're smarter than this, Adelaide," my dad said, though he never turned his attention from Wes. "You know he can't be trusted. Why in the world would you let him waltz back in here like nothing ever happened?"

"That's not what I'm doing, Doc," Wes said.

It was Sebastian's turn to step forward, and he went with a little more forceful approach than Cole's attempt. He grabbed both of my dad's shoulders and pulled him back. "Don't do something you're going to regret."

I'd never seen my dad in a physical altercation with anyone in my entire life. I'd never even seen him angry the way he was now, to the point that his ears were burning red and he had a crazed, intimidating look in his eyes. *Intimidating.* I had always placed him on a pedestal. I respected him. I honored him. I looked up to him. But I couldn't remember a time in my life when I had ever been intimidated by him.

And I wasn't going to allow that to start now.

"Daddy, *stop it!*" I shouted—not *thrilled* that I'd gone with "Daddy," which I feared made me sound a little too much like a teenager wanting to borrow the car keys, but satisfied with my tone overall. And the fact that every last one of them turned to face me helped confirm that I'd nailed it. "You stop it right now." I hurried over and squeezed my shoulder into the space between them, facing my dad. "You say I'm smarter than this? Well, you're *better* than this. If you want to talk, Wes is offering to sit down and talk with you. That's a lot more generous than *I'm* feeling right now. But this stupid, childish machismo is *not* how we're going to handle this. Do you understand me?"

We glowered at each other until he dropped his hands, and then I reached behind me and grabbed Wes's hand. "Come on. Let's go."

"Addie, hang on," Wes said softly as I pulled him toward Beulah. "If Doc wants to talk—"

"I don't," Dad grumbled from behind us.

"Let's go," I repeated and released his hand as I climbed into Beulah's passenger seat. Yes, because Wes already had the keys, and yes, because I was pretty sure Beulah's antique accelerator couldn't handle the speeds my adrenaline might have made me drive. But mostly—and I'm not proud of it—because I knew that seeing Wes climb into the driver's seat of his beloved truck and driving away with his beloved little girl would really tick my dad off.

## CHAPTER 25

# WES

**24 Years Since the Sex Talk**

Neither of them said a word until they pulled up in front of the Atwater home, where Wes had driven without really thinking about it. He certainly hadn't thought about *how* to get there. He hadn't been there since he was eighteen years old, and the route was still as familiar to him as the view from the steps of the Lincoln Memorial at sunrise. That was his favorite spot in all of DC, even though he was always just a little bit ashamed of himself for picking such a predictable location. But the fact was there was a reason every gift shop sold posters of that exact view and tours charged extra to groups that wanted to be right there right then. It was breathtaking.

When he'd first been elected to the Senate, he'd had so many sleepless nights that he had actually asked Wray, "How long will I survive if I never sleep again?" He hadn't meant how long would his career survive. He'd legitimately wondered how long he could keep living that way. The walks had been her idea. He would get up in the middle of the night and walk around their subdivision. Then when those walks grew monotonous, he started driving to Capitol Hill and walking around all the tourist locations in the dark, when no one else was around. If he actually got tired enough to sleep, he would go to his office and sleep on the couch for an hour or two.

One night about four months into his first term, he'd sat on the steps of the Lincoln Memorial at 2:00 a.m. and rested his head against a column, and he'd awoken with the beauty of the sunrise-lit pink and orange Washington Monument bouncing off the Reflecting Pool in front of him, cherry blossoms in bloom as far as the eye could see. It had been his longest night of sleep since Inauguration Day. From that point on, that was his spot. It got more difficult to get there as he regained the ability to sleep, since he was becoming more and more recognizable in the light of day, but he made a point to wear a ball cap and a hoodie and slip on a pair of sunglasses and head over with a cup of coffee in time for sunrise as often as he could.

He shifted Beulah into Park and unbuckled his seat belt. "How ya doin'?" he asked, turning to face Addie.

Her forehead rested against the window, and she was staring out at nothing. "I've never seen him like that."

"I know." He exhaled and reached out to gently rub her back. "What can I say? I provoke passionate responses in people." Addie cocked an eyebrow and slowly turned her head toward him. "It's true. Just look at my polling data. People love me or hate me. There is no in between."

He tried to make jokes because it seemed like what she would want him to do. It was what she would do if she felt up to it, he was pretty sure. But the truth was, he was feeling a brand-new heartbreak for the first time in a while. It wasn't that he'd been expecting Doc to welcome him back with open arms, of course. But he'd really thought he'd get the chance to sit down with him and at least try to talk it out. They'd always been able to talk.

When his mom was dying and all the other adults in town were showing their love for Wes by making him cookies and saying things like, "Let us know if you need anything"—which they sincerely meant but which also clearly demonstrated they didn't know what he needed any more than Wes did—Doc had talked to him. He'd walked him through test results and explained the chemotherapy process to him. He'd also taught him things his mom hadn't gotten around to showing him yet, like balancing a checkbook and negotiating payment arrangements for hospital bills.

In one of the more uncomfortable conversations of Wes's life, Doc had talked with him about the birds and the bees. And though he had wanted to climb under the table or maybe move to Uganda or something, Doc had respected him enough to talk to him man to man. Ultimately, he hadn't walked away mortified by an awkward conversation with his girlfriend's dad so much as doubled down on his levels of respect for Doc *and* Doc's daughter.

And when he asked for Doc's permission to marry Addie, they'd been able to sit down and have a calm, mature conversation about all the reasons why Doc thought they were rushing things and Wes believed they weren't. Once again, he'd respected him enough to hear him out and let his trust in Wes win the day.

Doc no doubt looked back on that as a conversation he wished he could take another stab at.

"You were about to tell me something." Addie sat up and faced him, and he ignored the temptation to smile at the red circle left on her forehead by the cold window.

"When?"

"Right before my dad came flying at you like Liam Neeson ready to demonstrate his particular set of dad skills."

Wes chuckled. "Oh. Yeah. Well, I'm not sure now's the time."

"Come on, please?" Addie rested her hand on his knee. "Distract me."

Her hand touching his leg was certainly doing plenty to distract *him*. He cleared his throat. "Okay, well, I met with Sebastian Sudworth—"

"Sebastian was there!" She slapped herself on the forehead and seemed to get momentarily distracted trying to make sense of why part of her skin was so cold before dropping her hand and moving on. "In all the hullabaloo I sort of forgot to even take note of that. Is that why Laila needed to see you?"

"Yeah. I guess Jo was putting in a good word for me over breakfast this morning." They both rolled their eyes in unison. "Sebastian had been hoping to talk with me, too, I guess."

"Why?"

"Ready for this?"

Addie grimaced. "I don't know. Am I?"

"Wray filed for an annulment about a week before I filed for divorce."

She did a double take and then tilted her head as she asked, "Aren't there only a few specific things that are grounds for an annulment? Like, don't you have to discover you're first cousins or impotent or something?"

"Or I suppose you can commit fraud by leading your husband to believe you're interested in men."

"Which Wray didn't."

Wes sighed. That was indeed one of the last remaining morally sticky wickets to confront. "No. She didn't." All the same . . . "But she filed. And she listed that as the reason."

Addie's eyes flew open. "Oh! So you don't have to worry about not being able to acknowledge the reason you filed for divorce."

"Exactly."

"So does that mean . . ." He watched her process the information, her eyes darting quickly from thought to thought but never really breaking their contact with his. "You can still run for president? I mean . . . you can. You can still run for president." Air escaped from her lips in the instant before she contorted them into a slightly upturned sort of something that he was pretty sure she had meant to be a smile. "You're running for president."

"I really don't know. As Sebastian said, Wray left me options where I thought none existed. I was hoping . . . You know . . . I was hoping we could talk about it."

"You and Sebastian?"

He shook his head. "No, you and me."

"Oh. Of course. Sure. Yeah, we can talk about it."

She once again contorted her face into that almost smiling expression and then pulled her eyes away and faced forward.

Both of their worlds had completely changed in the span of this one day, and it was still a few hours until sunset. What could she possibly be thinking? She had to know he'd meant what he'd said. She was it for him. If she was willing to keep moving forward with him, there was nowhere he had any interest in going unless they were together. That included the White House. But he knew she had also meant what *she'd* said. She wasn't in love with him. Not anymore and not yet. They'd had eighteen years of getting to know each other, so admittedly, they hadn't had to waste a lot of time on pleasantries over the past couple of days. But really, they were brand-new. They carried the comfort and intimacy of the past in harmony and tension with the self-consciousness and uneasiness of being strangers.

He probably at least needed to ask her out before he broached the idea of them running the country together.

"Addie, will you go on a date with me?"

*There we go. That* was an Addie Atwater smile. "A date, huh?"

He chewed on his lip, suddenly legitimately nervous for reasons he didn't understand. Maybe she would think this was stupid. Maybe she would say no.

Well, okay. Maybe he *did* understand the reasons.

"Yeah." He tried again after his voice cracked. "Yeah. Yes. I just thought maybe that would be the natural next step— *Hey*, stop laughing!"

Of course once she started laughing, he couldn't help but join in. That certainly didn't make things any easier. And of course, at the very same time, it reminded him that being with her was the easiest thing in the world. "*You* try being a forty-one-year-old man asking your former fiancée out on a first date."

"Your former fiancée whom you spent a good portion of the day making out with."

"Yes! Exactly. This isn't easy, what I'm trying to do. Show some humanity."

She unbuckled her seat belt and slid over to him and placed her hands on both sides of his face. "Of course I'll go on a date with you." She pulled him to her and kissed him, and having learned his lesson that morning, Wes didn't waste any time at all before wrapping his arms around her, dipping her slightly toward the crook of his shoulder, and making sure her brain didn't have time to misinterpret his tempo as lack of desire to kiss her back.

"Dinner? Tonight?" he whispered against her lips a bit later.

"Oh."

And with that, her lips were no longer engaged. He adjusted his shoulder and helped her back to a fully upright position. "What is it? Is that no good? Would you rather not be seen in public with me just yet?"

She smirked at him. "Wesley. I was canoodling with you on Main Street to the point that my dad was prepared to engage in fisticuffs."

"You're so weird."

"The point is I guarantee every single person in Adelaide Springs is now fully aware of the happenings of the day. Being seen in public with you does not intimidate me. I just can't tonight. I, um . . . I have to go to South Fork. For a meeting. Or not a meeting exactly. A group thing that I'm part of. On Sundays. And before you ask why I'm being weird—"

"You're *always* weird."

"About *this*, I mean." She sat back, putting a little more distance between them. "It's a support group thing. And it's not that I've been avoiding telling you. It just hadn't come up yet."

He grinned at her and shrugged. "Addie, I think that's great. Seriously. Really great. I, um . . . Would it be possible . . . I mean, could I come with you?" He covered his eyes and lowered his head. "Never mind. Forget I said that. I just meant because it probably wouldn't hurt *me* to do some grief counseling or whatever, too, but it probably came across like I just wanted to tag along with you to *your* grief thing, and *yowsers*—that's not cool. Please forget I said that. Just, um, maybe call me when you get back? If you want, I mean. Or actually, are you going to be at the inn again? No pressure, regardless."

Addie placed both her hands on his arm and said, "No . . . come with me."

He raised his eyes and studied her. "Are you sure?"

She cleared her throat and swallowed before nodding. "Yes. Definitely. And I'll tell you more about it on the way. Sound good?"

Nearly fifty miles round trip in a vehicle with her *and* their new relationship could start out with transparency and a focus on healing together? "Sounds good."

"Okay. Good." She nodded once and then leaned in for one more quick kiss. "I need some time to clean up. You take Beulah and pick me up at five thirty." She opened the door and jumped out, closing the door behind her. Just before she walked away, she tapped on the passenger-side window, and he leaned across to roll it down.

"Yes, ma'am?"

"Don't take this the wrong way, but maybe you could give that shirt an honorable send-off before being seen in public again."

---

Wes whistled all through his shower, and nondescript tunes morphed into standards. Classics. Frank Sinatra and Dean Martin. A little bit of Bobby Darin—the ballads, not the "Splish Splash" stuff. When had he become a ballads kind of guy? he wondered as he rinsed the shampoo from his hair.

In the old days, he'd considered himself to be much cooler than that. Of course in the old days he hadn't realized how cool the Sinatras and the Martins and the Tony Bennetts were. Now he saw no shame in admitting it. But once upon a time, "cool" had been Green Day and Nirvana. Cool had been The Cranberries—though of course he had been far too cool to own up to that one.

Throwing a football down the field to Cole while Addie, Laila, and Brynn cheered on the sideline, Soundgarden blaring. Slow dancing with Addie to every Radiohead song that came on the radio, whether it had any sort of beat to dance to or not. Indulging Addie when she didn't understand why Foo Fighters shouldn't be classified as a boy band, and splurging on an *NSYNC concert in Denver so she could finally understand the difference.

He had so many memories associated with music, and then it was like there were twenty-two years of silence.

He knew he and Wray had danced at their wedding, but for the life of him he couldn't remember the music that had accompanied them. Something made him think it had been in Italian. French, maybe. They'd gone to concerts at the Kennedy Center and Carnegie Hall, but it had always been about being seen, not making memories. And as much as he had loved spending time with Wray, those evenings were certainly never about enjoyment.

*I hate opera.*

Wes realized there was a possibility he had never been as sure of anything in his life as he was of that, but it had never occurred to him until just then, as he was stepping out of the shower. It had never occurred to him to have any sort of opinion about opera whatsoever. He wrapped a towel around his waist and grabbed a second towel to catch the beads of water as he flung them from his hair, and he smiled as he realized he was still whistling.

He raised a hand to the mirror to swipe away the steamy condensation, and as he did, he caught a glimpse of himself. More than catching a glimpse of himself, it felt as if he were catching a glimpse of the past. The worry—the constant worry—was gone from his eyes. For this moment in time, however brief, there were no thoughts of opinion polls or cabinet appointments or the wooing of donors and voters. The tiny lines at the corners of his eyes were still present, but for a change they seemed glad to be there. Perhaps they were relieved to be the results of an actual genuine smile with nary a photographer in sight.

In the mirror, right before his eyes, that actual genuine smile began to fade as the missing photographers, who were probably wondering where he was, reentered his thoughts—followed closely by opinion polls and cabinet appointments and donors and voters. Though who was he trying to kid? They hadn't ever left. Not really. *Could* they ever really leave?

Did he even want them to?

He opened the bathroom door, and a chill washed over him as the steam dissipated and he stepped into the dry, much cooler bedroom. But the chill continued—do you still call it a chill when the shudders throughout your body are tinged in warmth?—as he caught a glimpse of the future, every bit as bright and clear as the glimpses of the past had been.

*Addie.*

He grabbed his phone from its charging cable and strategically darted his eyes away from the screen until he got to Apple Music. He refused to look at the undoubtedly endless list of messages and missed calls from Phil. *Not yet.* He knew the bliss couldn't continue forever, but he wanted to hold on to it for as long as he possibly could. Instead, he flipped through his music library—album after album of artists and music that he couldn't remember ever liking. Maybe he had at one time or another, but he genuinely couldn't remember. Regardless, none of it fit his mood, and none of it fit what he wanted his life to be.

"Ah!" he exclaimed as he found one album he couldn't remember adding to his library and that he was certain he had never listened to. At least not since he got rid of his old iPod Nano from yesteryear. He hit Shuffle and allowed the long-forgotten sounds of Gin Blossoms to fill the room.

He began playing air guitar to the opening chords of "Follow You Down" and danced around the room, still-damp hair flinging beads of moisture everywhere as he jumped on the bed—a cross between a bratty child and a partying rocker. He honestly couldn't remember the last time he had heard the song, which made it all the more surprising that he knew every single note. Every single word. He hadn't even really liked Gin Blossoms in the beginning. But just as an *NSYNC concert had been Wes's attempt to show appreciation for the things Addie liked, Gin Blossoms had been her trying to understand his musical tastes. That was about as close as they had ever gotten in crossover appeal, so before long he was perfectly happy pretending to love them.

Before long he sort of *did* love them.

He jumped off the bed—air guitar still in hand—and turned his attention to getting dressed. He pulled his plain gray T-shirt over his head, having already thrown enough button-ups to fill a Men's Wearhouse into the corner of the room, and then slipped on a brand-new pair of Alexander McQueen jeans. What he would have given for a good old pair of Levi's right then so that he could fray the cuff or tear a hole in the knee without the guilt of destroying a pair of pants that cost as much as the 1996 Ford Windstar minivan with 125,000 miles that had been the first vehicle he bought with his own money—and his pride and joy all of senior year.

The song ended and "Allison Road"—just as distant but still so familiar—began next. This one he didn't know all the words to. In fact, the words "Allison Road" were the only ones he remembered, so he sang them at the top of his lungs each time those two words came around. It was just the soundtrack of a happier life. That's all there was to it. There were so many memories that he hadn't allowed himself to dwell on at any point throughout his adult life, but now they danced and mingled with new memories from the weekend and hope for the future.

Addie with him on the campaign trail. Addie holding the Bible on Inauguration Day. Addie with him on Air Force One. Addie living with him at the White House. Addie with him at the ribbon-cutting ceremony for his presidential library in fifteen years or so. Addie *with* him, the two of them making the world a better place together.

He sighed and muttered to himself, "Addie with you on a twenty-six-mile trip to South Fork, Colorado. How about we just focus on that for the time being?"

Yeah. Easier said than done. Because, yes, he loved her. Yes, he already knew he wanted to spend the rest of his life with her. Like he'd actually *always* wanted to spend the rest of his life with her. But it wasn't just that. It wasn't just emotion and sentimentality. Cole had hit the nail on the head.

Addie would go down in the history books as the greatest First Lady of all time. Wes was sure of it. And no, he didn't really need the help in the polls. Sure, there would be some fluctuation when news broke about Wray, and he would lose some support—though obviously not anything like what he had been anticipating before—but he didn't really see how it could be too much. And there would be some voters who would simply like him less when he was no longer single. There would be questions about how he could fall in love so quickly, but as Sebastian had said, they could offer up the childhood-sweethearts story.

Admittedly, it would be a little trickier to spin their backstory so he wasn't portrayed as too much of a villain for leaving her on their wedding day, but—

He felt the enthusiasm seep out of his smile and then just trickle its way out of the rest of him, and he sat on the edge of the bed, unsure of what had just happened.

Had he really just thought that? Had he actually just thought, even to himself, that he would need to figure out a way to spin the lowest moment of his life—the biggest regret in his life—in a way that would allow him to come out smelling like roses? He could almost hear Wray's voice saying, "*That's low even for you, Hobbes.*" He didn't want to think about what Addie's response might be.

And if he needed any further confirmation that he had to, as Wray would also advise him, run, not walk away, from those thoughts, he could suddenly picture the governor in front of him, beaming with pride.

"I won't do it," he murmured, bending over to slip on his socks and shoes. He was going to do it the right way, or he wasn't going to do it at all. And there was no reason, he told himself, that he couldn't do it the right way. He would be honest about the mistakes of his past. His opponents would use it, obviously, but if Addie was by his side, that would be what mattered. After all, if *she* could forgive him, what reason could anyone else possibly have for holding it against him?

"Eh." He wiggled his head back and forth, not too sure about the strength of that justification in his mind, but it was a start. He jumped up from the bed, grabbed his coat from the closet, made sure he had his wallet and all the keys he needed, and then headed to the door just as someone began pounding on the other side.

He opened it expecting to see Jo, who he figured would promptly tell him to keep the music down before also issuing a warning that Doc had put out a bounty on his head or something, but he didn't have time for lectures or bounties. The First Lady was waiting.

"Well, good evening, Senator." Phil stood in the hallway with a half-eaten chocolate-chip cookie in his hand. "So tell me, how do we want to spin this? 'Presidential candidate makes final trip to Colorado hometown before Super Tuesday' or 'MIA former front-runner for nomination tells American people, "Screw you!" as hopes for the Oval Office crash and burn into Colorado mountainside'?" He took a bite of his cookie and shrugged. "I'm ready to follow your lead on this one."

## CHAPTER 26

# ADDIE

### 8,303 Days Since They Last Ran Out of Gas

If there was one thing I knew for certain, it was that the food and the music were both better at Celebrate Recovery than they were at AA. It wasn't that AA hadn't been working for me. It had. In DC I'd actually really liked it. I'll be honest, I had been a little disappointed that I wasn't invited to be part of that super-exclusive Washington politico AA meeting that was disguised as a poker game in the basement of the White House. Of course I was also disappointed that that was nothing more than a plotline from *The West Wing*, so disappointment occasionally ran rampant. Still . . . I liked it. But if Adelaide Springs had any top-secret Alcoholics Anonymous meetings, I apparently hadn't made the list. And of course the thought was absurd, anyway. Adelaide Springs didn't know the meaning of the word *anonymous*.

But the weekly meeting in South Fork had been great. The drive was nice, and the people were nice, and everyone I knew there was someone I had met in the last year rather than someone I had known my entire life. That was nice.

When Wes called—no, I'm sorry, *texted*—to tell me he couldn't make it, I really didn't know whether to be disappointed or relieved. When he couldn't even be bothered to drive Beulah over to me himself and instead arranged for Neil to pick me up and drive me to the inn so I could take the truck, I started leaning a little more in the direction of relieved. He didn't even walk outside and kiss me goodbye as he handed me the keys. Nope. He just left the keys over the driver-side visor, and that was it. Not so much as a friendly wave from the porch.

I don't know what I'd been thinking inviting him anyway.

And still, it wasn't about hiding my alcoholism. Was I nervous about telling him? Sure. *Of course* I was nervous. But I wasn't putting it off. I'd been ready to tell him earlier, but he had assumed I was going to a grief support group. And Celebrate Recovery *does* have grief groups, and I'd spent a fair amount of time working through my grief on Sunday evenings as well. And when he'd wanted to come with me . . . well . . .

It only weirded me out to realize I was totally not weirded out by the idea of him coming with me. And that was when I knew. Or at least that was when I began to *think* that maybe he and I were actually heading somewhere. Sure, I'd already been thinking about spending more time with him. I'd already been realizing how much I liked all-grown-up Wes Hobbes. In fact, I'd say that I had been cautiously optimistic about a future with him—until about the time I found out he was running for president after all. (And no, he didn't come right out and say that, but it was pretty obvious where his mind was.) Because that couldn't work. I couldn't be part of that four- or eight-year plan. If I didn't want to stand in the way of that happening for him, then I couldn't afford to get too optimistic about the possibility of things happening for *us*.

Then he'd wanted to come with me. But he'd also felt like he made a mistake asking to come with me. He was real and transparent and vulnerable, and I *felt* it. Something about the fact that he was willing to put in the work. That he was already so naturally open with me. It just felt different. It felt like something I shouldn't think ahead too much on. Something I shouldn't give the answer to before the question had even been asked. I just needed to slow down my mind and take one step. And then another.

So I told him to come. And then I showered and got ready. And then I hurried downstairs and waited for him. And then I got a text that said, Can't make it after all. Neil's on his way to get you. Explain later. Sorry.

And then I had to admit to myself that maybe I hadn't forgiven him as completely as I thought. Maybe the past wasn't in the past as much as I'd been pretending it was. Because the very first thought I had after that text was, *Well, that's progress, I guess. At least he texted this time.*

"Good night," I said to various people on my way to the door after things wrapped up at nine. "Have a good week."

You absolutely could have knocked me over with all the breath it took to blow out a candle when I saw him stepping out of Jo's big red pickup truck in the parking lot of that little church in South Fork and walking toward me. Wearing jeans and a T-shirt under his unzipped coat. A ball cap. He still looked next-level handsome, like he would need absolutely nothing—not even a little powder on his nose—before he was ready to go live on national television or something. But he also looked, for the first time since he'd been back, like he belonged in our mountains again.

"Hey . . . What are you doing here?"

Clusters of people were congregated in the parking lot, but I noticed Wes didn't look around to see if any of them were looking at him. I'll admit it: that impressed me. He just walked straight toward me and said, "I'm really sorry to interrupt your group—"

"No, we just wrapped up." And dang it all if I wasn't super glad he was there. Relieved, even. When he canceled on me, I may have been trying to *convince* myself I was relieved more than I actually was relieved. But when he came anyway? Yeah, I was relieved.

It had been a real emotional boomerang of a day.

He held my elbow and pulled me aside, over toward Jo's truck. I wrapped my arms around myself to fend off the cold and swallowed hard. "I'm really glad you came."

"Addie, it's Doc."

I felt the throb of a nervous tic begin under my left eye as my arms dropped to my sides. "What about him?" And it was then that I saw it in his eyes. This wasn't about Wes being scared off by my protective dad, who had no doubt crossed a line. This was something else. "What is it?"

He held on to both of my arms and bent his knees so he could look into my eyes. And I'm not sure what *my* eyes looked like, but his were heavy and full of concern. "I'm going to drive you to Denver. They flew Doc to the hospital. I'm pretty sure he had a heart attack."

---

"This is all my fault," I said for probably the twentieth time just as Wes pulled onto Highway 285 and could finally drive at a speed more befitting the urgency of the situation. I scrolled through the messages on my phone, searching for something that wasn't there—just information—but Jo had only tried calling once while my phone was off for those three hours in South Fork. Rather than try again, she had called Wes and asked him if he knew where I was, and now here he was.

"It's not," he replied gently. "You know it's not. If anything . . ." He sat up a little straighter in his seat and checked his mirror before switching lanes. "No, you know what? He's going to be okay. And there's no point in feeling responsible. Ultimately, it's about arteries, right? Or blood flow or something?"

I placed my hand on his on the steering wheel and squeezed. "You're right. You're right. It's no one's fault."

*Except for mine.*

"So you said Jo's with him? In Denver, I mean?"

Wes nodded. "Yeah. Half the town tried to cram onto the plane, but—"

"Hang on. The plane? I assumed it was the Flight for Life helicopter. What plane did they—"

"My plane." I did a double take, and he began giving me the clarification I was seeking before I asked. "I mean, it's not really my plane.

I don't own it. It's more like a co-op jet. No, that's stupid. Maybe more like a time-share jet? Yeah, it's like a time-share." He activated his turn signal and passed an old Dodge Dakota struggling to make it up the mountain. "Except not really a time-share, because I get to use it as often as I want. Anyway, it was fueled up and ready to go, so it made the most sense."

I wasn't sure if anything about that information dump made sense, actually. "And how was he? Did you see him?"

"No. I didn't see him. Something made me think that maybe I wouldn't be the calming presence for him that I would hope to be." He glanced at me quickly and shrugged. "They were at Cole's restaurant, and Jo said Cole and Laila and Sebastian and everybody were around, and I guess your dad even talked them through what to do a little. Aspirin and such."

My hands were bunched up on my lap, holding my phone, and he reached over and placed his right hand over the cluster. "That sounded like a pretty good sign to me. If he was able to be his own doctor, that means he was awake and coherent and all of that."

He'd always had to be his own doctor. He'd always been everyone's doctor, of course, but apart from annual checkups with a doctor in Grand Junction, I couldn't remember him ever going to a doctor himself. Of course I also couldn't remember him ever being sick. Maybe he hadn't had time for it, or maybe I just hadn't been aware.

I pulled my phone out from under our hands, and Wes returned his hand to the wheel as I once again stared in frustration at a device that wasn't ringing. "Why hasn't anyone called? Should I call Jo, you think?"

"I really don't think you should. It's going to take a while to get him checked in once they get there, but you know she'll call when there's something to report. And you know what? I think it's a good sign if they aren't able to get him back right away."

I scoffed. "How is that good?"

"Because if it's an emergency, they will. But if they get there and Doc's doing okay . . . I mean, if they're busy treating broken bones and gunshot victims and people with weird things crammed into weird places because they aren't as worried about the picture-of-health that had a heart attack a little bit ago, how is that *not* a good sign?"

I chuckled softly under my breath. "You're all about the good signs tonight." I leaned as far as I could across the seat to try to rest my head on his arm. I got close enough for contact, but my seat belt wouldn't allow me to rest there.

He looked over at me and then glanced up into the rearview mirror before reaching out his hand and unbuckling my seat belt. "Why don't you come over here?"

He didn't have to ask me twice. I scooted into the center seat and buckled the lap belt across my waist as he stretched his arm behind me and wrapped it around my shoulder. I cozied into him as he muttered, "Much better."

I yawned, suddenly as tired as I had been in years, I was pretty sure. "This feels familiar."

"Driving with you was always one of my favorite things. Sometimes I wished we could just keep on going until we ran out of gas."

"I'm pretty sure a few times we *did* keep going until we ran out of gas."

"It was never enough." He kissed the top of my head. "We've got almost four hours to go. Why don't you get some sleep?"

"Jo might call," I protested through another yawn.

"I'll wake you."

"Who's going to help you watch for deer?"

"Jo has those deer whistle things on the front of the truck. I'll be okay."

I raised my right hand and rested it on his chest. "Okay." At least I think I said okay. I'm not sure if the word actually made it out of my mouth. At any rate, I'm pretty sure the last thing I meant to say—"Wes, why was the plane fueled and ready to go?"—got trapped inside when I noticed I could hear his heartbeat against my ear, and then my eyes fluttered shut.

CHAPTER 27

# ADDIE

**364 Days Since She Officially Stopped Being First Lady Material**

"Hey . . ." Wes woke me with a hushed tone and gentle pinches on my leg. "We're almost there."

I sat up, startled in spite of how carefully he had attempted to ease me into consciousness, and looked out the window. The lights of Denver shone all around—like a different world than the one we had come from, where a distant radio tower light on a mountain and the one intersection in town with traffic lights were the only things distracting you from the moon and stars at this time of night.

"Jo didn't call again, did she?"

Before I even asked, I knew she hadn't, of course. He would have awakened me, just as he had a couple of hours prior when Jo's first call managed to slip through while I miraculously had two bars of cell signal. They'd just been starting to get Dad checked into a room then, and she wasn't allowed to go back until that was all taken care of.

I tipped my wrist up to look at my watch. Two seventeen.

I leaned forward in my seat and curved my back and stretched as much as I could. After the call from Jo, I had moved back over by the window, which did provide plenty of support to lie against, but I hadn't slept anywhere near as peacefully without Wes's warmth against me and his arm around me.

"You doing okay?" I propped my knee up on the bench and my elbow on the back of the seat, then tilted my head over onto my hand and watched the city lights flash across his face. "I'm sorry I slept so much of the time."

"Don't be. I'm glad you were able to get some rest." He leaned forward and looked up at exit signs and then signaled to switch lanes.

"I bet you're used to sleepless nights. If you can ever actually get used to sleepless nights, that is."

He chuckled. "I have gotten sort of used to it, I guess. No one tells you that running for president is a lot of work. I thought it was going to be a lot of pie-eating contests and kissing babies. 'Hey, I like babies,' I told myself. 'Babies are cute.' And, you know, you get to travel a lot. But would you believe that *not once* has anyone let me pull over to see the world's biggest ball of twine or that park in Georgia with all the creepy doll heads? I've found that to be one of the most disappointing things about the gig. They should really be a little clearer in the job description."

"You mean the Constitution?"

"Yeah. The Founding Fathers dropped the ball on that one."

A couple of turns later, we were pulling into the hospital parking lot. "Want me to drop you off at the door?" he asked.

"No, I want to walk in with you, if that's okay."

He reached over and squeezed my knee. "Of course that's okay."

Thirty seconds later, Jo met us at the hospital door, took one look at our clasped hands, and muttered, "Nuh-uh. That is not okay. Your dad will have *another* coronary."

My breath caught, and Wes squeezed my hand tighter. "Don't say stuff like that, Jo. First of all, it's not like we're going to walk in there together when he's hooked up to machines and everything. You know us both better than that."

Jo spun on her heel and began leading us down a hallway past Admissions.

"Besides, I think we're both beating ourselves up enough for whatever role we might have played in all of this."

"Well, that's ridiculous. Neither of you caused this." Jo stepped into an elevator, and we followed. "Drinking eight cups of coffee a day and eating red meat for every meal caused this. Besides, he's been ignoring symptoms for weeks."

"He has?" I asked, a new, different wave of guilt beginning to pester me.

"Yeah, and don't you go thinking you should have seen it, Addie." Jo pushed the button, and the doors closed. "I've seen the man at least twice a day nearly every day for the past sixtysomething years, and a little bit ago he starts telling the doctor about fatigue and restlessness and pains and shortness of breath. Not for the past few hours or even the past couple days. No, for the past *month*. I guess maybe he just thinks that fancy medical degree of his is for picking his teeth. I'm so mad at him I could spit."

Wes and I turned to each other, eyes wide, as we stepped out onto the fourth floor, which was silent except for the beeps and whirrings of machines.

"You okay, Jo?" I asked her, placing my hand on her shoulder to get her to stop for a second.

She turned back to us and crossed her arms. "What are you asking me for? I should be asking you—"

"But I'm asking you." My lips rose in a subdued grin. "You take good care of us all. Especially him."

"Especially him." Jo repeated my words and looked down at her sensible snow boots. "I'm fine, darlin'. I was just . . . I don't know . . ."

"Scared?" Wes asked gently.

"No, mad!" she reiterated. Her voice was much too loud for the hospital hallway, and she knew it. She looked around and then back to us, once she was satisfied that—apart from one nurse at the nurse's station raising her head and glaring at us—no damage had been done. Then she added in a whisper, "And maybe scared. A little. But so help me, Adelaide, if you tell him that—"

"I would never. Cross my heart."

Wes squeezed my hand, and in that subtle gesture I felt him holding in the laughter and, I was guessing, some words that needed to wait as well. I figured he was probably dying to ask me what was going on between Jo and my dad, but the truth was, I wouldn't have any answers for him. They'd always been friends, but somewhere along the line it seemed like maybe the feelings had gotten deeper. At least for Jo. Just one more thing I hadn't noticed.

Jo walked a few more steps until she was just a few feet away from room 408. "He's in here."

In an instant, the beeps and the whirrings got personal. I took a step toward the dark room, but Wes planted his feet and pulled me to him before I could go in.

"I'll be right out here if you need anything," he whispered before brushing his finger across my chin and lifting my lips to his.

I nodded. "Thank you." And I wanted to say so much more. I wanted to say, "*Thank you for driving me to Denver. Thank you for still loving me. Thank you for coming home.*" And I would. At some point, if we kept going—or maybe even if we didn't—I would probably say thank you for all those things. Because it wasn't just the hard and painful things that needed to be said but the nice things too. But right then, for just the smallest percentage of a second, I wondered instead what might have happened if I had *asked* him to come home, even one time.

It wasn't my fault that he left. It wasn't my fault that he didn't come home sooner. And I'd had every right to sit there and wait . . . to be sad and wallow . . . to get angry and be hurt and allow it all to turn into resentment. I'd had every right to finally move on, and every single person—Wes included—no doubt thought I should have done that sooner.

But what if I had gone to Connecticut? It wasn't like I couldn't have found him. I could have flown into any airport in the state and asked a taxi driver to take me to the governor's house. I could have written him a letter. I could have called him. Rather than feel confused and hurt and sad—no matter how completely justified I may have been in feeling each of those things—I could have trusted in his love for me. I could have known that whatever was happening, he clearly needed me too. And maybe I could have helped, and maybe I couldn't have. Maybe it wouldn't have fixed things, but maybe it would have. And maybe—probably—I wouldn't have even wanted it to, knowing what I knew now.

But still . . . I could have at least *asked*.

Then again, as he had said, we were just kids. It was all so easy to see now, wasn't it?

I threw my arms around his neck and stood on my tiptoes to whisper into his ear. "I'm really glad you're here."

He looped his arms around my waist and sighed. "Not half as glad as I am."

---

"Hey, sweets," Dad greeted me groggily as I entered the hospital room. "I told you not to come."

He was receiving oxygen through his nose, and he was hooked up to various monitors via wires connected to his chest, but I have to say, I was greatly relieved. I think I'd been mentally preparing for the worst (the worst—in my imagination, anyway—being a repeat of thirty-year-old memories of my mom frail and unrecognizable in her hospital bed). But apart from the tube and the wires and the horrible lime-green gown, he didn't really look much worse than he had the time Maxine Brogan accidentally used flour instead of powdered sugar in the icing of the birthday cake she made him. (Come to think of it, the lime-green gown would have matched his complexion nicely on that day.)

"You didn't tell me not to come. I haven't talked to you."

"Well, I told Jo to tell you not to come."

I reached the bed and leaned over to kiss his cheek. "Thankfully Jo knew better than to pass along that message."

"Not that you would have listened, anyway."

I pulled the chair closer to the bed and sat beside him. "How are you?"

"I'm okay." I scowled at him, and he added, "That's the honest truth, Addie. I'll need to make some adjustments to my diet. Maybe scale back my schedule a little bit. Give up being mayor, maybe, and start putting out some feelers for nearby doctors to take some of the load. There will be some new medications in the mix. But I really am okay. I don't even feel all that bad right now. Just tired more than anything else."

"Oh!" I jumped up. "Of course. I should let you get some rest."

He grabbed onto my hand. "No, not yet. In a minute. Sit. Please." I did as I was told and returned to the chair, and my dad kept hold of my hand. "So he drove up with you?"

I took a quick peek at the monitor with his heart-rate and blood-pressure measurements so I could get a baseline. "Yes, *Wes* drove me here."

He nodded slowly and repeated "Wes" under his breath. "Well, I appreciate that. And the plane. And I want you to know I'm sorry about my behavior earlier—"

"I appreciate that, Dad, but I think maybe Wes is the one who is owed an apology."

He nodded again, but this time it was accompanied by a wrinkled brow and tight lips. "I know."

"You know what?" I stood from my chair one more time. "Let's talk about it later. I'm just so glad you're okay. Do you need anything before I go?"

"I wouldn't mind knowing if you and I are okay."

I raised my eyes to the monitor again. *Holding steady.* "Of course. We're fine. But you need to know that I've decided to forgive him—"

"And I think that's admirable."

"You do?"

He pushed himself up a little in the bed, as much as he could with the energy he had left in the tank for the day. "Of course I do. I'm proud of who you are. I always have been, and that right there's a good example of that. Of who you are. But that doesn't mean I'm there yet. Or, if I'm being honest, that I even understand how you got there. I'd love for you to walk me through that."

"Not tonight."

He chuckled. "No. Not tonight."

I leaned over and planted a kiss on his temple. "Good night, Daddy."

"Good night, sweets." I was almost to the door when he added, "I know he humbled himself coming back here. I get that. And I guess I respect it. Now, I don't know if I agree with Jo that that earns him an unconditional pardon."

"Wow." I leaned against the doorframe and smiled at him. "She just dove right in there, didn't she?"

I heard him sigh over the rustling of the bed as he settled into his pillows. "You know as well as I do that Josephine Stoddard isn't going to allow a little thing like a heart attack to get in the way of a good lecture."

---

I walked down the hall, looking for Wes and Jo, but didn't find either of them before the nurse at the desk asked me if I needed help with something.

"I seem to have lost my friends."

"The ones who came in with Dr. Atwater?" I nodded. "The lady went down to the cafeteria, I'm pretty sure, and the man is in the coffee lounge." She pointed past me. "Down there on the right."

"Thanks."

I chose to pursue the man, but when I got to the coffee lounge, I didn't see the man I had been expecting. In fact, I saw someone I was decidedly *not* expecting to see.

"Mr., um . . ." He looked up from his computer and smiled at me, but that didn't help me remember his name. "I'm so sorry. It's been a really long day. I'm afraid I've forgotten your name."

"Brewster." He set his laptop on the chair next to where he had been sitting and crossed the room to me. "Phil Brewster. How's your dad doing?"

I looked behind me, but alas, there was no one there to help explain to me what the snot was happening. I mean, Wes had said half the town had wanted to accompany my dad to the hospital. I wasn't surprised by that. In so many ways, he was the heart and soul of Adelaide Springs, and had been for many years. In addition to being their doctor and their mayor, he was their friend. Their moral compass. (Days like this one, during which their moral compass seemed hell-bent on beating his daughter's ex-fiancé to a pulp, aside, of course.)

Was it really supposed to make sense to me that the only person besides Jo Stoddard to make it on the plane was this random tourist?

"Um . . . he's resting. Sorry, why are you here?"

"Well, you know . . ."

"I clearly don't."

"There wasn't exactly reason for me to stay in Adelaide Springs if Senator Hobbes was going to be here. Besides, as much as I'm sure taxpayers want only the best for your father, it's not exactly accounting best practices to loan out the plane without making sure *someone* official is on board."

He was looking at me like there was nothing more to explain. Nothing left unclear. And he *kept* looking at me that way for far too long. Oh, it was only four seconds. Maybe five. But considering he was the outsider who had flown here with my ailing dad, and I was the daughter who had been running four hours behind, the impetus was really on him to do some explaining. At least that was how I saw it. Call me crazy.

"Who *are* you?"

"Philip Brewster."

"Yeah, got that much. *Who* are you?"

"I'm Senator Hobbes's campaign manager." His eyes widened and he tsked and slid momentarily into an unsettling toothy grin before adding, "I see. He hasn't mentioned me."

I still didn't understand the situation, but suddenly I felt a little more like I at least understood him. Yep. That made sense. The hesitancy to reveal any more than he wanted me to know. The fake smile, and then the other fake smile . . . and the other one. An endless revolving clothesline of fake smiles, made in every shade and texture, designed to coordinate perfectly with whatever room he stepped into. He was DC through and through. The parts I hadn't liked and didn't miss.

"I see." I mirrored his dominance smile, both impressed and repulsed by how easily playing the game came back to me. "Well, you have a good night, Mr. Brewster."

There were questions I wanted to ask, of course, but I wasn't going to ask them of him. Besides, my brain had already begun analyzing and sorting the data. I didn't intend to have all that many questions left by the time I found Wes. Mr. Brewster had flown into town today. I knew that much. And based on the fact that Wes had canceled on accompanying me to South Fork at the last minute, I was willing to bet Mr. Brewster's visit had not been expected. Add to that what I knew about Wes's dilemma as to whether or not he should run for president—a dilemma that, as of that moment, I was guessing Mr. Brewster was still unaware of—and I suddenly understood that wherever Wes was in this hospital, he was very much hiding from Philip Brewster.

I pulled out my phone, which was silenced, and saw the text from him.

I'm in the chapel.

I grinned, quite pleased with my skills of deduction—and, admittedly, pleased with how well I understood Wes Hobbes—and turned toward the door.

"It's a nice idea, the two of you. The senator sure thinks it has a lot of potential."

"Excuse me?" I turned back just as he pulled a file folder from his briefcase and opened it.

"Most of it does look good on paper. I don't have any trouble admitting that. You had a stellar record with the agency until your husband died." He looked up over the file folder and projected a downcast expression onto his face. "My condolences, by the way." His eyes returned to the papers in his hands. "You were well on your way to a great career until you started showing up at work inebriated—never a *great* idea when the safety of American operatives rests in your ability to make sound, expedient determinations. It looks like it didn't end *too* badly for Agent Stankowski." He met my eyes again as he said, "Thank goodness for that," then went back to the folder. "But it's probably a good thing you got out when you did. Not that you had any choice in the matter. Remind me, which rehab did they send you to?"

He stared at me, seemingly expecting an answer, but I just stared back, silent and unflinching. He cocked an eyebrow and looked back down to flip through a few papers in the file. "Aquila. That's right. That's a good one, I hear."

"Why don't we just cut to the chase, Mr. Brewster? What's your point? Because obviously you haven't told me a single thing I don't know. Is the point just that *you* know?"

*Ah. Of course.* The gears clicked into place in the instant before he spoke again. And though he didn't specifically say the words, Mr. Brewster's point was clear.

"The point, Mrs. Elwyn, is that my boy out there—"

"*Your boy?*"

"—is the most promising candidate in three generations. I've made sure of it."

I knew the sordid details of my separation from the CIA. Mr. Brewster knew. And now Mr. Brewster was threatening to make sure "his boy" knew unless I stepped aside. *That* was his point. He thought I was blocking the path to the White House, and he wasn't going to allow me to stand in the way for long.

"I'd actually say *Wes* has made sure of it. *He* is the most promising candidate in three generations. Not you."

He scoffed. "Okay. Sure. You believe that if you need to, though I'm fairly certain not even he *truly* believes it." He took a step toward me, his smile laced with disdain and every point of his outstretched finger drenched in threat. "I was there from the beginning, picking up the pieces—"

"What pieces?"

"The shambles of his broken heart, of course." Brewster tilted his head toward me and sneered, and I had to cough to cover up the laugh that nearly escaped. Not because the thought of Wes's heart in shambles after leaving Adelaide Springs amused me. It didn't. But I suddenly felt like I was in an episode of *House of Cards* or something. It was all so hilariously dramatic. "So believe me when I tell you I have a lot of time and a lot of effort invested into Wesley Hobbes. He's going to be president."

I crossed my arms and shrugged nonchalantly. "Great. I would hate for all your work to have been for nothing. Now, if you'll excuse me . . ." I gestured behind me toward the door with my thumb, but I didn't set my feet in motion yet. I instinctively knew he wasn't going to let me have the last word. And he certainly wasn't going to allow it to be something as civil and ordinary as what I had just said.

"I do want to thank you for one thing, however."

"Oh, goody! Let's hear it."

"I wasn't sure how long to wait to change gears from the mourning-widower platform. I see now I almost waited too long. He's growing restless—"

"Okay, you're an idiot," I said, finally allowing a laugh to fill the air between us.

I know it was immature and unbecoming of a disgraced former member of the intelligence community such as myself, but that didn't make it any less exhilarating to then take advantage of his stunned silence, do a one-eighty, and run out the door, down the hallway, and into the elevator before he could slip in an attempt at the last word.

## CHAPTER 28

# WES

### 8 More Years

Wes had always found churches comforting. He'd attended regularly with his mom growing up, or with Doc and Addie, and there was just something about walking into an environment where, at least in theory, you didn't have to think about yourself for a little while. Not that he had ever been able to stop thinking about himself, of course. Did anyone? But at least there had been an understanding that *he* wasn't supposed to be the point. The point was faith, right? The point was how he treated other people. The point, at least to him at that age, was that the world was a better place when he didn't try to put himself at the center of it.

He'd been in a lot of churches since then—for funerals and weddings and the occasional campaign rally—but now it was always about him. Even at someone else's wedding, it was a big deal if Wes Hobbes showed up. Even at a funeral, everyone was there to see and be seen. And for the past couple of years, no one in DC outside of a few top names was more highly sought after for the events where people went to be seen. He hadn't realized until just then, as he sat alone in the tiny chapel at the hospital, candles and stained glass casting strange shadows, just how offended he was by that.

Wes startled at a gentle touch on his shoulder. "Sorry," Addie whispered. "I didn't mean to sneak up on you."

He rubbed his eyes with his palms as he stood. "No, I'm sorry. I was pretty lost in thought, I guess." He wrapped her in his arms and rested his head on hers. "How are you? How's Doc?"

"He's sleeping. I think he'll be fine."

"Because he says so, or—"

"Well, yes. But I think he was giving it to me straight." Addie pulled back and looked up at him as he stepped farther into the pew and made room for her. "How about you? You doing okay?"

"On what scale?" he asked with a weary chuckle as he sat back down. He leaned forward and crossed his arms on the back of the pew in front of them and then laid his head down on his arms, facing her. "Nah, I'm okay. A little tired, but—"

"I just had a lovely time getting to know Philip Brewster."

Of course she had. He closed his eyes, hoping that would help him think and figure out what to say to her next, but even in the quick few seconds of darkness added to the silence, he realized how easy it would be to fall asleep. Especially if she kept rubbing small, soft circles on his back with her fingertips as she had begun to.

Wes sat up and opened his eyes as wide as he could to try to focus. "I'm sorry I didn't have a chance to tell you about him. He showed up right before I was supposed to pick you up earlier."

She smiled and nodded. "No, it's fine. I figured. I mean, it's a *little* odd knowing he was on the plane with Dad and Jo . . ." A snort escaped, and she rubbed her nose to get rid of the tickle.

"I know," he replied with a grimace. "I'm actually super annoyed that he showed up, but then I remember that I did lie to him and tell him I was in California all weekend."

"Oh. That." Addie winked.

"Yeah. That." He turned to face her and propped his knee on the pew between them. "I'm not sure that my annoyance has much of a leg to stand on."

"How did he figure out you were here?" She rested her arm on the back of the creaky wooden pew and mirrored his position.

He sighed. "I had him reach out to Heather McCord, deputy something of Senate what's-it—"

"Senate what's-it, huh? Is Senate what's-it an elected position, or is that a presidential appointment? Are there confirmation hearings?"

"Anyway . . ." He ignored her smirk. "I had Phil reach out to her to get me the intelligence reports on VE Ladder so that I could find out how much you'd been briefed."

She frowned. "Surely the clearance level on that goes higher than your campaign manager."

"Oh! No, totally. He didn't have access to anything." Maybe it was just because he was so tired and his brain felt like it was moving with all the precision of a janky lava lamp, but he didn't even know if anything he was saying was going to upset her. He hoped not, but he also had no desire to spin things in a way that misrepresented the truth. "I guess I said something about wanting to help out an ex-girlfriend or something. And I guess I forgot that Phil knows enough to know you're the only ex I care about." He shrugged. "I guess from there it wasn't too hard to start figuring things out. But hey, at least that meant the plane was available for Doc."

"Gassed up and ready to go?"

"I think Phil had images in his mind of grabbing me by the ear, throwing me on the plane, and being back in DC by dinnertime."

"Yeah." She smiled at him and even rested her hand on his arm and traced patterns on his skin with her finger, but he was pretty sure she was no longer with him. The smile was sad. The physical contact was absentminded.

"What is it?"

"I need to tell you something."

He stretched his eyes open wide again and blinked with his eyebrows raised as high as he could get them. "Okay. Shoot."

She chuckled and tried to cover it at first, but she quickly failed. "Sorry." She cupped her hand on his cheek and brushed her thumb against the grain of his quickly growing whiskers, then leaned in and planted a soft kiss on his lips. "Sorry. I had the benefit of a nap. Why don't you settle into a pew for a little while and—"

"Addie? What's going on?"

She kept her hand on his face and smiled sadly. "Your guy up there knows some things you don't."

Wes kept his cheek against her hand but darted his eyes to the altar at the front of the chapel. "You mean Jesus?"

She snorted again, but this time it was no cute little thing that she was able to cover daintily. She laughed into the crook of her elbow and finally managed to squeak out, "No, not Jesus, Wes! I mean, yes, I'm sure Jesus knows some things you don't know. But no." She sniffed and pulled a tissue from her jeans pocket and dabbed at her face. "I meant Philip Brewster."

He tittered as she continued laughing. "Oh. Okay." But his amusement fell away while she tried to compose herself. What didn't he know? "What is it?" His emotions were suddenly on high alert, and he didn't feel sleepy at all—even if he couldn't remember ever feeling so exhausted. "What does Phil know?"

She dug her top teeth into her bottom lip and reached down for his hand. Then she scrunched up her nose and said, "He knows that I can't be your First Lady, Wes."

He involuntarily scooted back from her on the pew, stunned. "He told you that I . . ." He cleared his throat. "He had no right. I mean, it wasn't like I was making plans. I was just . . ." Sheesh. What must she think of him? "Addie, I didn't have a plan. I wasn't *making plans*. It wasn't like I thought we were just going to fall right into that after three days—"

"I know." She nodded and smiled sweetly. "I didn't think that." Her eyes wandered off to one of the stained glass windows as a more quizzical expression overtook her face. "Huh. I'm surprised I didn't think that." She shook her head and turned back to him. "I'm surprised I didn't start second-guessing everything you've said to me over the past few days. I'm surprised I didn't begin to suspect that was your angle the whole time. Maybe even the whole reason you came back to town."

"It wasn't."

"I know. That's what I'm saying. And I guess I'm saying . . . that's not nothing. Between us, I mean. Trust and all that."

"Yeah. Trust and all that." He nodded. "That's not nothing." He squeezed her hand and weighed his next words carefully and decided it was probably best not to say what he wanted to say. And then he said it anyway. "But just because I haven't been making plans doesn't mean I haven't spent every single moment of the last twenty-two years wishing I was married to you. I have. I still do. And considering there are only two things I've ever really wanted in my entire life—you and the White House—I'd be lying if I said—"

"I'm an alcoholic, Wes." She sighed and shook her head before looking down at their intertwined fingers. "I haven't had a drink in 363 days. I know recovering addicts always know the number of days, but I've always felt like it's even easier for me to remember because it was 364 days ago that I reported to work having not slept for two days and having drunk an entire bottle of vodka since midnight. I spent the night drinking 100-proof, then I drove to Langley. I'll *never* understand how I got there without killing someone, but I did. Then I walked straight to my desk and mistook the operative on the ground—*our* operative—for the guy who shot Joel. Never mind that I was monitoring Nigeria and Joel had been killed in Venezuela."

Addie pulled one of her hands from his and brushed her fingers across his cheek again. "I don't actually remember much of it, but the report was pretty clear. Long story short, one of our agents—one of Joel's best friends, actually—got stabbed in the shoulder because I was freaking out and didn't send in reinforcements. He survived. He's fine. He even had the audacity to forgive me, I'm pretty sure. I don't think his wife ever will, not that I blame her, but that's another story."

The only sound filling the tiny chapel was the hum of the heater pumping warm air into the space and the creak of the pew as Addie's knee bounced up and down compulsively. Her leg bounced and her fingers twitched and her teeth dug into her lip, but she never looked away.

"And how are you now?" Wes whispered. "In your, um . . . in your recovery, I mean. Almost a year. That's amazing."

She squeezed his hand and grinned. "Thanks, but I don't know that it's amazing."

"I think it is."

"Well, I take it seriously. That's for sure. Beyond that?" She shrugged. "I go to meetings every Sunday—"

"Oh."

"Yeah. I was going to talk to you about all of this on the way to South Fork."

"Hang on." His grasp slipped from hers, and his knuckles hit the pew with a thud before he lifted his hand and ran his fingers through his hair. "You were going to let me go with you. That's . . ." He cleared his throat and swallowed down the lump. "That means a lot."

"It should," she responded, sniffing and chuckling at the same time. "My dad's the only person in town who knows about any of this. The addiction stuff, I mean. He can't know about Joel, of course, or any of the details about why I left the CIA. But yeah, he's the only one who knows I'm an alcoholic. Not because I'm keeping it from other people, really. Just . . . I don't know. It hasn't been the easiest to let anyone in. About anything. You know?"

He nodded. "Yeah."

"So . . . just you and my dad. Oh, and your campaign manager, of course." She laughed softly. Bitterly. "Sebastian should hire him to write an Adelaide Springs gossip column for the *Gazette*. He's getting all the scoop. Between plane rides and CIA personnel files—"

"Hold on. That's what you meant?" Wes leapt from his seat, whacking his hip bone on the too-close pew in front of them on the way up and, thankfully, managing to keep an expletive from escaping. He wasn't much of an expletive sort of guy anyway. The governor had taught him to always act as if potential voters might overhear anything he said. But he especially wanted to avoid the bad language in the chapel, in front of "his guy up there."

"Ouch. Are you okay?"

He rubbed the sore spot on his hip and carried on. "Addie, are you telling me Phil dug up dirt on you and this is why he says you can't be First Lady?"

"Yes."

"Well . . ." Wes scoffed and began pacing. He *wanted* to pace, anyway. There was nowhere to go, and he couldn't even walk the length of the pew without facing front and shuffling his feet like he was doing a lame version of the Electric Slide. "I don't care about that. We all have a past. Betty Ford was an alcoholic, and that ended up being a really good thing!" He reached the outside aisle and realized what he'd said. "I'm not saying it was a good thing that she was an alcoholic, mind you. Just that as First Lady she was able to bring awareness to it."

"To my knowledge, Betty Ford never got anyone stabbed."

"We don't know that." He hurried into the pew in front of her and sat on his knees, facing her. "The point is—"

"I don't want it, Wes."

"What?"

"I don't want it. I don't want to go back to Washington. I don't want to be First Lady."

"But you'd be so great at it."

"I know." She winked and offered him a downcast smile. "But . . . I just don't think it would be so great for me."

He thought of the long hours on the campaign trail. The receptions and the champagne toasts. The public scrutiny that, it wasn't difficult to imagine, would be so much more severe for her than it would be for other candidates' spouses.

He slipped off his knees onto his bottom. "Yeah. Okay."

"But you know what?" She placed her hands on his on the back of the pew and leaned forward. "As of Friday, I was as likely to vote for Elkrique Iglesias as I was you on Election Day. But you've won me over, Senator Hobbes. I mean, I still don't know where you stand on any positions, and I'll need to thoroughly examine your tax plan before making any promises, but I'm pretty sure I'm not going to vomit when I see your name on my ballot. That's progress, right?"

Wes chuckled and then tilted his head and lifted her hand to his lips. "I'm not going to run, Addie. How could I just leave now, like none of this ever happened? If you aren't with me—"

"I thought you hadn't made plans."

"I hadn't. I hadn't decided anything, and I certainly wasn't deciding things for *you*, without you. Obviously."

Addie smirked and rolled her eyes. "Whatever, Hobbes."

"But I do know that from the moment I thought of you with me in the White House, I haven't once thought of being there alone."

She leaned forward to rest her head on his arm. "That's really sweet."

"It's true."

She nodded against him. "I know." He brought his other hand up and combed his fingers through her hair. "Which is why we need to end this now."

Wes's hand froze on her neck. "End what?"

Addie sighed and raised her eyes, followed by her head. "We both got really serious really fast."

The panic tightened his shoulders first, then began making its way up his neck. "That's not true."

"It's been three days, Wes."

"It's been forty years, Addie." He shifted back onto his knees. "And okay, we were kids. I can't say for sure that I loved you every one of those forty years, but I know for a fact that in my entire life, I've never loved anyone else. This wasn't fast. Not for me."

"I get that. And yeah, on some level, I'm with you. You know I am. But I was married for nearly ten years—"

"And I was married for fourteen. What's your point?"

Addie tilted her head and smirked. "Really? You're comparing your marriage to mine?" Wes cleared his throat and motioned for her to continue. "So yeah, I've never had a serious relationship apart from you and Joel—"

He opened his mouth to speak again and she scowled at him, causing him to think better of saying whatever #samesies thing he had been about to say. His mouth closed again with a pop.

"—and I just think we probably need to slow this down."

He gulped. "You want to see other people?"

She cackled. "No! That's the point. Three days ago, I didn't even want to see *you*!"

"Um, in fairness, that was probably still true two days ago."

"You're not wrong." She smiled up at him and shrugged. "So maybe we should, oh, I don't know. Exchange emails? Text each other every day? Call each other on even days and talk about life? I can tell you how I sat at Valet Forge all day without getting a single call, and you can tell me all about winning the Michigan primary."

"So just normal couple stuff?"

She nodded. "Normal couple stuff."

"But . . . no commitments? Is that what you're saying? Just . . . we see where it goes?" He wanted to give her the time she needed. That was what he knew for certain, even if the idea of just casually dating Addie Atwater felt to him a little like wanting to keep his options open and not fully committing to the whole breathing-oxygen thing.

"Yeah. Exactly."

Three days ago, he hadn't expected to ever see her again. It never even would have occurred to him to hope they could be friends again, or to believe that he hadn't kissed her for the last time.

"Okay," he responded, disappointed in himself when his voice came out sounding every bit as sad as he felt.

"I'm not too worried about it, you know. Some time will be good for us."

Wes swallowed the lump in his throat and managed a half smile. "I'm sure you're right."

"I am. Besides . . ." She stood and held on to his hand, then sidestepped into the aisle and scooted next to him in his pew. "If you didn't stop loving me over the last twenty-two years, I'm not too worried about you getting over me in the next four."

"Someone's feeling very sure of themselves." He wrapped his arms around her and slid her closer. "And you said four years. You meant eight."

"Wow." Addie snuggled into the crook of his arm. "Now who's feeling sure of themselves, Mr. President?"

CHAPTER 29

# WES

### 26 Years Since He Wanted to Be a Rapper

Wes raised his wrist and angled his arm to catch the moonlight shining into the room through the blinds. Four a.m., and the plane was taking off from the Denver airport at five. That was the plan. It wasn't the plan he'd wanted to make, but he couldn't deny it was the one that made the most sense. He'd stopped by the coffee lounge long enough to tell Phil to make the arrangements with the pilot and then hurried away before any other subject could be broached. He couldn't avoid it for long. He had no desire to avoid it for long. He was furious with Phil for investigating Addie and digging up dirt on her. *Of course* he was furious.

But he also knew Phil was doing his job and, from what he could tell, doing it well. If things had been different, and if Addie were different—if she were someone who acted impulsively or recklessly or followed the whim of emotion—Wes would have married her today. Well, maybe not literally today. They were running on energy fumes, hanging out in a hospital, and he'd chewed his last breath mint about three hours ago. As desperate as he was to spend his life with her, he wanted forever to begin on a slightly mintier note than that. But if she hadn't slowed him down, nothing else would have. That much was certain.

She wasn't wrong, and neither was Phil, as much as he hated to admit it. If she was his wife, he couldn't be president. It was everything Addie had pointed out to him, but it was something else too. It was Joel. Yes, VE Ladder was classified. Yes, Joel's death certificate listed blunt-force trauma resulting from a head-on collision as his cause of death, and it listed the date as October 22, eight full months after the day Addie had to start grappling with the loss. But people talked. They lived in the age of WikiLeaks, after all. Be it reporters seeking a scoop or his opponents seeking a foothold, someone would find out things they shouldn't be able to, and Addie would have to live through it all again—this time on the world's biggest stage.

So that was one decision made. One possibility deemed impossible. Now he just needed to figure out if he wanted to spend any more time in a landscape that made it impossible for him to be with her.

He scratched the back of his head with both hands and then lifted them as high as he could to stretch out his tired back. At least on the plane he could sleep. He was going to hang on to that silver lining for dear life. At that particular moment, he wasn't having much luck finding another one.

Wes stood from the stiff upright chair beside Doc's bed and looked around for a piece of paper and a pen. He spotted a napkin under the tumbler of water on the table by the bed and a dry-erase marker on the board by the door. That would have to do. He grabbed them and tiptoed as quietly as he could back to the chair. He began by using the palm of his hand as a writing surface, but he only got as far as "Dear Doc"—which ended up looking more like an upside-down finger-paint interpretation of the section of Michelangelo's *The Creation of Adam* in which God's finger touches Adam's—before he gave up on that approach.

He stood and walked to the nearest hard, flat surface and began writing.

*Dear Doc,*
*I'm sorry we didn't get a chance to talk before I had to leave.*
*I really hope we can talk soon. There are things I'd like to*

*say, and I know there are things you'd like to say. For now, just know that*

Just know what? There was so much Wes wanted him to know.

Just know that I'm glad you're okay.

Just know that I'll never stop loving your daughter.

Just know that the best parts of me were instilled by you.

*I'll never stop being sorry.*

"You know that disconnecting my oxygen won't actually kill me, don't you?"

Wes jumped and turned toward Doc's bed.

"I am capable of breathing on my own, so you might need to try suffocating me with a pillow or something."

Yeah, okay . . . Wes could see, in hindsight, how huddling over the machines may not have been the best way to encourage peace and tranquility in an old man who had just had a heart attack.

"Sorry." Wes held up his napkin and marker. "Just leaving a note."

Doc pushed himself up in the bed. "Make yourself useful before you go, won't you?" He motioned behind him. "Pull these pillows up for me."

Wes laid his materials down on the top of the monitor and hurried over and followed Doc's leading. "Need to hang on to me and pull up?" he asked as Doc kept slipping out of his desired position.

"Stupid rubber mattress," Doc muttered, grabbing onto Wes's arm and finally making the progress that had been eluding him. "Thanks."

"Of course." Wes fluffed the top pillow one more time before Doc rested his head on it. "How are you feeling?"

"Fine. I'd be better than fine if I could sleep in my own bed." He pointed to the table. "Hand me that water?"

Wes scurried to the other side of the bed and handed the tumbler to him and watched Doc drink it up through the bendy straw until it started making the gurgling noises that signaled there was more ice than water. "Need me to get you a refill?"

"I thought you were heading out."

Wes glanced across the room at the note and then back to Doc. "Soon. But I can—"

"So are you leaving for good, or should we leave the light on for you for the next twenty years?"

Wes sighed. "Doc, I—"

"Here." Doc handed him the tumbler. "I'm good for now. Just set it over there."

He set it back on the table. "I don't know what I should say right now, Doc. I don't want to cause you to—"

"My heart's fine, Hobbes. Lay it on me."

Suddenly "I'll never stop being sorry" seemed so inadequate. What could he say to the man who had looked him in the eyes and told him he was proud of him just hours before he ran out of town?

Wes sat on the edge of the chair on the near side of the bed and took a deep breath. "You trusted me, and I let you down. I'm sorry."

"Tell me why you left."

"I wasn't good enough for her." Wes paused and waited, but Doc just kept looking at him. *Well, at least we agree on something.* "I'd been telling her for weeks that I thought we should wait—"

"I see." Doc pushed himself up higher in the bed after once again slipping down. "So it's Addie's fault."

Wes chuckled nervously. "See, um . . . that's my bad." He leaned over and adjusted the pillows again. "When I talked this through with Addie, I issued this sort of general disclaimer right at the top."

"What did you think would happen? For her, I mean. After you left."

"I don't know, Doc. I really don't. I'd love to tell you I was smart enough to have thought it all through, but clearly—"

"Well, clearly you weren't."

Wes cleared his throat. *Still stings, even when it's true.* "Yeah, I know. That's what I was saying. Trust me, no one sees what a putz I was as well as I do."

"Do you know that I couldn't get her to leave that tree until after dark?"

"What tree?"

"That tree in the meadow. She just sat there at the foot of that tree in her wedding dress all day long. And even then, it took Cole and me both dragging her away. She was so sure you were coming back. Did you think that would happen?"

He swiped at his nose. "No, I guess I didn't."

"You had to have thought *something*—"

"I guess . . ." He growled in frustration over not having any better answers than he'd had twenty-two years ago. "I guess I thought she'd be sad for a little while, and then she'd realize she'd dodged a bullet. She'd go to some Ivy League school or something, and then before long she'd meet some great, smart, really good guy who loved her as much as I did but who actually deserved her and who she wouldn't have to scale back all her dreams and expectations for." He shrugged. "I guess that's what I thought. That's definitely what I hoped."

The beeping of the heart monitor and the whooshing of the oxygen machine seemed louder as silence otherwise overtook the room.

"You sure you don't need some more water or something?"

Doc ignored the question and instead said, "It may have taken longer than you thought it would, but I guess you weren't too far off in the end. Joel was a good guy. And he sure loved our girl."

Wes sniffed and roughly brushed away the tear that fell. "How could he not?" He sighed and scooted the chair closer. "I never stopped loving her, Doc. I didn't. I haven't."

"So why are you leaving?"

"Yeah . . . that is the question of the day." He exhaled and laughed humorlessly. "Do you remember in ninth grade or so when I wanted to be a rapper? Never mind that I wasn't all that great at rapping. I mean, Cole had to do all my beats for me because I kept losing the rhythm. Nevertheless, I just listened to *The Slim Shady LP* on constant repeat and learned all the lyrics, and I knew that one of these days Dr. Dre and Eminem were going to be walking down Main Street in Adelaide Springs and maybe stop into my mom's restaurant for a cup of coffee, and they'd hear me spitting bars, and before I knew it I'd have a recording contract." He laughed softly as Doc nodded and rolled his eyes.

"I'll never forget what you said to me, Doc. You didn't discourage me or tell me how ridiculous that dream was. You just said, 'If that's what you want, go after it. But in the meantime, make sure you can pay your bills.'" Wes ran his hand through his hair. "My own father didn't always give me such supportive advice."

"Well, it's amazing what you come up with when you're just trying to make sure your little girl doesn't end up with a rapper who, let's face it, had a better chance of paying the bills with that buffalo-grooming business he tried starting."

"I still think that really could have taken off if the Fieldings had had more than just the one buffalo." Wes smiled as Doc chuckled softly and nodded.

"Seems like you're doing okay for yourself now. That was *your* private plane I rode here on, wasn't it?"

"I don't *own* the plane." And still, it had been a long time since he'd had to worry about making his own airline reservations or having enough money to pay the bills. For that matter, it had been a long time since he'd even received his own credit card statements. It was possible he wasn't even equipped for normal life anymore. "The thing is, I honestly don't know if I'm one of the lucky ones whose dream pays the bills or if I just gave up on dreaming. I really don't know. All I know is I don't have a backup plan. Twenty years of my life have been building toward the Tuesday after the first Monday in November. I don't know if I want to run for president or not, but I also don't have a clue what else I would do."

As long as Wes had known him, Doc had always been comfortable with silence. What Wes instinctively felt an itch to compensate for, Doc understood was a thing to be revered. It was beautiful not to feel a compulsive need to fill the gaps in conversation. To take the time to consider, or to be able to think without fear that you'd miss your chance if you waited too long, or even worse, that someone else would beat you to the words you should have said.

If Wes had finished out his formative years in the presence of Doc Atwater rather than Governor McNeese, would he, too, have someday shifted into that content, peaceful gear without the assistance of therapists and campaign strategists who never really helped him be content and only ever taught him how to bury and conceal his internal turbulence?

All he knew for sure was that in Doc's presence the silence was freeing rather than suffocating, and Wes was relieved that he didn't have to be the one to bring it to an end.

"Thank you for that, by the way," Doc muttered.

"For what?"

"The plane. Jo says . . . Well, she says you moved pretty quickly to make all of that happen."

"Oh, that was nothing—"

"It wasn't nothing. I probably would have been okay regardless, but I've been in Jo's passenger seat driving over those mountain passes when there *isn't* any real rush. It might not have been a heart attack that killed me if we'd had to go that route. And I'm saying I'm grateful."

The dim light didn't hide the sincerity and intensity in Doc's eyes as he stared at him unblinking, forcing Wes to accept the appreciation it would have been so much more comfortable to deflect. Because *of course* he was going to do all he could, and *of course* it was the least he could do, and *of course* he couldn't imagine a single thing he wouldn't do for this man who had never once expected anything from him apart from the one simple request that he be a man worthy of his daughter. Which *of course* had been too much to ask.

"You're welcome." The men nodded at each other, and Wes finally exhaled when Doc pulled his eyes away and began staring out the window on the other side of the room. "You know, if I get elected for the new job, I'll have a much bigger plane to fly you around in when you have your next heart attack."

"I think there will be a bunch of us having heart attacks, watching you try to land Air Force One in Adelaide Springs. I'm pretty sure the plane itself is longer than the runway."

Wes chuckled and raised his wrist to catch the light from the hallway on his watch. "Well, on that note, my paltry little non-nuclear-blast-resistant plane awaits. Tomorrow is one year since my father died, and the good people of Connecticut—or at least the people who want to make me president—just refuse to let him rest in peace." He stood from his chair and said, "I'm really glad you're okay, Doc."

"You said goodbye to Addie?"

He understood the subtext, and it was justified. But again, it stung. "I'm leaving but I'm not *leaving*. She and I are going to keep talking and figuring things out, and—"

"But you said goodbye to Addie?"

"Yeah, Doc." Wes slapped him gently on the shoulder and headed toward the door. "I said goodbye to Addie."

## CHAPTER 30

# ADDIE

### 50 Hours Since They Said Goodbye

"Laila. Laila? Are you awake? Laila!" My voice and my accompanying knock on the Kimballs' front door grew more and more urgent the longer it went unanswered.

Finally I heard footsteps. I could instantly tell they were not the dainty, delicate steps of Laila but the solid, manly steps of her husband.

"What time is it?" Cole greeted me as he opened the door. He tried to focus on me, but he couldn't do much more than squint, thanks to the beginning-to-rise sun streaming directly into his eyes from the east. "Everything okay?"

"Yeah. I thought you guys would be up." I pulled my phone out of my pocket. Six forty-six. Okay, so maybe I hadn't so much thought they would be up as not really slowed down long enough to decide if I cared. "Sorry. I just wanted to talk to Laila. I can come back later."

"Don't be ridiculous. Come in."

I followed after him and shut the door behind me. As soon as I turned back around, I shrieked a little at the furry things at my ankles attempting to trip me up with their cuteness (to which I was impervious) and their slithering (to which I was not) like feline skip ball toys.

"Watch out for the cats. Cocaine Bear takes no prisoners."

I stepped over them and joined him in the kitchen where coffee was already brewing. He didn't wait for the pot to finish and instead grabbed a mug and smoothly swapped it in place of the carafe so the dark, rich roast could go directly into his cup.

"Want some?"

"No, thanks. So is Laila up?"

He kept his eyes on his mug and deftly placed the carafe back under the drip. "Um . . ." He took a steaming-hot gulp and stared at me. "No. I don't think so. Oh, hang on. Yes. She went to the Bean early. She was expecting a delivery. I think." He closed his eyes briefly and then opened them again as he nodded. "Yeah. That's right."

I groaned and turned back toward the door. "Okay. Thanks. Sorry again."

"Well, hang on."

I stopped and faced him.

"I'm here. What do you need? Can I help with something?"

*What do I need?*

I needed to turn back time. Or better yet, jump ahead to some point at which my brain and my heart wouldn't be twisted and jumbled like old boxes of Christmas string lights. I needed to sleep. I needed to stop dreaming of Wes every time I *did* fall asleep, so that I didn't wake up more twisted and more jumbled and more unable to sleep.

"I think I need to talk to Laila."

"Okay. If that's what you need." He sat down on a stool at the island in the center of the kitchen. "But I have ears too. Just sayin'."

I closed one eye and squinted at him through the other. "I fear you may not approve."

"Ah. Would I be correct in assuming you wish to discuss Senator Hobbes?" He set his mug down and got up and grabbed another, ignoring my words and pouring me a cup of coffee anyway. He set it down at the spot across from him and then returned to his seat. "Sit. Drink. Talk."

I chuckled and took a seat. "Okay."

We sipped our coffee and looked at each other as if we were both waiting for the other to begin. Which was ridiculous, of course. He was supposed to be the listener. I was supposed to be the talker. But the fact was I had just barely worked myself up to the idea of talking to Laila—a person with whom I had once shared everything. Cole and I had been close, of course, and in so many ways, he had been the only person I allowed myself to feel close to at all after Wes left. But since I'd been back in Adelaide Springs, everything had been kept at surface level. Truthfully, I was confused even by the desire to talk to someone.

Wes Hobbes had ruined me yet again.

"Are you sure this won't be awkward for you?" I asked. *Yeah, because I'm so worried about it being awkward for* him. "It really can wait until Laila—"

"You do what you want, Addie, but don't forget, there was a time when I was the world's foremost expert on Atwater-Hobbes relations. If one of you had sued the other, both sides would have attempted to retain my services as the expert witness. If somebody had wanted to do a big news story on the two of you, I would have been the specialist they called in to give my objective opinion. I don't think there's a whole lot you could say that would surprise me."

"I think I want to be with him again." I allowed the words to dump out of me before I could stop them and then held my mug in front of my face and waited.

Cole took a leisurely drink. "As I was saying . . ."

My eyes flew open wide. "Oh, come on! You can't tell me you're not surprised by that."

"Are you kidding? I saw the two of you at dinner."

"Well, yeah, but at that point we were just being kind of flirty . . ."

"And then I saw you a couple days ago, evoking the spirit of *The Little Mermaid*."

"*What?*"

"Oh, you know, hiding behind your Prince Eric statue and crying out, 'Daddy, I love him!' to King Triton."

Drops of coffee dribbled out of my mouth as I sputtered laughter. "It was *not* like that." I leaned over and tore off a sheet of paper towel from the roll at the end of the island.

"It was a little like that," he murmured into his cup. "How's he doing, by the way? King Triton, I mean."

"He's good. He slept most of the way home yesterday. I think he was able to get better rest in Jo's truck than he was at the hospital, so I know he's glad to be home."

"Good. I'm working on some new heart-healthy recipes I think he'll like, so tell him to come to Milo's when he's up to it."

I smiled up at him. "That's really sweet. I will. Thanks." I tilted my head to survey the countertop at an angle to make sure I hadn't missed any wet spots. "I've been meaning to ask. Where did the name Milo's Steakhouse come from?"

"You know . . . Milo Ventimiglia."

"Oh, *obviously.*"

He laughed. "No, seriously. Because that week we were in New York with Brynn and Seb, Lai skipped out on her date with Milo Ventimiglia."

"*What?* You're serious?"

"Have we not told you about that?" He took another sip of coffee. "We really haven't spent much time together since you got back if we haven't even told you that one. It's one of our better stories."

I sighed. "Yeah. I'm sorry about that. You guys have made a lot of effort to welcome me back. Brynn too. I mean, I don't even feel like I've gotten to know Sebastian very well at all. I really am sorry. I'm going to try to be a better friend."

"I think more than anything, we've just felt like we haven't known how to be good friends to you." He stepped back over to the coffeepot and refilled his cup, then leaned his hip against the counter. "It's a weird thing, being as close as we all were for the first portion of our lives and then going in such different directions. We're family, you know? And we always will be. But you don't always stay tight with every member of your family."

I'd wanted to talk to Laila—a little bit because I just wanted to talk, like I would have talked to her about Wes in the old days, but mostly because something had changed in me over the course of the past few days. I didn't want to isolate anymore. I didn't want to do life alone. I'd enjoyed laughing again, and it had felt so good to cry, and I'd finally realized how exhausting it was to put in all that effort just to avoid feeling something.

"I've been sober one year today."

His eyes softened, and the corner of his mouth rose in a smile. "Congratulations, Add. That's huge."

"Thanks." I dabbed at the bridge of my nose where a tear had begun its ticklish descent. "Correct me if I'm wrong, but you don't seem all that surprised."

"I didn't know. But at one point I suspected something—only because I think Brynn and Seb suspected something." I quirked my eyebrow, and he continued as he returned to his stool. "Do you remember that one time we all got together for dinner a month or two after you got back to town?"

"Yeah."

"And we were drinking that bottle of wine—well, the four of us were—and obviously you didn't have any. And Laila was telling Sebastian that we'd all been such good kids growing up that we didn't drink in high school or anything. And it was the first time we'd all had anything to drink together."

"Yeah," I repeated.

"And then you went to the bathroom."

"That wasn't anything. I think I just had to go to the bathroom."

"No, I know. But while you were gone Laila asked me if we had any beer or something to offer you because maybe you didn't like wine, and I said maybe there was a reason you didn't want to drink." Laughter bubbled up in him and escaped. "Sorry. That isn't funny, of course. It's just that, like, at the exact same time, Sebastian said he thought you had an early-morning conference call, and Brynn said you were harvesting your eggs."

"*What?*" I set my coffee cup down with a thud, sending the brown liquid sloshing over and causing Cole to laugh even harder. He got the paper towels this time and began cleaning up my mess for me. "Harvesting my eggs?"

"Yes. And it was so beyond obvious that they were trying to act normal after that. Brynn changed the subject, and Sebastian just went silent, and then you came back and none of us ever mentioned it again. I kept waiting for Lai to bring it up with me at some point along the line, but she never did. So I figured she forgot."

He threw the wet paper towel into the garbage can and smiled at me. "Of course I'm realizing now that probably all four of us individually suspected something, and we love you far too much to gossip about it. And I'd be willing to bet money you haven't seen a single one of us drink a drop of alcohol around you since then."

I jumped up from the stool and hurried around to the other side of the island and hugged him. He held on to me, and I could feel him smiling against my head as he said, "We really do love you. And we love Wes. Nothing can change that."

"Can you believe he might be president?"

He pulled back a few inches to look at me. "I know he's all mature now and everything, but this is still the dude who used to belch all the words to 'Gettin' Jiggy wit It.' I can't shake the feeling that it would be a horrible idea to let him run the country."

"Yeah, I get it." I laughed and pulled him back to me. "We just know too much."

---

I had walked from my house to Cole and Laila's home, and I hadn't felt very nostalgic at all about the walk itself on my way there. Their place had once been Cole's family's house, where he grew up with his mom and grandparents, and growing up, his house and mine had been the closest to each other of anyone's. Not that any of us lived very far apart in Adelaide Springs, of course, but Cole's house was only about four blocks away. And it made perfect sense that the nostalgia didn't kick in until the walk home. The walk home was where the memories had always been made.

Cole would never allow Laila, Brynn, and me to walk or ride our bikes home alone, and because of the parts of town in which we all lived, Wes had always been tasked with being the escort of the other two girls. Cole and I, meanwhile, had many of our greatest conversations as we walked the four blocks between our houses.

The sun was finally all the way up over the mountains, and there wasn't a cloud in the sky. It was shaping up to be one of those breathtakingly beautiful Colorado January days in which the tingling of your skin and the steam in front of your face each time you breathed tried to convince you it was winter, but the blue skies and blinding sun made it nearly impossible to believe. Suddenly I didn't feel like just walking back home. I could go to the Bean Franklin and test out my new "Don't live life alone" initiative, but that didn't seem quite right either. Not right then. The day was too perfect to be spent inside.

Halfway between our four blocks, I turned down Elm and began heading toward my once-and-again favorite spot in town. And then, before I even knew what was happening, I felt myself lowering into a runner's stance, waiting for the starting pistol to give me permission to bolt. Permission came in the form of a brisk wind at my back.

I hadn't run in a very long time, and certainly not at high elevation, and for a moment there, as I felt the burn in my lungs and the tightness in my neck, I couldn't help but think about what a stupid, undignified way I had chosen to die. But then the tightness dissipated, and the burn spread throughout my entire body in a way that actually spurred me on rather than held me back.

"What shoes am I even wearing?" My voice bounced as I shouted into the morning air with a laugh. I really couldn't remember if I was wearing proper shoes or not—my feet were as unaccustomed to running in sneakers as they were in orthopedic kitten-heel mules at this point, so I really had no idea—but I instinctively knew not to look down at my feet for fear that I would tumble head over tail and make my impending death even more humiliating.

It was only a hundred yards. A hundred and fifty at most. But as I left the street and walked into the meadow that in just a couple of months would be alive with green grass and every shade of wildflower but which for now was still buried beneath a couple of feet of snow, I had to bend over, my hands just above my knees, to catch my breath.

"Don't worry, it's just the elevation. It gets everybody at first. You'll adapt."

I kept heaving as I raised my head and looked toward his voice, off to the left, farther into the meadow.

Well, *that* wasn't going to help me catch my breath—seeing Wes walking toward me in perfectly layered *GQ* casualness (white T-shirt under a V-neck sweater under a denim jacket under a slightly bulkier corduroy jacket, collars expertly popped), designer work boots clearly manufactured to help you believe the wearer just came from a construction site (where he served as the region's best-dressed foreman), aviator sunglasses, and blue jeans that, on him, could have served as a tutorial for fashion. ("See, men? *That's* how you wear a pair of jeans.") He also clearly hadn't shaved since I last saw him, which turned me into a bundle of indecision. Should I find a paper bag to breathe into or just spend my final moments creating a "Look how hot this guy is!" social-media post that could also serve as my autopsy report? ("Cause of death: well, just look at him.")

"Your perfect washboard abs intimidate me," I panted, still just because of the running, I'm *almost* convinced. "I, meanwhile, just ran the length of a football field and raised my heart rate enough for my Apple Watch to ask if it should call 911."

I wish I had been kidding.

"I'll let myself go if it will make you feel better."

I finally managed to stand upright and face him. "Now, now, let's not be hasty. This is clearly a me problem."

He chuckled and offered me one of the two disposable coffee cups in his hands. "Can your heart take a boost of caffeine?"

Let's see . . . I'd had two cups at home, one cup with Cole . . . "Sure. Thanks." I took the cup and wrapped my hands around it. "If my dad's heart attack taught me anything, it's that I only have thirty-something good years left before I need to start taking better care of myself."

Wes raised his cup in toast formation. "Happy Sober-versary."

I smiled and clinked my biodegradable cardboard against his. "Thank you very much."

He took a sip before asking, "So what are you doing out here?"

"What am *I* doing out here? What are *you* doing here? The South Carolina primary is in six days. Shouldn't you be in South Carolina? As of this morning they're saying you're only up four points in South Carolina. I know it's only nine electoral votes, but you really don't want to lose South Carolina."

An amused grin spread across his lips. "Please, Adelaide. Say 'South Carolina' one more time. For me."

"Okay, but I'm serious, Wes. If you're going to—"

"Hey, can we sit?" he asked, motioning back to the direction from which he had come.

I nodded. "Sure. If we can find a not-buried-in-snow seat, that is."

"I know a place."

He led me to the same log I had sat on to feel close to Joel a few days prior. The same log where Joel had heard every depressing detail of my Wes Hobbes sob story years before that. And the log where Wes had asked me to marry him twenty-three years ago, when life was nothing but possibility and everything else to come was still so unimaginable. It had already been cleared of snow, and when I sat, I could feel some still-present warmth spread through my legs.

"How long have you been out here?"

He sat beside me and sighed. "Awhile. It was just going to be a quick moment to think before I took you your coffee, but I got caught up watching the sunrise." He took another sip. "Sorry about the temperature of the coffee, by the way."

I raised the cup to my lips and felt the coldness before I tasted anything. "So tell me. What's all this thinking been about?" I took a deep breath and faced him. "If you've changed your mind, you can tell me."

That, of course, had been the uneasiness at the center of my restless night. It was so easy, I knew, to get caught up in a magical moment. When reality was put on hold and emotions were running high, you could envision whatever sort of future you wanted. Why *couldn't* he be president and still commute to Adelaide Springs a couple of weekends each month like it was Camp David or something? Thanks to some Brynn and Sebastian efforts, we had really great internet speeds. He could conference in to the situation room in the morning, give a speech to the Teamsters at lunch, sit down for a strategic planning session with the joint chiefs midafternoon, and take me to dinner at Milo's before a quick late-night check-in with the prime minister of Canada.

Easy.

But it wasn't difficult to imagine that the bubble had been burst for him in his first moments on the plane leaving Denver. Philip Brewster would have already had the schedule prepared, and it was no doubt unforgiving and unrelenting. In addition to quickly approaching primaries, he had several days of lost time to make up for. Add to that my 2:00 a.m. realization that Brewster was probably now hell-bent on finding Wes's next voter-friendly wife, and it made sense to think our take-it-slow-and-see-where-it-goes plan had been dismantled long before he crossed back over the Mississippi.

"I don't want to wait, Addie."

I nodded. "Of course. I completely understand. Thank you for coming and telling me in person. That means a lot."

His tilted head cast a shadow across my face, blocking the sun from my eyes. "I'm not sure you understand what I'm saying."

"No, of course I understand." I placed my hand on his and squeezed. "And I'm sad. Of course I'm sad." *Sad* didn't even begin to describe the disappointment coursing through my body like a faulty water feature that just dumped all the water from one level to the next, causing a messy splash that necessitated the use of Caution: Wet Floor signs, rather than slowly trickling it down in a way that was meant to be beautiful and mesmerizing. "But you're running for president of the United States, Wes. You're going to *be* president of the United States. It's difficult to compete with that." And it wasn't like this was the first sacrifice I had been asked to make for my country.

"Okay, Addie—"

"No, really, it's okay—"

My words were cut off by his fingers at the back of my neck, tilting my head toward his as he climbed onto his knees next to me on the log and brought his lips down on mine. I dropped my coffee into the snow and knotted my fingers into his hair to assist him in his absolute crushing of my senses. His other arm looped around my neck as he whispered against me, "I choose you, chucklehead. I want *you*. I'm not going anywhere." He nibbled gently at my bottom lip, then traced kisses across the phantom fire where his teeth had been. "Is that clear enough for you?"

I was rendered completely incapable of speech, of course, so I just nodded up at him, and he smiled and returned to his own side of the log. And once the branches of the tree above us finally stopped spinning, and my vision quit putting on its neon-colored kaleidoscope display, I couldn't help but compare our two states of being. Wes sat there smirking, sipping his cold coffee and watching me, one of his rugged construction worker boots (Givenchy, I could now confirm) crossed onto his knee. I, meanwhile, was sweating and surrounded by brown snow, and my watch had just offered to notify the authorities for the second time in a span of six minutes.

"You look like Mountain Town Ken," I finally said.

A laugh burst from him, but he squelched it quickly in favor of pretending to take offense. "Hey, I worked really hard to make sure I brought the right clothes this time!"

I grinned and looked down at my fingernails, digging into my knees. "You're really staying?"

"Yep. If that's okay with you."

I nodded. "It's okay with me."

"And look, we can still go as slow as you want. I just . . . I don't know, Addie." He lifted his sunglasses and rested them on his head. "I can't deny there's a part of me that wants to be president. But *every* part of me—every single part—knows that if I could go back and do one thing differently in my life, I never would have left this place. I never would have left you. And I was standing there at the statehouse yesterday, making this incredibly saccharine political poppycock speech about the governor, all about the 'wise' things he used to say and how much I missed being able to go to him for counsel." He rolled his eyes. "And in the midst of it all, I heard Doc in my head, *actually* giving me good advice. If he told me once, he told me a thousand times: 'Smart people make mistakes. Only idiots make the same mistake twice.'"

"I believe his word was *clodpoles*. At least that's how he said it to me."

Wes laughed and nodded. "I don't want to be a clodpole." He used his thumb to absorb a line of moisture on my cheek.

"You could still seek reelection, you know. You could keep being a senator."

"I don't want to."

"You're going to put a lot of people out of work."

He did a double take and watched me out of the corners of his eyes. "'I want to be with you, too, Wes.' 'I'm so glad you chose me over being the leader of the free world, Wes.' I feel like there are so many things you could say that *wouldn't* make me want to go drown myself in a frozen lake."

"I'm just saying—"

"I know." He nodded. "There will be a lot of new jobs opening up in DC thanks to this little shake-up I'm causing, and I intend to write every last one of the people I'm laying off a glowing letter of recommendation." He took a sip of coffee before adding, "Well, except for one."

"Phil was just doing his job."

"No, see, that's what I told myself, too, at first. But that should never be the job. Hurting people? Trying to intimidate people? Acting like it's all for my own good when he's personally witnessed how lost I've been without you for more than half my life?" He shook his head. "Nah. I left him in Denver."

"You didn't!"

"I did." He turned to me and smiled, quite proud of the moral stance he had taken. "I mean, he was at a major international airport, so it wasn't like I dropped him in the desert or anything, but he doesn't get to do that to the woman I love and then fly back with me on a comfortable private jet with leather seats and a surround-sound entertainment center."

I laughed and then asked the one last question I had—the one last thing I needed to make sure he had thought of—before I could finally give in to the romance of it all. "So what will you do? For a job, I mean."

"I genuinely have no idea. Although I did hear Adelaide Springs may be in search of a new mayor soon . . ."

I tsked and shook my head. "Just like a politician. Roll into town and immediately believe you're qualified to run the place."

He smiled and stood from the log, gathered my dropped cup, and slipped it into his empty one before stretching out his hand for me. "Well, can I at least buy you breakfast and start running some campaign-slogan ideas past you?"

I placed my hand in his and allowed him to pull me to my feet. "Sure, but you should know—if people see us together, they're going to talk."

"About how much my clothes make me look like a local and it's easy to forget I ever left, you mean?" He threw his arm around my shoulders and pulled me against him as we began walking back toward town.

I chuckled. "Yeah. That's it." I wrapped my arm around his waist and reached up with my other hand to snatch the sunglasses off his head and slip them over my eyes as we walked toward the sun. "And by the way, I'm glad you chose me over being leader of the free world."

He kissed the top of my head and pulled me closer. "The free world never stood a chance."

# EPILOGUE 1

## WES

### Day 1 of the Second Blessing

"*Wow.*" Wes's mouth dropped open as he turned his eyes toward the wooden staircase in the Atwater house. Addie was gingerly dipping from one step to the next, careful not to snag her heel on the satin train of her gown, but her lips curled up in response to his one-word show of approval. He hurried over to offer her his hand as she took the last few steps onto the landing.

"We're too old to be doing this." She squeezed his hand once she reached the ground level, but he wasn't so eager to let go. "I feel ridiculous dressed like this."

"Um . . ." He shook his head, words still failing him. "You . . . nope . . ." He swallowed hard and allowed his eyes to indulge in a leisurely stroll down the length of the dress, lingering perhaps a little too long at the spot where her leg became visible via an expertly placed slit above her knee. "I mean . . ."

"Hey, Lai?" Cole came up behind Wes and shouted into the other room to his wife. "Don't quote me on this, but I think—I *think*—Wes approves of Addie's dress." Cole slapped him on the shoulder and then added, "You look gorgeous, Add," before scurrying into the kitchen to check on his hors d'oeuvres in the oven.

Laila squealed as she joined them at the bottom of the stairs. "Oh, yay! You're stunning, Addie. It's official. I'm adding a wedding line at the boutique." Her hands ran down Addie's abdomen, straightening out perceptible-only-to-Laila wrinkles. "Aren't you glad we went strapless?"

"Yes," Wes answered, quickly realizing—when both ladies shot him a gently chiding glance—that the question hadn't been directed toward him.

"I guess. It's just that these arms turned forty-one a couple weeks ago—"

"Oh, I don't want to hear it," Brynn called out from the hallway where she was putting the final touches on her makeup in front of the mirror. "My arms have been forty-one for four months already."

Sebastian stood from the couch and walked toward them. "And my arms are already happily settled in their mid-forties. Now that that's all established and it's been acknowledged that we all look fantastic—especially you"—he playfully whacked Brynn on the bottom as she passed from the hallway to the kitchen, causing her to turn back and exclaim, "Watch it!" through her giggles—"are we ready to get this show on the road?"

"Almost," Laila answered. "We're just missing one thing."

"What's that?" Addie asked.

"The groom." Cole came back around from the kitchen and leaned against the log column beside the staircase as he brushed a fleck of oregano off the cuff of his shirt. "I'm pretty sure Jo will kill us if we show up without him."

Addie sighed. "I'll go check on him." She turned to head back up the stairs, but Wes stopped her with a hand on her lower back.

"No, let me. As spectacular as those forty-one-year-old legs of yours are, I fully expect them to revolt if you make them go up and down these stairs in heels too many more times."

He covered her mouth with his as she laughed, then ran up the steps and hurried toward the master bedroom. "Doc?" He knocked and then opened the door slowly when there was no answer. "Doc? Everything okay?"

Doc stood in front of the antique mirror over his dresser and grumbled as he threw his hands up in the air. "I give up. I'm not wearing a stupid tie."

"Oh no, no, no." Wes crossed the room and joined him at the mirror. "That is not the note you want to start your marriage out on. Here. Let me help."

Doc sighed and turned away from the mirror. "Thanks. Truth is I can't get my hands to stop shaking."

"That's understandable." Wes nodded and unfurled the mess Doc had created, then took it from around his neck and straightened it out. He laid the tie over his shoulder temporarily while he popped up Doc's collar and then looped the tie back around. "It's a big day."

"I guess."

Wes laughed. "You guess? You're getting remarried after thirty years alone. I'd say that makes for a pretty big day."

"Except I never really was alone. Jo was there the entire time, which is what I guess makes this feel weird and right all at the same time." He slipped his fingers between his collar and his Adam's apple and attempted to stretch his neck away from the constriction.

"Would you stop?" Wes lifted his hands, waiting for Doc to remove his. "We'll never get this done if you don't stop wiggling."

Doc huffed and lowered his arms to his sides.

"Thank you." Wes picked up where he'd left off, looping the wide end over the small. "So listen, Doc. I just want you to know that if you have any questions, you can feel free to ask me."

Doc's eyebrows rose. "What kind of questions?"

"You know." He shrugged. "About the wedding night. It's perfectly normal to be nervous—"

"Shut up, will ya?" Doc grumbled.

Wes grinned as he brought the wide end down through the loop he had created and tightened it against Doc's neck. "All done. A perfect Windsor. Just like you taught me."

Doc turned back to the mirror. "Not bad," he acknowledged. "Thanks."

"My pleasure." He spotted the suit jacket on the bed and grabbed it and held it open for Doc to slip his arms into. "Need anything else?"

"Nah. I guess I'm as ready as I'll ever be. You're giving her away, right?"

Adelaide Springs was a town full of people who viewed Josephine Stoddard as a mother figure, and he was pretty sure he'd never get over the honor of being the one she had asked to walk her down the aisle.

"Yeah. Any requests? Should I take my time or make quick work of it?"

"Eh . . . better make quick work of it. I guess we've waited long enough."

Wes nodded. "Got it." He gestured for Doc to go ahead and prepared to follow him to the door, but he couldn't let him go without saying one more thing. "Hey, Doc?"

"Yeah." Doc took one last look in the mirror and smoothed down his hair.

"I just want to say . . . You know I didn't have a dad growing up. And when the governor came into my life, all I could think about was what I had been missing. Or what I *thought* I had been missing. Because the truth is, the only reason I'm able to see what a horrible father he was is because I spent the first eighteen years of my life seeing what a great one you are. I'm sorry I didn't realize that sooner. And I'm sorry if I never thanked you."

Doc met his eyes in the mirror and swallowed. "You taking good care of Addie is all the thanks I ever need." He turned and faced him and stretched out his arm. As they shook hands, Doc added, "But if you don't mind me saying so, from one second-chancer to another, I think one slow mover in this family is plenty."

"I assure you, I'm not the one controlling the tempo."

He thought of how far he and Addie had come in the six months he'd been back. There hadn't been a day for three of those months that he hadn't had a ring in his pocket, but he was scared of rushing her. She seemed as happy with him as he was with her, but Wes couldn't help but feel like he needed to wait for a sign or something. He wasn't sure what that sign needed to be, but he'd been on the lookout for evidence that complete healing had taken place.

Of course, if he was being honest, he'd felt like there'd been complete healing between him and Addie for quite some time now.

He choked down the lump forming under his tight collar. "Are you saying you're ready to give me your blessing, Doc? I honestly wasn't convinced you were too sure about me yet."

Doc shrugged and opened the door. "I wouldn't have given you my blessing the first time if I wasn't sure about you, kid. I just ask one thing . . ."

Wes shook his head and sighed as they stepped out onto the second-floor landing. "Yes, Doc. You have my word I'll show up this time," he said softly, and Doc laughed all the way down the stairs.

# EPILOGUE 2

## ADDIE

**Day 1 of No Regrets**

"Would you hand me those last couple glasses?" I asked Wes over my shoulder as I lifted my gloved hands from the soapy dishwater and air-dried them by flinging drops back down into the sink.

"Nope," he responded from behind me.

"Nope?"

"Nope." He brushed my hair away from the nape of my neck and then wrapped his arms around my waist as he began kissing a path down the back of my neck and onto my shoulder.

"Come on," I protested, even while I leaned against him and welcomed the distraction. "That's all I have left to clean up, and then—"

"Nope!" he repeated and lifted me up and spun me around to face him. "No one as beautiful as you should have to wash dishes."

I directed my eyes to the dozens of pieces of drying china and stemware, laid out on dish towels across the entire countertop, representing the hour or so I had already committed to dishwashing. I returned my focus back to him, my eyebrow raised.

"Well, okay . . . no one as beautiful as you should have to *finish* washing the dishes." He smiled and kissed me, and I laughed. I knew his heart was in the right place, and if he hadn't been so busy taking down strings of lights in the backyard, he no doubt would have called off my dish crusade much earlier. "Seriously, I'll finish up before I head home. Right now, just sit with me for a minute."

I pulled the rubber gloves from my hands and draped them over the faucet, then took his offered hand to walk with him to the living room.

"Actually . . ." He stopped in the open space between the kitchen and the living room and twirled me around, then captured me in his arms and pulled me against him. "How about one more dance before we return to the land of hoodies and sweatpants?"

"Aww!" I clasped his face in my hands and kissed him. "That was sweet of you to say that in a way that made it sound like we *both* live in that land." He chuckled and pulled me tighter against him, resting his cheek against mine. "You really should join me there sometime. It's a lovely place."

"I honestly find you just as irresistible in your sweats as I do *this*." He twirled me out and gently tugged me back. "Though, let me say again, this dress . . ." He growled softly against my ear.

I melted against him and counted on his arms to keep me upright as the warmth of his breath heated me from head to toe. "Thank you. I won't deny it was fun getting dressed up for a change. Not that I want to do it again anytime too soon."

"No?" He tilted his head back to look at me. "This is just a wedding occurrence, huh?"

"Yeah, I think so. Weddings, cotillions, Truman Capote's black-and-white ball, occasional Hollywood awards shows maybe, but otherwise . . ."

"Just think. If I'd stayed in the presidential race, Laila might have needed to design you about eleven different gowns for eleven different inaugural balls."

"Don't tell her that. You may find your name mysteriously back on the ballot."

It had been a bittersweet thing, watching him maneuver through all of that back at the end of January and into the beginning of February. I was so glad he'd made the decision he made, of course, and it was obvious he was at peace about it all. But certain things had been difficult for him to swallow. Things like finding out that Phil Brewster had been the one to hide his divorce filing, and—much more offensive to Wes—that he'd also been Sebastian's anonymous, untraceable source.

I'm pretty sure he'd spent most of February wishing he'd ditched Phil in the middle of the desert after all.

The bittersweet part, at least for me, had been watching Wes on television, answering in a dignified and somehow endearing way every question they threw at him and realizing just how great he would have been.

Ultimately, he'd refused to go through with the annulment, which could have been legalized posthumously, since Wray had been the one to file. Instead, he sat down with Sebastian on national television and told the truth about a marriage that had been based in friendship and honesty and mutual respect. Not fraud.

I leaned my cheek against his shoulder. "Any regrets?"

"About dropping out?"

I nodded.

"Oh no. Not about dropping out. Not one."

"About other things, then?" I lifted my head and looked up at him. "Things we haven't already dealt with, I mean."

He shook his head and stopped swaying. "I don't think so." He put a few inches between us and reached into the inside pocket of his jacket. "And if it's okay with you, I'd really like to keep it that way—"

"Yes."

His hand wasn't even fully out of his pocket yet, and I don't think he registered what I said. "Addie, I have loved you since before I had any idea what love was. All I knew was *you* were the thing that mattered most, and—"

"I said yes, Wes. I'll marry you."

His eyes flitted back and forth, and then he squinted a bit and leaned in. "But I haven't even—"

"Okay, fine." I shrugged and walked over to the couch and leaned up against the back of it. "Do it your way. Go on."

He scoffed. "Well, it doesn't seem very romantic now, does it?"

"No, by all means, go ahead. Had you prepared a speech? A seventeenth-century sonnet recitation, perhaps?"

He attempted to hide his smile as he crossed his arms and walked slowly toward me. "If you must know, I was going to read you the vows I wrote for our first wedding."

I gasped and covered my mouth. "Really? Now I do feel bad! Please read them. *Please.*"

He snapped his fingers. "Shoot! No, I was just making that up. But now I wish I had them. How great would that be? I could try to remember what I wrote, I guess. It probably rhymed. Maybe I was going to rap for you?"

I laughed and reached out for the lapels of his jacket and pulled him to me as he continued. "I probably said something about your rockin' bod. Actually, I can almost guarantee I did." He reached into his pants pocket and pulled out his phone. "Let me call Cole real quick. I bet he'll remember."

I wrapped my arms around his neck and captured his mouth and had the genuine pleasure of being the one to take his breath away for a change. "Shut up and give me my ring," I muttered against his lips, and he smiled and threw his phone on the couch before raising my left hand between us and slipping the ring onto my finger.

"Well, *now* I guess I regret not asking you sooner. If I'd known it was going to be that easy . . ."

I lifted my hands to his face and shook my head. "This was the right time."

He nodded. "I know."

"I love you," I whispered.

"I love you too."

He kissed me again—softly and slowly in a way that somehow carried promises of an unhurried life.

"Besides," I added when he pulled me back into his arms and once again began leading me to the tempo of music only we could hear, "where's the fun in easy?"

# AUTHOR'S NOTE

More than ten years ago, I started writing a love story about Senator Wes Hobbes, a presidential candidate going back to his hometown and ultimately reuniting with Addie Atwater, the childhood sweetheart he had left at the altar. After I received my first publishing contract for a completely different book, I began pitching Wes and Addie's story as the book that should be published next—and thus began a seemingly endless cycle of rejection for Wes and Addie. It would go something like this:

PUBLISHER: So what do you want to write next?
ME: I have that one about the presidential candidate . . .
PUBLISHER: Anything else?
ME: Um . . . I guess I could write something about [insert hastily pulled together plot idea here].
PUBLISHER: Yes! Let's do *that*!

After a while (and at least five rejections from multiple publishers), I finally started giving up on Wes and Addie's story, but their hometown of Adelaide Springs, Colorado, refused to quietly step aside. So, okay . . . fine. Wes and Addie weren't going to happen. But this fictional town of Adelaide Springs would also make a great little hometown for this new character I was whipping up for a new book. Brynn Cornell could have grown up there, surrounded by these same quirky characters. And you know what else? I really liked those supporting characters from Wes and Addie's story. Why couldn't Cole Kimball and Laila Olivet become Brynn and Sebastian's supporting characters instead? And hey . . . what the heck! Why couldn't they have all grown up together, maybe even alongside Wes Hobbes and Addie Atwater? And you know, maybe I could plant some little seeds along the way. Sure, that book was about Brynn and Sebastian hating each other, but it could also be fun to make readers wonder if Cole and Laila were really just friends, and if Wes and Addie had already had their chance.

So, you may be wondering, what's the point? The point is I'm so grateful for the years of being told it wasn't Wes and Addie's time. They were right. Everyone who rejected "the one about the presidential candidate" was right. To me, it was always about Wes and Addie. There were no other Adelaide Springs stories to tell . . . and there never would have been if I had gotten what I wanted. (Do you understand what I'm saying? Without rejection and disappointment, I never would have met Sebastian Sudworth. Unacceptable.)

I'm talking to you, writer friend lamenting that manuscript you have stuffed in the drawer or tucked away in the cloud. You know the one. The one you believe in so fiercely but that, for whatever reason, you can never get anyone else to appreciate. Keep working on it. Make it better. (For the record, Adelaide Springs was originally named Rier Ridge, which is not very catchy.) As you grow, make sure *it* grows. (Um . . . my original version of Wes and Addie's story wasn't a rom-com. At all. What was I even thinking?!) But don't give up. Don't lose heart. And don't stop writing. You just never know when those characters you love may finally get their chance.

# ACKNOWLEDGMENTS

Golly, Laura Wheeler . . . I adore you. Thank you for continuing to believe in me and for being brilliant and so much stinking fun to work with. And truly, I feel that way about the entire Thomas Nelson team. Thanks especially to Savannah and Leslie who, alongside Laura, helped whip this bad boy into shape.

I went for quite a while without an agent because I believed it was worth waiting for the *right* agent. Emily Sacks, thank you for being the right agent and for wanting to work with me. I mean, *what*?! And thanks to Berni Vann, Allegra Craver, and my entire incomparable team at CAA. I'm so excited to head into the future with y'all by my side! (Thao Thai, thank you for making the initial introduction, my friend. You inspire me with your talent, your artistry, and your generous spirit.)

As always, I'm so grateful to the writers, performers, and musicians whose voices fill my head and help build a story. During Wes and Addie's season, my brain was overtaken by Annabel Monaghan, Zibby Owens, Paul Simon, Amy Sherman-Palladino, Ann Patchett, Taylor Swift, Janine Rosche, Bonnie Garmus, Ryan Gosling, Delia Ephron, Gin Blossoms, Carrie Fisher, and perhaps a little too much Michael Bolton.

Reader friends, library friends, bookseller friends . . . you continually dazzle me. Thank you for all the support and encouragement.

I have two friends who read Wes and Addie's story while it was in various stages of a very long development process. Caitlyn, thank you for helping to keep my enthusiasm for the story alive, even when I was dragging, and for your great catches and suggestions. And Jenny

. . . good grief, BP. Can you believe this one is finally seeing the light of day? Thank you for being my very first reader of a very different version of this story more than a decade ago.

And of course I would have long ago lost whatever remaining sanity I possess if not for my IRL community of family and friends: Ethan, Noah, Dad, Mom, Missy, LeeAnn, David, Tonya, Robert, Anne, Sharon, Laura, Janine, and Kelly Turner, my once and forever favorite.

Thank You, Lord, for all the blessings, and for the gift and privilege of storytelling.

# DISCUSSION QUESTIONS

1. What were your first impressions of Addie upon meeting her? How did your opinion of her change throughout the story?
2. What were your first impressions of Wes upon meeting him? How did your opinion of him change throughout the story?
3. Our three Adelaide Springs couples have explored the tropes of enemies-to-more (*Brynn and Sebastian Hate Each Other*), friends-to-more (*Cole and Laila Are Just Friends*), and second-chance romance (*Wes and Addie Had Their Chance*). Do you have a favorite romance trope?
4. Upon seeing Wes for the first time in so long, did you identify more with Laila's reaction or Cole's?
5. If you've read the other Adelaide Springs books, you've known Doc Atwater as a welcoming and forgiving father figure to the town's prodigal children. Were you surprised by his reaction to seeing Wes? Do you believe his anger was understandable? Was it justified?
6. Wes muses about having so many memories associated with music. Are there certain songs that bring back specific memories for you?
7. Do you believe there can only be one great love for a person, or do you believe that, like Addie, someone can truly love two different people?
8. Who would you cast as Wes and Addie in a film version of the book?

# ABOUT THE AUTHOR

Photo by Noah Turner

Bethany Turner has been writing since the second grade, when she won her first writing award for explaining why, if she could have lunch with any person throughout history, she would choose John Stamos. She stands by this decision. Bethany now writes pop culture–infused rom-coms for a new generation of readers who crave fiction that tackles the thorny issues of life with humor and insight. She lives in Southwest Colorado with her husband, whom she met in the nineties in a chat room called Disco Inferno. As sketchy as it sounds, it worked out pretty well in this case, and they are the proud parents of two grown sons. Connect with Bethany at bethanyturnerbooks.com or across social media @seebethanywrite, where she clings to the eternal dream that John Stamos will someday send her a friend request. You can also text her at +1 (970) 387-7811. Texting with readers is her favorite.

bethanyturnerbooks.com
Instagram: @seebethanywrite
Facebook: @seebethanywrite